hastybooklist.com

Censored Angel
Anthony Comstock's Nemesis

By Joan Koster
Book 2 in the Forgotten Women series

Tidal Waters Press

NEW YORK

Published by Tidal Waters Press
Copyright © 2023 by Joan Koster
All rights reserved.

e-Book edition ISBN 978-1-959318-11-8
Paperback edition ISBN 978-1-959318-12-5

No part of this book may be reproduced or transmitted
in any form or by any means, electronic or mechanical,
including photocopying, recording or by any information
storage and retrieval system in use now or in the future,
without the written permission of the Publisher, except where
permitted by law. All inquiries should be addressed to Tidal
Waters Press.

Cover design by
Book Design by Kristin Campbell

This is a work of fiction. While some characters and
circumstances portrayed by the author are based on real
people and historical fact, references to real people, events,
establishments, organizations, or locales, are only intended to
provide a sense of authenticity and are used fictitiously. All
other characters and all incidents and dialogue are drawn from
the author's imagination and are not to be considered real. In
all other respects, any resemblance to persons living or dead is
entirely coincidental.

Dedication

Dedicated to every author who has ever had their books censored.

To the Reader

This is a work of both historical fact and historical imaginings. The majority of characters you will meet lived and worked in the late nineteenth century. Many have well-documented lives; some do not.

From the existing writings, diaries, letters, magazines, court documents, and news reports, I have conjured their thoughts and feelings as best I can. In particular, the role played by Ida Craddock in this narrative is entirely fictional. My imagined Ida does, however, abide by the generally known facts of her life, and I have sometimes quoted from her works, diaries, and letters, passim. The angels and all the passages relating to her mysticism and sexual experiences have no factual basis

This is a novel about sex, obscenity, and censorship. Any resemblance to current social issues is astonishingly remarkable.

Warning: This book contains blunt descriptions of sexual relations judged obscene in 1902, and of suicide

The Comstock Act
As passed by the United States Congress in 1873

Be it enacted . . . That whoever, within the District of Columbia or any of the Territories of the United States . . . shall sell . . . or shall offer to sell, or to lend, or to give away, or in any manner to exhibit, or shall otherwise publish or offer to publish in any manner, or shall have in his possession, for any such purpose or purposes, an obscene book, pamphlet, paper, writing, advertisement, circular, print, picture, drawing or other representation, figure, or image on or of paper or other material, or any cast instrument, or other article of an immoral nature, or any drug or medicine, or any article whatever, for the prevention of conception, or for causing unlawful abortion, or shall advertise the same for sale, or shall write or print, or cause to be written or printed, any card, circular, book, pamphlet, advertisement, or notice of any kind, stating when, where, how, or of whom, or by what means, any of the articles in this section . . . can be purchased or obtained, or shall manufacture, draw, or print, or in any wise make any of such articles, shall be deemed guilty of a misdemeanor, and on conviction thereof in any court of the United States . . . he shall be imprisoned at hard labor in the penitentiary for not less than six months nor more than five years for each offense, or fined not less than one hundred dollars nor more than two thousand dollars, with costs of c

List of Characters

Historical Personages

Philadelphia

Ida Celanire Craddock (1857-1902): Author, spiritualist, mystic, and marriage counselor.

Elizabeth (Lizzie) Craddock Decker (1833-1904): Mother of Ida. A staunch temperance supporter and distributor of Craddock patent medicines.

Ida (Nan) Craddock (1856?-1859?): Sister of Ida, died of whooping cough at age three.

Thomas Decker: Third husband of Lizzie Craddock.

Katie Stuart Wood (unk): Ida's best friend and life-long correspondent. Both attended Friends Central Academy.

Annie Shoemaker (unk): Instructor in biology at Friends Central Academy.

Dr. Henrietta Payne Westbrook (1835-1909): Doctor, journalist, and follower of free love.

Richard Westbrook (1920-1899): Methodist minister, lawyer, and judge. Served on the board of Girard College, Wagner Free Institute, and the American Secular Union

Frederick Allen Hinckley (1820-1917): Unitarian minister, dedicated to women's suffrage.

Voltairine de Cleyre (1866-1912): Essayist and anarchist.

Carrie Burnham Kilgore (1838-1909): Doctor, instructor in physical culture, first woman to graduate from University of Pennsylvania Law School, first woman lawyer in Philadelphia, and the first to argue a case before the Pennsylvania Supreme Court

Dr. Charles Turnbull (1847-1918): Philadelphia occultist and hypnotist.

San Francisco

Euclid Frick (unk): Ida's boarder in Oakland, a premed student.

Alexander Badlam (1836-1898): President of Bankers and Mutual Life Association, Treasurer of the Russian-California Fur Association, which worked to purchase Alaska. Author of *The Wonders of Alaska* (1891), Transcribed and edited by Ida Craddock.

Chicago

Dr. Alice B. Stockham (1833-1912): Physician, gynecologist, and author of *Tokology: A Book for Every Woman* and *Karezza: The Ethics of Marriage*. A close friend of Ida and of Leo Tolstoy.

Moses Harman (1830-1910): Publisher of *Lucifer, the Light Bearer*, a radical magazine devoted to the separation of church and state, free love marriage, sexual questions, and population control.

Otoman Zar-Adusht Hanish (1856?-1936): A self-styled mystic of German descent who advocated healthful living, hypnotism, and naked sunbathing.

Clarence Darrow (1857-1938): Lawyer famous for his defense of evolution.

England

William T. Stead (1849-1912): Newspaper editor, an early investigative journalist, a social reformer, and publisher of *Pall Mall Gazette*, *The Review of Reviews*, and *The Borderlands*, a spiritualist magazine. He is credited as the originator of the tabloid. He died on the Titanic.

Ada Goodrich or Miss X (1857-1931): British clairvoyant, psychic researcher, author, and folklorist of the Middle East.

Alma Gillen (unk): British author and poet, follower of Divine Science and Theosophy, and editor of the magazine *Expression*. Books include *The Law of Expression, The Passion of Passion*, and *Mind and Thought*.

New York City

Anthony Comstock (1844-1915): Founder of the New York Society for the Suppression of Vice and active member of the YMCA. He lobbied for the passage of the Comstock Law and was appointed United States Postal Inspector. Credited with destroying over fifteen tons of books, he drove over fifteen people to take their own lives and made over four thousand arrests.

Dr. Edward Bond Foote (1854-1912): Founder of *Dr. Foote's Healthy Monthly*, secretary of the New York Liberal Club, founder of the Manhattan Liberal Club, supported free thinkers and reformers.

Hugh Pentecost (1848-1907): Baptist and independent minister, lawyer, briefly NYC District Attorney, considered a brilliant orator but waffled on the issues of the day.

Edward C. Walker (1849-1931): Lawyer, author, a founding member of the Free Speech League, and husband to Lillian Harman, Moses Harman's daughter.

Theodore Schroeder (1864-1953): Lawyer, author, free-lance psychoanalyst. A founder of the Free Speech league.

All other characters are fictional.

PART 1

"Our route of travel is so varied. Now up the mountain of joy, now down in the valley of gloom, or maybe straight across the marshes of disappointment."

Ida C. Craddock, Letter to The Pleiades, September 10th 1879

Chapter 1

"The passions of the child must be kept subdued and
wholesome."
Anthony Comstock, 1873, *Traps for the Young* p. 41

Monument Cemetery, Philadelphia, 1875

The angel is my favorite. I trail my fingers over the
polished folds of cold marble and stare up at the
monument. Stone curls, frozen in wind-tossed
perfection, frame a radiant face that shows no anger—only
enduring love. I could stand here forever, basking in his gaze.

"Come, Ida." Mother's voice is icier than the December
gusts whipping at my skirts.

I hurry down the cemetery path, an armful of evergreens
clutched tight to my bosom. Up ahead, she stops beside the
half-buried stone marking the grave of my long-dead sister.
Shears flicking, Mother trims the dried grasses around the
granite marker with the same attention to detail she gives
everything.

I turn my head. Sometimes, I wish I lay beneath that
stone. Maybe then, she would love me, too.

Ignored again, I inhale the sharp scent of the fresh-cut fir and set a bough at the foot of my father's headstone. The simple limestone slab is gray-green with moss. I press my palm to the chill stone.

There will be no wreath for my father. His weathered tombstone lies untended. No carved angel stands sentinel at his grave. No loving sorrow from my mother marks his passing.

I trace the date, December 1857. He died a mere four months after my birth. How different my life would have been if he had lived.

"Forget him," Mother hisses. "Bring the garland here."

I wipe my damp hand on my cloak and slip to her side.

Mother tugs at my sleeve. "Wreath, Ida."

I hand her the pine circlet with its black ribbon, and she sinks to her knees and rests it on the most elaborate of the six small tombstones.

"Dear lost child, would that you had survived." Her breath trembles.

She peers up at me. "Men will have their way, Ida. Heedless of the consequences. I begged your father to wait, to let me grieve. Recover my health. But no. An heir to inherit the business—that was all he wanted from me. What choice did I have? Wives must submit to their husband's will. It is our duty in marriage. Our duty as women. Our path to heaven."

I pinch my lips together and watch the wind rattle the bare branches of the poplars. It is always the same litany when we come here. If she wants to ensure I never marry, she has done well.

Mother straightens the wreath. "And then to suffer the pain of bearing children"—she runs a hand down her face—"only to lose them."

I want to shout that I am here. I am alive. But it will do no good. I was not the desired child. Instead, I humble myself, as always. "I know, Mother. But think—she is with God, a blithe spirit cavorting forever in heaven."

"Does she, daughter? Or does she hover in the borderland?" My mother kisses the damp stone.

Beneath lies my sister, dead from the swoop of the strangling angel—the dreaded diphtheria. Dear Nan. We would have played, shared secrets, and known each other's innermost thoughts. She would have clasped my hand as we sat straight-backed, feet flat on the floor, for hours during Mother's wearisome lessons.

But heaven wanted her more than me.

Sometimes, I despise the angels.

For a moment, it is all too much—the cold, the wind, the moldy scent of death. The memories. I fall back on the Bible, more for myself than for my mother. "The Lord loves the little children. The kingdom of God belongs to them."

Mother pushes to her feet, her eyes wild, the traces of her French accent strong. "The séance table at the Hunters. It moved, Ida, when I asked if my little ones are at peace."

I rub one foot against the other. "Perhaps, that was a yes?"

She glares at me. "What do you know of the spirits? You are but a foolish child, Ida Celanire. Now stand up straight and stop dirtying your stockings." She seizes my hand as if I am a disorderly toddler instead of an eighteen-year-old on the cusp of womanhood. "Come. I have borrowed one of those new spirit boards. Together, we will learn the answer."

"A spirit board?"

The tree branches sway. Bitter cold crawls under my petticoats. I do not need to know if spirits are real. I already know they are.

The house is dismal and dark when we return, the fire in the parlor grate reduced to embers, the Irish day girl long gone. But the aroma of the stew she made lingers. My stomach growls as I slip off my wet cloak. I can't wait to fill my icy insides with a bowl, and then warm my freezing toes and fingers at the still-hot cook stove in the kitchen. But Mother is on a mission.

"Come, Ida." She presses her hand against the small of my back and hurries me into the drafty dining room. "We must call the spirits while they are foremost in our minds." She lights a candle. The flickering flame illuminates the spirit board in the center of the tabletop. The pale, polished wood glows ominously. The black alphabet and red YES and NO spell disaster. The triangular planchette hovers on its tiny feet like a spider come to entangle me in its web.

A chill worms its way through me, and I look longingly toward the door. But escaping my mother's will is not an option. I am too hungry and too cold to bear a night shut away without my supper for disobedience.

"Sit, Ida." She points to the chair on the opposite side of the table.

I dutifully take my place, roll my shoulders, and stare at the board. I have heard of these instruments designed to call forth the departed. Something slithers down my spine.

I focus on the stale scent of the dusty drapery and the hard needlepoint cushion on the seat. I am safe. This is our dining room. I have eaten every meal here since I can remember. A candle, a piece of wood, and a metal disk cannot change that.

I hope.

My mother caresses the ever-present, pearl-trimmed pendant of baby hair at her neck, the chestnut brown so unlike my own pale locks. "We must concentrate. Think of the dead. How much we love them."

I tip my chin. "Yes, Mother."

4

"Now place your fingers on the planchette." She says the word in the French way—*planchet*—all nasal and arrogant. When she takes that tone, I know better than to disobey.

I set my fingertips on the smooth metal as Mother does the same. She whispers her question with a hesitancy surprising for her. "Are you at peace, my dear Nan? Are you?"

For long minutes, nothing happens. Then, beneath our hands, the planchette moves snail-like across the talking board, heading toward the *YES*.

My stomach knots. My breath rasps. Shadows dance. Drapes rustle. All my life, I have seen spirits. Are they here?

"Mother," I whisper, "you're making it do this, aren't you?"

"Hush. Of course not, Ida. Our loved ones draw near. Can't you feel them?"

Another chill wafts over me, raising all the hairs on my body. I tuck in my chin and shut my eyes. Is the ghost of the father I never knew manifesting behind me? Are the shades of my sister and the stillborn babes from Mother's second marriage to Mr. Brown, the ones that gave my mother her sad eyes, hovering above us?

The planchette vibrates as if in answer. The proof of the unseen grows too close.

I jerk my fingers up.

"Don't," Mother chides.

I tentatively touch the corners of the cold metal as the planchette alights atop the *YES*.

"See? They have come. Now, Ida," Mother says, "ask a question."

Above the mantle, my father's portrait stares down at me, his eyes heavy, his mouth pinched down. I cannot bear to think the shadows are real. Ghosts are not angels, but they can be demons.

I choke out the words, "No, you . . . you first."

5

My mother's taut body melts into itself. She rocks back and forth. "Oh, my lost babes." She seizes my hand. "I am afraid to ask. You must help me be brave."

Brave? If I knew how to be brave, I would not be sitting here. I hunch lower.

"As you wish."

She resets the planchette at the center of the board and closes her eyes. "Are you safe, my children? Are you with the angels, my darling little ones?"

The candle flickers. The shadows settle in around us. Cold wraps over my shoulders like a shawl. I do not want to talk to the dead. All I want is for my mother to be happy. Everything is better when she is light-spirited and not focused on my failings.

I hold my breath and place the tips of my fingers on the edge. The planchette lies still beneath our hands. I pray the angels forgive me and press a little. It moves slightly. Stops.

"Please"—Mother's voice wavers—"please say yes."

Her words float in the air like mist. I give another nudge. The planchette glides across the board, the black lace at my mother's wrist sweeping after. Then, as if by some unknown presence, it settles into place.

YES.

My mother lifts her hands, her face transformed by a smile. "Now, Ida, your turn."

I know what I am supposed to ask—the name of my future husband. That's what my silly schoolgirl friends would want to know. That's what my mother expects—for me to be normal. For me to marry a fine gentleman who will treat me like a china doll and keep me quiet and forever pregnant.

Instead, I test the spirits. "Who—" My mother catches my eye, and I correct myself. "*Whom* do I love?"

On its tiny wheels, the iron disk skitters across the board like a flea searching for the sweetest patch of skin. This way and that, it slithers until it comes to a stop near the A. Ghostly fingers sweep along the back of my neck.

I barely touch the metal, but it moves again. Only an inch. But it is enough. I go cold all over. Holy awe fills me.

It is true then. Spirits *are* here. And they know my secrets.

My mother clasps my hands. "A and S, Ida? What unknown suitor has claimed your heart?"

I am too shocked to pinch my lips closed. The name bursts out. "Annie. Annie Shoemaker. The spirits speak true."

Mother shoves my hands away, pushes the board aside, and stands. "Of course, they do. And I am glad they have revealed this weakness in you—this schoolgirl fancy. I will not have it. My only daughter pining over a spinster schoolteacher. I send you to Friends Central Academy to acquire a bit of ladylike polish in a staid Quaker setting as your long-departed father wished. Not twaddle on about biology and history and teachers you swoon for. I fear I was wrong to enroll you in that school."

The trembling starts in my toes and twists its way upward until it clamps around my skull. I cannot lose my place at Friends. I cannot lose the one breath of freedom I have.

I glance about the room, willing a spirit to come to my rescue. But any specter with sense is long gone.

I give a slight laugh and lie. "Just fooling, Mother. I have no care for Miss Shoemaker or any of the teachers. I cheated. I moved the planchette. Made it pick those letters."

She turns up the gas lamp. The edges of the shadows shift. Her face contorts. "Shame on you. The spirits must not be abused in such a way." She looks me straight in the eye. "I do not like the change that has come over you ever since I placed you at that academy. You are of marrying age, no longer some dreamy child prone to unruly fits and imaginings. I am of a mind to remove you before the end of the term."

Panic sweeps through me. If I don't graduate from Friends, I won't be able to get my medical degree and save sick babies like our Nan.

I raise my chin and try to be enthusiastic. "I need to graduate so I can continue my studies. Just think, if I were a doctor, I could be a great help in the apothecary. I could improve Papa's bitters and give them a proper endorsement."

Mother waves her hand in dismissal. "A patent medicine business is no place for a lady. I run the apothecary because I must—so we can live well, so you can attend Friends and become acquainted with the daughters of the better families in the city, meet their marriageable brothers. That's all. And you can be sure that tomorrow I will be in the headmistress's office, reporting this unwholesomeness you are displaying and having you removed from that woman's class. What was her name again?"

I lower my head and pretend my blood is not boiling. There is no stopping Mother when her course is set. "Shoemaker. She teaches science."

My mother's mouth twists. I know what is coming next.

She points her finger at me. "Now, in punishment for your tomfoolery with our new spirit board and for offending the spirits, it is off to your room."

I swish around her and stomp down the hall and up the stairs. Eighteen and still being sent to my room, if you can call it that.

Behind me, Mother jingles the keys. She can jingle-jangle them all she wants. She can lock me in all she wants. The tiny space partitioned out of Mother's sitting room so she can rent out the other bedroom to a boarder is my refuge. Always has been.

At the doorway, I stop to glare at her over my shoulder then throw myself onto my narrow cot and listen to the key turn in the lock.

My stomach cramps. There'll be no stew to warm my insides. No hearth to huddle by. I burrow my head in my pillow. It is not I who has disturbed the spirits, but it will be I who has to face them.

Chapter 2

"A terrible responsibility rests upon parents who fail to early
fill their children's minds with wholesome thoughts."
Anthony Comstock, *Traps for the Young*, p. 18

Craddock residence, 1032 Race Street, 1875

It doesn't take long before a warning chill sweeps over me.
I curl up on the mattress and draw my knees to my chest,
but it does no good. Invisible fingers pinch my toes.
Thorny prickles prowl along the back of my hands and up my
arms. My whole body trembles.

The whispers start. I burrow deeper into the covers.
Huffing, hissing, humming in my ears. Louder and louder,
closer and closer.

I slap my palms to the sides of my head. I hold my breath.
Tighten every muscle. But it makes no difference. My demons
are here, and nothing I do will make them go away.

Later, much later, I find my breath. I rediscover my bones
and blood. I crawl back into my skin. I untwist the sheets from
my legs, relieved to see I am not bound or being prayed over.
For once, my attack has escaped Mother's notice.

I shake off the lingering malaise and roll over. There will be no sleep for me tonight.

I wiggle my hand between the iron headboard and the rough wood bedframe. Long ago, I discovered there are other ways to spend my hours. Other ways to fly free.

There. I grasp the binding of my latest treasure, *Gray's Anatomy*, borrowed from my dear Annie Shoemaker.

I set alight the candle on my nightstand and lay the heavy volume on my lap. In the flickering light, I thumb through the pages, stopping here and there to admire the intricate workings of the body.

Slowly, the ghost-bidden cramps and chills fade into blood-warmed flesh, and I solidify. I am alive. I am myself.

My fingers reach my favorite illustration: *No. 348. The Uterus and Its Appendages*. I trace my finger over the finely drawn lines. How like the diagram of the flower Annie Shoemaker drew in biology class. I press my hand to my belly. My dearest Annie says the organs of plant generation are like a holy temple. How much more holy must be the ones inside our womanly bodies?

I press a little harder, careful not to go too low. It will not do to finger my untouchables, even if I would love to see if mine match the illustration in *Anatomy*. I wore thumbless mittens too many childhood nights to succumb to that temptation. I must not defile what God has created, Mother says.

But no one can stop me from looking at the drawings.

I squint, the tiny lettering barely visible in the settling dark. Here is where a child will be planted for better or for ill. Though how, I have no idea.

I picture the gravestone marking the short life of my sister. How can such a small organ be responsible for so much wonder and so much pain?

Thumping on the front door thunders down the hall, up the stairs, and over the thin partition that walls in my room.

I jerk upright.

Mother's feet stumble past, a sure sign she's been dosing with her own laudanum-laced Craddock concoction.

Downstairs, the door bangs open. I hear the night watchman shouting the dreaded word. *"Fire."*

"Mother!" I scream. I rush to my door and pound on it. This is the thing I fear most in the world—being trapped, forgotten. Smothered.

My limbs tremble. The windowless walls of my room crush in around me. I pray to the heavens. I beg the angels.

Don't leave me to die, locked in, with only the demons to comfort me. I have too much to learn. Too much to do. Too little time to escape my mother's strictures and make my mark on the world.

"Mother!" I yell again. I kick the door and twist the knob, to no avail. I ram my ear against the wood panel and strain to hear, but my blood pounds too loudly in my ears. My breath turns solid in my lungs. I gasp again and again. I am going to die here. I can already smell the smoke wafting over the space between the ceiling and the walls of my cubicle.

Pain whips through my head. My pulse thunders. My muscles twitch. The unwelcome chorus of voices invades my brain. My demons hover and, for a brief second, I fear I will suffer another of my fits.

Shaking, I cling to the doorknob. Not here. Not now. I am not ready to die.

And then Mother is there, the key turning in the lock, fresh air rushing in.

"Ida." My mother's voice is sharp. "Take this." She shoves my dead stepfather Brown's portrait into my arms. "Now, come along. The fire is three houses down, but we have been ordered into the street just in case it spreads this way. Not that it is likely—there is no wind."

I cling to her arm and stumble after her, the left-behind portrait of my father casting recriminations as we rush by.

Outside, flames lick the sky, billowing smoke chokes the air. A huge crowd presses around us, cheering every time a rafter falls and sparks fly up. Despite the December cold, the heat of the fire warms me through.

"May I help you with that?"

I turn. It is the young man from the rooming house next door, a student at the University of Pennsylvania.

A twinge of jealousy twists my empty stomach. He is no older than I, and yet, unlike those of the female persuasion, his educational horizons are unlimited.

He tips his head at the gilt-framed oil I am clasping. "That looks heavy. Shall I hold it for you?"

I find my voice. "That would be kind." I put dour Mr. Brown's portrait into his capable-looking hands and smile. Perhaps this is someone I could befriend and share my discoveries with.

I take advantage of the crowd and my mother's fascination with the burning building to introduce myself yet keep my tone low. If Mother were to hear such forwardness, I would draw a whipping. "I'm Ida Craddock. I've heard mentioned you are at Penn. What are you studying?"

"Frankie Bradley, at your service." Despite the bulky painting in his grasp, he manages a brief bow. "I am in the philosophy department."

I clap my hands together. "Fantastic. I love philosophy. So, what do you think of the works of Immanuel Kant and his transcendental idealism?"

"Who?" He tucks the painting beneath his arm and leans in so close that, despite the smoke, I can smell his off-putting hair pomade. The boy pinches his lips to the side. "Never heard of the man. But, I say, why not come with me, away from this commotion, and we can discourse about him at our leisure?" He puts his free hand on my elbow, and the warmth of his palm seeps through the cloth.

My face heats. My toes curl. It is almost pleasurable—and then it is not.

Bradley's eyes have narrowed. His hand cinches tighter. I still.

Mother says I must allow no man except my future husband to touch any part of me. Some men are wily, she avers. Some men are of the devil. Some men will drag me down the path of ruin and get me with child then leave me weeping in the graveyard.

Is this Frankie such a man?

My empty stomach tightens. I should yank free and run, but he holds my mother's dearest belonging. I take refuge in polite behavior and hard-won knowledge.

"First, you must meet my mother."

I tug on Mother's shawl. She turns with a jerk and wrinkles her nose.

"Mother, this gentleman kindly offered to hold Mr. Brown's portrait for me."

Like an avenging specter, she straightens her already poker-perfect back and gazes at his hand on my sleeve with knife-edge intensity. No one can bear that scrutiny for long. Just ask the boarders who stiff her on the rent and the suppliers who deliver late.

And me.

Bradley's leer vanishes. His cockiness subsides. His hand falls away.

She thrusts out her hand. "I'll take the painting and would have you leave my daughter alone."

"Yes, ma'am." He hands the portrait to my mother then slips into the crowd before I can introduce him by name.

It is just as well. Frank Bradley might be at Penn, but he is no one I want to cultivate an acquaintance with.

My mother lifts her chin. "Come, Ida. The fire is under control."

I trail back into the house behind Mother, up the stairs, and down the hall. I stop and take a peek out the sitting room window at the dispersing crowd. There. There he is. Bradley, standing with a group of dandies jeering at the firefighters with their soot-blackened faces. No scholar, that one. Sometimes, I am glad my mother protects me so firmly.

"What's this, Ida?"

I spin around.

And sometimes, I am not.

My mother stands in the entranceway to my cubbyhole, holding Annie's *Gray's Anatomy*.

Blood pounds through my head. How could I have left my treasure to be discovered?

She shakes the book. "I demand an explanation for how this disgusting volume came into my home."

"I borrowed it."

"From whom, Ida?"

I pinch my lips tight. She can lock me away and toss out the key. She can whip my shins until I am covered in scars. Never will I tell.

But my resolve does no good.

Mother flips the cover over, finds the owner's name, and snarls it out. "I see. Annie Shoemaker."

Clutching the book, she stomps into the sitting room, stokes the embers in the stove to red-hot, and then throws Annie's *Grey's Anatomy* in.

Pinned like a butterfly by my mother's glare, I do nothing as the flames lick and tear at the precious pages.

I shift from one foot to the other and tuck the coil of hurt under my heart. I want to please my mother. But sometimes, it is like trying to lift Sisyphus's boulder. I will always be the inept replacement for the first babe she lost.

Nan wouldn't have let strange boys touch her. Nan wouldn't have had dreams of being something more than a wife. Nan would have been perfect.

I raise my head as she comes toward me with the cane.

"Lift your skirts, Ida Craddock. I will make this clear. You will not study medicine. I will not pay for any more schooling than this last year at Friends. You are not a son. Your future is marriage and child-bearing."

I close my eyes, clasp my hands together, and brace for the blows. The cane strikes. The pain whips through me.

I stifle my cry. There is no future for me here in this house. All I want is to escape and find love and freedom where I may.

Chapter 3

"To please the eye, charm the ear, or to entertain any of the senses, is often the way to the heart."
Anthony Comstock, *Traps for the Young*, p. 168

Craddock residence, Race Street, 1876

The day maid stands in the parlor doorway. "That Irishman again—Mr. Sullivan—asking for Miss Ida."

I drop the book I am reading to the floor and jump up from my chair. Clever man to come when Mother is out at her Temperance meeting. For a half-hour or so, I will have my Angel Prince all to myself.

"Let him in, let him in." I run my hand over my hair and tuck in the curls that have gone astray.

The girl glares at me with narrowed eyes. "But madam said—"

I hold up my hand and speak with more force than warranted. "He is my friend. Let him in."

The maid tips her chin in judgment and goes to escort him in.

Heart thumping against my ribcage, I rock on my feet and wait for him to appear.

Clasping his brown bowler to his chest with one hand and a small velvet bag dangling from the other, Charles Sullivan, the oldest son of my father's best friend, steps through the doorway. Not tall, but pale-haired and sweet-faced, he is my angel in the flesh.

I smile.

We are no longer children playing hide and seek while his father does the accounts for the apothecary. Still, I am so happy to see him I bounce on my toes as if I am a spoiled child instead of the staid nineteen-year-old my mother expects me to be.

Sometimes, he brings me sweets or bouquets of wildflowers picked from vacant lots. But more welcome are the books and the piano sheet music purchased or purloined, if I were to believe my mother, from the bookstore he works at, always accompanied by teasing and Irish tales of ghosts and pookas. However, the velvet bag he carries is too small to hold a book or music.

What has he brought me today?

"Ida, my little bird." Charles rests his hat and cane on the side table then holds out the bag. There is a new steadfastness about his posture. "I have fetched you a treasure in honor of your graduation from Friends. Take a peek."

I step closer. He smells of exotic cedar wood and the camphor compress he uses to suppress his cough. Mother believes him consumptive and on death's doorstep. She wants me to stay far away from him, but the Charles I know is so jolly and well-fleshed. I do not believe her. He looks nothing like the desiccated images in the medical manuals.

Nevertheless, I avoid approaching as close as I wish and instead take the bag from him and look inside. Something silver glitters in the sunlight streaming through the window.

With a glance at my dear friend, I draw out an oval locket embossed with a bee hovering above a lattice of vining flowers.

His mouth turns solemn. "It was my mother's."

"Oh my, I am honored." With my thumbnail, I work at the tiny catch. It springs open, revealing my Charles's handsome face on the underside.

He folds his hands. "Can I be so bold as to ask to see your own beautiful visage placed beside mine?"

"I beg to differ as to my beauty, but most assuredly, I will add my own miniature and wear it close to my heart, always." I pinch the locket closed then lift the chain over my neck.

"A delightful image, my princess. One I will cherish all my life." He heads to the box grand piano, my most prized possession; the only thing inherited from my father. He shuffles through the sheet music. "This one. Will you play for me?"

I perch on the stool, arrange my skirts so my feet fit the pedals, and place my hands on the keys. I do not need see the notes. I know the piece by heart, as Charles has asked so often for it.

My fingers dance against the ivory, and the strains of Chopin's second *Nocturne* fill the room, the ethereal harmony cascading over me and through me as I lose myself in the melody.

Charles stands behind me, a warm, comforting presence. Contentment fills me. If only it could be like this forever.

Suddenly, he steps away and doubles over. A wet cough wrenches through him and leaves him gasping.

I rush to his side and guide him to the best chair in the parlor—Mother's chair. With a whoosh, Charles lowers himself on to the rich burgundy cushion. I rest a hand on his shoulder. He does seem paler and more tired this afternoon. Could Mother be right?

For a moment, worry niggles at me. I could not bear to lose this kind friend who's brought me treats and laughter since I was a child.

He runs a finger down my cheek then lifts the locket from my breast and cradles it on his palm. "I think the bee so appropriate. My mother was as busy as a worker bee from day to night. Raising us young ones, seeing to the family business after my father died. A worker bee." He peers up at me. "But you are a different type of bee, my dear. You are the searcher bee. The one who flits from place to place, thought to thought, idea to idea. I predict that, like a bee in search of sweet nectar, you will wander to-and-fro, sipping of knowledge and sharing what you learn with all mankind. You will make a difference in this world, Ida."

My heart leaps, and I want to tell him every dream I have kept hidden. But fear holds me back. Instead, I seek his advice. "I can't wait to start my advanced studies, but I don't know what to choose. I always thought medicine would be my field, but I am not sure I will be satisfied dealing with the everyday ailments of the populace. I think I would rather pursue the sciences. Perhaps investigate spiritualism using scientific methods?"

"My princess, whatever you seek will be yours. And I would happily join you in those pursuits." He stares into my eyes. "I am a man who keeps promises. Marry me, and I will see that your dreams come true."

My pulse thunders in my ears. "You want to marry me?"

"I have always loved you." He presses the pendant to his lips, and then lays it gently on my breast.

Heat warms every part of me. Should those lips touch mine, would they set me afire like the kisses in the poems? Would I melt into accepting his proposal even though I do not want a husband?

This is my chance to find out.

I lower my face to his. Our foreheads touch.

"Ida C. Craddock, what is going on?" Mother stands in the doorway, her hat half off, her purse dangling from her wrist, the bone-white ribbon of the Christian Women's Temperance League pinned to her lapel like a brand.

I jump back, and the locket slips from his grasp. I clench his gift in my fist and think fast, but all I come up with is the truth. "I was thanking Charles for his graduation gift." I touch the delicate image of the bee, still warm from his kiss.

"That's apparent." She flicks her fingers at me. "We will discuss your behavior later. What is not apparent is why Sullivan's bastard and his confounded cough is sitting in my chair, in my parlor? Did I not tell the maid-of-all-work not to let him in?"

I take a deep breath. I will not cause another poor girl to lose her position. This one's been here less than a month. "I instructed her to do so."

Handkerchief pressed to his mouth, Charles struggles to his feet. He swallows down a cough. "It is not Ida's fault. I thought to bring her a graduation gift and"—he gives me a shy smile—"to ask her to marry me."

"*Marry you?* It's bad enough you expose her to your diseased breath just by sitting here. You will not take my daughter to the grave with you." Mother straightens to her full height. "And if you truly love her, you will walk out that door and never come back."

He looks at me, eyes glossy with tears. Two bloodred spots blossom high on his cheeks. "You will accomplish great things, Ida. Do not let anyone dissuade you otherwise. Be brave, be bold, and be assured that I and the angels love you and watch over you, and will for all the days of your life."

Mother jerks her hand toward the door. "You dare call on the spirits and make empty promises to my daughter? Better you beg God for forgiveness, for I fear you will face His judgment soon enough. Now, get out of my house and never cross this threshold again."

And he does. Head bent, he slips away like a ghost, leaving behind the barest wisp of cedar and an unanswered marriage proposal.

Heart thumping, I press the locket to my breast and glare at Mother. "How could you treat anyone so cruelly? Charles is my friend, and he wants to marry me."

"*Ha*. That shows what you know about men. Charles Sullivan is a good-for-nothing, like his father. He hopes to wheedle his way into your heart so he can get his hands on the Craddock fortune. Not that it will do him much good. Boy is at death's door."

I cross my arms in front of me. "He is not."

"For such a supposedly bright young lady, you can be exceedingly blind. That boy is riddled with the consumption that took his father and mother, and he risks your future by exposing you to his foul miasma. With your delicate constitution, you are just the type to succumb to the death cough, and I refuse to lose you. You are my only child. I have expended too much effort and money on your upbringing. And despite the vile words of that man, I care deeply. Now go pack. We will leave at once for the Freehold cottage. This entire house will need to be aired and scrubbed from top to bottom."

My head pounds. We can't leave now. I have a momentous decision to make. Should I marry Charles? Give up my resolve to never bear children in return for his loving support for my dreams? I know so little about him as a man, not even where he lives.

I bite my lip. Charles has always been kind, but can I trust him? Is Mother right? Does he just want our money? The Craddock patent medicine business is highly lucrative.

And even if he is honestly in love with me, do I want to relinquish my freedom as a woman to the domination of a man just for some kisses and a vague promise to help me pursue my dreams? After all, what use are dreams of a career if I am burdened down with children?

My brain whirls, searching for some excuse to delay our precipitous departure and give me time to think my choices through. Then I remember one.

"But we can't leave yet. I promised Katie she could borrow Daisy while we were at the cottage."

Mother shakes her head. "Sorry I ever bought you that stupid horse. I'll pay a boy to take your old cob over to their stable. Now, get a move on. And hand over that locket. I will dispose of that contaminated thing."

Blood roars in my ears. I shove the pendant under my collar. "You might have gotten rid of Charles, but you will not take away his gift."

Mother crooks her finger toward the door. "Fine. I'll see to your defiance later. Getting you away from his foul sickness is of utmost urgency. I want your bags packed and on the front stoop in half an hour. The Nelson boy can fetch the horse and buggy from the livery.

I draw out the locket and press my lips to the warm surface. I hope I do get consumption and die like the heroine in one of those French novels she hates. It would serve my mother right.

Chapter 4

"Lewd thoughts soon overcome native innocence."
Anthony Comstock, *Traps for the Young*, p. 8

Craddock Apothecary, 1034 Race Street, Philadelphia, 1879

I slip through the side entrance and wrinkle my nose against the carbolic reek of my mother's apothecary shop.

Three years after my graduation, and I am still at Mother's beck and call. Today, she has set me the task of polishing every medicine bottle in the store.

I don my white apron and pick up the polishing cloth.

Someone knocks on the front door.

I spin around. There aren't supposed to be any customers at this early hour. My mother would never have left me alone while she supervised the unloading of the latest supply order, if she'd thought I'd have to deal with the public.

A familiar face peeks through the glass.

"Annie Shoemaker." I drop the cloth and rush to meet her. I throw open the door and give my former teacher a hug. "I am so glad to see you." I draw back. "Are you still teaching at Friend's?"

"No. I . . . I left at the end of this term. I have married."

"That's wonderful news."

Her mouth forms a pinched smile. "I guess." She runs her finger along the edge of the oak counter. "I need some medical advice, and I remembered your mother ran an apothecary."

"Are you ailing?" I wave my hand toward the bottles of cure-alls on the shelves. "I would advise seeing a doctor over any of these concoctions."

She studies the floor. "I can't. It's . . . well, I thought perhaps . . . your mother being a woman, might have a suggestion as to how to deal with a female problem."

"Oh. I don't normally work here, but let me see. We stock lots of female remedies." I circle the counter and stare at the rows of jewel-toned bottles. Surely, there is something I can give the teacher who taught me so much? I take a ruby-red vial from the bottom shelf. The label claims it is a tonic for the blood. I look over my shoulder. "Annie, what exactly is your problem?"

"Ida." My mother's voice slashes through me. "What are you doing?"

I shove the bottle back in its place and turn around. "I was helping this customer." I take care not to say her name. I would not remind Mother of the anatomy book incident.

"That is not your job. Now leave."

I give Annie a crooked smile. "My mother will help you." I undo the apron, hang it on a hook, then hurry out the door. I stop just past the shop window and wait.

Annie emerges a few minutes later, her hands empty. She frowns at me and swerves to pass by.

I catch her sleeve. "Didn't my mother have anything to help?"

"No."

"But I know she sells many popular remedies. Mother swears by our Craddock Bitters for pain at that time of month."

"None of them will help with my problem. I misjudged her. I thought, since she sent you to a liberal school, she'd be sympathetic."

"I'm sorry. My father was the Quaker. He required my attendance at Friends in his will. Thank goodness, or I would never have received any education."

Annie huffs. "I knew your mother was a prude after she destroyed my *Grey's Anatomy*, but I thought she would have some womanly feelings. She's the only female apothecary proprietor in this part of the city."

I cannot stand the look on her face. "If you want, I could go look for something after closing hours."

"Dear heart, while everybody at Friends Central touted your brilliance, I always found your kindness and empathy to be your most attractive feature. But I don't think you can help with this problem. You are so very young."

"Not that young. If my mother has her way, I will be married soon, too."

"Oh, Ida. Why are we kept so innocent?" She gazes off down the street. "How can I say this?"

A pair of women decked out in flower-trimmed bonnets stare at us as they walk by.

Annie glances around. "We can't talk here. Come." She grabs my arm and pulls me across the way and down the nearest back alley. The reek of the outhouses and stables makes my eyes water, but Annie doesn't stop until we are totally in the airless shadow of a brick wall.

"I probably shouldn't say anything"—she looks up and down the narrow passageway—"but what kind of teacher would I be if I didn't share my knowledge with you? I wish I had known more before I ended up in this mess." She peers up at the sky. "I thought that if you loved someone, the marriage bed could be quite lovely. My mother died when I was young, but she and my father were so loving to each other. I believed I would have the same."

She shakes her head. "My husband, George Whitby, is an up-and-coming lawyer. My father liked him. I liked him. He courted me for a year and was most attentive, bringing posies and taking me on long walks. I could talk to him about everything. He seemed open to my continuing to tutor. It was all so perfect. He proposed. I accepted. And then . . ." Annie draws a breath. "We kissed, and I felt such desire. Such love. I had no idea what would happen, but I wanted him so much."

She places her hand on my arm. "I'm not a complete fool. I knew what takes place physically between a man and a woman, but I thought it would be wonderful, romantic. Instead, the man I loved turned into an unfeeling beast. The pain was excruciating. I thought I would die. I begged him to stop, to be gentle." She sniffs back a tear. "He said it would get better, but it hasn't. The pain is worse. And he wants it all the time." She sobs loudly now.

Her news explodes in my brain like a bombshell. I wrap my arms around her and cry with her.

Hasn't my mother warned me of the pain of the marriage bed? I thought she meant childbirth, but it seems there is more to fear. This could be me. Annie is only a few years older than I.

Her voice sinks to a whisper. "I can't bear him to touch me. And I thought there must be something to help."

"Have you seen a doctor?"

Annie nods. "He prescribed cold baths and laudanum and told my husband I was the hysterical type. Me, a teacher of the sciences, hysterical? Now my husband looks at me like I am some crazed imbecile and checks every day that I have taken my 'sedative.'"

"You're actually taking it?"

"Dumped the stuff out and filled the bottle with weak tea."

"Good for you." I glance toward the end of the alley. "My mother has been married twice. Surely, she could have helped. What did she tell you?"

"To bear it. That once I was with child, I could maybe ask him to respect my delicate condition. And what will that earn me? Six or seven months free of my wifely duties? And then it will start all over again. I would escape this marriage if I could. I can't face the idea of a lifetime in that brute's bed."

"You shouldn't have to." I hug her tighter. I can't believe there is no help for her. "You could ask for a divorce."

"George would never agree. It would hurt his political aspirations." She pulls away. "I'm trapped, and there is nothing I can do about it."

For a moment, we stare at each other in silence. Annie's face is pale. Sallow skin underlines her eyes. This is not the brave, bold teacher of my last year. The light has gone out of her.

If I could, I would run away with her to someplace where women could not be mistreated by the men who profess to love them. But I have no idea if such a place exists.

She brushes the wet from my cheek. "I'm sorry I upset you. Now I know why they keep girls in the dark about what happens on the wedding night."

I grasp her hand. "Not all marriages are horrid. You said your parents were loving."

She shrugs. "Who knows what goes on in other people's bedrooms? Wives are supposed to accept their lot and not complain. Perhaps my mama put on a good show in front of me."

"I can't believe the poets could get it so wrong."

She gives me a modicum of a smile. "Maybe all that romantic balderdash is just that—a trick to get us to marry."

"Well, I think doctors should help women with problems like yours."

"Why would they? Almost all are men. And men like their women quiet and docile and soused in laudanum."

"How about a woman doctor?"

Annie huffs. "There are so few, and they're all overworked. I tried to see the two nearest to where I live and couldn't get an appointment. Come back when I am pregnant, they said. And I can't travel farther without George knowing."

At the other end of the alley, a horse neighs. A door slams. She stiffens. "I have to go."

I clutch her hand tighter. "I refuse to believe there is no help for you. If marriage is such a horror, surely someone has written about it. There are books about everything. I am going to find out the answer for you."

"Your mother would be outraged. Someone who burns anatomy books will never allow their daughter to read about what happens between men and women."

"I'll figure out a way. Mother has never been able to control all my reading."

Annie presses her fingers to her lips. "Oh dear. I should never have said anything. I can tell by the set of your jaw you are determined to pursue this. Please, don't get in trouble on my account. I would never forgive myself." She kisses my cheek then hurries away.

The kiss leaves a warm spot on my skin. I place my fingers over it.

Annie was my heroine at school. She welcomed curiosity and experimentation, made me open my eyes to the inner workings of nature. Forced me to think more deeply.

To see her brought so low sends spirals of worry through me. I made a bold promise to help her, yet I have no expertise. No freedom to pursue investigations. Limited access to books.

I would study medicine, but Mother has sworn she will not pay the fees. Still, I can't believe every marriage is so terrible. If it were, women everywhere would rise up against the institution.

The answer to her problem must exist. Marriage can't always be a nightmare.

I will just have to figure out a way to find the answer.

But weeks later, I am still searching.

Katie Stuart, my boon companion from Friends Central, tugs me closer. "I can't believe that clerk wouldn't let you buy the book you wanted. What was it called? *Female Physiology*?"

I glance back at McGrath's, the fifth bookstore we'd tried. "I hadn't realized how precious Annie's *Grey's Anatomy* was. I feel even worse now about my mother burning it."

"I think she'd said it had been her brother's."

"That's it. We need a man to buy the books." I grab her hand. "Your brother could get the volume for us."

Katie sniffs. "My brother, the horse trainer? He's not a great scholar, you know. Rarely reads. Only cares about horses and prize fights. My parents despair."

"Maybe once he discovers there are marital relations books for sale, he'll become an avid reader?"

She lifts one shoulder. "I don't think men need books about that."

We turn off Market Street and head up 12th.

"Well, Annie's husband needs something. I have a mind to go tell him to leave her alone."

Katie slaps her hand to her mouth. "Ida, you can't tell Mr. Whitby what to do. He's her husband."

"And there's the problem right there. Men and women should be equal in all things, including marriage."

"That's what Susan Anthony is trying to do."

"We can't just rely on other women to fight for our rights as woman. Sometimes we have to take action on our own." I avoid stepping on a crack in the pavement. "I know. Annie should run away."

"Be sensible. Where would she go?"

Where *could* she go? I've thought about running away forever, but the options for a young woman alone without financial resources or family support are few. "Maybe she could find a teaching position in New York or Boston, or even out west."

"Really, Ida? With no references? No money? Always looking over her shoulder for an irate husband. Why, he could even call in the Pinkertons."

"So, you're saying she can do nothing? We can do nothing?"

"You could study to be a doctor. Then you'd have access to those medical books, and you could help many women with Annie's problem. You're brilliant. You should have no trouble getting into Women's Medical College of Pennsylvania."

"It's not the getting in that's the problem. It's money. My mother refuses to pay the fees for me to study medicine. She considers any discussion about the human body vulgar. In fact, if you listened to her, you'd think nothing but cotton stuffing fills our clothing."

Katie squints at me. "But she sells patent medicine."

"And hates every minute of it. Heavens, she'd make a fortune if she'd only be more specific in the advertisements. Blood purifier? Pain reliever? We are being outsold by kidney cures and stomach easers and female trouble remedies of all kinds, and still, she will not list a single organ on the label of Craddock Bitters' cures."

"So, you're giving up on the idea of going to medical school? What will you do instead? Marry?"

Annie's pleas ring in my ears.

"No, I won't marry. Not without knowing what happens between a man and a woman. I must keep at my research, no matter how long it takes. It's the only way to help women like Annie."

"I don't know how you can help her. No one will tell us unmarried girls anything. Before I left, I asked my mother what happens on the wedding night. She said my husband would teach me what to do. She told me not to worry. With a loving man, it would all work out fine."

"Fine? But what if your loving man turns into a monster like Annie's? We can't rely on luck-of-the-draw husbands to teach us. Unmarried women must gain their own knowledge. We need to be prepared for the marriage bed so we can make our own decision about whether we want to marry or not."

"But, how will you do that? Even if you find a bookseller who will sell you that one book, it won't suffice. You will need more. You'll need access to libraries."

What Katie says is true. I will require scores of books and time to read and write. I think hard.

"I know. What if I were to claim to be writing a book on something, like the beginnings of religion?" I catch her hand in mine. "Religion is a subject my mother would find suitable for me to study. I could start with the ancient ritual practices— looked at from the perspective of history, philosophy, and science—with a woman's viewpoint, of course. I know my mythology. I've read Bullfinch's *Age of Fable* and White's *Student's Mythology*. Mother goddesses, like Isis and Demeter and Freya, once were venerated."

My mind whirls. I stop and turn to face her. "Past peoples exalted fertility and motherhood. That would give me the perfect reason to take out books on sex and marriage."

Katie lets go my hand. "It sounds grand, but don't you need a university degree to get such a work published?"

I drop my head. Katie is right. No one will respect my research unless I have a degree—an advanced degree—a *bona fide* Doctor of Philosophy. And how in the world am I supposed to get that?

The brick façade of my home looms up in front of me. The wagon outside reminds me that we are heading off to the Jersey shore on the morrow.

I stop at the steps. "Come in, Katie. Maybe my mother will let me stay with you instead of going to Ocean Grove for our yearly summer pilgrimage. That will give us time to convince your brother to buy the medical books I need."

Katie frowns. "I doubt he will." But she follows me in, anyway.

Mother stands in the hall, surrounded by her trunks and suitcases.

She speaks before I can get a word out. "Late, as usual."

I look over at Katie and strive for a light tone. "I have terrific news. Katie has invited me to stay at her house while you go to Ocean Grove so I can attend the last meeting of the Pleiades."

Mother taps her foot. "No, you're not. You can meet with your silly girlfriends when we get back from the shore. Or write them a letter."

I widen my smile. "It could be the last time we are all together." And the last time, I can maybe advise them before their wedding nights. "Three of my friends will be getting married this summer."

"I congratulate them and hope their good fortune rubs off on you, but I will not let others' social engagements spoil our summer respite."

"But it won't. It will only be for a week. I can take the train and meet you in Ocean Grove."

"Don't be ridiculous. An unmarried girl cannot travel on a train alone."

"Why not? I'm twenty-two—old enough to marry."

"But you are not married yet, are you, young lady? After you marry, it will be up to your husband to escort you. But, for now, it is my duty."

She tips her chin in that way that spells trouble coming. "You are my only child. I have expended much effort and money on your upbringing and keeping you safe. And despite the hateful expression on your face, I care deeply. This discussion is over."

I can't let Annie and my friends down, no matter how much my stomach clenches and roils.

I take a step forward. "I just can't leave now."

Mother points her finger at me. "I'll see to your defiance later. I want your bags packed and ready to go, or I will stop paying for all those correspondence courses you are taking."

Blood roars in my ears. Those courses are my path to freedom. Maybe I could just ask her what happens between a man and a woman? But I am not the brave person my friends think I am.

I hesitate.

A mistake. Mother can sniff out weakness like a mosquito hones in on bared skin.

She advances on me. "You knew we were going to the shore. What are you up to, Ida?"

I retreat. "Nothing. I just wanted to see my friends."

"I doubt that's the truth. However, to assuage your need for companionship, I will write a note to the Stuarts inviting your friend to come to Ocean Grove with us. Would that be to your liking, Miss Stuart?"

Katie nods so hard her dark curls bounce against her neck. "It would be an especial treat. What with Papa having to work all the time, I so rarely get to the shore."

My heart soars. I have begged and pleaded for years to have Katie vacation with us. Alone, I can go nowhere. With a companion, I can escape Mother's careful eye for hours. For the two weeks of our stay, I can act the independent woman I've always wanted to be, free to think and to plan. Free to play.

I can't turn down this generous offer. My research for Annie will have to wait until we return at the end of the month.

"Thank you, Mother."

She turns to Katie. "See? I am not the tyrant she tells you I am." A toothy smile, as falsehearted as her words, appears on her face. "I will write a note to Miss Stuart's parents for her to take to them."

In minutes, Katie is on her way.

But Mother is not done with me.

She seizes me by the shoulder. "How dare you defy me in front of Miss Stuart? And to think you thought to travel alone. What if your fellow travelers witness you in the grip of a fit? Such humiliation."

Her words knock the breath out of me. Will I never be free of that curse?

I throw up my hands. "But—" The lie twists on my tongue. "But I haven't had a spell in a long time. Not since I started at Friends."

"Then you're due for one."

"*Due*? No. What happens to me isn't like some kind of clockwork."

"It's a weakness in your brain that you have no control over."

I stumble back, any confidence I held battered away. My knees tremble. My words waver. "You think something is wrong with my mind?"

"Enough talk." Her voice becomes a steely swish. "I can see you've had too much exertion today, wandering who knows where with your Katie. Indeed, your face is flushed. Go to your room and rest till supper."

I turn and shuffle up the stairs. It does no good to rail when she uses that tone. Instead, I will dream of the days ahead—two weeks of freedom with Katie by my side.

Two wonderful weeks of misadventures my mother will never hear of.

Chapter 5

"Evil thoughts like bees, go in swarms."
Anthony Comstock, *Traps for the Young*, p. 1

Ocean Grove, New Jersey, 1879

For the first time since Annie's plight became an obsession, I am filled with contentment. I put my arm around Katie's waist and snug her closer. I can't believe she's here at Ocean Grove with me. No longer do I have to take tea with the biddies who rock away the summer days on the rooming house porch with nary a step in the ocean, nor do I have to sit next to my mother at the sunset services like the one being held tonight.

I squeeze Katie's hand. "I'm so glad you are here. Tomorrow, in the morning cool, we can go horseback riding on the sandy trails over among the pines. And later, when the sun burns hot, we can go splash in the waves."

Katie peeks up from beneath the shadow of her straw sunhat. "I can't wait."

I nudge her with my elbow. "But let's not go wading in our dresses like old ladies. I have saved up some coins. We can rent bathing suits at Ross's Pavilion, share a changing room, and then dash out into the surf."

"Oh, Ida." Katie wags her finger at me. "I don't think our mothers would approve."

"Those long-sleeved, below-the-knee woollies and baggy pantaloons show far less skin than these summer dresses we are wearing." I kick my feet beneath the layers of petticoats. "Though, wouldn't it be wonderful to not have to wear all these clothes in this heat? You know what? I wish we could wear short pants like little boys do."

Katie giggles. "Really, Ida. Sometimes, you have the most outrageous ideas."

"It's the clothing we have to wear that's outrageous." I pull her toward the big tent. "But first thing we're going to do is attend the sunset service. You can't visit Ocean Grove and not experience a revival meeting."

We duck under the flapping canvas and find seats at the back, as far from where my mother is sitting as possible.

All around the open-sided pavilion, daily life goes on. Campers living in the neighboring tents prepare their evening meals. Pots and pans clank. The aroma of smoke and frying meat whiffs past. From the beach come the shouts of the sunset swimmers facing down the waves. On the path behind us, children race by, playing tag, their bare feet throwing up sand.

Katie whispers from behind her hand, "Is it always this noisy?"

I laugh and whisper back, "Yes. And it's going to get noisier once the singing and preaching starts. I hope you find it entertaining. I always do."

She gazes around. A growing crowd fills the benches. Women place white sheets over the wooden altar.

She nudges me. "I have never seen the like. Religious services should be solemn. The quiet communication between you and God."

"That's the Quaker in you. But that's not the point of a camp meeting." I wave toward the musicians and choir gathering up front. "Revival meetings are intended to entertain. That's how they get so many people to come and listen to God's word. Wait till you hear the hymns and the preachers."

At that moment, the musicians strike the opening chords of "Holy, Holy, Holy." The chorus members raise their voices, and the people around us join in. Before the altar, men in white collars gather.

My gaze lands on the minister coming forward to preach first. I murmur in Katie's ear, "Look, the Methodists have brought in a young preacher for the service tonight."

Katie crooks her neck to see past the heads in front of her then whispers back, "Handsome fellow. Quite Byronesque, don't you think?"

She's right. This man of God is well-chosen by the bearded elders sitting to the side. Angel-faced and sweet-tongued, he is a fine specimen of manhood. He spouts the same scripture all of them sputter, but he puts more passion into it. And it is working.

The low hubbub that usually goes on throughout the preaching has quieted down so much you can hear the collected breaths of the congregation. Women, old and young, peer up at him, their faces flushed. Men shuffle on the hard benches.

I shift on the bench to gain a better view. He has power, this man. Perhaps today is the day spiritual ecstasy will overtake me, and my mother's prayers will be answered. Maybe at last, my demons will be exorcised for good.

The too-handsome holy man calls on the Lord for our salvation. "Rise, my friends. Shed your sins and take the Lord who died on the cross into your hearts. He is waiting. Come." He tilts his head back and spreads out his arms as if he were on that self-same cross. "Arise and be saved."

In front of me, a girl stands, and then another and another. The tent fills with song as the penitents tread the sand-packed path to the altar and bow their heads in submission. Forgiveness descends in the form of the minister's hands. Girls visibly tremble at his touch.

I hold my breath. Is the Holy Spirit truly here in this place, flowing through this man's fingers? Is that why the women are quaking?

A sinful thought strikes. Or is it the effect of the handsome minister himself?

The idea shocks me.

I clasp my hands to my heart and beg forgiveness for such a wanton sentiment. I hurry to repent my sins. I ask forgiveness for being a perpetual disappointment to Mother. But most of all, I pray for my unearthly fits to flee and leave me normal.

The preacher's hands alight on the head of a kneeling, pink-faced girl, dressed in virginal white. The soles of her sand-scuffed slippers peek out from beneath the hem of her skirt. I imagine his hands on my own skull, the weight of them, the power of them, and chilly bumps skitter across my skin.

Could it be that simple? Could all my problems be solved so easily by a preacher man's touch?

Katie's elbow nudges me in the ribs. "I dare you to go up there."

For a moment, I'm tempted. I could confess my sins and feel those holy hands on my own head. For once in my life, I could do the expected and make my mother happy.

I half-rise. My demons cast off, I could go home, and perhaps Mother and I might live together in peace under God's blessing.

I peer over the shoulders of the people in front of me and spy my mother. She, too, is mesmerized. Not by the descending of the Holy Spirit before us, but by the red-haired, bewhiskered man sitting beside her, the one whispering in her ear.

Two unhappy marriages, a litany of dead children, and still Mother is looking to attract a man? Surely, marriage cannot be as horrible as Annie says.

Mother rubs her shoulder against the stranger's and laughs in that under-the-breath way she usually reserves for the handsomest tradesmen who come knocking on our door. She wouldn't marry this man, would she?

My temples pound, and my skin crawls. I tuck my elbows to my sides. My ears buzz. Have my demons invaded this holy space?

I must not have a fit here in the presence of God and His followers.

I seize Katie by the hand and drag her out into the dusk.

"Please." Her hand twists in mine. "You're embarrassing me in front of all these people."

"It doesn't matter what they think. They don't know us. We don't know them." I wrap my fingers more firmly around Katie's and tow her down the well-trod path to the ocean.

Out in the open, the sea breeze ruffles my hair and buffets my skirts. I breathe deeply. The salt air calms the pounding in my head and drives the impending demons away.

At the water's edge, I stop, inches from where the waves lick the sand. How could my mother be interested in a man like that? Or any man? My mother's advice to Annie gave no hint she found a man in her bed pleasing.

A gust of wind steals Katie's bonnet. I watch it tumble down the beach, cartwheeling left and right like the crazed ideas tumbling through my mind.

She races after it. Happy and free, Katie returns, laughing, the hat dangling from her fingers, two marble-pink whelk shells in her hand.

"Thank goodness, those little boys caught my straw hat before it flew into the surf. And look what they gave me." Katie drops the shells in my lap. "See? One for you and one for me, so we will always remember these days at the shore."

I hold one of the fragile shells to my ear. The whispers of the sea swirl through me like the winging of ghosts.

She plops down in the sand and loops her arm around my waist. "You're trembling. What's wrong?"

Overhead, gulls soar against a lavender-blue sky. Green-blue waves wash in and out over white sand.

I drop the shell in my lap and let out a long, faltering breath. "I saw my mother being way too familiar with a gentleman. I fear she is thinking of marrying again."

"But she's a widow. She's free to do so."

"The only reason anyone would marry a twice-widowed woman of forty-six is for her money. Everyone knows my mother is wealthy. The law gives a husband total power over his wife's possessions. If this man marries her, he would have legal rights over our property. Run the business or, more likely, ruin it."

"You're jumping to conclusions. Just because she's flirting with someone doesn't mean marriage or ruin."

"You don't know my mother. She'd marry someone to spite me."

Katie's brow furrows. "I find that hard to believe."

"That fiery-hair stranger could join forces with my mother and force me to marry."

"But you will have to marry sometime."

I lean back on my elbows. The warm sand cups my body. "I had a marriage proposal, you know."

"*What?* And you didn't tell me?" Katie puffs out a breath. "So, who proposed?"

"The son of an old friend of my father's, Charles Sullivan. My mother believes he is dying of consumption. Banned him from seeing me ever again."

"Charles? I remember meeting him once at your house. He is good-looking, in a delicate way. All that white-blond hair. So, are you considering his proposal?"

"Of course not. I'll never let a man own me. Be my master." I squint out at the horizon. "But I was tempted. I've known him from childhood. Charles has always been kind to me. He promised to help me follow my dreams if I accepted his proposal."

"You don't need his help."

I sit up. "I'm going to need someone's help. I'm going to do something outrageous."

Katie wrinkles her nose at me. "What else haven't you told me?"

"I'm going to apply to the new undergraduate program at the School of Arts and Sciences at the University of Pennsylvania."

"But Penn only accepts men."

"Exactly. And it's time that changed. Why shouldn't I be the first woman to trod those ivy halls?"

"Oh, Ida. If anyone can get in, it is you. You were a tyro at school. And you are the most persistent person I've ever met. I have no idea how you managed to study German and Latin, as well as French, and graduate at the top of our class. But why not attend a woman's college, like Pennsylvania Female College or Vassar?"

"Because if I am going be recognized as an expert, I have to do it in the world of men."

"I don't know, Ida. If your mother won't pay for medical school, she surely won't pay for you to go to an all-male university."

I grasp both Katie's hands. "But I'm going to be the first. Imagine how honored I'll be when I'm accepted. How celebrated. How can my well-to-do mother deny me the fees then? She would look petty. And I am sure I will find plenty of women who will support me in the effort to bring down those unjust barriers—our teachers at Friends, the girls in our Pleiades club, and you. Right?"

"Of course."

"Then, how can I fail?"

Katie grins. "That's what I love about you, Ida—nothing can stop you. Someday, I'll be able to tell people I knew you."

She rises and pulls me up. "Let's get an ice cream at Day's to celebrate Ida Craddock, the woman who will change the world for women."

Twenty minutes later, I stand on the porch of the rooming house, my dripping cone forgotten. I grasp Katie's arm so tightly I am sure I am hurting her. I can think of nothing to say.

Now I know why Mother let me invite Katie. Not because she wanted me happy, but because it gave her the freedom to bring a man into our household.

The man holding my mother's hand is large and jowly and familiar. Thomas Decker has often stayed at this rooming house during our summers in Ocean Grove. He has eaten at the table with us, blotted his mouth, folded his napkin. Never has he paid a bit of attention to my mother, as far as I know. No more than a greeting in passing. A tip of the hat. A closed-lip smile.

But he sat beside Mother today at the service, and he is smiling broadly now.

"Lizzie and I have an announcement to make."

I close my eyes and hum beneath my breath in an effort to shut out Thomas Decker's next words, but I hear them, anyway.

"I have asked her to become my wife, and she has accepted."

Traitor, I want to shout. *Go away and leave Mother and me alone. I do not need a father to control me. I don't need someone to interfere in my plans.*

But I say none of those things. I hold my fingers to my lips. Surely, this is just a whim on my mother's part? Or has he bamboozled her?

Or worse—compromised her?

I stare at the pair. My mother looks too happy for this to be unwanted.

She wags her finger at me. "Ida, come get a hug from your soon-to-be father."

A hug? After years of being warned never to let a man touch me, it is fine for this one to do so?

I shrink against Katie. What in the world must my dear friend be thinking? She knows how I feel about men. About marriage.

The interloper doesn't wait. He steps forward and traps me in his arms. He presses me to his pungent body and buries me beneath a shadow I will never escape. Then he lets go, and I fall back into a world turned upside down.

For years, it has been the two of us—Mother and me. Choosing which maid to hire. Worrying that the next shipment of Craddock Bitters won't sell. Disagreeing over what I can and cannot read. Fighting and hating and living close.

But that mother is no longer mine. Once she marries, she will no longer be head of the household. Decker will be. No longer will she run the patent medicine business. Decker will. No longer will she be in charge of me. Decker will. Nor will she be the one deciding to pay for my university education.

My heart skips a beat.

Decker will.

Later that night, I lie beside Katie in the bed we share and stare at the two shells resting side by side on the windowsill. I cannot sleep. Fear of the changes coming slash through my brain. The pounding at my temples drums like the surf against the jetty. A shiver runs through me, cold as the undertow that pulled at our feet during today's swim. Tingles like the touch of a thousand fingers start in my toes and ripple over my skin. I have been on the edge of losing control all day. Can I stave it off again?

I sit up. Breathe in. Breathe out. Over and over. Until the impending terror subsides. Until all that remains is a tightness across my chest.

I cover my face with my hands. So close. I came so close to succumbing.

"Katie," I whisper, "you awake?"

"Uh-hum." She flips over.

I can barely see her in the dark. Not that it matters. I can feel her body heat. Smell her salty-sea scent.

I run a finger down her arm, soak in the reality of her. "Promise me you will always be my friend."

In a rustle of bedclothes, Katie pushes up on her elbow. A stray ray of light streams through the window and highlights the contours of her body, the softness of her face. "Of course."

"No matter what I say or do?"

"You are my one true friend. You helped me in my studies, taught me how to ride, showed me so many small and large kindnesses, like this holiday at the sea. You are the sister I have always wished for."

Dear, dear sister. I clasp my hand in hers. "I have something to tell you. A secret." I crumple the bed sheet in my fist. "I have fits."

"Fits?"

"These . . . spells come over me. My head aches. My skin tingles. My ears hum. It feels like invisible beings touching me, whispering to me."

Katie sits up and wraps her arms around me. "You sense spirits? But that's amazing."

I rock back and forth. "Not amazing—horrible. I'm ungodly, my mother says. Possessed by demons. When I was little, she'd tie me to the bed or lock me in a closet."

"How cruel." She hugs me tighter and rocks with me. "Not all visitations are demons, you know. Do these spirits make you do bad things? Do they hurt you? Make you scream?"

"Never. They touch me, caress me, murmur in my ears. They make me feel all prickly inside until I tremble all over. It's unworldly. Strange."

"Oh, Ida, that doesn't sound at all like demons. More like guardian angels come to earth."

"Angels? But you are a Quaker."

"I thought you knew every word in the Bible. Does it not say in the Psalms: *For he shall give His angels charge over thee, to keep thee in all thy ways*?"

I wrap my hands over her enfolding arms. "I could be sensing angels—benevolent spirits come from God? Have I been afeared for nothing? Have I let my mother control me for no reason?"

Katie nestles her chin against my neck. "Do not be hard on your mother. I am sure seeing a beloved child in the throes of a manifestation would be fearsome."

Many people sense spirits. Why not me?

The tightness in my chest loosens. No longer do I need to fear being exposed to ridicule. No longer do I need to worry about leaving home.

I twist around and put my lips on Katie's. The warmth, the connection, soothes in a way nothing else ever has. "Thank you, dear friend. You have given me hope."

I wrap the end of her braid around my finger, the chestnut brown of it blue-black in the night. My brain spins with possibilities. "Oh, I do pray they are angels. But from where and why? Oh, Katie, I must learn more about the world of spirits and spiritualism. Will you help me?"

"I'd love to. . . but—"

"But what?"

Katie stays silent for a long time. "I was going to wait to tell you this."

My chest constricts. My breath loses its rhythm. "What?"

"My parents and I will be traveling to England come fall. My father is looking to invest in manufacturing equipment for the wire works."

My pulse pounds in my ears. Katie leaving? I can't lose her. "You're going to England? What will you do there?"

"I assume we will be busy seeing the sights. My mother wants to go to France and Italy."

"But don't you want to stay here and further your education? Become a doctor or a lawyer? It is what smart women must do if we want to change the world."

Katie rests her hand on my back. "I am not you, Ida. I don't want to shake up the world. I will be content to experience being a world changer vicariously—through you." She slides her hand around my waist. "Promise me you will write me regularly. I will want to know everything you discover about your guardian angels and about marriage relations. And in return, I will tell you all about my Grand Tour."

How can I not promise to write? Katie is my heart. My soulmate. She is the one person who truly understands me. I want to say, stay—that I can't live without her. But it is not in me to spoil her amazing opportunity. Instead, I suck in a strained breath and say, "Of course, I will write. You know what an avid letter writer I am."

I put my lips on hers again. They are warm and moist, fleshy and soft—special. Sparks fly through me. Tentacles of heat stretch out deep inside me. I draw back.

"Did you feel anything?"

She scrunches back down. "I will miss you." Her voice is muffled in the sheets.

"And I will miss you." I give her another hug and vow to correspond, no matter what. But will I have something to share?

Can I win a place at Penn, or will I be a female Don Quixote, tilting at men with windmills for brains, defending their fiefdom from uppity women? And if I do win, will Despicable Decker, my unwanted step-father, support me?

I snuggle closer to Katie and fight back tears. Katie's leaving hurts, but we can stay in touch through letters and, hopefully, she will not be gone forever. If I become desperate enough, I could escape to England, or to wherever Katie is.

But Mother remarrying and bringing a man into our home? There is no escape from that. All I have are some unknown angels to protect me.

I rest my head on Katie's shoulder and pray they will.

Chapter 6

"Our youth are in danger; mentally and morally they are cursed by a literature that is a disgrace to the nineteenth century. The spirit of evil environs them."
Anthony Comstock, *Traps for the Young*, p. x

Craddock residence, Race Street 1880

*T*ump.

I shake myself awake.

The door to my sanctuary flies open.

I jerk upright and wipe the late-night-reading grit from my eyes. Sun blasts through my window. I have overslept.

My mother looms over me. Eyes narrowed into unforgiving slits, she pivots slowly, her heaving body filling the room with her nose-turning perfume. She points to my stack of library books. "Ida, where did all these books come from?"

I fight for calm. She mustn't know that I've cajoled the penniless old lawyer living next door to sign out books for me in return for a kind smile and a coin or two. "The library."

She lifts the one I've been reading off my coverlet. *"Primitive Marriage?* What are you up to, Ida?"

"It's a history of folk beliefs about ancient marriage customs."

She flips open the cover. "Marriage capture? Totally unsuitable reading for an unmarried girl. It belongs in the trash." She tucks it beneath her arm. "And that is where it is going."

My voice turns small, no louder than the squeak of a mouse. "Mother, please, I have to return it to the library."

She points to the pile of books. "And these?"

"Nothing to concern you."

"Everything you do concerns me, daughter. I have been way too lenient. To be honest, Thomas and I thought you'd come to see marriage as your best choice. But here you are, still unmarried. Still living under our roof. It is time you abandon this constant reading and studying and assume you proper role."

I throw up my hands. "No. I will never give up my books. Nor will I marry."

Mother sucks in a breath and gazes heavenward. "You are just like your beast of a father—headstrong, stubborn, foolhardy. A trial to those who love you. Would that your angelic sister had survived instead of you."

Every part of me goes numb. I have always known the truth of it, but she has never said so aloud.

She gives me a piercing look. "You have never been normal, Ida. A fidgety child, prone to fits and unable to sleep the whole night. You were always asking ridiculous questions, telling incomprehensible stories. Insisting invisible beings spoke to you. So immersed in reading a book you didn't hear me calling your name. I would have done better to tear your eyes out than to teach you how to read."

She swings her arm into the precarious pile of books. Volumes go flying. They land every which way on the floor, pages bent, covers dented. She pushes aside a sprawled book with her toe and steps toward me. She stops bare inches away, so close I can see the broken blood vessels on either side of her nose.

"Reading has ruined you. Your head is full of radical ideas and ambitions inappropriate for a daughter of mine. Just look at you. Still abed while the rest of the household is up and working."

She backs to the door. "Accept that you need the guiding influence of a man. Put away those fool books and marry. Deliver me a grandchild or two before you cannot. Before you have lost all your decency and must come begging for my forgiveness."

Mother puts her hand on the doorknob then stops and spins around. "Oh, I almost forgot the reason I came." She tugs a black-edged card from her pocket and hands it to me. "This arrived in the post this morning. That teacher of yours, Annie Shoemaker Whitby, has passed from this earth."

Every part of me stills. I pinch the card between my thumb and index finger and blink back tears until the writing comes clear. "She's dead?"

"Gone to hell. Committed suicide, is what I hear."

"No." A high-pitch buzzing fills my ears. The bright woman I knew would never have snuffed out her own life. "No, you lie."

"Do I?" She wags her finger at me. "I know the aunt. She says your *friend* was a trial to her husband and addicted to laudanum. She was one of those bookish women who think they know as much as men but are ignorant about how to live as a proper wife."

"That's because no one tells girls how men turn into beasts in the marriage bed."

Mother draws herself up to her full height. She is not tall, but she is taller than I. The skin below her eye twitches. "Ida, did that Shoemaker woman complain to you about her husband? Is that why you're reading this garbage? Why you refuse to marry?"

"What are you talking about?"

"You think I didn't recognize your *beloved* teacher that time she came round asking stupid questions about how to avoid doing her wifely duty to her husband?"

I shift from one foot to the other. "Oh, is that why she came?" My voice comes out as a squeal. Even I can tell I am lying.

"So, that spineless creature *did* share her complaints about her husband with you. I pray that woman is in the lowest level of hell."

I put up my hands, as if to bat her foul curse away. "That's a horrid thing to say."

"Not when she has poisoned you against marriage."

"If anyone has turned me from marriage, it is you. All those dead babies. Your disdain for my father."

"Little fool. The world out there is ruled by men. A woman needs a man to protect her and support her family. Yes, sometimes the marriage bed is unpleasant. Sometimes babes die. It is our inheritance from Eve. But you do your duty and, in time, if you are smart, you learn to twist your spouse to your will."

"It shouldn't be that way."

"Well, it is. So, get yourself married to some piddle-brain who will tolerate your crazy ideas. I will not support a spinster daughter who defies and embarrasses me at every turn. I'd rather see the Craddock fortune go to the Temperance League."

She thinks beggaring me will get me to marry? I can't tell if I feel stone-cold or boiling hot.

"Keep your money. I will never marry."

Her eyes narrow into dark slits. "Fine." She looks me up and down. "Nothing will come of this fool idea of living and supporting yourself on your own. You'll see. Sooner or later, you will come running home, begging for me and my dear Mr. Decker to support you."

"*Never!*" I yell then point to the door. "Go."

"Fine. Have it your way, little fool. *For now.*" With a swish of satin and a crinkle of starched lace, she finally leaves.

I slam the door behind her, and she's gone from my sight. Gone from my space.

No, not gone. Mother's dead-rose scent remains. Her cruel words remain. Her prophecy remains.

Hands trembling, I restack the books, smoothing out the pages and setting the volumes into place. A faint breeze, as soft as an angel's wings, sweeps the air around me. I give a little shiver and close my eyes. The touch of invisible fingers runs up my limbs.

For the first time in my life, instead of fighting the spell, I welcome the feeling in and let it consume me. Shaking, I fall to my knees.

"Have you come, my guardian angel? Come at last?"

Whispers swirl around me. They are light, gentle tones that chime like bells. Not the screams of evil manifestations. I breathe deeply. For the first time, my heartbeat settles, my shoulders relax, and the tension disappears. Katie is right. I am not haunted by demons, but guarded by angels.

I'm not alone. I can stand up to my mother. I can stand up to these monstrous men. I am going to *fight* for my place at Penn.

I am going to fight for women like my poor Annie. I have failed her with my procrastination in leaving home, and my inability to find clear writing on marital relations.

But there are other women out there; I am sure of it. Women whose husbands use and abuse them. I cannot fail them.

Monument Cemetery is no less dank in early spring than it is in winter. I stand toward the back, cowering under my veil, hidden in the protective shadow of my stone angel. At the gravesite, the minister drones. Dirt splatters atop the coffin. An elderly woman sobs. Black arm-banded men console Annie's pale-faced husband.

Outwardly, the funeral proceeds with proper decorum, but beneath the surface, I know, as does the beast she married, that all is not as it should be. The world believes my Annie committed suicide, overdosing on that laudanum so nicely provided by her physician. I do not.

I think her husband rid himself of a troublesome wife. Had he found her doctored laudanum and replaced the innocuous tea with something far more lethal? No one will ever know.

Annie.

Tears blur my vision. Grief squeezes so tight I cannot draw a single breath. I have never felt so angry nor so sad. Dear Annie. Dead. Buried. A beautiful bright light snuffed in the marriage bed.

It is my fault she is in that grave. While she was in pain, I dithered and dabbled, more concerned with getting into Penn and acquiring the skills I need to survive on my own than helping her.

I know more about marital relations, thanks to the books I have been reading. But while I may now understand the basic physical act, despite the curious euphemisms used by even the most eminent doctors, I do not know how to make it better for the women condemned to bear it.

I turn away and stride toward the cemetery gate, wishing my Katie was by my side. But she's gone across the sea, leaving me alone with my grief.

My body sways, my fingers tingle, and I pray a fit does not overtake me on the way home.

No matter what the Bible says, God could not have meant women to suffer so. I must do what I have been dreading. I must set out on my own.

So, I bury myself in learning a marketable skill.

"What's this?" Decker stands in my doorway, slapping an envelope against his palm.

I raise my head from the stenography book I am studying and push a wisp of hair out of my eyes. "A letter from Katie, I hope." I stand and hold out my hand.

He jerks the envelope away from me. "It looks official. Something from the University of Pennsylvania."

My heart rate speeds up. Is this the answer I have been waiting for?

After a year under this bully's thumb, the lie comes easily to my lips. "I made an inquiry about some research I am doing."

"*Research?*" He shakes the letter at me. "I'm tired of you sitting around, reading who knows what and filling your head with grandiose ideas that are of no use to a female. Tired of you having me pay money for home study courses. Time you were married, young woman, living in a household of your own and raising children. Being supported by someone else. And your mother agrees."

He taps his chin with his index finger. "The bookkeeper I have hired to keep the business accounts would be a perfect husband for you. I'll see what I can arrange. Perhaps a dinner to start."

I scuff my foot back and forth. He can arrange, and Mother can proclaim, but I am not marrying anyone. Ever. If I were to have married someone, it would have been Charles, who at least supported my dream of a career.

Decker turns to go.

"My letter." I reach for it again.

For a moment, I think he will not give it to me, and then he does. But I don't like the look on his face, all furrowed brow and steely eyes.

My stomach churns my long-ago-eaten breakfast into an acidic knot. Has he read it?

I wait for him to leave for the apothecary next door. With my mother's benign supervision, he has penny-pinched the patent medicine receipts so tightly that despite the current economic upturn, we are living like it were still the Panic of 73. So much for her twisting her husband to her will.

Only when I hear the front door slam do I examine the seal on the envelope. It looks untouched. But what about the next time?

I must put my plan in place as soon as possible. Maybe this letter will help.

I bite my lip, hesitate, and then tear the envelope open and pray for good news.

Yes. I have passed the exams. I throw out my arms and do a little jig.

I fall back on my bed and kick up my feet. I have done it. Won entrance to Penn. A true miracle. If only my beloved idol, Lucretia Mott, hadn't died two years ago. She'd be so proud of little me taking this major step forward for women.

Not that I did it alone. Without pressure from my teachers at Friends Central and from the Quaker community, and a good word from Anna Broomall, head of the Women's Medical College, and from my real father's lawyer, a Penn graduate whose always had a sweet spot for me, they'd never have let me sit for the exams.

I scan down the letter. *Oh my.* Due to my exceptional scores in Latin, Greek, history, and geography, the faculty has voted six to five to provisionally admit me to the spring undergraduate class. All I require is board approval, and I will have turned one of the oldest, most renowned men's universities co-educational.

My brain whirls. I sink down at my tiny desk and draw out a piece of stationery. I can't wait to tell Katie. She will be thrilled.

Dear, dear Annie. At last, I am on my way to making good on my promise.

Four days later, I slide into my seat at the dining table. My news tugs at my insides, but I dare not mention my plans. Not yet. First, I have to discourage the frog-eyed bookkeeper sitting opposite me, who thinks marriage to me is a *fait accompli.* Second, I must get through this meal with some semblance of manners. I owe that much to my mother for her years of chiding. That accomplished, I will make my announcement.

We are having a roast tonight. I have smelled the delicious aroma all day. The baggy-chinned maid, hired for the evening, places the platter before Decker. Across the way, my reedy suitor licks his lips. I bet he thinks we eat like this every day. To his hungry eyes, we surely look rich, what with velvet drapes at the windows, vases *a la chinoise,* and silver-plated place settings. And I, as the heiress to the Craddock patent medicine business, must appear a delicate morsel just waiting to be ingested as dessert.

Mother doesn't help. She has gained weight since marrying. Still, her mauve satin jacket, trimmed with lace, is right out of Godey's magazine, and her smooth hands, with their manicured nails, are those of a lady of leisure.

She smiles across the table at her husband. As far as she is concerned, her marriage to Decker is all she could wish. No longer does she have to run the patent medicine store and rub shoulders with the help and suppliers. No longer does she have to worry about facing customers on a daily basis like the shop girl she once was. She is free to sit in the parlor and entertain the callers come to gossip—a true lady of leisure.

Now I understand why she married this man after all those years of being just the two of us. Clever woman. She has all the benefits of a husband with none of the angst of bearing a child at her advanced age of forty-nine. The only thorn in her side is me, hogging up space, reading too much, and capable of having an embarrassing visitation at the most inconvenient time. But no worries. Her husband is working on ridding her of the problem.

Decker slices off the choicest piece of the roast and places it on Frog-Eye's plate. Me, on the other hand, he gives a thin morsel that is barely more than one bite.

I stare down at it. The penny-pincher will live on this lump of beef for the rest of the week, and he knows it.

I suck in my stomach and pretend I don't mind. I don't, really. Soon, I will be able to buy all the food I need and eat when I like.

The maid comes around with a bowl of buttery potatoes, well-mashed, followed by a dish of boiled carrots. I fill the empty spots on my plate. Then I cut off a tiny piece of meat and fork it into my mouth. Despite its delicious aroma, the actual product is tough and stringy, as befitting a cheap cut of meat.

Across from me, my would-be-wooer fills his mouth. Good. He will be kept busy gnawing on his wad of meat while I chisel my way through his armor.

For a moment, I hesitate. Am I strong enough to do this? I glance at Mother. Yes. I'm going to the University of Pennsylvania, and she isn't going to stop me.

I lay down my fork. "Mr. Gill," I say in my most fluted voice, "have you read Henry James's newest novel?" I lean in slightly. "*Portrait of a Lady*? Surely, you have encountered it. It was serialized in *The Atlantic* and just came out in print a few months ago."

Frog-Eyes glares at me over his loaded fork, swallows hard, and mumbles something.

"You have?" I state, all smiles and batting eyelids. "And what did you think of the heroine, Isabel Archer? Is it not a shame she married so wrongly? A wise lesson for all, I should think."

Decker turns a flushed shade of red. At the other end, my mother sits frozen, her fork midway to her mouth. And somewhere in the vague shadows in the corner of the room, I pray the ghost of my father is cheering me on. If he ever loved me, I am sure he'd not find this limp affront to manhood a suitable match for me.

The clerk finally finds his voice. "Uh, no, I have not read that work. With my job and all"—he glances at Decker—"I have little time for reading."

And little time for a wife. I can see that woman's future—cooking, cleaning, bearing child after child after child. That woman will not be me.

I tap the tabletop. "But reading is all so important for the cultivation of the mind, don't you agree?" I rush on before he can answer. Before Decker can shut me up. "How about I loan you my copy, and when you finish, I will be happy to discuss it with you?"

If anything, the man's eyes grow wider, but he gives it a valiant effort. "I had thought to ask you to take a walk over to the park. But—well, most certainly—we can talk about your book—*The Portrait*, did you say?" He looks at Decker, who shrugs.

I guess they cooked up something compromising for our little after-dinner outing.

I lay my hands flat on the table and look into Decker's eyes, and then the bookkeeper's. "Well, I am glad we have that settled. Now I have some news to share."

I go silent for the drama of it and to calm the trembling racking through me. When I speak again, my tone is stronger, deeper. "I have taken a job teaching phonography at Girard College."

"Phonography . . ." My mother's voice falls away. I know she has never heard of phonography, and I bet all sorts of crazy things are whipping through her head.

I decide to help her out. After all, it is not worth antagonizing her any more than needed.

"It's a way of writing down spoken speech at a rapid pace. All bookkeepers need to be fluent in it, don't you agree, Mr. Gill?"

Since Frog-Eyes probably has no more idea what phonography is than my mother, I get a muted grunt from him.

"Well, the board of directors at Girard," I continue, "thinks this notational system will be an excellent skill for their young orphans to acquire so they can be court recorders."

Mother's mouth twists. "But you don't know . . ."

"I taught myself through a correspondence course. It's amazing what you can learn through the mails today. Besides, after learning Ancient Greek and Latin and German, mastering a few squiggles was no challenge at all." I press my fingertips together. "Anyway, I am quite skilled, apparently. Girard couldn't wait to hire me as an instructor."

Mother reaches across and clamps her hand over mine. "When do you start, Ida?"

"Next week." Despite the antipathy I feel toward her, I pat her hand then withdraw my own. My mother made her choice to marry. I must now stand by my choice to leave the lopsided triune she has condemned me to. "Oh, and I will be moving out. Girard has offered me a room on campus in the matrons' wing."

I turn my attention to Frog-Eyes and risk a question. "I won't be allowed any gentleman callers, I'm afraid, Mr. Gill. Perhaps you can mail me your thoughts on James's novel. That is, if you wish to pursue our acquaintance?"

He glowers and gives a shrug-it-off nod.

I smile back. "Grand. So, that's settled."

Actually, nothing is settled. But the recriminations will be held in abeyance until our guest is gone.

It does not take long for my unwelcome suitor to gobble down his meal and take his leave, my copy of *The Portrait of a Young Lady* beneath his arm. It is no great loss. I can always take it out of the ladies' section of the City Library.

I close the front door and let out a slow breath.

"Ida, in here." My mother, arms stiff at her sides, awaits at the parlor door.

I scoot past and sit myself in the most deeply upholstered chair in the room—her chair. The one she bought to dazzle her daily callers.

I settle back against the mud-colored, horsehair cushions. No reason my body can't be comfortable, even if I fully expect to leave with an uneasy mind.

Her usual chair taken, Mother sits on the loveseat and folds her hands in her lap, a perfect picture of discomforted motherhood.

I straighten my back and lock my hands in perfect reflection.

"Now"—Mother begins—"this position at Girard you mentioned? Tell me what it entails." Her tone is chillier than the unheated room.

I smooth out the folds of my dress, wishing for my shawl. "Of course. It is quite ideal. I will be an instructor of the older boys—those ready for gainful employment. The sixteen- to eighteen-year-olds."

Mother purses her lips. "I don't know. That doesn't sound like an appropriate occupation for a young lady."

I keep the growing annoyance out of my voice. "I am going to be a teacher, Mother. That's all. A perfectly suitable occupation for a woman."

Mother gives me a too long glare. "I suppose. But this ah . . . thing you will be teaching—phono. . .?"

"It's also called stenography. It's just like teaching handwriting. I fully expect no problems." And if there are any, she will be the last to know.

"Well, I'd rather see you married. That fine bookkeeper would be a kind husband, I believe."

I stifle a snort. "That remains to be seen."

Decker steps inside the parlor. He glares at me. "She's got a job and room and board? Let the ingrate go, Lizzie. You've spoiled her rotten. Let the brat see how harsh life for a woman on her own can be. Cut her off from her allowance. She'll come running back in no time and marry as we will."

I curl my fingers in my lap. I will not come back. I will not kowtow to him or any man. But I am not opposed to his suggestion. Not at all. Decker is an unlikely ally against my mother, but his chance of success is much higher than mine. He is a man, after all.

Mother's hands twist together. Her head drops. She's a forceful woman, but she can't fight us both. "Yes, teaching will do, I suppose. It is respectable, and the work should not overly strain you. However, I will not allow you to live at that school.

What will people think of us? They will assume we have driven you away."

Though that is the truth, I soften my voice. "They will assume nothing of the sort. They will think I have found a fine position." Before she can ask my salary, I throw her a bone. "It is not far from here by horse car. I can visit often."

Mother leans back. "I would hope so. You will always have a home with us. You may not be quite the disciplined young lady I hoped, but I love you, Ida. Always."

Years ago, I would have melted at those words. But it is too late. There have been too many degradations and constrictions. Nevertheless, I rise and go to her, wrap my arms around the stiff corset holding in her well-padded body, and inhale the sour-sweet scent of her. She is my mother, and I have not been the best of daughters.

Soon though, I will show her and her misbegotten husband that I am much more than dessert for a bookkeeper. How grand that will be—to see their faces when they hear I am the first woman to enter the undergraduate school at the University of Pennsylvania.

I rise to my feet and pull myself to my full height. I am leaving home at last. A dream come true. I will be the first woman to uncover the role of women in ancient religion and to write the truth about marriage relations.

Without looking back, I march out the door and head up the stairs. I should feel exalted. Instead, unease snakes its way across my shoulders and settles in my stomach. If only I could have saved Annie, my happiness would be complete.

PART 2

"I want the universe to myself to make my experiments in."

Ida C. Craddock, Letter to Katie Stuart Wood, June 5, 1879

Chapter 7

"These obscenity defenders shout 'liberty' and 'freedom' on all
occasions. It is chronic with many of them."
Anthony Comstock. *Traps for the Young,* p. 186

Girard College, Philadelphia, 1882

My room in the matron wing at Girard is bare bones
and cramped. My trunk and book collection take up
half the space. A hard little cot, the other. Not that it
matters. The important thing is that it is my own for the
semester.

Through the open window, the sound of boys playing
baseball on the lawn sweeps in. Balls whack against bats.
Raucous cheers arise when someone scores.

I throw my brown paper-wrapped package onto the
mattress. No one cheers when I deliver my lessons.

Teaching is not what I thought it would be. The work is
unrelenting. Every day, I face down recalcitrant boys whose
interest in phonography waxes and wanes in direct

relationship to the level of heat and sunlight streaming in the classroom window. However, I do love my paycheck.

I untie the string and unwrap the paper from my newest purchase—an emancipation waist. I hold up the finely knitted merino garment that will replace not only the stiff bones of my regular corset but also the annoying corset cover that pinches me under the arms and the uncomfortable bunched-up chemise trapped beneath them.

My mother would be scandalized to know I am wearing one of those fiddle-faddles—as she calls them—dress-reform garments. I unbutton the bodice of my dress. I can't wait to put it on.

It takes a few minutes to sew loops to my petticoat and skirt so I can hang them on the buttons placed on the emancipation waist for just that purpose. But oh, what a difference when I am fully dressed. I can breathe freely, and my skirt feels so much lighter.

I spin around and clap my hands. New funds. New clothes. Next, a new religion.

I finish dressing, affix my new beribboned hat with my hatpin, then leave the campus and stride down Corinthian Avenue, past the city reservoir. The trees are adorned in the changing colors of autumn. Brittle leaves crunch beneath my feet. Crisp September air fills my lungs.

I'm free for the first time in my life. Free to roam the city. Free to read what I will. No mother or stepfather stands by to criticize my clothes or choices.

I catch the horse car at the corner, as I do every time I visit Mother, and settle in for the ride down Ridge Avenue to Spring Garden Institute. Little twinges run through me like rivulets of ice water. Am I being too bold? I have no idea who or what I will find at the meeting.

I extract the flyer about the lecture from my pocket and reread it. *"For all who love liberty,"* it says, *"the Spring*

Garden Unitarian church invites those interested to a new talk by Edward Bond Foote on 'The Comstock Laws and Free Speech.'"

I have no idea what the Comstock Laws are about, but I am sure I will find out.

The streetcar halts opposite the Institute. I tuck the brochure into my purse, cross the street, and pass beneath the columned portico. It takes me a while to search out the room where the Spring Garden Unitarians meet. Only a plain doorway with a hand-lettered *Welcome* sign at the end of a long hallway marks the meeting place.

Imagine, they have no formal church building; no gilded trappings of Christianity to announce their place of worship. It would appeal to Katie's Quaker aesthetic. It appeals to mine.

I rest my hand on the doorknob. Can I barge into a meeting of strangers?

I smooth down my bodice. Will they be able to tell I'm wearing such a radical undergarment?

My stomach pinches tight and, for a moment, I consider fleeing back to my tiny room and the waiting stack of student papers. Still, I am curious about these Unitarians my mother reviles, and I can't resist taking a peek.

I push the door partially open. Deep in discussion, a small congregation of men and women encircle a rather short gentleman with wide-set eyes, long, flowing black hair, and a chin-sweeping mustache. But it is not the speaker who interests me. It is what they are discussing. They are arguing about marriage and childbirth in mixed company. My mother would be outraged.

This, I must hear.

I gather my lagging courage and enter as quietly as I can, slipping in behind a tall woman with glossy chestnut hair, gathered up in an intricate arrangement of braids. She is perfumed with something light and sweet with a hint of lavender so different from my mother's musky rose. Surely, someone who would choose such an enticing scent will also be kind?

And she is. The woman turns and signals me to stand by her side. She takes my hand and gives it a gentle squeeze. "Welcome, my dear," she whispers.

For several minutes, I listen. To my long cotton-woolled ears, the discussion is beyond scurrilous. But oh so interesting.

Every idea proposed by Dr. Foote—for I have determined that is who the animated young man in the center of the group is—would leave my mother aghast. He argues that all social ills would disappear if the propagation of children was controlled in the marriage bed. I wonder how this would be accomplished. But it is what he says about science that wins my heart.

"Science is argus-eyed," he says. "It searches in all directions for truth, accepts it from any and every source, and assimilates everything that will bear investigation."

I clasp my hands to my bosom. This is who I want to be. A searcher bee, like Charles predicted, scientifically testing and observing as I uncover the truth about angels, about religion, about marriage.

Dr. Foote finishes and is drawn into conversation with a pair of men on the other end of the room.

The lovely lady at my side offers a smile. "I am Dr. Henrietta Westbrook, and you?"

I shake her hand, thrilled to meet a woman doctor at last. "Ida Craddock. I'm an instructor in phonography at Girard." I bite my lip and confess my indiscretion, "This is my first time here. I came alone."

But she is not my mother. She pats the back of my hand before letting go. "How brave of you. Come; let me introduce you to our members."

To her left stands a tower of a man with a prominent nose, strikingly dark eyes, and a noble brow. The distinguished white of his hair contrasts with the strength of his face and the athletic build of his shoulders. Already, I respect him. He has defended Dr. Foote's ideas on every point during the discussion. And though he is far my senior, I am unexpectedly attracted.

If I could find a man as straight and true, who acknowledges that childbirth should be regulated and the marriage bed a place of gentle love, I might consider marriage.

My newfound acquaintance rests her hand on his arm. "My husband, Richard Brodhead Westbrook," she says. "We call him the Rev, but he left the Methodist ministry years ago to serve the law."

Her words hollow me out. The best man I've ever met is taken.

"Richard," she addresses her husband, "this young lady is Ida Craddock. She is an instructor at Girard." She looks at me, and the corner of her lip tips up. "Richard is on the board of the college."

Oh. He's effectively my boss. My breath catches. If only I could turn invisible, but it is too late. The gentleman holds out his hand, and I clasp it gingerly.

"I remember your application well, Miss Craddock," he says. "Quite a Renaissance woman. All those languages. An outstanding academic record at Friends Central. Self-instructed in stenography to a master's level. And I hear you are doing miracles in the classroom."

I retrieve my hand and gather my courage. Teaching is something I can talk about. "I've discovered that boys learn phonography best when we start with the basic elements and master them before attempting dictation. And . . . I've discarded the official instruction manual and written some exercises and stories for them to practice. That seems to have made a difference."

"How interesting. Have you considered publishing your method?"

"Publish my exercises?" The thought that a prominent man would deign to offer such a suggestion sends shivers through me. "They would sell?"

Westbrook rubs his chin. "A book or a pamphlet might profit quite well. There's a growing demand for stenographers. Court clerks are always needed, and more businesses are finding people skilled in the stenographic technique to be of great value. In fact, I am anxious to hire one of your students as soon as he graduates to work in my law office. Yes, indeed, I believe you could earn a pretty penny with a text that provides a basic introduction to the craft."

The thought of earning an income from a stenography textbook overwhelms me. Then reality hits me smack in the gut. I am barely out of high school myself. Who am I to claim expertise in any subject?

I gaze down at my feet. "The suggestion intrigues, but I have no idea how to go about publishing a book. Besides, I fear I do not have the funds for such an enterprise."

"Henrietta and I would be happy to invest in a publication on stenography. Wouldn't we, my dear?"

His wife smiles broadly and tips her head in agreement.

For a moment, I see the possibility—a glowing accomplishment that is within my reach. My name forever bound between the pages of a book to be read by hundreds, maybe thousands, of people. Even my mother would applaud such a work.

But, how can I take advantage of this kind couple who have no idea I intend to leave Girard come February? That I must help women like Annie, like Katie, like me. I owe the Westbrooks the truth.

I lick my lips and clear my throat. "I fear I will not have time for such a project. I have plans . . ." My voice falters. I have told no one except my dear Katie of Penn's decision. Speaking about it aloud will make it all too real. But why shouldn't my accomplishment be shared?

I pull forth the words. "I have passed the entrance exams for the undergraduate school at Penn. The faculty have invited me to enter the university for the spring semester. I am waiting on board approval."

Henrietta gives a whoop and claps her hands. The room falls silent. All eyes turn toward us.

"Everyone. A miracle is standing here in our midst. This young lady, Miss Ida Craddock, has passed the entrance exams and been accepted into the University of Pennsylvania. A first for women. Those ivy halls will never be the same again."

Hands reach out to shake mine. Congratulations resound in my ears. I stand taller. If only my mother could see me being acknowledged for what I can do rather than how demurely I comport myself.

A middle-aged man with gray eyes and a soft mouth comes up to me. He takes my hand and embraces it between his two. For a fleeting moment, I think of how many men's hands I have touched in the last few minutes, and I want to laugh. Forget what my mother says. There is no harm in touching a man or in touching anyone. It is a mark of respect and trust and, for me, another freedom.

The gentleman bobs his head. "Reverend Hinckley, at your service. I am the minister here, and I want you to know that speaking on behalf of the members of my congregation and all the Unitarians in the city, we will fully support you in paving the way for women in higher education. It is well past time these male bastions of academia realize women are as intellectually powerful as men. Now, please meet our guest of honor whose come all the way from New York City. He, too, will support you in your efforts."

His words are like salve on the wounds inflicted by my mother. I gift him a smile. He leads me forward.

Dr. Foote greets me with a wide grin. "My, Miss Craddock, it is an honor to meet such a remarkable young lady." He offers me his hand, and I slip mine into a clasp that emanates warmth and protection. No wonder my mother doesn't want me touching men. You can learn too much about someone from placing your bare skin against theirs. I know nothing about this man except his radical ideas, and yet I would trust him with my life.

I give his hand a squeeze. "Dr. Foote, the honor is mine. I have never heard such amazing ideas as those you have shared today. The social ills of society are immense, and it is a pleasure to find someone who has a rational plan to address them."

"My dear, call me Dr. Ned. Everyone does. Now, it is you I want to know more about. So, what do you intend to study at Penn?"

He is the first to have asked, and my wildest dream pours out. "You may not approve, but I intend to focus my research on the ancient origins of religion with an emphasis on the worship of goddesses and the feminine in primitive societies and how it relates to current marriage practices."

"I most certainly do approve. It is the kind of study that is sorely lacking and for which there is a great need. But such a work is certain to stir up those stuck-in-the-mud Christians who think there is only one right way to worship God." He presses his palms together and touches the tips of his fingers to his lips, as if offering me a prayer. "I want you to know that I will always be ready to assist you in any way possible."

And I believe him with bone-deep trust. Despite his youth, this is the wise father I've always yearned for. One who will accept me for my own worth, protect me from those who would do me harm, yet still let me fly free.

But the dear man has problems of his own.

I bite my lip. "In your lecture, you mentioned Anthony Comstock. I know little about the man, though I intend to learn more. I do hope he no longer causes you trouble?"

"The Inquisitor of Smut is trouble with a capital T. He arrests without cause and drives men and women to suicide. I have personally been immune from his assaults. However, anyone he troubles, troubles me." He tugs on the end of his mustache. "And there are many—way too many—under attack. Freedom of speech is guaranteed in the First Amendment to the Constitution, and Anthony Comstock has no right to throw people in jail who speak the truths about religion and give medical advice about proper sexual union in the marriage bed. Things all people need to hear." He glances at me. "But perhaps I speak too freely to a young unmarried woman?"

My face warms. "No, not at all."

An arm slips into mine. "I have come to take you and your young lady away." Henrietta loops her other arm into his. "The reverend's wife is serving tea in the next room over, and it grows cold."

I glance about. We are the only ones left in the room. Another first. I have conversed alone with a gentleman, and my virtue has been perfectly safe. My mother can take her rules of decorum and stuff them in her pillow.

Henrietta hugs me as I am leaving. The tea was insipid, and the small cakes dry and tasteless, but none of that matters. I have found kindred souls.

I give her a huge smile.

"You are unmarried?" she asks. "But you do know what happens in the marriage bed?" She winks.

My stomach cramps. Something animalistic. Something awful enough to drive Annie to commit the worst of sins.

Something to be borne, according to my mother. But how can I admit my ignorance after attending this lecture?

Henrietta would think me a foolish girl, unworthy of her attention. And I need her. I need these Unitarians who aren't afraid to talk about marriage and childbirth. Other Annies are suffering. My friends are on the verge of marriage.

I give her my boldest look, the one I wore when I took the exams at Penn and tell myself I do not lie. I will know soon enough. "Yes, of course."

Henrietta smiles. "I have a manuscript for you to read on marriage and pregnancy. I will have someone deliver it to your room at Girard. It is by my friend, Dr. Alice Stockham. She will be speaking to our group early next year. You will join Reverend Hinckley's congregation, I suppose?"

I look over to where the Reverend stands in conversation with Henrietta's husband. I certainly want to know both men better.

I nod again. "Most assuredly. It's lovely to have found so many friendly people in one place."

A schedule of meetings in my hand, I say my goodbyes then hasten back to my room.

Storm clouds darken the sky. But the threat of rain and the looming towers of Eastern Penitentiary fail to dampen my joy. I give a little skip. What devilishly fine compatriots I have discovered. And I have even been promised a book on marriage that might answer my questions.

I turn into the gates of the Girard estate. My mother is wrong. The hunger for more knowledge about marriage is perfectly normal, and my research will help add academic strength to these people's arguments and make life better for women. I picture Richard Westbrook—and for me.

Chapter 8

"Foul thoughts are the precursors of foul actions."
Anthony Comstock, *Traps for the Young,* p. 16

Girard College, 1882

H ow quickly one can go from elation to the pit of despair. My whole body shakes as I stare down at the letter. The bastards. The idiots. Despite the support of the faculty, despite my top scores, Penn's trustees have voted against my entry into the university's hallowed halls. It will cost too much money to refit the buildings to assuage the sensibilities of a female, they say.

Sensibilities? Bah. I run my hands over my breasts, my neat waist, my feminine hips. What does my anatomy have to do with my academic ability? Rotten know-nothing men. They don't want a woman outshining silly college boys like that Frankie Bradley. They don't want *me*.

I pick up my pillow and toss it across the room with all my might. It just misses the teetering stack of books on top of my chest. The volumes I've purchased and borrowed with my heart so full of hope in preparation for starting my university studies.

Now useless.

What's the point of learning five languages and absorbing the world's history? What's the use of reading all the philosophers? I choke back a sob. What use having dreams and ambitions if you are born a woman?

I throw out my arms. Am I condemned to spend the rest of my days teaching stenography? Reading the same student exercises over and over. Finding the same stupid errors again and again. Answering the same naïve questions ad infinitum. And once a week, sit in my mother's parlor with my knees pinched together like a proper old spinster. I will go crazy from the tedium.

I puff out a breath. I could look for another position, but can I leave Girard? Despite the dull work, my situation is ideal. Where else can I live for free and earn seven dollars a week—a decent salary for a woman?

By scrimping on food and taking on outside students, I have saved half as much as I need to buy the new Remington No. 2 writing machine I've been coveting. A typewriter that I will require even more if I hope to carry out my scholarly research.

Research? Who am I kidding? I stare up at the plasterwork on the ceiling as if rosettes and meanders are a spirit board that can foretell my future. What paths are open to me now? How will I ever face all the people I regaled with my acceptance at Penn? The Westbrooks. Reverend Hinckley. The kind Dr. Ned. The embarrassment of it all.

I toss the horrid rejection letter to the floor, flop down on my cot, and thrash the mattress with my fists, wishing I could pummel the Penn board members instead.

Over and over, I pound until my temples throb, my vision blurs, and my body shakes. The old familiar chill sweeps across my shoulders. In a blink, a flash of light blossoms. Voices flutter around me, whispering incoherent messages. I scrunch into a ball and wrap my arms over my head. I rock back and forth and latch on to my only coherent thought.

Not demons.

Angels, Katie says.

I squeeze my eyes closed and try to understand the words, but numbness and nausea overtake me and carry me to oblivion.

Two weeks later, I stare across the street and take a deep breath, failure heavy on my shoulders. The entrance to the Philadelphia Institute is mobbed with people. It hasn't taken long for everyone in the city to hear of my battle with the University of Pennsylvania. How could they not when Susan Anthony, herself, has come to Philadelphia to speak out on my behalf?

Today, I will stand beside her and beg for my dream.

The thought makes me want to turn around and run. How can I convince anyone I belong at Penn when I cannot even control my own guardian spirits nor help women like Annie.

I hesitate then step off the curb and straighten my shoulders. I can do this. Men do it every day. Other women do it. Why, Philadelphia's own Anna Dickinson, the celebrated orator, has stood on this platform many times, enthralling crowds.

But I have no idea how to enthrall anyone.

I take another step. My stomach clenches so tight I can take only shallow breaths. My foot falters. I would rather sit for another round of entrance exams. I would rather be hiding beneath the sheets of my bed. If I could be anywhere but here, I would be.

But I cannot turn back. My friends and supporters are expecting me.

I work my way through the crowded doorway, my heart thundering in my chest. I scan the faces but do not see my mother. Good. She hasn't come. She has no place here among the women of the future. But I do see someone who does.

I hurry down the aisle and slide in next to Henrietta, the marvelous woman who has arranged all this for me. I want to throw my arms around her and kiss her and thank her with all my being. But such a public display of emotion is too shocking, even for me. Instead, I clasp her hand and squeeze it, perhaps too tightly. But later, at the celebratory dinner she has planned, I will find a way to tell her how precious she has become to me.

I settle in my seat and gaze up at my supporters. On the stage, flanked by the three lucky women who have gained entrance to the medical and law programs at Penn, Anthony prepares to speak. For a giant in the suffrage movement, she is more diminutive than I imagined her to be. Her face is thin and sunken. Dark circles ring her eyes. Her hair is pulled back in a lifeless bun. My mother would disdain her appearance, although they'd agree on the temperance issue.

But how Anthony looks or her stand on alcohol consumption doesn't matter. What matters is she has filled the hall with supporters for my fight against the one board member who has refused me entrance, Reverend William Bacon Stevens, the Episcopal Bishop of Philadelphia.

Henrietta clasps my hand in hers. Soon, it will be my turn to perch on that platform and make my case. My first time speaking publicly.

I give her my best smile, though deep in my heart, I know that we will fail.

Penn will never let me in. All I need do is glance around me to see the truth of it. Women fill the hall, not men. The sprinkling of Unitarians, reporters, and good male friends do not count. The powerful men are missing. The fat, arrogant men on Penn's Board of Trustees dorichard's scentn't have to listen to such as us.

"Ready?" Henrietta asks.

I nod in affirmation, even though every part of my body cringes more now that I have seen how large the audience is. I stand, despite my weak knees, move toward the platform as if through a fog, and take my place next to the grand lady.

Miss Anthony sweeps me forward, and I turn and face my supporters. I raise my chin. I will not accept this rejection. I will not run back to my mother's skirts. I promised Katie that I would make a difference.

Win or lose, I will show my mother, and all women, that birthing babies and suffering under a brute of a husband is not the only thing a woman can do.

Chapter 9

"...takes the word 'love' that sweetens so much of earth, and shines so brightly in heaven, and making that its watchword distorts and prostitutes its meaning."
Anthony Comstock, *Traps for the Young,* p. 158

Home of the Westbrooks, Oxford Street, Philadelphia, 1884

I love the Westbrook's home. Light and airy and littered with books and newspapers, it is nothing like the dull, formal rooms I grew up in. I can't believe they have invited me to the dinner being given in honor of today's guest speaker, Dr. Alice Stockham. Maybe it's because I praised her upcoming book, *Tokology,* at the public talk she gave this afternoon.

I toy with the food on my plate and glance around. Richard Westbrook commands from the head of the table. Henrietta occupies the end nearest me. Beside me sits Reverend Hinckley, and directly across from us, his soft-spoken wife, Sarah. She gifts me with intermittent smiles.

But it is Alice Stockham who holds my attention. She is precisely the kind of woman I thought she'd be—powerfully built, strong-featured, but with gentle eyes. Nothing seems to faze her as the conversation bounces around the table, skipping from one outrageous subject to another. If I were delivering a child, I would want her by my side.

As the guest of honor, she sits to the right of Richard, whose booming voice dominates the discussions. I smile at her, feeling so young.

My subtle movement catches Stockham's eye. "My dear Miss Craddock, please let me thank you for reading the draft of *Tokology* and providing such useful feedback. I am always concerned that women with little experience will not understand all the technical details of pregnancy, so your notes helped me hone my words better."

"Thank you for the opportunity." I clasp the edge of the table and lean forward. "Your book is just what girls and women need. I was never instructed by my mother, or by any teacher, on what happens inside a woman's body or how a child is conceived. All I had experienced was the sorrowful result when things did not go as nature intended. I sat beside Mother, her hand in mine, too many times as she mourned the loss of another babe."

Stockham presses her palm to her bosom. "How sad for your mother and for you. But knowledge brings power. You are just the sort of audience I hope my book will reach."

My pulse rises. I can't believe we are discussing women's matters at the dinner table. "What I truly appreciated was the clear, straightforward writing."

Do I dare say more as an unmarried woman? My mother would be aghast to hear me speaking on such topics. But she isn't here, and these are my friends—my extremely liberal friends.

I glance around the table, swallow hard, and then plow forward. "There is just one thing. You mention the law of continence. But I am not quite sure how that works from what you have described."

Next to me, the reverend inhales an audible breath, Henrietta's face flushes, and Richard's lips turn up slightly, as if he is holding back a laugh.

Sarah Hinckley carefully lays down her fork. "That is probably something that would be better understood once you marry."

The reverend's wife means well, but I will not be relegated to the when-you-are-married category by the least important person at the table. I have been named a trustee of the church. I have a right to speak my thoughts.

"But Dr. Stockham, you just said knowledge is power. What if a woman didn't want a child immediately and wants to experience marital relations on a mental and spiritual plane at first? Shouldn't she know more details about this method and any other similar ones beforehand?"

An odd silence meets my question.

My stomach cramps around the rich food I have just eaten. The only person who is looking directly at me is Stockham.

She takes a sip of her lemon water and clears her throat. "I agree with you. I wished to add much more detail in several sections, but I must be careful." She sets down the glass. "I don't know if you have heard of our postal inspector, Anthony Comstock? He reads any books that deal with the subject of pregnancy and marriage, looking for reasons to get them banned."

"*Banned*? But you are a doctor. *Tokology* is a medical book."

She shakes her head. "Doesn't matter. There is a reason other writers on the topic bury the science under bad prose and flights of poetry. Anthony Comstock is an evil snake. He ferrets out a sentence or a phrase, and suddenly you're thrown in jail and your books destroyed. I can't risk that. My information for pregnant and new mothers is too valuable to be condemned to the trash heap."

I frown. "I've heard of Comstock. Dr. Foote calls him a spider. But I thought that he only attacked obscene materials sent through the mails. *Tokology* is a medically necessary book, written in scientific language by a doctor."

Her lips form a semi-bitter smile that really isn't a smile. "We shall see. I hover very close to the edge in *Tokology,* especially in that section on chastity that you referred to. And I hope that my medical degree and the staid presentation will keep my work from his censors."

Heat floods my body, but it is no longer from embarrassment. "But that's wrong. Don't we have free speech in this country?"

Richard Westbrook snorts. "Only on paper."

I look around the table. "We have to do something about this. It is unjust for women to be kept in the dark about things concerning their own bodies by one bigoted man. Why should this Comstock person have the right to interfere in people's private lives? People should rise up and bring him down."

Richard wipes his mouth on his napkin. "That's what the American Secular Union is trying to do."

I turn to face him. "I am not familiar with them."

"It is a new organization, devoted to the separation of church and state, made up of people who believe religion should be a private matter, as guaranteed in the First Amendment, and not sanctioned or given special benefits like non-tax-paying status by our government."

"Of course," I agree.

Richard folds his hands in front of him. "Well, you see, many of us Free Thinkers, following that same line of argument, believe that marriage, universal sexual enlightenment, and sexual guidebooks are part of our spiritual and religious lives and should be free of government oversight. Have you heard of the Free Love Movement?"

I shake my head.

He gives me a wink. "Time for a little lesson in radical thought. You know that, in many states, while divorce is on the books, it is near impossible for a woman to obtain one, condemning many women to loveless, abusive marriages, and perpetual pregnancy.

"Many of a liberal mind, and those who advocate for women's rights, maintain this is wrong. Women should be able to decide whom they wish to have as a spouse and be free to choose when they will become a mother. The state should have nothing to do with their decision."

Henrietta chimes in, "Why, we must give Ida a subscription to *Lucifer, the Light-Bearer*. A good friend of Alice's, Moses Harman, just started publishing it."

Reverend Hinckley clears his throat. "I am all for women's rights, especially in liberalizing the divorce laws. But, Richard, do you really think we should introduce this young lady to the most radical ideas of the Free Love Movement before she has explored the more socially acceptable ideas of mainstream marriage reformers?"

Henrietta tips her head. "I think our Ida has way more knowledge than we give her credit for."

All eyes focus on me, and I want to shrink into nothingness. What has given Henrietta the idea that I have had sexual experience of any kind? Yes, I have book knowledge, but nothing real.

I twist my fingers in the wool of my skirt. Is it the radical way I dress? My forthright speech on sexual topics? Or is there some sinful defect in me that my mother never succeeded in whipping away?

"Of course," Henrietta continues, "it may be a moot point. You never know when Comstock will close Harman down for obscenity and throw him in jail."

"*Jail?* This Comstock person can put someone in jail just because he doesn't like what a someone writes?" I stare at Henrietta. "I can't believe one man is given that much power. Before I joined the Spring Garden Church and met Dr. Foote, I'd never heard a word about him."

Henrietta slaps the table. "The man thinks he alone is all that is standing between the devil and the American people. He believes he has the right to stick his nose into the private parts of our lives. And do you know how he got to be so powerful, Ida?"

I shake my head.

"He gathered stacks of pamphlets, books, and photos of the lewdest kind and went from one Congressman to another, dumping his supposed proofs in their laps and claiming all of those vile materials were being sent through the mail for the purpose of corrupting their children. None of which was true. He bought all that stuff himself."

Henrietta thumps the table again. "But the Comstock Laws were passed, and now we and our dear friends suffer. Doctors and pharmacists, and any who are concerned about the welfare of mothers and children, are at risk of being swept up in the postal inspector's wild purges."

Stockham clenches her fists. "He knows the only way to get books like mine to our far-flung populace is through the post."

"Don't you worry," Henrietta says. "We will help get your book distributed and into as many women's hands as possible. When does it go to print?"

"Early in the new year."

"Well, it will be none too soon." Henrietta glances over at me. "I have many contacts in Pennsylvania. For example, I'm sure Ida would be an effective manager for the dissemination of *Tokology* here in Philadelphia and environs."

I rub my ankles together. How exciting to be part of this worthy effort. But reality intrudes. My heart sinks. With my position at Girard, I have no time for such a task.

I tap the table. "Of course, I will do what I can. But with my teaching schedule and the extra tutoring I do, I don't know how much help I can provide."

"Ah," Richard leans forward. "That is one of the major reasons we asked you to join us tonight. I have a new position to offer you."

I hold my breath. Maybe this is the chance I've waiting for?

Richard looks around the table then focuses in on me. I resist closing my eyes under his intense gaze.

"As you know, I'm head of the board at the Wagner Institute, and I have authority to name you the secretary. It will be a perfect fit between your secretarial skills and your scientific bent of mind."

The Wagner Institute. My heart rate soars. I couldn't ask for a better position. It will allow me access to the amazing library and to the writings of so many famous investigators in the sciences. As secretary, I will correspond with scholars from all over the world.

I picture myself meeting academicians and impressing them with my knowledge. Perhaps one of them will take me under his tutelage and give me a chance to gather the academic qualifications I need to publish my research on religion and female fertility.

Henrietta pokes me in the shin. *Oops.* Everyone is waiting for my answer.

I clap my hands. "Oh, yes, of course. I would love to work at the Institute."

Congratulations rise around me. The reverend comes and shakes my hand. His wife beams at me.

Alice reaches across the table and bestows a sturdy handshake. "We'll talk later," she says.

For the first time since Penn rejected me, I have hope.

Everyone rises from the table and gives their compliments to the hosts. Henrietta and Richard escort the Hinckleys to the door. I turn to follow.

Alice Stockham steps up to me. "I am quite taken with you, my dear. Such intensity in a young woman is a rare find." She half-covers her mouth. "I don't think our liberal gentlemen were ready to discuss male continence at the dinner table, but let me assuage your curiosity. You probably noted that I make the point that release for men is not a necessity, as so many believe. This mistaken idea leads to women sacrificing themselves in the marriage bed. But there is another way. Men can maintain control while giving the women they love great pleasure and receiving equal pleasure in return."

"*Pleasure?*"

"Oh, you poor girl." Stockham places a hand on my arm. "Of course. Women can experience immense pleasure in the arms of a loving man. The repression of womanly sexual feelings so prevalent in our society is not natural."

Henrietta comes up, hooks her arm in mine, and winks. "Come with me for a minute. I have something to give you."

She guides me to the hallway and signals me and Alice to follow her up the staircase. The second floor is less elegantly furnished than the downstairs rooms, and far more lived in.

Henrietta opens a door off the hall and turns up the gaslight. "Come into my study for a moment."

I slip inside. The room is redolent with her soft lilac scent. It looks homey and comfortable with faded wallpaper and woven rag rugs on the floor. Shelves stacked with books line the walls, and a desk overflowing with papers stands in front of the windows. I can imagine Henrietta sitting here, writing letters to people from one end of the country to the other and composing her storied newspaper articles about Philadelphia life.

I run my hand over the books lining the nearest shelf and dream. Someday, I will have a study like this. A place of my own where no one can interrupt me. A place where I can carry out my scientific experiments on spiritualism and write my dissertation on the role of women in religion and marriage.

"Now, where is that book?" Henrietta hunkers down and searches the bottom of the tallest shelf. "Ah-ha." She yanks out a thin volume. "Perfect. I knew I had a copy here." She turns and offers it to me.

I stare down at the dusty tome in my hands. *"Kalogynomia?"*

"Bell's book is full of crazy ideas about medical treatments for women. Ignore the title and most of the recommendations. But I think you will find the short section on female orgasm enlightening."

"Female orgasm?"

"I know this probably goes against everything your mother has drilled into you, but women are fully capable of great passion and release during sexual relations." She pulls several more books off the shelf and hands them to me. "Even more so than men. A woman's capacity for sexual pleasure is one of life's greatest secrets and one, perhaps, not best learned from books." She dumps the books into my arms. "But you can try."

I must look like a startled pigeon because she takes my hand, turns it palm up, and runs her fingers across the tender skin. My breath catches.

She moves closer. "Have you ever been touched by a man? Felt that special tingle of awareness?"

I nod, remembering my former suitor's, Charles, brief touch to my forehead on the day he proposed.

"And the meeting of lips? Have you been kissed by a lover, Ida?"

I remember the feel of Katie's warm lips against mine. How different can kissing a man be?

I glance at the two eager faces. I want them to think me experienced at least a little. I swallow and lie.

"And it felt good, right? Well, that is just the tiniest taste of what a woman experiences in the arms of the person she loves. It is the most existential experience a woman can have."

Is this why my mother keeps remarrying—solely for her own pleasure while sealing my own away?

I withdraw my hand from Henrietta's. "So, why don't mothers share this with their daughters? My mother made the marriage bed sound like a place of torture."

Alice puts her arm over my shoulders. "And that is what we have to change, my dear. Are you willing to help us?"

I lean into the warm embrace. Why couldn't my mother be like this woman? There would have been no secrets between us. She would have welcomed my curiosity, nourished my yearning to scale the heights of knowledge.

My stomach twists tight. She could have helped Annie.

"Of course, I will do everything I can to help disseminate your book and any other materials you have. I am not afraid of Comstock, or any man."

Alice stands me at arm's length. "Well, you should be, my dear. Anthony Comstock and his legions are a threat to every woman. Be wary. Let our free-thinking men deal with him. It is better to stay out of his purview and do what women have always done—work behind the scenes."

I open my mouth to protest.

"And don't forget you have your research to do," Henrietta says. "Producing a major work on ancient feminine ritual power will go far in furthering our cause for free love marriage. This new position at Wagner is going to let your great intellectual imagination soar. That's why I encouraged Richard to appoint you over one of those stodgy Penn graduates who usually apply for the post."

I reach out and take her hands in mine. "It was your doing, my landing the secretary job?"

"Well, it didn't hurt that Richard is amazed at your prowess with the new stenography. Expect to be taking down a lot of letters for him and the rest of the board and managers. My husband finds you quite attractive, too. Thinks you will add a more feminine tone to the museum offices."

Richard Westbrook thinks me attractive? My heart does a little leap then tumbles. I picture Henrietta and her handsome husband in the throes of passion and blink my eyes. I want to experience that. But without the fear of bearing children.

I remember my initial question. "Dr. Stockham?"

"Call me, Alice, please. I just know we will be the best of friends."

"Alice, about this male continence; can you tell me more?"

She gives a laugh. "Planning on some fun explorations with your lover?"

I shake my head. "No. I have no lover. He, uh, died." My stomach cramps, and the food I have eaten turns heavy. I hate to lie to these two women who have been so kind.

Alice takes me in her arms and gently rocks me. "It's okay, Ida. There is no worse pain than to lose one you love."

I think of Annie, and I curl against her. This is what my mother should have done the day she brought me the news.

I press my hands to my cheeks and discover them wet. If I could sink into the rug, I would. What must these two fine ladies think of me?

I pull away and struggle to regain control. "I am so sorry." I suck in a breath and change the subject. "Do either of you believe spirits are real?"

Henrietta tips her head. "There are so many unexplained phenomena it is hard to believe they are not. Still . . ." She peers at the drapes, as if a host of phantasms hides behind them. "I also believe there are many charlatans out there who prey on people's grief."

"It's just"—I hesitate—"well, I have never admitted this to anyone before, but sometimes I feel angels nearby, hovering and watching over me." A tingle runs through me. What I used to hate, I now desire with all my being. But no fit has come in the last two years. "Do you think me foolish?"

Alice shakes her head.

Henrietta pats my back. "Never. We feel what we feel. Now come; let's go get a cup of coffee and together plan our little Ida's future."

Chapter 10

"But worse than any cyclone or tornado is this silent influence,
this breath of poisons. . ."
Anthony Comstock, *Traps for the Young*, p. 48

Craddock residence, Race Street, Philadelphia, 1884

The light of dawn creeps between the draperies. I pull
another book off the pile Henrietta has lent me and flip
the cover open then slap it closed.

Of all I have read so far, Alice Stockham's *Tokology* is the
best. I draw out the well-thumbed book. I scan the pages.
Stockham's work is in plain language and assumes women are
sensible, not flighty creatures, fully capable of understanding
their own bodies. And her advice on food and diet make
tremendous sense. But it is her section on the law of
continence that fascinates me.

I may not know exactly what happens between a man and
woman, but I have seen dogs rutting in the street and imagined
it to be much alike. But that animalistic joining is not the way
men and women were meant to act. Stockham writes that

intimate relations of men and women must be elevated to a spiritual plane. We are the wisest of creatures, and the union of male and female must be more than animal lust. There must be control, and care, and love for each other.

I close the book. The problem is Alice doesn't explain enough.

Nearly everything about women is written by men. What did they miss? What did they leave out? I must go farther back into ancient history. Mine the depths of mythology and folklore. But, most importantly, I need access to books titled *Primitive Symbolism* and *Sex Worship*. Books that say right inside the front cover: "*Not for women's eyes.*"

The question is how to get my hands on them.

It takes me a week to gather up my courage. Even so, I can't stop the trembling in my knees as I climb the steps to the trim rowhouse on Cherry Street. I glance over my shoulder. This is way too close to home. One of the Craddock patent medicine customers, who knows my mother, is sure to see me and wonder why I am visiting a known bachelor at his home. But it is worth the risk.

Fellow Unitarian and trustee, Mr. Quincy, seems a kind, intelligent man, and he is one of the few to write a scathing letter to Penn upon my rejection. Surely, he will help me.

I grasp the door knocker and tap the magical three times that always works in fairy tales. Then I tuck my head down and pray—hard. *Please be home. Please open the door. Quickly.*

But Mr. Quincy has no idea I am coming, and the reason I'm here is rapidly becoming one I wish I never had.

Seconds tick by. A whiff of a cesspit somewhere down the street assaults my nose. Horses and wagons clomp past. Two gossiping maids stroll down the sidewalk, arm-in-arm. A nosy matron stares then hurries on. A cloud scuttles across the sky, blocking out the sun, and the air chills.

I shuffle my feet on the stone step. Should I go? Knock again?

I turn. The door opens.

Jacob Quincy, Esq.'s overly handsome face peers out. "Miss Craddock?"

Quincy's voice rumbles through me. My breath turns heavy in my chest and clogs my throat, as if evil spirits would smother the life out of me for what I dare do. I tense my shoulders. No, there are no evil spirits.

"Miss Craddock?" he repeats. Despite a raised eyebrow, Quincy's face shows the soft concern I am relying on.

I peer up at the man I have gotten to know over the last few weeks, and the pressure in my chest lightens. This is Always-A-Gentleman Quincy. He will help me. Once I get the courage to ask.

I half-whisper the words, "Can I come in?"

He opens the door as I hoped he would, and I step inside.

With a bow, he points the way to the parlor, and I move forward, aware of the rustling of my skirts and the whiff of my scent invading his home. What would it be like to be a free woman, come to spend an afternoon with this man like a trollop in a novel?

I shake off a vision of me gliding up the stairs to the private rooms and turn into the parlor.

The elegance surprises me. Spread out before me is a masculine space hung with gilt-framed portraits and exotic objets d'arte from places I have never been. I pick up a smoothly carved wooden bowl. The scent of cedar tickles my nose.

"You have traveled?"

"In my youth. I visited South America and the Pacific Coast." He stands in the doorway, a hand on the doorknob, his eyebrow still raised. "How may I help you, Miss Craddock?"

I set the bowl down and edge toward the fireplace. I hold out my hands and pretend to warm them. At this moment, I doubt they will ever feel warm again.

"I have a favor to ask." There, I have made a start.

I give up on warming my hands and wander around the room.

He stays in the doorway. "Would it not have been better to ask at the next meeting?"

I stop in front of a curved glass curio cabinet. "No. My favor is a private one."

He inhales and steps back. "Explain what you mean."

Now comes the hard part.

I draw on the tiny flame of righteous anger that has been propelling me ever since I had this outrageous idea and turn to face him. "I have decided to write an original thesis and prove to the world I am as good a scholar as any of those University of Pennsylvania graduates with their high-and-mighty Doctors of Philosophy."

Quincy's eyebrows settle into a more natural position. "I am sure you would succeed at such a task. I have never met a more agile mind."

Why does he have to be such a sweet-tongued man?

I press my palms together. "I knew you would be a supporter, from things you have said about women and from the letters you wrote to Penn's Board of Trustees on my behalf."

He steps into the room, and tingles flutter up my spine. I take a breath. I liked it better when he was more on guard. He will not care for what I say next.

"For my topic, I have chosen Sex Worship."

His Adam's apple bobs as he swallows down what I am sure is a gasp, but that is the only outward sign he makes. For that, I am grateful.

"And your reason for this choice?"

"I plan to write a history of religion and sex from a woman's point of view."

"Is that wise?" He comes and stands beside me.

"Curiosity is always wise. It is how we learn." I turn back to the curio cabinet. Among a hodgepodge of blue and white vases are small jade figurines, seashells in wonderous colors and, on the bottom, a stuffed baby alligator sitting next to a naked porcelain Greek goddess.

I tip my hand toward his assemblage. "Isn't that why you collected all these artifacts from your travels? Cultural objects. Folktales. Myths. Rituals. These are the keys to our past. Anthropology is the rising science of our time. We must draw on the primitive in order to delineate the evolution of the beliefs and practices of today, especially in the relationship of men and women and marriage. This area of scholarship needs a woman's voice. But how can women analyze these myths and folktales when books in this field are forbidden to them. That is wrong, is it not?"

"I do believe women are in all respects equal to men, but society is not ready for a woman to take on such a subject."

I squeeze my hands into fists. "Society will not be ready until some woman does it. In my lifetime, women have crossed the boundaries and become doctors, and lawyers, and scientists. I am going to cross the one that says women cannot study the religious and social foundations of sexual conduct. Sexual behavior is the root of all society's ills, from unbridled passion to marriage slavery. And I need your help."

Quincy holds his hands palm up, as if to push me away. But I will not be dissuaded. This man—my friend—is my best hope.

"All I am asking is for you to take the books on this topic out of the library for me."

He steps back. "No. You ask the impossible. Were it discovered, I would be seen as a corrupting source. Your mother would expect"—he tips back his head—"marriage."

"I will never marry. And I will not be corrupted. I have read *Gray's Anatomy*. I know about phal. . ."—the word sticks—"uh . . . how men are made."

"Do you?" His lips pucker. His tone turns all-knowing. "You think you can learn everything from books?"

Awareness washes over me. I am alone with a man, the one thing my mother insisted would lead to my ruin. And Quincy is right. Not everything can be learned from books.

I touch my lips. How would it feel to be kissed by a man. Could I experience that secret pleasure Alice and Henrietta raved about—an orgasm?

I give him a sideways glance. Could I ask him to kiss me? Would he stop if I asked? I trust him. I really do. And then it strikes me. It is not him I do not trust.

It is myself.

I want to be ruined. I want to know what sex is all about, and why the ancients worshiped it. I want to see a naked man. A real man. Not a marble sculpture in the museum. But I don't want a baby nor to become some man's chattel.

And I want pleasure.

Quincy is still staring at me, awaiting an answer.

I tip my head down but peek up at him. "I don't know everything."

"Of course not. But your choice of topic—you must admit, it is beyond the bounds of what an unmarried woman should concern herself."

"Is it? I should think it is exactly what every virgin should know before committing to the intimacies of marriage."

"Miss Craddock, you have no idea what you are saying."

But I do.

I move closer. So close the heat of his body soaks through the fabric of the bodice and liberty waist, warming my skin. My nipples tighten as if I am cold, but I am not. I am on fire. For the first time, I understand why women wear all these layers of cloth.

I lick my lips. "Not every woman marries, but that doesn't mean she need live a spinster." I throw caution into the trash bin with the rest of my mother's warnings, reach up, curl my arms around his neck, and press my lips to his.

His mouth against mine is stiff and dry. His teeth beneath hard. It feels nothing like how kisses are described in the penny romances, nor how I imagined kissing a man would feel. But how can I judge—a corseted girl with little true knowledge beyond books? It is my first kiss.

I fumble at his suit buttons.

"Oh no, you don't." He grips my arms and sets me back away from him. "I will not be toyed with, Miss Craddock."

"Ida. My name is Ida. And I am serious. I want to learn—everything."

He hesitates, looking to his right and his left, as if searching for escape. "Not from me, you won't."

I shrug to cover my anger. "Then it will have to be from books, I guess."

He flicks his fingers at me and turns toward the doorway. "I think it is time you left. The neighbors will think me disreputable for entertaining a lone woman this long."

"It is past time I left if you are concerned about what your neighbors think. Now, about the books. I have a list."

His shoulders slump. "You have compiled a list of works on *sexual worship*?"

"I have. Gleanings from ones I have laid my hands on." I open my purse and draw out the paper. It is one thing to talk generally, but the titles make me blush.

He unfolds the paper and scans the list. "You *are* serious." He refolds it, as if that act alone could make the reality of them disappear. "I think you wrong-headed, but I will not stand in your way. The books would have to be read here. You cannot carry them around on your person. It would be unsafe to be found with them in your possession."

That is exactly where I want them, in my hands, in my mind. What would be unsafe is reading them here.

"I live in the matron wing at Girard. I will be discreet, I promise."

Within minutes, I am out the door, and after a quick glance up and down the street to make sure no gossipy acquaintances are passing by, I hurry up the street. My heart thunders in my chest. I have done it. I have unlocked the key to reading about the sexual mysteries that women have been banned from for so long. Wait until the world reads my master work. Never again will sex be a forbidden topic, and never again will men be able to prevent women from learning about it.

I peer back at Quincy's and sniff. Mother is wrong about men. Not all of them want to ruin women. Or—I picture the marble nude in his cabinet and give myself a shake—is something wrong with me that a man like Quincy would have no sexual interest in me?

I look down. Is my figure too thin? My chin too pointed? My eyes too intense?

I cross the street and wave the horse car to a stop. I scramble aboard and find a seat across from a factory girl and her beau. I study the girl, her coarse, heavy body draped in an unstylish dress of gray, her face adorned with an over-long nose and wide-spread eyes, none of which seems off-putting to her swain, whose adoration is more than apparent.

They kiss, and I turn my face away, watching the buildings go by. Is there no man for me? No chance of experiencing that secret passion?

I refuse to believe it.

I just haven't found the right man, yet.

Chapter 11

"That 'appearances are deceitful' is especially true when Satan sets a trap for victims."
Anthony Comstock, *Traps for the Young*, p. 168

Wagner Free Institute of Sciences, 1886

The Wagner Free Institute of Science is a palace of scientific marvels, collected from all over the planet. I love the museum. I love my job.

Two years working at the Institute, and I am living my dream. My salary is double what I earned teaching. My rented room is neat, and clean, and perfect. The minute I saw that the landlady was nearly deaf and blind, I knew it would suit me fine. And it has.

She never complains about the noise as my fingers pound away on my new Remington typewriter all hours of the day and night, writing and writing what little I have learned about the role of women in religion in the past.

I snap my umbrella closed and stroll down the center aisle. The iridescent wing of an African butterfly glitters like fire in the light from the gallery windows. The convoluted surface of a brain coral catches my eye. But today, the pearlescent tones of the shell collection draw my attention.

I lean over the newly installed cherry wood specimen case, careful not to get fingerprints on the highly polished glass, and study the intricate whorls of a bisected nautilus shell that are as complicated and baffling as my current research into the history of what is called sexual worship.

The medical books Henrietta has lent me tell me nothing. The studies of the sexual religious practices of antiquity Quincy has obtained for me leave me unsatisfied. I can read the words, but without real experience, I understand nothing about how men and women come together for passionate lovemaking.

With a sigh, I turn away and head up the stairs to my office, hoping that today will be the day I make a breakthrough about fertility cults, and what I have discovered is called phallic worship.

At the top of the stairs, I spot Richard standing on the threshold of my office. My hopes fall. He smiles at me as I head toward him.

When he is here, I get nothing done. Not that I dislike his lively conversation, but the attraction between us makes me shudder with need. From the first, there has been an electric spark that has only grown more powerful over the weeks and months.

In some ways, he would be the ideal subject for my foray into sexual knowledge. I find him attractive; he finds me the same. And I know he is experienced in giving pleasure to a woman, and living with Henrietta, surely familiar with the practice of this mysterious male continence.

But I cannot approach him. He belongs to my best friend, and I would never come between them. Henrietta has been more than good to me, and she loves this man with the roving eye with all her heart.

"Ida." Richard waves a flyer at me. "I thought you'd be interested in this lecture on spiritualism."

Spiritualism. A much safer topic. I take the proffered paper from his hand and glance at it. "Another detractor, I see. Friend of yours?"

"An acquaintance. One of the professors investigating spiritual occurrences for the University of Pennsylvania. But you know where I stand on the issue. I want to see proof—scientific proof—before I succumb to the belief that apparitions make tables dance and that ordinary people can speak with the voice of some famous personage. Your own experiments . . . have you made contact?"

"Not really." Sure, I have felt the whisper of what might be angel wings and the tingles of their touch. But a message, a meaningful message from the other side—a reaching out from my angels, if that is what they are? Not at all. My spirits have abandoned me.

I fold the flyer in half and pinch the crease with my fingernail. "Well, my experiments with crystal gazing have come to nothing. Not one ghostly image has appeared, no matter how I prepare myself or what kind of crystal I use. But I am having some success with the automatic writing. If I clear my mind enough, my hand begins to form words and sentences unconsciously, but as yet nothing meaningful."

"We could hold a session together. I just purchased a new table board."

I tuck the flyer into my pocket.

Richard moves closer. His musky pomade, rich with some expensive wine-based aromatic, envelops me.

It is not Richard's scent that attracts me, but rather the chance to expand my knowledge of sex from the minuscule bits

I have gleaned from the medical books and Henrietta's hints. And that is the problem.

I imagine his fingers on the planchette, brushing against mine, my truths revealed letter by letter, and shiver. Dare I agree? Every part of my intellect says no, yet my body sends other messages. But I dare not act upon them.

"I am not using a table board. It is too easy to cheat. I am using pencil and paper and trying varying means of reaching a state of trance using automatic writing."

"And this is working for you?"

I glance down the hallway to my office where my research notes on mythic sexual symbolism wait. "A bit—as I said before."

"Fascinating. Perhaps you could demonstrate for me?" He steps closer. "I would be happy to be an outside observer for you."

It is not an outside observer I desire, and I should give him a flat no. A great big never. If we were to meet, the two of us alone in the dark, I do not think I could trust myself. I am so desperate to know what the love relation feels like. How else can I write my book and bring knowledge to other women? But poor Henrietta, as liberal as she is, would never understand. Richard is her choice. The man she loves.

And I love him not at all.

Nevertheless, I cannot wrap my mind around the definitive no that comes so easily to my lips when facing my mother. Instead, "Maybe," rolls off my tongue and turns my stomach to jelly.

I know what comes next—setting the time and place for our assignation—making my cowardly *maybe* a yes.

Trembling from head to foot, I want to pull back my words. But it is too late. Way too late.

I straighten my shoulders, determined, at least, to put him off for as long as possible.

The Director of Acquisitions pushes out of his office across the way, and I jump back. He appears oblivious to our behavior, but I know better. He has long suspected I got this position over all the better qualified male applicants because of some special relationship with the dapper Mr. Westbrook.

"Morning, Ida. I left some paperwork on your desk," he says through the thick mustache overhanging his lips that makes him look like one of the walruses at the Philadelphia Zoo. "See that they are in the mail today." He rests an arm over Richard's shoulders and guides him away from the temptation that is me.

But not for long.

Just as I settle into typing the orders for another set of cherry wood display cases, Richard peeks in my door. He winks. "How about you come around to my house this evening at seven with your planchette or whatever you're using, and we'll give it a try?"

His house. That seems safe enough. Henrietta will be there. This time, the *yes* comes effortlessly from deep inside me.

By evening, all my anxieties have returned. In my petticoat, I pace back and forth the narrow length of my rented room. Will there be other people at the Westbrooks'? I never asked. Will Richard expect to see me fall into a trance? I haven't had much success contacting the spirits or angels who speak to me during my fits.

Right now, my mind is tipping toward believing all the spiritualists' hubbub a big hoax. Weren't Jennie and Nelson Holmes found to be great frauds right here in Philadelphia, just a few blocks from Mother's?

What if Richard and Henrietta think I'm the same and disparage any scientific claims I might make? I could become a pariah. I could lose my position at the Institute.

Pressing my hands to my face, I sink down on my bed. Spiritualism had seemed such a safe topic to broach with Richard. So much safer than my real interest—sex.

A whisper of air caresses the skin of my arms. The fine hairs rise and calm settles over me. Not a real calm like the kind you feel lying in the warm, embracing sand at the beach, but an imposed calm, like the stillness soldiers say envelops them right before battle.

What do women wear to battle? I look over my few dresses and take the brown wool off the peg, the one my mother hates for its nearly bustle-less skirt. A working girl dress, she calls it. But that is what I am—a working girl.

I lay the one-piece garment out on the bed. I like the loamy color. And tonight, it will be perfect. Drab brown to fade into the shadows. Mud brown to hide the burning lust that consumes me.

But the gold buttons. They are too shiny. Too bright.

In a fit, I snip them off then cut the jet ones off my mourning black. As quickly as I can, I stitch them on then slip into the dress and glance at my pocket watch. It is past time I should leave.

Way past time.

I arrive out of breath, a half-hour late, my hair slipping out of my hurriedly whipped-together topknot, my skirt hem wet-stained from dashing through the passing rain's leftover puddles. I knock on the door, expecting Henrietta to welcome me in with her darling, crooked-toothed smile, wrap me in towels, and help fix my ragged bun.

Instead, it is Richard. He gives me a too big grin and opens the door wide.

"I was getting worried you'd decided not to come. Henrietta is out attending a lecture on childbirth or something equally obscene, and it was looking to be a lonely night."

Henrietta is out.

Richard is lonely.

My heart pounds so loudly it blocks all the warnings slicing through me. I stop in the entryway, alongside the massive pedestal table, and seize the edge just to keep standing upright. I should leave. Make an excuse. Turn around and head back to my room. Henrietta trusts me.

Then he holds out his hand. "Come, my dear. Did you bring your equipment?"

I nod. "There's not much. Just my notebook and a pencil. They're in my bag."

"Excellent." He tugs, and I follow, like a cob obeying its master.

Richard has dimmed the gas sconces. We step into the shadowy dining room. The familiar cabinets, vases, and oil paintings lie hidden. The only light is from a candle flickering on the table. The silence of the room rings in my ears.

No longer is this the place I have shared many a meal, where I have raised my voice in argument, and where I have seen the grand love between Richard and his wife play out across the table expanse.

"Where do you want to sit?"

I jump at the sound of his voice. It is softer than normal. Quieter. Almost a whisper. But with an edge of hunger in it.

I glance around the empty table, avoid Henrietta's usual place, and whisper back, "At the head."

He pulls out the chair, and I gather my skirts and sit. He pushes me closer to the table then steps to the other end and takes Henrietta's place.

There is something disorienting being in this position and looking at Richard full on. He looks smaller, tamer, and less the bulldog. He stares at me, and I hurriedly lay out my pencil and notebook.

I tip my chin. "Do you have a question?"

He leans back and gazes up at the ceiling, or rather toward heaven. "Ask my mother if she is well."

For a skeptic, it is the last question I would expect him to ask. But I pick up my pencil, semi-close my eyes, take ten deep breaths, and then wait.

For once, the words come quickly, spilling over the page, crissing and crossing, veering up and down, crowding against the margins. They come and come and come, and when I look up, the seat opposite me is empty. I inhale with a hiss, and two hands float down and rest upon my shoulders. A thumb caresses my neck.

"I was worried. You have been writing for near an hour, oblivious to everything. You must be exhausted." Again, his thumb swirls beneath my ear.

My blood thunders through me, igniting the fire that stretches from the tips of my toes to that place between my legs where the secrets lie.

I twist my head so I can see his face. Will him to kiss me. That is all it would take—a kiss, and I will explode.

There is a click of a lock, a draft of outside air, and then Henrietta, her coat half-off, peers in at us. Richard's hands are frozen on my shoulders. If I could vaporize into a spirit at that moment, I would. But I am no spirit, and Henrietta is no fool.

I shove the chair back into him, knocking his hands off me, and rise. "Henrietta, I was waiting for you." I sweep my hand toward the notebook. "Richard asked to watch me do an automatic writing demonstration. He says I have been writing for upward of an hour."

I stop. An hour? What am I saying? I can't possibly have been here so long.

I babble on, "I must have sunk into a trance. It felt like minutes. Would you like to see what I wrote?" I look down. The notebook lies open, a glaring white rectangle against the mahogany tabletop. There is plenty of writing, all right. Mostly gibberish. And a few things about angels and devils and about Richard that I want no one to read. I flip it closed.

"So, tell me about the lecture."

And she does. We retire to her office, sip tea, and talk about the use of forceps in delivery while I keep my eyes cast down, unable to look my dear friend in the face. She must think me a seductress, come to defile her husband.

Every part of me is icy-cold, and I slump over further. Why had I come here tonight? To show off my treasonous automatic writing skills? To get information for my research? No. I came because of lust, pure and simple. I want Richard Westbrook with every sinful fiber of my soul.

My mother is right. I am a fool—I shift on the chair—and I should leave. But I can't find a shred of will left. If only my dear friend would yell at me. Show anger.

But Henrietta is just too good a woman.

"Richard and I are not married."

I jerk my head up. "What?"

"Not in the way you think we are. Not on official paper. Not before the church. We have a Free Love marriage, firmly established with our own personal consent and sanctified by God." She sets down her teacup. "Far stronger than anything created by man."

"I have seen the love between you."

"Have you? Because my Richard, he's a good man, but he has appreciation for feminine beauty that can be misunderstood. And I wouldn't want to think you fell for his charm and expected—"

"Never." I rise to my feet. "I would never do anything to come between you."

Henrietta stands. "You are young and curious about sex relations." She puts a hand on my cheek. "That's understandable. A woman's desire is a mighty power. But my dear." She runs a hand down my bodice.

I look down. Two of the buttons I sewed on so hastily, too small for the buttonholes, have come undone. My breath stops. I blink back tears. She will never believe me innocent, no matter what I say.

She slowly rebuttons my dress. "You are very sweet, Ida. But I think you should find another man."

Chapter 12

"Tastes and appetites are perverted, evil habits are formed, vicious and filthy practices encouraged and death and destruction escort our youth on every side."
Anthony Comstock, *Traps for the Young*, p. 92

Wagner Institute, Philadelphia, 1887

You have to leave. Immediately."

Richard Westbrook stands in my office, the veins in his neck bulging, his face scarlet.

"I'm sorry, I'm sorry." I hurriedly gather up my precious research notes and stuff them into my carpetbag. I swing the bag off the desk top. Pens and pins go flying, along with all my dreams.

"Here." Richard holds out a small slip of paper. "It's an address in San Francisco. A friend of Henrietta's. Now hurry."

I rush down the hall, past the director's office. I can hear my mother screeching at him.

I reach the top of the stairs.

"Ida, don't you dare run away from me." Mother's voice rattles the paintings on the walls, shakes the glass in the cabinets. How she ever found out about my supposed assignation with Richard, I'll never know. But she has.

On the landing, I glance over my shoulder and cringe as the puffed-up, satin-ruffled she-demon who is my mother strides out of the office, leaving my career in ruins and my self-respect trampled beneath her feet.

"Halt."

I freeze, one foot midair.

The nasty names she called me upon arriving in my office still ring in my ears.

Trollop.

Whore.

Ingrate.

Destroyer of the Craddock good name.

And still, I cannot tear myself away.

I turn and meet her eyes.

Then Richard—dear Richard—seizes my mother's arm and pulls her around.

The connection broken, I run.

In hours, I am on a train, heading west, rocking and rolling and coughing my way to a new life in San Francisco. I twist my fingers in my lap. I have pinched and saved near three hundred dollars from my salary at Wagner. Let's see how far it will take me.

I smooth down the wrinkles in my skirt. What will Mother think when she finds me gone from the city? All her and Decker's plans to *fix* things by marrying me off to cover up my wanton behavior turned useless?

Wanton behavior? I peer into the window glass and study my reflection. Some wanton. A wanton woman would have succeeded in actually seducing some Free Love Unitarian bachelor, like Quincy. But not me.

So much for free love. A woman's choice? Bah. No man I was attracted to gave me a second look. Too intense, they said. Too forward. Too unfeminine. Only Richard is interested, and he's off-limits.

Thirty years old and still a virgin.

I force myself to peer out the window. I am doing the right thing. I am off to have a grand adventure, traveling through some of the most amazing parts of the country—the Great Plains, the Rockies, the Sonora Desert, the High Sierras. I will see the length and breadth of America. Something I have dreamed about for years.

If only I had a companion, a friend, to join me. Oh, Katie. Why didn't I follow you to Europe all those years ago? The weight in my chest grows. Maybe I could have stopped her from marrying some career diplomat who will never bring her back to the States.

I rummage in my bag and take out my newest acquisition—Spencer's *Principles of Psychology*. I can't wait to see how he has applied scientific principles to the workings of the mind. Maybe I will finally understand my own.

Two weeks later, all I desire is to get out of the rain. It is the rainy season in Southern California. Rain patters down on my umbrella as I direct the men hefting my trunk and assorted bags into the tiny cottage I have rented in Oakland. The slightly crooked, two-bedroom bungalow is built of slapped-together clapboard and furnished with battered furniture redolent of the last tenants. But the rent is far lower than anything I could find across the bay in San Francisco, and it is only a mile walk or a quick horse car ride to the ferry terminal and my new job as a lowly clerk.

Best of all, one of the few oak trees left in the city stands in the front yard. The gnarled old tree is more scrub than towering oak, but having a bit of green outside my window makes me feel a little less homesick in this burgeoning place where everything is rough, rushed, and raw.

"Ma'am?"

I turn around, expecting the hauler to be waiting with his hand out. Instead, I find a disheveled young man in a dripping wet suit, a stained travel sack at his feet.

"Is this your place?"

"I have just rented it." I thumb a finger at the carters as they come out the door. "Moving in."

"Would you be renting out a room?" He gnaws his lower lip, like an embarrassed schoolboy, and shakes the water out of his hair. "I've been searching for a while."

Dare I take in a border, especially a rather disreputable looking one? It would certainly help my money go further. Still, this one has just appeared out of nowhere.

I look up and down the rain-empty street and raise an eyebrow. "I am far from the only person in the city with a room to let"—I correct myself—"a possible room to let."

He scuffs his feet. "I heard you talking at the depot, arranging for your trunk, so I followed the cart. Your accent says you're from the East Coast, and that you're a lady and, well, I trust you more than the others around here." He drops his chin. "I have been robbed twice and beaten too many times to tell."

"Do you have a job?"

He nods. "I am working on the docks for now, trying to save up money to go to Toland Medical College."

For a moment, jealousy whips through me. How easy it is for a man to have such hopes.

"You want to be a doctor?"

"It has always been my dream. I thought to earn enough in the gold fields, but there are no opportunities left there."

I glance at the small cottage. I have just run away from gossip about my morals. Dare I welcome in an unattached young male who, despite the dirt and grime and obviously unwashed state, has the most luminescent green-gray eyes I have ever seen?

I give myself a shake. His eyes have nothing to do with this. My mother has rented to gentlemen for years. And who among these Oakland strangers, half or more of whom do not even speak English, knows enough to judge me? Far more important is the extra money his rent will bring in until I find a full-time position.

I tip back the umbrella. "The place is a mess. I planned to hire a girl to clean it up and to cook. I suppose she could sleep in the loft."

He pushes a lock of his hair out of his face. "I knew you were a lady." He puts out his hand. "Euclid Frick, at your service. I would be happy to help straighten the place up; hammer in some of those slipshod clapboards. If you approve?"

I clasp his hand and mimic my mother's tone of voice. "A dollar fifty a week. Payable in advance."

He gives my hand a confirmatory squeeze. "Agreed."

I try not to melt at the way his workingman's hand, rough and callused, wraps around mine and sends warmth streaming through me. Euclid is a boy. Much younger than I. No one I should lust after. Still, I can't stop the flutter that starts in my bosom and wells up into a breathless laugh.

I smile. "Then let's get in out of the rain and see if we can put this place to rights."

Bang.

I turn over in my bed, suddenly awake. Had I heard a sound?

A thud. Then another. My pulse rises. I sit, drawing the sheet up to my neck, as if a flimsy piece of cotton can protect me from whatever stalks through my cottage.

I hold my breath. A shadow passes my door and slips into my room.

The shadow man, for surely it is a man, shuffles around the room, pawing here, burrowing there, a rat in search of treasure. I can't see his features, but I can hear his breath hovering in the air like a whispered threat. I shrink back, heart thundering, sure I am going to die, murdered in my bed with no one to save me.

"Lady, where's your money?" His voice is gravelly deep, the way I imagine a devil might sound.

I scrunch back against my pillow and pray. I am not ready to leave this earth and join the angels, my work unfinished. God would not be so cruel.

The intruder steps closer, and I scream. I scream until I have no breath left. I scream until the shadow man runs from my room and into Euclid's. The boy was dead tired when he came in from the docks.

I yell his name over and over. Will he even hear me? Or has the thief already snuffed his life out?

The German girl thumps around in the loft above my head. An eye appears in a knothole. "Vas is it?" she calls down.

I yell back, "A robber. A robber in the house. Help."

There's a crash from Euclid's room.

"Stop," I hear him shout. "I have a gun."

All the hairs on my neck stand up. A gun?

The robber stumbles, tumbling past my door. A bowl smashes to the floor in the kitchen. The back door slams and, for a moment, all falls silent. Then the dogs up and down the back alley raise a barking chorus, and I know it is over. He's gone.

I suck in a breath. Then another. To no effect. My lungs are paralyzed. My limbs frozen. I could have been killed in my bed. Left for dead. Far from home. My grand work on the worship of the feminine and marital relations undone.

Euclid sticks his head through the doorway. "Are you all right, miss?"

All I can do is stare at him. I am alive. I have survived. But I can't stop shaking. I can't speak. Never have I felt so cold, such terror. It is as if one of San Francisco's earth tremors has rolled over me and left me marooned in some new world.

All my life, I have been cocooned, kept in wraps, living the life of the mind, not the flesh. And only today have I realized how weak I truly am.

I gaze up at Euclid and don't even try to fight back the tears as he strides toward me and gathers me into his arms. He smells of sweat, sunbaked skin, and man. He crushes me to him, and I am in heaven—heaven on earth. A heaven I do not deserve.

He rocks me back and forth as if I were the child, and he the parent. "It's okay. It's okay," he croons over and over. "He's gone. He's gone, miss."

He is right to call me miss. He is ten years younger than me. It is a mark of respect. But I'd rather he said my true name, the one only my mother knows. Not that prudish Ida, but my middle name, Celanire, the one I write little fiction pieces under and send to the *American Monthly* and *Saturday Evening Post*.

Ulla stands in the doorway, holding a broomstick. "Is she okay?"

Euclid doesn't even make a pretext of pulling away but snugs me tighter to his chest, which makes me cry even harder.

"Had the bejeezus scared out of her," he answers. "Fetch the mistress some hot tea, Ulla."

"*Ja*, sure." The girl trips off, broomstick held high.

"Do you really have a gun?" I squeak out between my sobs.

"No. But I will get one. I will not be robbed again. Or let you be terrified."

"Robbed?" I swipe at my eyes and force some air down my throat. I've had a horrible scare, but if the thief got away with Euclid's savings for school, he has sustained a grievous loss. I choke out the words, hoping I am wrong. "He stole all your money?"

"Not my cache. That's well hidden. But the bastard made off with my work jeans. Today's pay was in the pocket. Must have seen me tuck it there down at the docks. Followed me home."

I put a hand against his chest. "We must call the police. Get it back."

He places his hand on top of mine. "Too late. He's long gone by now."

My heart turns. How I wish I had the money to replace what he has lost. But I do not. I have barely twenty dollars left. Working as a fill-in clerk pays less than what a dockworker earns. Still, as the landlady, I have some responsibility for the safety of my boarder.

I clasp my hand in his. "As soon as I have a full-time job, I will repay you what was stolen."

"You are too kind. I know you're penny-pinched. Well-paid work is not easy to come by with all the immigrants streaming into the city." He looks directly into my eyes. "What is important is that you are unhurt. It could have been much worse." His mouth flicks up in a tentative smile. "Besides, I have dreamed of seeing you with your hair down since that day I met you."

I jerk back, suddenly aware of my state of undress, and tug the sagging sheet back up to my neck.

He lifts a tangled lock, running it through his fingers. "It is as lovely as I imagined it, like pale satin. You are always a lady, Miss Craddock. But I wonder . . ." He makes a rumbling sound in his throat that might be a swallowed laugh or the hum of desire. I assume it is the first, but dream it is the second.

"Your tea." Ulla swishes into the bedroom, sets a pair of mismatched cups and saucers on top of my chest, gives me an ah-ha glare, and swishes right out again.

Euclid moves closer. "Smart girl."

"Ulla?"

"No, you. You know when to scream and when not to." Then his lips are on mine, smooth, soft, and hungry, and I am melting, every part of me flaming, thrumming, and throbbing, wanting more and more and more. He wants me with all the lust a man can have, and yet he is tender, respectful.

I kiss him back with total abandon. Tasting him. Sucking him in. This is the kiss I have dreamed of ever since I learned that what passes between a man and a woman does not have to be unpleasant.

I wrap my hands in his hair and pull him closer, kissing him again. This is mutual desire. This is what it means to experience sexual arousal.

Euclid pulls back, and our eyes meet.

Ah, now I know true lust. I never was attracted like this to Richard Westbrook. I wanted to use his sexual expertise for my own purposes, and he wanted to use me for his.

But Euclid? He wants me as a lover, an equal, skin to skin, body to body.

And I love him for it.

Chapter 13

"Lust. . .reaching out like an immense cuttlefish, draws in,
from all sides, our youth to destruction."
Anthony Comstock, *Traps for the Young,* p. 13

San Francisco 1889

L ove is an amazing thing. It makes you feel lighter, as if
bubbles of joy have replaced muscles and blood and
bone.

I slip off my stool and glare at the back of my current
employer as he heads out the door. If I didn't have hope in my
heart and a handsome young man to run home to, Mr.
Batterson, Esq. would hear a thing or two from me about how
first-class stenographers should be treated.

I toss the expenditure reports and client billings onto his
desk. I hate figure-work. It is sad enough, after working a year
and a half in San Francisco, that I have to take half-pay just to
land a secretarial position. But then to be condemned to do the
accountant's work, too, burns in my craw.

But it is done, and I am free for the day.

I rush out the door and hurry down to the train ferry. The sooner I am back in Oakland, the sooner I will be with Euclid. No more haunting dreams for me. I have a real man to love.

Passersby stare after me. I slow to a ladylike walk. My dear boy has no idea how I feel, of course. Up to now, I have contented myself with a shared conversation about our workday over dinner and, later in the evening, snuggling close on the divan as I help him understand the medical textbook he is struggling through. If our time together is sprinkled with a few kisses and touches, then that is all for the better.

I arrive just as the ferry is getting ready to leave. I hurry up the gangplank and push my way to the bow. In minutes, I will be home.

Maybe tonight, Euclid's lips will meet mine. He will snug me tight against his chest and openly declare he loves me. Maybe tonight, he will unbutton the top button of my bodice and kiss my neck like a lover in a French novel. Maybe he will kiss lower. But not so far as to join in the most intimate way. Never that. I do not want a child. Yet, perhaps I will come a little closer to that ultimate pleasure Henrietta talked about.

Just the thought sends shivers through my body, and I grasp the railing of the ship and inhale the fresh scent of the sea. I have never been so happy in my life. I have never felt so near to God and the understanding that we live and move and have our entire being through Him. His beneficence grows more vivid in my heart and mind at the same time my growing love for Euclid gives me wings.

I gaze out at the incredible aqua-blue of the bay and the golden glow illuminating the western sky and shake away the bitterness and loneliness that have weighed me down all these years.

For a long time, I have held my feelings back. After all, Euclid is everything I have ever been warned against. Despite his intentions to study medicine, he's no man of leisure and scholarship like Westbrook. Nor a man of principle like Mother's Mr. Decker, who abstains from alcohol and coarse language.

Euclid is merely a dock worker with aspirations and sexual hunger—a creature of smoke, and whiskey, and male desire. But he is a man, an attractive one, and I want him, and I am going to have him as my Free Love lover.

I prepare to disembark from the ferry. Mother can no longer shame me for who and what I am, or what I feel. I am three thousand miles away. I am totally free.

Euclid is waiting for me when I arrive at the cottage. He sits at the kitchen table, his head resting in his hands.

I send Ulla off to do the marketing then hurry over to him. We will have an hour or so to immerse ourselves in each other.

"Bad day? Shall I rub your back?" It is forward of me to ask, but I tingle with the need to run my hands across his broad shoulders and feel his muscles relax beneath my palms.

He looks at me, his expression full of pain. But then it often is—working on the docks can be a punishing experience.

"What is this?' Euclid's voice is tight.

I look down at the papers on the table. Somehow, he has found my research notes.

A quiver runs down my back. My writings are far from ready for the eyes of others.

I shrug. "Oh, just research for my book." I go to pick them up.

He slaps the papers with his palm. "You're studying sex? This . . . this . . . *phallic worship*?"

Something catches in my heart. I peer down at the floorboards. "Well, yes—the science and history of religion's relationship to sex—on a spiritual level, of course. It is to be my masterwork."

"I thought you collected folktales, wrote little fables for magazines. But this . . . this is obscenity—pure filth. The kind of thing the Comstock Laws are supposed to stop." He pounds the tabletop. "I believed you a lady. Someone I shared interests with. Someone interested in helping me get into medical school. Someone I might . . . marry. But now I see you are not a respectable woman."

He shakes his head. "Did you think to seduce me as part of your research? Take advantage of my youth? Practice this male continence thing you write about?" Euclid shoves back the chair and rises. Hefting bales on the docks has made him broad and muscular. He glares at me as if I have been a bad girl. As if I am no longer an equal, but rather, just another female.

"You want sex?" he says. "I can give you sex."

Something breaks inside.

I shake my head and stumble away from him, fighting back tears. "No. I want love. I want you to love me."

"You think I could love you? Some sex-crazed lady who wants a toy you can turn on and off when you want?" He shakes his finger at my manuscript. "Like you say here? Male continence. Bah. It doesn't work like that."

"I am not crazy. It can work. Dr. Alice Stockham says—"

"I don't care who says what. Sex isn't fancy words and careful sensibilities—some special way to communicate with God as you seem to think. Making love, as you call it, is sweaty, and smelly, and wildly satisfying. It's the animal inside us. Once you set it loose, it is impossible to rein in."

My whole body trembles. How could I be so wrong to think him capable of a higher plane of existence? He is a beast, like Annie's husband, like all the others like her who share their horror stories in Harman's *Lucifer, the Light Bearer*.

I fist my hands. "For you. For the man. But not the woman."

"Really?" A lopsided grin mars his handsome face. "Only a virgin would say that."

He stalks up to me and stops so close I can feel the heat rolling off him, smell the liquor on his breath. "Want me to show you? I've put up with your teasing looks and touches for weeks now. I've commiserated with you over your mean employers and the cruelty of your mother.

"I've come to your bedroom to assuage your nightmares and listened to your rave about angels and demons, all the while trying to be the gentleman and ignore the hunger in your eyes, the glory of your hair. And now I find you have been writing this . . . this filth." He sweeps my manuscript off the table. The pages fly in every direction like feathers torn from an angel's wing.

My heart screams. My head pounds. "No. You don't understand. We are not animals. Having sex is a spiritual joining, a pleasure given us by God."

"Let's find out." He seizes my hand, trampling my hard-won words underfoot. "Come."

His hand fits perfectly around mine and, for a moment, I consider doing what he asks. I might never get this chance again. Surely, despite his harsh tone, he'll be gentle.

I stare into his narrowed eyes and read the truth there. He is like all men. He will use me like George Whitby used my Annie, and then leave me pregnant and alone.

Still, I don't want to lose him. I want him to touch me. I want him to make my blood thrum. Surely, with more time, I could convince him to try Noyes method. Prove the truth of my words. I bite my lip, searching for an excuse.

"I'm not sure we should—Ulla will . . ."

Euclid snorts. "It doesn't take that long, Miss Virgin Sex Scientist."

That most decidedly male snort of superiority decides me. This not the quiet, studious Euclid I thought I loved. This is a man turned demon by drink and anger.

I yank my hand back and take refuge on the other side of the table. "No."

"Ha. You can write about sex but not face the reality of it?" He circles around the table.

I cringe away. "I didn't think you a cruel man. To force a woman."

My words halt him.

He gives a huff, looking me up and down. "A cruel man would have already fucked you."

I flinch at the crude language. "That's the drink talking. Not you, Euclid. You're not a crass man. You are intelligent. A scholar."

He steps back and puts up his hands. "Fine. Think that. I'm done resisting your come-ons. I'm done with you." He tosses some coins on the table. "There's what I owe in rent. I'm leaving." He kicks through my papers and heads into his bedroom.

I sink down to the floor and snatch up the trampled pages, no longer trying to stop my tears. I don't even bother to look up as he stomps past me and bangs out the screen door.

For long minutes in the ensuing silence, I stare down at my mutilated manuscript. Have I made a mistake?

"Miss Craddock?" Ulla stands on the threshold with the grocery basket slung across her arm. "Was that Mr. Frick heading down the street with his duffle bag?"

I wipe my nose with the back of hand. "He will not be rooming with us anymore."

Ulla's eyebrows rise beneath her kerchief. "But we will be alone, miss. No man to protect us."

I smooth the crease from a page and set it carefully atop the pile. "Young men are streaming into the city every day. Don't worry; there will be another soon enough."

But not another to love. I will never give my heart again.

Months later, I am still reminding myself that not all men are like Euclid.

Alexander Badlam sets down the manuscript I have polished up for him. "You've done a wonderful job on this, Miss Craddock. Are you sure you won't accept any payment?"

I shake my head. "I wouldn't think of it."

How can I charge Mr. Badlam? The scholarly gentleman has given me not only two months of peace to recover from my heartbreak but also the most wonderous experience of a lifetime—a trip to Alaska aboard one of the first steamers to explore the glaciers. Singlehandedly, he has restored my faith in the male sex. Despite my lowly position as his copyist, he treated me as an equal, including me in every part of the expeditions.

And now he's fallen on hard times.

I glance around at the unfaded wallpaper squares where paintings once hung. His insurance agency is being sued in court. It will take his remaining funds to publish his amazing book, *The Wonders of Alaska*. We worked so hard on it. I must do nothing to hinder its release.

He gives me a smile so sad I know I have done the right thing. He rests his hand on the manuscript I have laboriously edited and typed. "Are you sure? Not even a bit to tide you over until you find another secretarial position?"

I shake my head. "I wouldn't think of it. Not after the incredible experience you have given me." The letter in my pocket crinkles. "Besides, I am not totally without hope."

He steeples his hands. "It was an amazing tour. What impressed you the most?"

Images flash before my eyes. "The whales. The icebergs. Walking on a glacier. Visiting the Alaskan natives and listening to their myths."

"And those amazing totem pole of theirs. Have you written your article about them, yet?"

"I have."

"Bravo. Publication is just around the corner, I am sure, my dear."

I am not sure if he means for his book or my article, but I rise, gift him my truest smile, and leave him a happy man.

Outside, the air blows hot as the inside of a furnace. I lift my hair to cool my neck and glance back at the Baden mansion. Despite his straits, he has far more than I. Sometimes, I can be too kind. I should have charged him.

I owe money to everyone I know, even my dear Katie, who sent one hundred dollars, though she has problems of her own. Secretarial work that pays a living wage is impossible to find in the city. I have my name in at six temporary employment agencies and have heard nothing.

I take out the crumbled letter that arrived three days ago. Richard Westbrook is offering me a position as secretary at the American Secular Union, the organization he mentioned so long ago. It would be a fine job, even if it does pay less than I earned at the Institute. I fan myself with the missive.

But why does he want *me*? Did Henrietta put him up to this out of our past friendship? Surely, she has heard of my dire straits. I have borrowed money from too many shared acquaintances.

Or is this solely Richard's doing? A way to get me back where he can try to seduce me again?

I watch the mothers pushing baby carriages, the strolling gentlemen in their top hats, the daring bicyclers whizzing by.

Everyone seems to have companions, lovers, places to go, things to do. Everyone but me. Without money, it doesn't matter what quality of scholar you are or how important one's research is. No one wants to be associated with the taint of poverty.

I waft the letter again. Study my scuffed shoes. If I stay here, my only choice is to become a house servant. At least then I would have food and board instead of this pinching in my stomach. But if I stoop so low as to wait on those who are the thinkers and doers and people of power, I will never be considered a lady again.

I tap my notebook containing my finished article on the phallic symbolism of totem poles.

I will never find someone to publish my writings.

I picture my crumpled research notes buried at the bottom of my trunk ever since that fateful night when Euclid turned into one of my demons. He was right. No man will accept a woman's research on sex worship. Once again, I have aimed too high.

I fold up the letter, decision made. I'm going back to Philadelphia.

But I am returning a different woman. From now on, I will proclaim to the world that I'm studying spiritualism and the occult. No one questions a woman doing that while, on the side, I use what I have learned in my research on sexual worship to write a pamphlet on the marriage relation.

I know so much more now. Annie is far from alone in her trials. Every issue of Harman's *Lucifer, the Light Bearer* carries articles decrying the abuse women receive in the marriage bed from the husbands who proclaim they love them. How can I ignore their suffering any longer?

I join the afternoon strollers and head to the horse cars. Now that I have stood in the ranks of the miserable workers whom I once despised, I know how they feel, every day facing the prospect of starvation and misery. God helping, I want my work on marriage relations to benefit ordinary people, one and all, as long as I live.

And I will have help.

Another breath of air flicks over my heated skin and raises the hairs on my arm. There are spirits, perhaps angels, all around us, and I am going to uncover them using science.

Chapter 14

"Satan by these agencies sets doubting traps, defiant traps, faithless traps, prayerless traps, blasphemous traps, fear-not-God traps."
Anthony Comstock, *Traps for the Young*, p. 200

American Secular Union, Philadelphia, 1891

Two years later, I am still wondering if my choice to return to Philadelphia was for the best. With a flick of the wrist, I insert a fresh piece of parchment into the typewriter, a move so practiced I can do it without thought, which is just as well, as the job is so time-consuming. Since taking up the secretary position, I haven't had a moment to concentrate on my research or on establishing communication with my spirits.

I rub my aching forehead then sling the carriage over.

It is hard to call up spirit visitations or write a dissertation when I toil away in an ordinary office, surrounded by mounds of undone work. Academics have secretaries. Here I am, the secretary.

I roll the paper into position and type in the Secular Union address. If only I could devote all my time to my research instead of working at this infuriating job.

I glance up from my typewriter. At least the office will be quiet for a change. The officers are off to the Girard Hotel for oysters and a drink after the board meeting, leaving me behind to do the grunt work—typing up the minutes, filing the paperwork, sending out the letters.

I type the date and stop. This is so unjust. I write all the official documents, author the Society's pamphlets, and correspond with the most eminent scientists and philosophers of our time.

I slam my fingers down on the keys. As secretary, I literally run the place, but an unmarried woman is no fit equal to join a group of supposedly liberal-minded men for lunch.

I tear the paper out of the typewriter, ball it up, and throw it at the wall. A glorified clerk is all I am and all I will ever be. For all their proclaiming of women's rights, the Union is a bastion of men and their ideas. I am voted down on everything I propose.

Without a degree and associated academic recognition, I have no standing in the intellectual world of men. Not one of the members takes my suggestions seriously. My plans for Free-Thought Sunday schools meet deaf ears. Worse, my calls for a unified front to stand against Comstock and his ilk have been argued down to the point of absurdity.

"Miss Craddock?"

I jerk my head up and fight back a grimace. Another man come to plague me. This one is wider than my desk and twice my height. His cheeks glow red from the climb to the second floor.

Hat in hand, he lumbers to my desk. "Otto Wettstein. We've corresponded. You got the solid gold pin I sent you for your consideration?"

My stomach knots, which only adds to the pounding in my head. More trouble. I pawned the stupid pin to return the money I owed Katie.

I swallow a curse. Stupid men on the board haven't given me a raise since I started here. Sure, my wage is better than what I was earning as a temporary clerk in San Francisco, but it is not adequate to pay off my debts and provide an income I can live on in some manner of style. But that's a problem to deal with another day. Right now, I have to get rid of Wettstein.

I fumble through the papers stacked on my desk. "Yes. Yes, I did. I appreciate you sending your idea for our insignia, but I have proposed a pansy and"—I pull out the design I had drawn up and lay it before him—"I have received much positive feedback from the committee."

He puts his meaty palm on top of the paper and leans toward me. "A pansy, madam?"

His size overwhelms, but I resist pulling back. "From the French *pensée*, meaning thought."

"You propose a womanish flower as a fit emblem for the champions of free thought?" He points his finger at me. "Any priest, parson, or schoolgirl might be happy wearing a cheap girlish pin you can purchase at the five-cent counter in every millinery and jewelry shop. But not bold men such as I. Men taking on the establishment need a manlier symbol. An erect torch blazing science's triumph over superstition." He holds up his lapel. "In solid gold. Like the solidity of our beliefs."

Wettstein's pin sparkles in the sunlight streaming through the blinds. "*Reason*" is emblazoned on the torch handle. "*Free Thought vs. Superstition*" encircles it.

I tug on the corner of my pansy design, but he holds tight. I pull my hands back and fold them on the desk, prim and proper. "We'll see." I glance at my day book. "The board is scheduled to vote on the design next week. And I am sure—"

"That they will select my design. You accepted my pin. Sent me a receipt." He pulls a paper out of his pocket and waves it in front to me. "See? Says right here, '*Your gracious sample pin is accepted on behalf of the American Secular Union. Signed by Ida C. Craddock, Corresponding Secretary.*' You."

"As far as I am concerned, that is official recognition from the Society. I've already produced a first run of one hundred pins to offer for sale. I expect your total support before the board, or I will sue you personally for all my costs, including the patent applications and the gold I have expended in producing these pins."

My breath lodges in my throat. I have no money, only debts. A lawsuit would be a total disaster. Still, I cannot let a man intimidate me, especially a bully like this one.

I rise to my feet. "You cannot. The Union—"

"But I can." He seizes my pansy design sheet with his thick fingers and tears it into tiny bits. White scraps with blotches of purple litter the desktop. "Just try me, girl."

I don't want to try anything. I want him gone. I lift my fingers to the bun on back of my neck and feel for my hatpin. I have a new one. Long and sharp.

Not that I could use it on a member, but it gives me courage.

"I think you should leave, Mr. Wettstein. The board will take up your proposal next week"—I sharpen my tone—"as I said."

Men's voices echo down the hall.

I glance over Wettstein's shoulder. The board is back from their all-male repast. A half-a-head taller than the rest, Richard, as president, leads the group. But I will get no help from him. He might have offered me this job in hope of pursuing his attraction to me, but I have built a wall between us, one that will topple and crush Henrietta if either of us interact in more than an official capacity.

Wettstein turns and heads toward the officers, grinning broadly. He fastens a pin to Richard's lapel and slaps his back. In seconds, every board member is sporting a pin and a smile.

I flop down in my chair and shift through the torn bits of paper, puzzling together the purple pansy. I am competent enough to be in charge of the Union's business, but there is no way for me to compete in a man's world when I am treated as a mere secretary with womanish ideas.

I sweep the scraps from my desk. My abilities are wasted here, and I worked long enough to know that there is no money in wage work, nor in publishing articles in free thought and academic journals. My dream of being independent from my mother and living an intellectual life will never happen if I continue working here. My salary will never be enough to pay off my debts. If only I hadn't exhausted my savings on that ill-fated trip to San Francisco.

I glance up as the last board member hurries down the hall to get his pin. There is only one way I can earn enough money—do as my mother has done and run my own business.

But what business?

I press my fingers to my lips and think of Katie and her excitement that I could sense spirits. Spiritualism. That's it. I could become a medium. People pay grand money to contact their passed-on loved ones, and they don't care if the medium is male or female. In fact, it is the one field where women, being more intuitive, have the advantage.

All I have to do is advertise my experiences with clairvoyance, and people will be begging for me to intercede for them in the spirit world. I could hold readings, sell pamphlets. Write a book. A book like Madame Blavatsky's spirit-given history, *Isis Unveiled*. But better. A book based on real scientific research, not plagiarism.

But how will I gain followers or a publisher? To rise above the ordinary, I need something earthshaking, something that will set me apart from the other mediums. Something that will get people to notice me.

I roll another paper into the typewriter.

But what?

Huddled in my cold rented room, I work late into the night, struggling to make contact with the beings that once haunted me.

I stare into the crystal ball, the pool of water, and the reflecting mirror, and sense nothing. Not a flicker of light. Not a ghost of a sound. Not the wisp of an angel's wing.

The séance table does not move for me. The spirits do not manifest after I've spent hours staring into space. No borderland chill brushes over me. No tremors rise from within.

Only my automatic writing experiments come close to touching the spirit world. Words come and go, scrawled across my pad, but never do they make as much sense as they did that fateful evening with Richard. My stomach flips at the memory.

The problem is that, for years, I lived in fear, blocking those visitations with all my strength.

I toss down my notebook and pace up and down the room. I need a powerful spirit guide, and I know where to find one, if I can call up the courage to do so.

The next day, I stand before my mother's house, the place I swore never to return to, hand ready to knock.

I steady myself then rap the knocker. A new serving girl answers the door. There is always a new servant. No one can stay long under my mother's rule. I don't intend to stay long, either, but I have a request to make.

Mother appears in the hallway. "Ida, my dear child." She rushes forward and wraps her arms about me as if she truly loves me.

I shake her off then step around her and turn into the parlor. I sit in her chair and fold my hands in lap.

She sweeps in after me. I can see she has been ill. Her face is puffy, her eyes glassy.

I harden my heart. "This is not a social visit, Mother. You have something of mine."

Her nose pinches in. "I've heard you are secretary for the Secular Union." She presses her palms together. "Oh, Ida, those people are crazy. They want to remove God from our lives. I can't believe you would work for such people."

I sit up straighter. "Actually, they don't want God eliminated. They want religion separated from the state, as is laid out in the First Amendment to the Constitution. But that is not what I am here to talk about."

Mother sits in the chair across from me. She leans forward. "You've changed. Gotten so thin. And that outfit . . . is that what they are wearing out west? Plain blouses and skirts? Quite unfashionable." With a sniff, she rests back in the chair. "And your skin, it's become so freckled. Why haven't you been applying lemon juice to your face like I taught you? Everyone will think you have been laboring outdoors."

I bite my lip to keep from screaming. That is all she has ever cared about—my outward appearance and how it reflects on her.

I flick my hand. "It is hot and sunny in San Francisco, and I have made it clear, and will make it clear again, my fashion choices are my own." I tuck my feet back. "Now, the reason I'm here is I would like the pendant Charles Sullivan gave me when he proposed. It was in the jewelry box I left in your safe keeping."

She lurches upright. "What is the problem with you, child? How can you still be fixated on that fool after all these years? Thomas and I presented you with so many quite suitable men. Sickly boy like that had no business courting you. And I will have you know he has long ago rotted in his grave."

I clench my teeth. "I am *fixated,* as you say, because he loved me." *Unlike you,* I whisper under my breath.

"Loved you? Don't tell me you are lost in that crazy world of yours again. God knows I tried to beat those fantasies out of you. All those rolling-around-on-the-floor fits as a child. The ridiculous stories you made up about spirits whispering to you. That boy is dead and burning in hell. And he needs to stay there."

I hiss through my teeth, "How do you know? Why not call up his spirit and find out if that is the truth of it? You believe in phantasma, attend seances, seek your dead children; why can't I summon my departed Charles?"

She wrings her hands in her lap. "That's different. Those seances are led by recognized spiritualists. Experts."

"Most of those *experts* are fakes. I have studied occultism for years using scientific methods. Done hundreds of observations. Read thousands of pages on the topic. I will use the pendant in my experiments. Perhaps I will prove you right—Charles is in hell. Now fetch the locket. I know you have it."

"Ida—"

I hold out my hand. "Now."

A strange look comes over her face. "Fine. You never have been a proper daughter. You deserve a comeuppance."

I have no idea what she intends, but I don't care. I expect her to rise, go upstairs, and unbury Charles's gift from wherever she has secreted it. But she doesn't move.

I tap my foot and open my mouth to urge her on. Then stop in shock.

Button by button, my mother undoes her bodice, revealing the pendant lying on the mottled skin above her corset. She grabs hold, breaks the chain, and whips it at me. I watch it spin through the air and leap up to catch it. I whirl and advance on her, struggling to believe what I have just seen.

"You're wearing my locket? Why?"

She presses a hand against her heart, her eyes as cold as Alaskan snow. "You're so smart. Figure it out."

Fingers trembling, I flick the tiny clasp and open the locket. No, no, no. My mother's portrait sits beside Charles's father's.

"Ida, listen—"

I snap the locket closed and wrap the chain around my fingers. No one will ever take it away from me again. I rise.

"His father loved me, but I refused. In revenge, he set his son on you—a sickly boy who'd break your heart and steal away the Craddock business."

"No." I cover my ears. I do not want to hear any bad about Charlie. I do not want to know if he were honest with me. Or maybe I want to know too much.

I rock back and forth again and again. And it happens.

A freezing cold enwraps me. I shiver and look up.

He is here. Charles. A gray shadow hovering over my mother's shoulder. Holding his finger to his lips as if he has a secret.

I try to reach out to him, but my limbs are too heavy to move. My breath too painful to draw in. All I can do is stare at the familiar face and feel the calm seep in. My head falls back, my eyelids close, and I let the feeling wash over me.

"Ida! Stop this." Mother grips my shoulders.

Her touch, so hard and cruel, shatters the moment.

I take a breath. Then another. My blood settles. My vision clears. I find my voice.

"He was here, just now."

Her neck spins from side to side. "Who?"

I look down at the pendant. "Charles." I push to my feet. "And he is no demon from hell. He is an angel—a glorious, ageless, divine spirit. You felt his presence, right?"

Mother stiffens. "I felt no spirit here." She waves her hand. "The room is warm, sunny. No trace of ozone. Your eyes rolled up in your head. You touched yourself in that lewd way you always did. It was one of your fits, not a visitation."

I glance around. Mother is right. The room looks perfectly normal. But I can feel the cold of the Borderland still clinging to my skin and the tingling deep inside. The heavenly scent of cedar curls around me.

"He was here. I know he was."

Clasping the locket in my fist, I rise from the floor. Energy fills me. I need to rush to my rented room and bring Charles back to me. Only careful scientific observations of our interactions will prove to the world that spirits exist.

I head down the hall and out the door, ignoring Mother's pleading. I will never forgive her for what she has done.

On the doorstep, I open the locket and scrape out my mother's image, and that of Charles's father. Everything she has ever told me has been a lie. I will never get the truth from her, only concocted stories that put her in the best light.

I throw the mutilated photographs into the gutter, along with her tale of unrequited love. If there is one thing I am sure of, it is that there is no love in Mother for anyone but herself.

I pass by the apothecary. Inside, her third husband stands at the counter, waiting on a customer. For a moment, I pity poor Mr. Decker, whose surname she has not even deigned to assume. Then I laugh.

She married the baggage out of some misguided idea he could control me, and instead, he's driven me from the house and taken over her business. How fitting. Serves her right for thinking marriage is the way to solve a woman's problems.

Never has. Never will.

PART 3

"In the ideal honeymoon, the bridegroom will not seek genital contact until the bride herself shows indications of desiring it. 'But she might never want it?' My dear sir, you must be indeed lacking in manhood to be unable to arouse sexual desire in a bride who loves you with even a halfway sort of affection."

Ida C. Craddock, *The Wedding Night*, 1900

Chapter 15

"Lewd thoughts soon overcome native innocence."
Anthony Comstock, *Traps for the Young,* p. 8

Rooming House, Philadelphia, 1892

Thunder booms over the city. Lightning flashes across the wall. I curl up in bed and pull the covers over my head. I hate storms. Always have. It is when the demons inside me were always the worst. But perhaps, angels like storms, too.

In the dark, I clasp the locket and picture Charles smiling at me. I press my lips to the engraving. He is the only person who cared enough to want to further my dreams. I loved him for that. Surely, his spirit knows how I feel? Surely, he will come again, if only I concentrate hard enough.

The storm rumbles overhead, and I close my eyes and wish him near. I picture his long-fingered hands, his sparkling silver eyes, his wayward blond hair. He looks less like an angel than a rogue and, for a minute, I am frightened. What if Mother is right? Am I summoning a soul from hell?

I burrow into my pillow. So what? No one cares what happens to me. I am alone. Loveless. Floundering.

If I could make contact with one spirit, I would know that I have the power to accomplish all I dream, and at last prove Mother wrong.

I roll over. Maybe this heavenly being is waiting for a complete invitation.

I push down the covers, open the buttons on my nightdress, then spread it wide. Surely, the Divine Powers will answer my plea.

"I am so sorry," I whisper. "I may have refused to marry you in life, but I am older and wiser now, ready to proclaim my vows."

I press the locket to my breast and concentrate, all my senses alert but focused, and call out, "Come. Come, be my lover in truth."

Humid air and electrical currents, left from the storm, settle on my bared skin, leaving me cold and clammy and covered in gooseflesh. I close my eyes and suck in a breath then exhale it. I do it again and again, slowly, deeply in the proscribed way of the *Yoga Sutra*. My body sinks into the mattress. My mind hones in on only one thought—Charles.

"*Ida?*" The voice is soft, gentle, otherworldly, and rich with Charles's Irish vowels. Every muscle tenses. It's finally happening.

"*Ida?*"

The voice is closer, nearer my ear. I can almost feel his breath, smell the cedar.

Something brushes over me.

"Charles?"

The scent intensifies.

I keep my eyes closed. My body still. But my mind calls out, "*Is it you?*"

A touch as soft as a spring breeze runs down my neck, flows over my clavicle, and alights on my breast. The feeling is exquisite, and I welcome it with a release of breath. Heat radiates out from that feather of a touch.

I arch my back. I want more. Need more. This is what I have lived for.

I picture the boy I knew transformed, a new wiser being—a divine angel—leaning over me. And my heart fills. He has come for me. All the love I have kept bottled up all these years flows forth.

"I love you," I whisper.

The touch disappears, taking the warmth away, leaving my skin chilled.

I cry out, "No. Don't go. Stay."

Silence.

Long minutes pass. I hold my breath, afraid to speak. I wait. I listen. But only the pounding of my heart and the suck of air in and out of my lungs answers.

Finally, I can bear the quiet no longer. I open my eyes slightly.

The room is dark and empty. But that means little in the shadow world of the spirits.

A storm-damp draft stirs the curtains. I sit up and peer into the night. If my angel is here, he is cloaked in invisibility, or else he is a figment of my mind.

I button up my nightgown. He will come back.

He must.

But he doesn't.

Days go by. Weeks pass. At the Union, I have one more argument with the trustees about stopping the evil that is Anthony Comstock, to no avail. So, I quit.

I will write about my sexual experiences with my angel. Soph, I am calling him. For he will bring me great wisdom. If people think I have a close relationship with the denizens of the borderland, they will flock to my door. I could even offer—dare I say it—divine marriage advice.

I hold the pendant to my lips. But first, I need my angel to come again. And I will do whatever I must to make that happen.

Days pass.

Weeks.

And I hear nothing from the spirits. My Soph has not returned to my bed. No spirit has reached out to me with a message from the beyond. The planchette refuses to glide over my new Ouija board. My renewed efforts at spirit writing produce gibberish.

I glance down at the scratchy lines and odd words on my paper from tonight's session. Not a readable bit of spirit communication appears beneath my pencil nib. I crumple the paper in my fist. Again and again, my feeble attempts at automatic writing resemble crudely drawn pot-hooks and handles.

But that is not the worst of it.

I throw the paper wad into the wastebasket and stand. I have been a terrible fool. I have resigned from the Secular Union before I was financially ready.

So, now I am back to teaching at Girard for pitiful wages. If I can't commune with the borderland soon and find some paying customers, I will end up living with Mother and Decker again.

A shiver trails its way down my spine, like a droplet of rain. I can't let that happen. To reach the spirits, I need to stop feeling sorry for myself. I need to clear my mind and practice right living as the *Yoga Sutra* advises. But it is hard to bury my hate and resentment. Hard to ignore my growling stomach.

But I must. I must be pure in all ways.

For weeks now, I have given up meat and dairy and my beloved coffee. I stand at the washbasin and dribble cold water over every part of me until my skin is covered in chilly bumps and my hair squeaky clean. Then I towel dry and snug beneath my blanket.

I am as perfect as I can be. If my spirit lover doesn't come tonight, I will abandon the idea of becoming a medium.

Thunder rumbles across the rooftops. I huddled deeper under the covers. Soph came before in a storm. Maybe tonight will be my lucky one.

I turn down the gaslight, drop the blanket, and lie naked on my mattress in the semi-dark. I concentrate on clearing my mind and breathing with control. Inhale through the nostrils. Hold. Exhale through my mouth. Push away all thoughts.

With each breath, the silver pendant rises and falls on my chest. I outline the tiny insect with my fingertip. The bee is the symbol of wisdom. The symbol of nature. For the Druids, the bee was the divine messenger to the gods. I lift it and deposit a kiss.

"Tell him I need him." I close my eyes and picture the golden bee zipping its way to my Soph. My ears buzz, and I follow, despite the cold that strikes out of me.

Thunder growls. Lightning flashes.

"*Halt.*" A voice rings out, not Soph's, but another far more commanding. "*Come no further.*"

For a moment, fear fills me, but then I fling it away. I cannot fail. Not now when I am on the precipice of understanding. I draw in a long, deep breath.

"Soph, please. I need you. I love you with all my soul. Come to me."

I peer up into the dark. My eyes blind. My heart drumming.

"*Hush, Ida.*"

My breath stalls in my throat. Soph! He has come back.

I struggle to still the anger at his lengthy absence by rounding my voice into sweetness. "Where have you been?"

"Here. Watching you."

"Here?" My blood runs chill. Does he know I doubted? I push the thought away. "But I could not sense you."

"You weren't ready. You needed to prove your perseverance and your love." A whiff of air moves over me. *"Can you feel this?"* The touch on my cheek is surer this time, as if my angel has studied my body and learned my sensitive spots.

"Oh yes, I can. I can feel it."

"And this?" The touch comes again.

Heat flares through me, making my toes curl and electric currents swirl beneath my skin.

"Yes," I whisper. It is the last thing I say, my voice stolen by his charged breath.

"Then welcome in the pleasure," he murmurs, and I lie still and open all my senses to the heavenly sensations swirling through me.

Soph's kisses wisp over me, fragrant with jasmine and cedar. His airy breath brushing across my lips is like magic. Nothing like Richard's almost kiss. Nothing like Euclid's lustful one.

He blows his breath down the side of my cheek, and my heart flutters. I want more. So much more.

I bend back my head to give him greater access to my mouth and neck. I feel as light as a cloud and as insubstantial as a feather. My angel has no weight, only heat and magnetism that flow in and around me.

His caresses come and go, setting every nerve afire. Sometimes, so close and tangible I can feel Soph's smooth skin brush mine. Sometimes, so ephemeral I wonder if this is all in my imagination. Either way, I would let this angel do anything to me as long as he keeps touching me.

And touch me he does. With lips and hands, breath and tongue, worshiping my breasts, nuzzling my belly, running his palms over my hips, the heat and pressure building inside me and setting me quivering everywhere.

His hands move lower. His being presses against mine. Outside, thunder roars and lightning crashes. Inside, lightning hot heat whips through me, gathering deep inside at the seat of my womb. I have never had an earthly husband, so I have no idea what should be happening, but whatever my spirit lover is doing is all I could wish and more.

He moves slowly as we join and then stills. Entwined, he holds me in his arms as we melt into each other and become one in spirit and soul. We lie still for long moments, my angelic lover and I, and then it happens.

Between us, fire ignites, holy divine power floods through me. Pressure builds and twists inside me and—oh, Divine Spirit—releases, leaving me boneless, and gasping, and fulfilled.

Is this what Henrietta means by an orgasm? Is an angel's ethereal touch enough to bring it on?

"*Celanire*," he whispers in my ear. "*It is enough. This pleasure is yours . . . and mine.*"

His presence lessens. A draft of air, redolent of the borderlands, seeps between us. My body chills. I am losing him.

"*It is not enough to love me,*" he says. "*You must ask the Divine Spirit to join us in this holiest of bondings—marriage.*"

I find my voice. "I will. I must. I love you."

He rises above me in a wafting of wings. "Then it shall be so."

I reach toward him. "Don't leave, please."

I strain to pull him to me but grasp only empty air. He is gone, my heavenly bridegroom. And I can't wait for him to come again.

I curl up on my side. If this is a dream, I want it to never end.

Chapter 16

"It should be spelled l-u-s-t, to be rightly understood."
Anthony Comstock, *Traps for the Young*, p. 158.

Rooming House, Philadelphia. 1892

And come he does. Over and over, my Soph joins me and teaches me how to be a loving partner. Not always alone. Dr. Jason, who attended me at birth, and who unknown to me has been my spiritual protector all these years, maintains a constant vigil over me, lest I be injured when I am in the in-between. My dear, departed sister, Nan, whispers encouragement from the beyond. The spirit of her heavenly husband, Iases, comes to hone my self-control.

Day after day, I learn more about my body. How to please my lover. How to find my own pleasure. Finally, I understand what the medical books I have been reading are talking about in their convoluted way. Women need more time to become aroused than men. They need touching, caressing, and words of love.

I say nothing of my visitations to anyone. Locked in my room every hour I am not at Girard, or tutoring, or selling Alice's books, I see no one. Talk to no one.

Except the spirits.

Every time I think to share my experience, I lose courage. I have seen too many spiritualists debunked. How will I prove to my skeptical friends that my spirit husband is real when I'm not even sure he exists?

Katie's letter, when it arrives, whips me into a frenzy. She is coming to see me.

I scrub, and dust, and worry. Once, I had hoped to have a pleasant residence where I could set up my own salon and foster those delicious conversations about philosophy and psychology and the place of women in it all. Instead, all I can afford is a dreary room in a battered brick house dating back to the Revolution, the worn leavings from the past tenant covered with coal ash and soot from the ill-drawing chimney.

I toss my merino shawl and the brilliant china silk scarves I bought when I was still working at the Union over the threadbare sofa and pray I have done enough to cover over my straightened circumstances. At the last minute, I retrieve the whelk shell from my trunk, my tangible link to Katie. It has traveled across the continent and back, carrying the whisper of the sea. I set it on the windowsill in a tiny patch of light.

A slight knock on the door sends chills up my spine. I brush the dust from my skirt then open the door. Suddenly, everything is right in this world.

My darling Katie, home from Europe at last, peers back at me. Oh, how I love her.

I grasp her by the hands and draw her in. "It has been too long."

"That it has, dear friend." She snugs out of my clasp, steps back, and smiles. That little turn up of her lips takes longer than it should.

The cramp in my stomach steals my joy. Something is wrong. Is it her child?

I glance behind her. "You did not bring your little Constance?"

She drops her head. "I hope you don't mind. I left her at my mother's. I know you would have loved to meet her. She is a darling child. But she's a chatterbox, and we haven't had a chance to talk in so long." She takes my hand in hers and squeezes. "A letter, no matter how long, just isn't the same."

"So true." I wrap my arms around her waist and lay my head on her bosom. The rich velvet of her dress cushions my cheek, the jewels at her neck catch the light from the window.

My schoolgirl friend has become an elegant woman, arrayed in the highest fashion, her hair upswept beneath a perfection of a bonnet, her body softer and rounder. But her scent hasn't changed. I would recognize her anywhere, even with my eyes closed.

I guide her to the battered divan. She sits, her hands curled in her lap like wilted lilies.

I pick one up. Her palm is cold against my own. I rub it between mine. "Have you been ill?"

She shakes her head. "No. Not really. It's just—" She breaks off then starts again. "Oh, Ida. I have never fully recovered from Constance's birth. The lot of woman, I suppose."

She sounds so like my mother that my stomach turns. Not my dear Katie, too.

"You are in pain?"

"No. Not anymore. But I am always tired and irritable. And . . . my husband, he desires another child. It took a long time for me to conceive, and I'd hoped . . . well, one would be enough. But Constance's a girl, you see, and he wants a son." She lets out a long sigh. "And I can't stand him to, uh . . . do what married couples do in bed. Never could.

"I love Guy. He's a good man." She stares down at her well-shod toes. "Ida, I hate to ask, but in your research on, uh . . . what happens between husband and wife, have you learned something that would help?"

I send a quick thank you prayer to Soph. "I have." I get up and retrieve a copy of *Tokology* from the pile in the corner and hand it to her. "This book is a great place to start. You must read it. But it doesn't tell us women everything we need to know about sexual relations."

"It doesn't?" Katie lifts her head. "You have learned something more?"

I draw in a breath. How best to explain? Suddenly, every medical book I have read, every mythological goddess, every hour spent cuddling with Euclid, every touch Soph has given, plus the wisdom of the Divine, come together. I know what to say. I have the answer that would have saved Annie all those years ago.

I lean my shoulder against hers. "Have you ever had an orgasm?"

"A what?"

"In an orgasm, your whole body spasms in delight and joy until every atom of your being tingles with energy, and you feel one with the world. It is the most pleasurable thing about lovemaking."

Katie twists her fingers together. "No. It hurts. Every time."

I snuggle closer. "That's because you are not ready. Your Mr. Wood must prepare you with gentle touches and kisses, so your vagina becomes lubricated and ready for his penis."

She slaps a hand to her mouth. "Ida, how boldly you talk."

"Well, someone has to. It is time women use the proper medical terms instead of hide-behind-the-hands euphemisms. We have an entire generation of women who know nothing about their own bodies or how to enjoy being with their husbands. Instead, we are told it is Eve's fault that lovemaking is something for a woman to grit her teeth and suffer through rather than the God-given joy it truly is."

"I don't understand." Katie's voice is small.

"Being with your husband becomes a wondrous experience when performed with self-control and in communion with the Divine." I flash back to my first lesson in women's pleasure in Henrietta's study then pick up Katie's hand again and run my fingers across her palm and along her wrist. "You like that?"

She gives me a genuine smile. "Oh, yes. Brings back memories of lazing late in bed that summer in Ocean Grove and drawing pictures on each other's backs."

I grin at the memory. "Yes. And remember the kiss we shared? How sweet it was? Does Guy touch you like that? Kiss you like that?"

She squirms on the cushion. "He did before we married. But then, after the wedding, he rarely bothered. Always in a hurry to . . . to get it done."

Poor Katie.

I continue tracing the lines on her palm. The head line. The heart line. I tamp down the ping in my heart. "You still love him?"

"He's a good man, Ida. You know I wouldn't have married someone cruel. Guy is wonderful with Constance and always solicitous of my health and safety. We enjoy traveling and seeing new places, and he's for women's equality. We have had many fine talks about it."

"Women's equality? Well, it is time for him to learn about equality in the bedroom. You deserve as much pleasure as he does."

She extracts her hand and rubs her palm along her knee. "But how?"

"You say he listens to you—loves you, right?"

She nods.

"Then it's time for you to teach him a new way of lovemaking."

Katie shakes her head. "Oh, I couldn't."

I tip up my chin. "If you don't, you will end up hating him. Besides, it is not as horrible as you think. You liked the way I touched you. All you need do is ask him to touch you like he used to before you were married. Explain you want to be courted again. Start fully dressed. Have him touch your neck, your hands, your wrists. Share some gently kisses like lovers in a storybook. And you do the same to him. Could you do that?"

She looks away then nods.

I focus on the pale oval of her face. I want so much to help her. "Good. That's my Katie. The next stage is to do the same thing—but unclothed, skin to skin. Touches only. Nothing more. Start for five minutes." I remember how long and wonderful Soph's touches were. "Then, each day, extend the touching session up to twenty minutes or even longer. Do this until you are wet down there at your vagina, until you don't want him to stop because you are so full of desire."

She draws back. "And all this time, my husband does not . . ."

"If he loves you, he will exercise self-control, because he wants to give *you* pleasure. Wants *you* happy."

Her lips quiver. "I know he does, but how can I ask him to hold back?"

"You will ask him because you want equality in your marriage. You want as much pleasure as him. So, only when you are wet—only when you are begging him to complete you—do you proceed to lovemaking in all its glory."

"Oh." She purses her lips. "But how do you know this works, Ida? Have you . . . been with a man?"

It is my turn to look away, but I cannot deny the truth to my dearest of all friends. "I have had an orgasm—several."

Katie's eyebrows rise.

I can't bear her to think I am a loose woman or vile masturbator, so I hurry to add, "I have married."

Katie's head pops up, the beginning of a smile tipping up the right corner of her mouth. "And you didn't tell me?"

I knot my hands in my lap. "It just happened."

"Recently? So, who is the lucky man?"

But I can lie no further. "Charles Sullivan."

Her hand comes up. "Wait. Not the same man who proposed all those years ago?"

I toy with the trim on my sleeve. "Yes—"

A frown line mars her beautiful face. She shakes her head. "But he's dead."

"Oh, Katie. The most amazing thing has happened. He's an angel now. A spirit come from the borderlands to be my husband."

Her mouth opens, and I rush on before she can interrupt.

"He has taught me so much about my body—women's bodies—and Divine sexual union." I lay my hand on her arm. "Believe me; I was a virgin until just a few weeks ago. Never lain with a man. You know my disappointment with that young man in San Francisco that I wrote to you about. And now, I am a fulfilled woman."

Katie's eyes widen. I have frightened her.

I hasten to add, "All I say is the truth. Put my advice to the test, and you will see I know what I am talking about."

She runs her finger along my cheek. "Ida, I love you more than my own self. And I will try what you have suggested, though it sounds incredible to me. Asking Guy to show more physical affection can do no harm. But I am worried about you."

"Why?"

"Because I know you won't keep these wild ideas to yourself. The world isn't ready for frank talk about what happens between a man and wife in the marriage bed, and women are definitely not ready for the advice to come from an unmarried woman, even if you pretend to have learned from a spirit husband."

The skin beneath my eye twitches. "I am *not* pretending. My Soph is as real as your Guy." I spread my arms out. "The spirit world is so close to us, Katie. My angels come to me. Talk to me. Dictate what I write. Even now, they are listening to us—right in this very room. Surely, you believe me?"

"Guy and I have attended several seances and, while highly entertaining, never found them to be scientifically convincing. A lot of nonsense and knocking."

"Most of them are frauds. But the American Society for Psychical Research has many well-documented cases."

Katie hesitates. "If anyone can reach the spirit world, I know it is you. Your powers of observation and perseverance are greater than I have seen anyone display. And you have always talked about the phantasms that haunted you as a child."

I stare at my hands in my lap. "They were not fantasies. And neither is the borderland where the Divine and human interface. Where Soph and I are husband and wife." I look up. "I can prove it. I have never lain with an earthly man. You can look far and wide for a lover of mine, but I am not a virgin. And the neighbors, they will attest to my cries of delight."

"Oh, Ida." Katie bites her lip. "Think of your mother. She's such a maven for gentility at all costs. What if she were to hear you say these things?"

I straighten up. "My mother will never dictate what I say, or write, or do."

She pats my hand. "Of course not. But do have a care. Promise me? I do not want you hurt." She gathers up her beaded purse and fine leather gloves. "I must be leaving. My mother will be weary of Constance by now."

She stands, and we walk to the door like two old friends who have just shared tea and gossip, not discussed what happens in the marriage bed.

Katie turns at the threshold. "Thank you for the frank talk. Even if nothing comes of it, I now have some hope for my marriage. As hard as it will be, I will talk to Guy."

"And you will let me know how it works out?"

Katie hesitates then puts her chin up. "Yes, I will."

My heart does a little leap. Maybe if I can help one woman find Divine pleasure in marriage, I can help others.

She fumbles at her purse. "If you need money . . .?"

I refuse to take on more debt, especially from Katie.

I shake my head. "Oh no, I am doing fine. I know the place is ragged, but I will be moving from here shortly."

Her lips turn under, but she sets her purse back on her arm.

I close the door after her and lean against it. All the arguments in support of free love are worthless without women demanding equal pleasure in the marriage bed. Katie chose her husband. She loves him. But if he uses her only for his own pleasure, her love will sour.

I cross the room, pick up *Tokology*, and weigh the volume in my hand. Stockham touches on this when she talks about girls being taught repression and boys expression through passion. She doesn't go far enough. She doesn't detail what women should do to get the pleasure they are entitled to from the men they love.

I set the book down. Medical books are even worse. If they talk about female orgasm at all, they condemn it as something that degrades a woman and reveals her a whore.

I can't let that to continue to happen. It is time someone talked in everyday language to men and women about loving sexual relations.

A knock sounds on the door. "Miss Craddock, rent due."

Ugh. The landlady.

I tuck my freezing fingers under my arms and pretend I am not home.

She raps again. "I know you are in there. Either pay me what you owe or vacate by Friday."

I take in the worn surroundings, my foolish attempt to brighten the space with old shawls. Katie must have thought me on my last legs to offer me another handout on top of all she has given me.

I let out a breath as another shiver racks my spine. I am tired of being cold. Tired of not being able to entertain visitors. Tired of living poor.

The lack of money is crushing me. Without money, I can't publish my second stenography book and gain some small income that way. Nor can I set myself up as a spiritual marriage counselor. Even more pressing, at the end of the week, I will be evicted onto the street.

I swallow hard. There is only one thing left for me to do. The one thing I swore not to.

Go home to Race Street and beg Mother to take me in.

I spin around and throw open my travel trunk.

But just for a few weeks. That's all.

Chapter 17

"To please the eye, charm the ear, or to entertain any of the senses, is often the way to the heart."
Anthony Comstock, *Traps for the Young,* p. 168

Race Street, 1892

I hurry past the open parlor door. It is always better when Mother doesn't notice my comings and goings, especially when my goings have to do with giving talks about my sexual awakening.

"Ida, where have you been?"

Caught, I slow and turn halfway toward her. "A lecture, Mother. I have to run upstairs and jot down my notes." I put my foot on the first step.

"Stop this minute." She stands in the doorway, arms crossed. "I have had enough of this running in and out of the house at all hours. When I agreed to let you come home to live, I thought you were ready to be the young woman I raised you to be. But no. If anything, you are behaving worse. Now, come have tea with our long-time friends, the Montgomerys."

I cast a glance up the stairs. Up there in my little room, Soph awaits.

"Right now." When Mother puts that edge in her voice, I know better than to disobey.

I need the room and board she has gifted me a while longer. I have made no progress in acquiring a paid following as a medium in the last three months. Not even my most supportive friends believe I have an angel lover.

I bite my lip and follow her into the overheated room.

Mother hands me a cup of tea, and I find a seat as far as possible from the beribboned and befrilled mother and daughter.

Mrs. Montgomery sets her teaspoon on its porcelain saucer. The imported Hammersley bone china, trimmed in gold, is Mother's best, the set intended only for show. But then she has always toadied to the hoity-toity rich. And the Montgomerys are not only wealthy but also friends of the mayor. Just the combination Mother loves to cultivate.

The elder Montgomery tucks in her chin. "What was the lecture about, Miss Craddock?"

I bite my lip harder. It is so trying to live a lie. And why should I? These two ladies mean nothing to me and probably care little for my mother, a fussy old woman with pretensions.

A little shock will do them good. "Free love."

Their unitary gasps are almost laughable.

"Ida has liberal leanings," Mother says, giving me the you-be-good tip of head that worked when I was a child. Still does, sometimes.

The younger Miss Montgomery looks puzzled but takes up the topic I have thrown at her. Just because they are wealthy doesn't mean they're stupid. "I have never understood why a woman would want to have more than one man." She lets out a half-snort, half-laugh. "I should think one man is quite enough."

I shake my head. "Don't believe the church's propaganda. That's not what the Free Love Movement is about at all. It is about women's rights. It is about what happens in the marriage bed. One, a wife should not be used like chattel. Two, her husband has no right to act like an animal. Three, she should have the right to tell her spouse when she wants to lie with him and when she doesn't. And most importantly, she should insist that he give her as much pleasure as he gets in the act.

"*Pleasure.*" My mother clanks her teacup down so hard I am sure she has cracked the saucer. "Ida, where in the world do you get these ideas?"

I should get up. Beg my leave. But I have withstood two months of attacks from friends I had thought liberal-minded for daring to speak openly about my sex life and too many days being treated like a leashed poodle by my mother.

I can hold in no more.

"From my husband." All three women turn and stare at me. I sit up straighter. "That's right, I am married." I set my teacup aside before my trembling hands lose control and send it smashing to the floor. "To the most wonderful of men."

Mother's face is whiter than the porcelain of her cup. "What . . .? How . . .?"

For the first time ever, I have struck my mother wordless.

I smile. "You know of my experience with the occult and my skill at mediumship. Well, my spirit husband is of the borderland. You can style me Mrs. Craddock from now on. He has initiated me into the wonders of Divine love." I lean forward slightly. "Why, just last night I had five orgasms."

The quiet that fills the room would match the stillness of a grave. Three pair of eyes look everywhere but at me.

Mrs. Montgomery stands. She tugs her daughter up by the hand. Then she casts a sympathetic glance at Mother. "We must be leaving."

My mother gives her head a shake and rises. "Of course, you must." She trails them out into the hall, murmuring words of outrage and apology.

I do not move. Why bother? I have overstepped the line of all propriety. I will be cast out from the house in moments.

I fold my hands in my lap and stare at the piano Charles enjoyed hearing me play. The Chickering with its rosewood trim has always offered me comfort. It is the one thing in my mother's house that I have missed in my years away. But there will be no comfort for me today. I have stepped beyond the bounds.

As I wait, I search inside myself. I know I have spoken only the truth, and that women need to hear about the joys of the marriage bed.

I pat my pocket. Katie's letter is my constant companion. It works, she wrote. She has never loved her husband more. And she will never be able to thank me enough. But she is off to Italy with her peripatetic foreign-service husband, and not here to defend me.

Still, I fear I am not brave enough to carry through and spread the news to all women. I rub my forehead. Why have the spirits laid this burden on me?

A faint wisp of air floats over me. Oh, my dear Soph. I must not sink into despair.

I rise and seat myself at the piano. My fingers settle on the ivory keys, and Charles's favorite nocturne fills the room. I haven't played it since the day he proposed. As the notes ring out, so does my heart. Over and over, I play until my spirit flies free.

"Ida."

I drop my hands from the keys, my soul yanked back to earth.

An overstuffed man accompanies Mother into the parlor. "This is Dr. Turnbull," she says by way of introduction. "I asked Thomas to fetch him."

Every part of me tenses, and I draw back. I have heard of the man. He is the worst type of fake spiritualist. He believes he can cast out demons.

"Why is he here?"

"You need help." Her lips curve up into the simper of a smile she uses when she wishes me to do something for her.

I glare at the man. "He's a fraud, Mother. I am far more qualified to deal with the occult than this man whose been debunked over and over by the American Spiritualist Society. He wants only your money." I point my finger at him. "Remove him at once."

Mother pinches her lips together. "Now, Ida, stay calm."

Turnbull moves toward me. "I mean you no ill," he says, but his eyes say the opposite.

I back up until I am pressed against the keyboard. I throw my hands back to support me and accidentally hit the keys. A cacophony of notes assaults my ears. Chills sweep over me, and I squeeze my fists tight and raise them. He would take my Soph away from me. He would muffle my voice.

I gather my strength. "If you take one more step toward me, Dr. Turnbull, I will . . . I will—"

Decker, wearing his white apothecary apron, appears behind Mother, his eyebrows raised high. The door is fully blocked. I have no way to escape. No way to fight.

I let my arms fall. I must rely on my wits instead.

"Sit down, Ida," Mother says. "All we will do is talk."

I sit on the newly upholstered couch and fuss with my skirt, setting the pleats in alignment, flicking the lace at my wrists. It does not take much to reduce me to a child again.

So, I sit, and I dream, and I wish, and I fume. All the while, these people who know me not at all tell me I am crazy—

actually, the good doctor propounds that I am suffering hysteria—and need to be confined for my own good while he treats me.

"Just in your room for a short time, my dear, to give you time to settle your nerves," Mother says in a soothing voice so fake that even Decker's mouth twitches.

"If you want sex," Decker sneers, "then marry. However, I know you have rejected that option quite firmly. I doubt there's a man I could convince to marry you with your history." He softens his voice. "Accept our help. The good Doctor Turnbull is recommending nothing extreme. Merely bedrest."

And probably a stiff course of something much stronger than Craddock's Bitters.

I look from face to face. I should stay quiet, but my tongue has become less than well-behaved.

Besides, I am beyond angry—my whole body pulsates with outrage.

"Let me get this clear—I need bedrest because I used the word orgasm? It is a perfectly fine word. One every woman should hear. Something every woman should have." I turn to my mother. "Has any of your three husbands ever given you one, Mother?"

The looks that greet me make me want to laugh. But I know better than to do so in front of the quack. That is all these people need to have me incarcerated in an asylum.

Mother's face flames red. "How dare you speak to me so? I will not have my daughter talking about marital relations like some . . . some . . . woman of the streets." She extends her hands toward Turnbull as if to say, "*See what I have to contend with*," then focuses back on me. "I don't want to know where you got this knowledge, Ida, but you will not talk about spirit lovers in this house. And you will not style yourself *Mrs.* Craddock ever again in public."

It is better to be tossed out than treated as insane. With a longing glance at my piano, I rise from the sofa. I will probably never see it again.

"I am no longer a child as much as you wish to treat me as one. I am a woman of thirty-six years. I have run the Wagner Institute and the American Secular Union. I have written numerous articles and pamphlets. With your help, for which I am most grateful, Mother, I have published *Intermediate Stenography* and am well along on my grand masterwork. I appreciate you putting a roof over my head for the last three months, but I see it is time for me to leave."

Turnbull steps toward me. "I don't think—"

I push past. "No, you don't see. You touch me, and I will complain loudly to the Spiritualist Society, of which I am a member. One medium cannot effectively lock up another because she has misguided parents."

Turnbull has the common sense to step back. "I only wished to relieve your stress."

I point toward Mother. "Relieve hers." I head to the door.

But my mother is not done. "You will regret this, Ida."

Decker puts a hand on her shoulder then glares at me. "Your mother is too good a woman. She has forgiven you much. We have paid off your debts, subsidized the printing of that stenography book of yours, put up with your wild liberal ideas, your little tantrums, and your obscene talk. We are done. You will receive no more money from us, even if you are lying half-dead in the street. Which is where you will certainly end up, if you continue this foolishness."

I firm my jaw. The Interloper may be right, but I cannot change my course. Not now. Not with Katie's success.

I may have failed at getting an advanced degree. I may not have completed my masterwork on women and religion.

But I have made good on my promise to Annie, and I can now bring Katie's happiness to other women.

My enthusiasm is gone by the next morning. A night spent hiding in the stable has reduced me to a hungry, shivering fool.

The auditorium where I have taken refuge only chills me more. Rain patters against the windowpanes. The acrid stink of wet wool irritates my nose. I pull my shawl tighter, my fingers numb with cold, and try to listen to the lecturer. Not so long ago, I was the secretary who'd arranged for speakers to come. Now I have come as a beggar with only the clothing on my back and my notes.

I blot my nose with my handkerchief and focus on the raindrops trickling down the glass. Hopefully, one of the wealthy people come to jeer the National Reform Association's amendment to declare our country a Christian nation will have an opening for a competent secretary with a liberal bent and an angelic lover.

Women may titter behind their hands when they see me, but I am still held in some admiration among the members of the Union for the work I did.

On the platform, the lecturer rails on. I curl and uncurl my frozen toes and look forward to the hot coffee and refreshments to follow, and a chance to make my inquiries. But first, I must survive the lecture.

I bury my chin in my shawl and let my thoughts drift. In my mind, I am shouting my sexual awakening to the world. But I don't know how to make that happen. In the bag at my feet is my recounting of my nights in Soph's arms. My lessons with my spirit guides. The research and history I have done to support my spiritualism experiments. But what can I do with it?

Mother and the Interloper will have me declared insane were I to publish even a small bit of it. But without it being made public, I will never be accepted as a renowned medium whose advice about marriage relations is taken seriously.

There is a rustle beside me, and I glance up. "Henrietta?"

She slips into the seat next to mine, leans over, and whispers in my ear, "I heard you're looking for a secretarial position. What's happened? I thought you were doing better since you paid off your debts."

I let her lovely scent wash over me. I have missed her so much.

I sit up straighter. Dare I tell her the truth? Maybe. But not all of it to start.

"I had hoped to be established as a medium by now," I whisper back. "My experiments in the occult have gone exceedingly well. But I need money to publish my work and gain renown in spiritualism circles, and my part-time teaching at Girard, and the few students I tutor, do not bring in enough."

"I thought your mother was helping you?"

I bite the inside of my lip. "Mother has been most helpful. But we have parted ways, for now."

"A difficult woman, as I remember." She lays a hand atop mine. "I am sorry for what happened between us. I have always cared for you deeply. I know it was Richard's fault—he led you on." Her mouth purses. "But forget him. Come"—she slides out of her seat and waits for me to join her—"we women must stay together."

Ignoring the turning heads, I pick up my bag and follow her out the door and into the rainy street.

She throws her cape over me, and we hurry to her waiting carriage. Suddenly, I am young again and full of hope. We jump inside, and I pull her close.

"You are such a precious friend. I am so sorry for the mistakes I made."

"No, you have nothing to apologize for. I regret what I said, how I have behaved to you, Ida. Jealousy is a terrible beast. I have much to make up for. I should never—"

"No, I understand completely how you feel. You love Richard with all your heart." I gather my courage. "I, too, now have someone I love with all my heart and who loves me back equally."

Henrietta squeezes my hand. "I am so happy for you. But who—"

"His name is Soph." I hesitate then push the words out. "And we are married. Surely, you've heard?"

"Richard mentioned that you're styling yourself Mrs. Craddock."

I stiffen. What has he told her? Richard has made perfectly clear that he thinks me totally inappropriate.

I squeeze her hand back and pray I have not misjudged. "My experiments into spiritualism have borne a truly wondrous result, Henrietta. Soph is my heavenly bridegroom. He comes to me from the borderland and lays with me in Divine love. I have experienced orgasm, Henrietta. It is the most marvelous thing."

Henrietta blinks. Her mouth opens and closes.

My shoulders fold in. Have I made a mistake telling her?

I close my eyes and wait for words of shock and dismissal. The weight of my manuscript presses against my ankles. If Henrietta, with her open mind and desire to spread sexual knowledge, does not believe me, who will?

"Help me understand better," Henrietta says, her tone far gentler than I expected. "You have a spirit lover?"

"A spirit *husband*." I must make that perfectly clear from the start, or women will never accept my spirit-gleaned advice. "We have married ourselves before God. Here." I lift the bag from the carriage floor and take out my draft manuscript. "I have written what I have learned about spirit husbands in this—the first volume of my grand work on sexual worship."

"Oh, Ida, how wonderful. May I read it?"

"Of course. Anything you can offer to make it better would be most appreciated. After all, my research got its start right in your study."

She smooths her palm over the top page. "So, you have experienced an orgasm finally?"

I nod. "Several. But I must prepare myself most rigorously for it to happen. I no longer eat meat or milk. I practice deep breathing and yoga daily—sometimes for hours. My spirit guides are teaching me how to maintain my self-control during my joining with Soph."

"Would it work for other women?"

"Oh, yes. I am sure that if a woman truly concentrates and lives a blameless life, she can find satisfaction with a spirit lover. But even more importantly, it will transform the marriage relation. My friend Katie has taken my advice and swears it has revitalized her relationship with her husband."

The carriage halts in front of the Westbrooks' stately white-faced townhouse with its columned portico.

Henrietta offers her hand. "Come; you must tell me all."

Clutching my manuscript, she leads me inside the home I have not visited in over seven years. It is as elegant as ever, but that is not my worry.

I glance around. "Richard is not here?"

"No. Besides, he will trouble you no longer. You have my word on it." She tips her head. "I have made my own progress in the lovemaking department. His eye roves no more."

I am not sure I believe her, but I have nowhere else to turn. So, I follow her to the study, where we held so many intimate talks, and over cups of Earl Grey and delicate lemon teacakes, plan out my future. It feels like coming home.

"You must go to Chicago," Henrietta insists. "Far away from your mother. I don't trust her. Not if she is calling in quack doctors. It is too easy for a woman to be shut up in an asylum by supposedly well-meaning relatives. It's happened to too many women I know."

"But what can I do in Chicago?" I take a bite of the lemon tart and let the tangy sugar melt on my tongue. I don't want to go anywhere. I want to stay here, with Henrietta, curled up on the divan in a mess of silk shawls, drinking tea, eating cakes, and talking about sexual pleasure. I play with the short hairs at her nape.

Katie believed me enough to try my method, but Henrietta's eyes glow and her breath slows when I tell her about how Soph touches me.

She sits up suddenly. "I know. You can visit Alice Stockham. Tell her about your research. She will support you, I am sure. And Moses Harman's farm is not too far from there. Spend some time with him. He will be fascinated with your work and excited to publish it in *Lucifer, the Light-Bearer*."

I rub my toes along Henrietta's calf. "But won't that bring Comstock down on me?"

"That's the risk you take, if you pursue this course. But Chicago is much more liberal than Philadelphia and New York. You might slip under his notice, as long as you don't send anything mentioning women's parts through the mail. Mustn't offend him and his hypocrites."

She drapes her arm around me. "Besides, the World's Fair will be opening soon. I would give everything to go, but with Richard's court cases, we are stuck here all through the summer and fall. You must go and write me all about it. And don't delay your departure. Sooner or later, your mother will come after you."

I know she is right. I kiss her cheek. "Then that is what I will do." I stop. "But most of my things are at my mother's."

Henrietta lays her head on my shoulder. "Don't worry; I will retrieve them for you and send them on."

I remember my sojourn to San Francisco. I had such high hopes, only to end deep in debt. Now I am going to do it again—take off with no funds to a place I have only visited once before. But how else can I spread the knowledge Soph has gifted me? How will I fulfil my promise to Annie now that I know the way?

I am either a fool or a zealot. I know which one my mother would choose. So, I must choose the other.

Chicago, here I come.

Chapter 18

"[Lust] sinks man, made in the image of God, below the level of the beasts."
Anthony Comstock, *Traps for the Young,* p. 132

Chicago World's Fair, 1893

It is still early in the day, but already the sunbaked Columbian Exposition is full of thousands of gawkers like me, kicking up dust. I hurry to catch up as my companions squeeze their way through the crowds, exploring the exhibits on the Midway Plaisance.

Alice Stockham might be ten years older than I, but she has more energy than six locomotives. In the last four hours, I think we have seen every inch of the exposition, from Columbus's three amazingly tiny ships to one too many lace doilies in the Women's Building.

I push back the brim of my much-traveled straw hat, rub one sore foot against the other, and look longingly at the Viennese Café. A coffee and pastry would not come amiss right now. But Alice insists we must first check out the most popular exhibit at the fair—the camel ride at the Street of Cairo. It is all Helena, Alice's little adopted daughter, has gabbled about since we arrived. Not that I am averse to visiting the Egyptian exhibit. So, I pay my quarter admission and step through the gates and into a colorful and authentic looking Arabian bazaar.

Striped awnings flutter in the sultry breeze. Men in caftans and turbans stroll past. Splendidly draped camels and chubby little donkeys await riders in the center of the plaza. A woman squeals as the camel she is astride folds its legs and tips, toppling her on the way down.

Far braver than I, Alice negotiates with the driver and is soon sitting atop the same beast, Helena in her arms. Helena's governess, Addie, snaps a photo with Alice's new Kodak camera, and then the beast is off, rocking and rolling down the street.

But it's not the camels I am interested in. It is the outrageous Danse du Ventre I want to see. Alice, as bold as she is, swears she will not go in. Of course, with Helena with her, she is right to stay away if the performance is as inappropriate as the Board of Lady Managers thought it to be. Even I have a qualm or two.

The music is supposedly so grating that women with their delicate hearing can stand no more than five minutes of the performance. More off-putting is the fact that most of the people lined up outside the Cairo Theater are men.

We'll see about that.

I join the queue and buy a ticket for ten cents. I pat the coins in my pocket. Thank heavens, I have found a temporary stenography position here in Chicago. The fair is not cheap. This one day will cost me more than a day's wages. But I would be so embarrassed if Alice had to pay my way. And she would have, if I asked. A more generous and kinder soul I have never met.

I find a seat on the end of a bench near the front of the theater and set my bonnet in my lap. Jasmine and other exotic perfumes fill the air. After the heat outside, the cool of the interior raises the hairs on the back of my neck. Tingles run up and down my body. I shift on the hard bench. Are my spirits guides here with me? Are they sending me a message?

Two men slide in next to me. More men file into the rows behind me. Their voices are rough, their comments ribald. I tuck my skirt in closer. Pin my elbows to my sides. Have I been a fool to come alone?

Electric lights click on, and a wild piercing sound assaults my ears. Drums thump in rhythm with my heartbeat, tambourines rattle, and a woman steps to the front of the stage. She is not what I expected. Short and chubby, she is dressed in a colorful flowing skirt. A netted-silk undervest covers her arms and torso, while an embroidered cloth enwraps her breasts. Despite snipes in the press, she is garbed more modestly than many a woman on the beach at oh-so-religious Ocean Grove.

Then she dances.

At first, I am lost in the wonderment. Around her neck hang beads and bangles that clink and chime. Around her waist, six tassels spin and jiggle as she moves. And how she moves.

She sways her body using her pelvis as a fulcrum, powerfully contorts her abdomen, and undulates her hips, the movement clearly visible above the waistband dipping below her navel. Her ugly black stockings, wide, white muslin drawers, and pointy-toed, high-heeled slippers but rarely show when she spins and play no role in the dance. Everything is concentrated in the way her torso moves.

It does not take long before most of the spectators realize the dance mimes the movements of a passionate woman, conventionalized and performed in harmony with the beat of the drum. The young men in the audience whoop and yell. The prudes rise and leave, ejaculating words like disgusting and obscene.

Transfixed, I stay seated as one after another of the dancers come forward from the bench along the back wall and perform the dance over and over, each in their own unique way.

In their hands, they hold castanets, which I immediately recognize from my research as a female phallic worship symbol, representing the agitation of the female in ecstasy. As their movements increase, so does the clicking.

Several times during the performance, the dancer stops and holds perfectly still, then slowly begins shaking and undulating, moving faster and faster until it seems she will be too exhausted to continue. Never is she overcome and swept away with passion, but each time recovers and continues the dance.

I grip the edge of the bench. *Oh, spirits, you have guided me well to bring me here.* This is a dance of ancient origins from the time when Sex Worship was the uplifting religion of the whole world. What a striking lesson in feminine power and the ability for self-control in the act of passion. This is what my spirit guides have been trying to teach me all these nights. I must tell Alice.

I stand, whip my hat onto my head, and rush into the aisle, only to smack into a bull of a man with wild mutton-chop whiskers and the reek of a sweaty, overweight male.

He grasps my arm. "You do well to flee this obscenity, madame."

"No obscenity, sir." I attempt to shake myself free, but the idiot's hold only tightens. "This is the most marvelous thing I have ever seen. I must tell my friend. She will want to see it herself."

He maintains his grip. "A pretty woman such as yourself does not belong in a place of filth. Is there no man with you?" My captor draws in his upper lip so his chin juts out like a determined bulldog's with a rag he won't drop.

"No, there is not."

"Then come with me. I will chaperone you from this den of immorality, which I fully intend to see closed down within the hour." He loops his arm around mine, as if he were a gentleman, and drags me with him as he stalks up the aisle, all the while muttering to the snip of a man hurrying to keep up with him.

Just who does this bully think he is to treat me so? I should yell and cause a stir at being manhandled by a stranger. But I do not want to interrupt the dancers or spoil the show for others. However, once we are outside, I plan on reporting him to the first authority I find.

We step out into the sun, and I glare at the fool man. In the daylight, he is larger and more intimidating. A white scar mars his whiskered left cheek. His eyes glisten the metallic silver of the Exposition's commemorative Columbus dollar coin made of the new metal called aluminum.

He halts. "Now, where are your friends?"

I squint then point. "There, just getting off the donkey."

"Ah, that Stockham woman, I see. You are one of those. What a waste of your beauty." He releases me with a jerk then storms off and out the gate before I can say a word.

"Are you all right?" Alice wraps me in her arms.

I rub my arm where he gripped me. "Horrid man. Dragged me out of the theater."

Alice hugs me tighter. "Don't you know who that is?"

I shake my head. "No. And I need to tell a law officer that he assaulted me in there."

"No, you don't. That was Anthony Comstock."

The name sucks all the breath from me.

She slides her hand into mine. "You didn't tell him who you are, I hope?"

"There wasn't time. He took offense that I was watching the show unaccompanied." I squeeze her hand. "Oh Alice, the Egyptian dance is amazing. You must come see it. Totally eye-opening. Just what every woman must learn to do in the marriage bed."

"Hush. Not here, Ida."

"What?" I scan the Arabian market square. "Comstock's gone, right?"

She takes Helena's hand and starts toward the gate. "He has spies everywhere, and he doesn't like what I publish."

"His persecution of liberal-minded thinkers and medical doctors is outrageous. We shouldn't let a fat old man boss us around like that. Tell us we can't talk about sex. It's against the First Amendment, *and* it's a women's right's issue. Someone like you should take him on. You have the renown as well as powerful friends. Women love your books. They'd support you."

Alice shakes her head. "Not me. I can't go to jail, Ida. I have patients who rely on me. I have a daughter." She rolls her shoulders. "And maybe I am not that brave. He's a fearsome man with the power of the United States government behind him."

My blood runs hot. I massage my arm where he touched me. "Someone has to challenge Comstock. He's a disgusting bigot."

"How about you, Ida?" Alice says. "You know as long as he controls the mails, you will not be able to publish your sex worship research as written. I certainly won't take that risk."

Despite the blazing heat of the July sun, every part of me chills. Alice had been my best hope.

Something pinches me inside. The words boil up. "Maybe I *should* take Comstock on . . ."

Alice squeezes my hand. "That is something you have to decide for yourself, my dear. Now, let's go to the Vienna Bakery and Café and enjoy a pastry while we rest our feet. We still have miles of exhibits to explore."

Helena tugs on her mother's arm. "And the Ferris wheel to ride."

I peer up at the monstrous wheel dominating the skyline at the end of the Plaisance. No way am I going on that.

I retie my hat beneath my chin and trail after Alice. Am I really brave enough to face Comstock?

I guess I will have to find out.

Two weeks later, I am in Valley Falls, Kansas. I heft my valise and head down the broad main street, the hot sun of July soaking my back in perspiration.

Alice says Moses Harman is my best hope for getting my writings published. She has sent a letter ahead, but I have no idea of the welcome I will receive. The poor man was released from jail a few months ago after serving a year's sentence on obscenity charges. Will he be courageous enough to publish my new article on the Danse du Ventre?

Harman's white clapboard house sits on the edge of town, sheltered beneath two spreading elms. I make my way up the curved carriage path. Whether my breathlessness is from the walk from the train depot or from fear, I cannot tell.

A heavily bearded man rises from a rocker on the porch and gives a wave. "Miss Craddock? You should have sent a boy, and I would have fetched you in the wagon."

I wave back. "No need. The exercise is much needed after all those days in Chicago, inhaling that sooty air."

In minutes, Harman has me settled on a creaky porch swing, a large glass of creek-cold, sweet lemonade in my hand.

"So, Alice says you have an interesting article for me to publish."

"If you are willing to risk it?"

He laughs. "I am willing to risk much to bring enlightenment to the American populace."

I take a sip and let the cool, tart drink wash the dust from my throat. "I would not wish to be the reason you are returned to jail."

His whole face smiles. "I have not read your piece yet, but I assure you, you need assume no responsibility for what the law chooses to do to me. Chose the wrong title for my magazine, that's all. *Lucifer, the Lighter-Bearer* seems to strike Christians wrong, even though it is right from the Bible. Between that, and the universal misinterpretation of what free love is, means Comstock and his cronies won't leave me alone. He's a bulldog, that man. Once he's on your scent, you can never escape."

A rabid bulldog, for sure.

I rub the place where the tyrant touched me. "I met Comstock at the Exposition. He is a frightening personage."

"That he is, my dear." His eyebrows flick up. "You met him, you say?"

I nod. "He was there to close down the Cairo dance theater."

"So, at least you have some idea of what you are up against."

That I do.

I chew my lip. "Well, I have written an article about the Danse du Ventre. Alice thought it too outrageous to publish herself. She suggested I talk to you about it."

"Outrageous, huh? Sounds exactly like what I publish." He puts out his hand. "Let's see what you have."

I dig the manuscript out of my case. My pulse rises. Have I dared too much in tying the Danse du Ventre to preparation for marital duties and my research on sex worship? It is the boldest thing I have ever penned. But Harman is waiting, and it is too late to hold back. I didn't travel all this way to turn coward. I hand him my article, and he leans back in his rocker.

While he reads, I sip my lemonade and attempt to relax for the first time in months. I have no secretarial temp job to rush off to. I have no mother casting a disapproving eye on all I do. I am even glad to be away from Alice for few days. As kind as she is, I do not fit in with the wealthy and rather opinionated friends and relatives who constantly visit her grand house in Evanston. Nor did I enjoy all the formal meals served by the most elegant of servants after years of living on my own and eating as I would.

Though one thing is for sure—writing a popular book or two can certainly provide a fine income for a woman. If only I could accomplish as much as Alice has.

I glance over at Harman. Publication in his journal would expose my ideas to his thousands of subscribers. If well-received, I would have a potential audience for a marriage guidebook. Surely, there is a hunger among married women and men for information that will make their sexual relationships more pleasurable? It could be more popular than for another book on spiritualism, I suspect. A best-selling book for married couples would set me up in funds so I could pursue my real dream in life—completing my too-long-set-aside scholarly history of women and religion.

I set my glass down, rise to my feet, and lean against the railing. No use thinking too far ahead. Harman has not said yes . . . yet.

All around me, crickets chirp and cicadas whir. The scent of new-mown hay fills the air and mixes with the faint perfume of the white roses surrounding the house. The combination is intoxicating in the best of ways.

It has been years since my long summers at our cottage in Freehold—my beloved little bungalow sold long ago by Mother. Living in one city or another over the last ten years, I have missed the joy of being outside in the wide-open spaces of the natural world.

Moses flips the manuscript back to the title page and signals me with his finger. "Interesting reading, Miss Craddock. I would be happy to publish your article. It is important to be timely in the magazine world, and this is sure to prove of exceeding interest what with Comstock in Chicago trying to close the exhibit down." He pushes up from the rocker. "Yes, indeed. This is just the kind of material the *Lucifer, the Light-Bearer* accepts. Though I suggest you might look into publishing even more widely than my small newsletter. In fact, I would gladly send it to my contacts in New York, who might facilitate getting it into the newspapers there."

I turn and lean back against the railing, my stomach suddenly sour. I picture Comstock looming over me. Remember the stink of him. The violence in his eyes. Do I want to challenge The Inquisitor of Filth?

Someone has to, Alice says.

Someone has to be brave.

Why not me?

I roll my shoulders and tip up my chin. "Mr. Harman, I'd be happy for your assistance."

An hour later, I find myself beneath the speckled shade of Harman's orchard trees. Back at the house, Harman is penning the letter to his reporter friends. I have made the right decision . . . I hope.

I take a deep breath. Ripening apples and pears hang from the boughs above me. Birds flit about. A butterfly floats past. I raise my hands over my head and sway my hips like one of the Cairo Street dancers, glad I gave up my corset so many years ago.

I spin around and snake my torso. It's been years since I took dance lessons, but my daily round of yoga has kept me limber. I do it again. There is nothing complicated to the Danse that a willing woman could not master. Surely, other women will benefit from learning the dance of passion. And I could teach it to them.

I peer heavenward into the blue of the sky. "Is that what you want me to do, Soph?"

A light breeze wafts the apple leaves.

Is that him saying yes?

I wander deeper into the orchard until I am sure no one can see me from the house, find a thick patch of grass, and sink down. Heedless of my white muslin blouse, I stretch out on my stomach. Beneath my cheek, the grass is soft and fragrant, the earth-scented loam sun-warmed. I press my entire body against the earth and open myself to the Divine Spirit, Creator of All. Life flows through me like a river. My blood hums. My heart beats. My breath slows.

I settle deeper into the soft earth, pressure building against my abdomen. I move gently, slowly, undulating and mimicking the movements of the Danse du Ventre. And it happens.

Warmth gathers at the seat of my womb and builds. I control my breathing, tamping the growing tension down, holding it in as it expands through me, beyond, and becomes part of the universe. My limbs quiver. My fingers fall open against the earth, drawing in its power. My mind floats free. My body convulses.

And the earth beneath me moves.

When I recover enough to be aware again, I roll on to my back and stare up at the blue of the sky, in such total relaxation that my thoughts are more of sensation than logic.

"Soph," I whisper.

He does not answer, but I know he is here. Only my spirit guides could have led me to this place and shown me in such a wondrous way that I am on the right path.

Chapter 19

"They publish their false doctrines and theories, hold public meetings where foul-mouthed women address audiences of males."
Anthony Comstock, *Traps for the Young*, p. 163

Race Street, Philadelphia, 1894

Six months later, I'm certain publishing the *Danse du Ventre* article has been the worst mistake of my life. My stomach knots, partly with hunger, but it is the gut-gnawing fury that hurts the most.

I turn the corner and trudge up the second flight of steps. I stop and peer into the narrow stairwell, lit only by the moonlight creeping in through the hall window. Almost there. One more flight.

I swallow down a curse at the state I have been reduced to. Why is it that other people find renown and a goodly income from their writings, and I publish a simple article to help married couples and receive only notoriety?

I tuck my lecture case under my arm and unlock the door to the tiny attic room above the Craddock apothecary I am using as my office now that I am back in Philadelphia. Once inside, I toss the case on the cot and light the kerosene lamp on my makeshift desk.

Another lecture on the history of sex worship and its relevance for marriage reform delivered and paid for. This time to the Manhattan Liberal Club. I untie my hat and hang it on its peg with more force than needed.

More like the Un-Liberal Club.

I unbutton my shoes and kick them off. I can understand the uneducated public's outrage over my *Danse du Ventre* article. Publication in the *World* attracted far more attention than any of us expected. Most of it disgusting. And the post-Exposition craze for lewd, half-naked belly dancers in Burlesque shows sealed my fate.

But I hadn't expected the most liberal people I know to accuse me of indecency or to be offended by the idea of an unmarried woman speaking openly about sex and giving marriage advice. Richard Westbrook, the so called-women's rights supporter, has tried to get me off the speaker list for the Ladies Liberal League of Philadelphia. Though maybe Henrietta had a hand in that. She has not been happy since I came home to pursue reconciliation with my mother and help her care for Decker, who is ailing. She insists I should have stayed in Chicago.

And maybe she's right.

I tear off my coat and let it drop to the floor. Then I throw myself on to the hard cot. Despite dear Dr. Ned's glowing introduction, last night was the worst. The outcries during my talk. The so-offended women and men walking out. The personal attacks afterward during the discussion.

To be called immodest by the same people who should support me makes me want to cry. But I am too angry to let my tears free. A shiver racks my body. My head pounds. I rock back and forth. *Oh, Soph, I need you.*

Voices echo up the hallway, footsteps clomp up the stairs. I pull the pillow over my head and grit my teeth. Peace and quiet isn't going to be forthcoming tonight.

Thwack. Thwack.

"Ida," Mother screeches through the door in a voice that drives nails of pain blasting through my head. "Open the door."

I roll over. "Go away. I'm working."

More banging. "Open this door at once. The climb up these stairs near killed me."

I hold my breath. What does she want at this hour of the night? We haven't spoken in days.

"Go away."

The doorknob rattles. "Don't you dare tell me to go away, young lady. Draw the bolt. This is an emergency."

What could make Mother sound so desperate? Has something happened to Decker? He has looked sicker every day, his once rotund body slowly shrinking in, his jowls hanging low. His legs constantly swollen and sore.

His illness is the only reason she has let me live here. She needs my help to maintain the books and serve at the till.

I push my hair from my face and stumble to my feet. "Coming."

I open the door a crack. "Is Decker okay?"

Mother pushes the door all the way open and shoves a piece of paper in my face. "Here. You have finally done it. They're going to arrest you."

I fall back, the pain ballooning in my head and pressing against my temples. "Arrest? What are you talking about?"

"Read it." She presses it into my hand.

I turn up the kerosene lamp and hold the message under the light, my fingers trembling. "No, no, no. A warning from the Philadelphia postal inspector. It can't be."

"Of course, it can," Mother spits at me. "What do you think happens to people who broadcast obscenity to the world?"

"I do not lecture about nor write obscenity. Medical doctors use the same words every day. No one throws *them* in the insane asylum." I wrinkle my nose. "Oh, but of course, they are men."

"Stop being snippy. You are a woman, Ida. An unmarried one. And you are not behaving normally. Claiming you are married to an angel? What rot. And now this? Sending obscenity through the mails? How dare you?"

"I sent nothing but letters of gratitude to the women who wrote me about how changed they were by my *Danse du Ventre* article."

"That stupid article. The disgrace you have brought on this household. It is a wonder people patronize the shop, and that I am still accorded my place in the Temperance League." She seizes me by the shoulder. "Put your coat on."

I jerk away. "Do you think it's right for the post office to open my personal mail? It's against my First Amendment rights. It's against the rights of all women to keep them ignorant of how their bodies function and how the marriage relation should be."

Mother raises her eyebrows. "*Bah.* Don't feed me that liberal swill, Ida. Now come. I have a hired carriage waiting."

A hole opens in the pit of my stomach. "A carriage? Where do you plan to take me?"

"I have enlisted the services of two excellent doctors. They have agreed to help you calm down and cease this wild behavior. A month at the Philadelphia Asylum will give them time to exam you."

"*Insane asylum? Examine me?* You have no parental rights over me anymore. Now get out." I give her a shove, and then another. My mother has always been the stronger, but fear-filled anger fuels my strength. Besides, it is not far to the door. I push her out and throw the bolt. Then I plant my feet and flatten my back against the hard wood and yell, "And don't come back."

The door jiggles as she tugs on the doorknob. She screams my name over and over. From down below come howls from the other lodgers so rudely awakened. My mother yammers on and on about a crazy woman. Heavy footsteps stomp up the stairs. Men's voices grow louder.

Mother has fetched help.

My head pounds. I press my hands to my temples. I can't be locked up in the asylum. The idea of being confined for months—maybe forever—in a tiny cell, unable to read or write as I wish, sends ripples of panic radiating through me. I can't let it happen. I must escape.

I glance around the bare little room. First, I must block the door better.

I pull and shove my trunk over until it stands before the door. Then I cross the room, throw up the sash, and look down at the second-story extension below. I am not a young girl anymore, but I am fit from my daily cycle of yoga and dance. If I hang from the sill, my feet would be three feet or so from the roof below. A jump would be possible.

I study the flat expanse of roof, the neighbors' windows on every side. I'd also be completely visible. And how could I get down from there? Someone would need to bring a ladder to rescue me. I'd be just as trapped as in this attic.

I turn back and scan the room again. My gaze alights on the old cupboard beneath the dormer where I hid as a child when I wanted to escape my mother. Set behind the cot and in the dark, strangers will never see it.

I rush over, push the cot out slightly, and lift the rusty latch on the slated wood door. Then I bend down and peer inside. The hole is darker than a starless night sky. Anything could be living inside.

I glance over my shoulder. Men grunt as they shove against the door. Any minute, they will break through and seize me. I have no choice.

I grab my coat at the last second, and creep inside. I was much smaller the last time I hid under the dormer, and the space is far dirtier. My heart thunders as cobwebs sweep across my face, and the reek of mouse droppings attacks my nose. I pull my knees to my chest and scrunch myself as tightly as I can.

I peer at the crack of light coming around the cupboard door. Shivers run up and down my spine. My pulse races. I hate being trapped. I hate being in closed spaces. But what choice do I have? Anything is better than being locked up in an insane asylum.

I wrap my coat around me then, grasping the small nut holding the handle on, close the door.

Crack. And none too soon. The door to my room slams back against the chest, the sound sharper than a gunshot. My trunk grates along the floor. Crashes and bangs echo through the cupboard door. China shatters. I hold my breath. They must be tearing the room apart, destroying all my beloved things. My gut clenches at the thought.

"Your daughter's not here, ma'am," one of them calls out.

Mother answers from down below, her voice muffled by layers of plaster and wood. I curl up tighter, praying she does not decide to reascend the stairs and remember my old hiding place behind the bed.

Eventually, the bangs and crashes end. The men shuffle out, and all falls still.

Are they truly gone? I wait for what seems like hours. My fingers chill. My toes numb. The skittering of the rodents in the walls haunt me. All the while, I imagine the destruction wrought by those men. Has my precious typewriter survived? Did they destroy my manuscript? Is the much-traveled whelk shell from Ocean Grove broken?

There is no way to tell the time. My head droops, and I think I sleep. Maybe not. But it is not sleep I need. I need guidance. I practice my controlled breathing, clear my mind, and wait.

Will they come? Iases with his kind suggestions? Soph with his feathery touch? My sister, Nan, with her gentle voice? But my spirits have abandoned me. I am alone.

So, I sit in the dark with the scurrying mice and the cold night air sneaking through the cracks and ponder my revenge.

It takes me until morning to wrangle my way out the back of the boarding house with no one seeing me. Mother's doctor goons have seemingly disappeared, though I would not put it past her to set spies on me.

I eschew the horse cars and wend my way on foot to the Westbrooks by way of back alleys and side streets, fingers crossed that only Henrietta is there. Of all the people I know, she is the most likely to welcome me and know what to do, even if she wears her told-you-so face all the while.

To insure I do not meet up with Richard, I sneak around to the back of their house and knock on the kitchen door. Their live-in maid cracks the door ajar and gives me a pinched mouth glare. "No beggars allowed."

I brush my hands over my bodice and skirt. Cobwebs still cling to my clothing. My buttons are mismatched, my bonnet askew, and my hair hangs unpinned about my face. But to be mistaken as beggar? Have I been brought so low? Somehow, I find my voice.

"I . . . I'm a friend of the Westbrooks. I need to speak to Henrietta."

The maid closes the door in my face. Minutes later, it opens again.

"Oh heavens. It's Ida Craddock. Let her in, Milly." She throws her arms around me and draws me inside. "Oh, my darling, what's happened to you?"

I glance around quickly. "Richard?"

"He's in court, defending a case." She pushes my hair behind my ears. "Why? What's wrong?"

The knot in my stomach loosens. I curl into the safety of her body, the warmth of her friendship. "It's Mother. Last night, she brought doctors to have me committed to the asylum. I've been in hiding in a cupboard for hours."

"You poor dear." She rubs my back and ferries me into her small breakfast room.

The yellow-flowered, wallpapered space is sunlit and well-heated by the kitchen cookstove. Still, shivers ripple through me. I fear nothing will ever be warm inside me again.

I choke back a sob. "I had to leave everything behind—my typewriter, my manuscripts, my books. All my clothing and little treasures. If old Mr. McCauley, the first-floor tenant, hadn't let me slip out his window, Mother would have succeeded in having me locked up."

Henrietta taps her mouth with her index finger. "She's threatened this before. Is there no hope of changing her mind?"

"I fear not. Not this time. Mother wants me to be conventional, to stop lecturing on sex worship and marriage relations. But it's too late." I withdraw the crumpled paper from inside my bodice. "I've received a letter from the postal inspector." I smooth the wrinkles from the cursed summons. "What am I going to do?"

Henrietta clasps my hand. "Hush, you're safe now. That is just a warning. Even Richard got one for some article he wrote on free love. Nothing to panic over. Let me have Milly draw a bath, and I'll find you something to wear from my closet. We're about the same size. You will feel much better once you clean yourself up and rest for a bit. Oh, I almost forgot. Guess who is in Philadelphia today? William Stead."

"Stead? The British reformer? Alice Stockham raved about him. She had every copy of his *Review of Reviews*. I regret that I missed meeting him when he was in Chicago." I sit up straighter. "Oh, I must speak to him, tell him about my occult discoveries. Perhaps, he would support me in my fight?"

Henrietta clasps her hands. "Then we shall go. He's giving what he calls a snapshot talk about Chicago to a group of reporters at the *Inquirer*. I have plenty of friends there. And you know Fred Case—you did copy work for him. He'll be there."

Four hours later, I am feeling more myself, even if Henrietta's flouncy blue silk dress is tight in the bust and way too long after wearing my ankle-length skirts all these years. But I manage not to trip as I step up to shake hands with the oh-so-famous and oh-so-handsome William Stead.

I put my hand in his. Tingles spread across my palm, up my arm, and settle deep inside. I can barely get my planned words out. "Mr. Case suggested I speak with you. I have conducted numerous experiments in automatic writing and have established contact with several spirits. I was wondering if you might consider some of my work for your new publication *Borderland*?"

Stead focuses his pale gray eyes so intently on me that, despite the crowd milling around us, we might as well be in the middle of an empty room.

He leans toward me. "Possibly. Automatic writing is a major interest of mine, ma'am."

A knot forms in my belly. Dare I tell him of Soph? Dare I not? If anyone would be accepting of my work, this man ought to be.

I dip my head unable to withstand his gaze. "My name is Ida Craddock. Perhaps you have heard—"

His mouth turns up, and he claps his hands. "Mrs. Craddock. Of course, the secretary Mr. Case spoke to me about, who has written so many interesting articles. I read the *Danse du Ventre* essay while in Chicago and visited that Cairo Street exhibit myself. Alice Stockham has told me all about your work on marital relations. She says you have a spirit husband?"

I can barely answer. I am standing the proper distance away, and yet the magnetism emanating between us feels hotter than flames. "That is correct."

"And you communicate via automatic writing?"

"I do."

"We must talk more." He glances around. "But these gentlemen have arranged a dinner in my honor for this evening, and I leave for the port of New York and my ship to England on the morrow. I sail two days hence. Is there a chance we could meet over breakfast?"

Who knows where I will be tomorrow?

I look over my shoulder. Henrietta is flirting with one of the newsmen. Will she let me stay the night? In the same house as her untrustworthy Richard? I think not.

"I am not sure. It is dangerous for me to be seen in public. I have received an obscenity warning from the postal inspector on account of my Egyptian dance article. And in consequence, my mother has threatened me with incarceration in an insane asylum. I know you have been a strong voice for causes such as mine. Would you be willing to offer me support?"

Stead runs a hand through his thick, brunette hair. "In a perfect world, I would plant my feet and fight this battle with you. Institutionalizing women because they are bold and speak things men do not wish to hear is barbaric. Our most creative and spiritual minds are always under pursuit by those with no imagination. But my time is limited. Have you considered throwing off your pursuers by leaving the country? Giving yourself at least a year's breathing time?"

I shift from one foot to the other. "At times. I do keep a passport by my side always. This is not the first occasion I have been under threat."

"Then that is what I recommend. I propose you accompany me—as my secretary, of course—aboard the ship. Once there, you can work as a researcher for my new magazine on spiritualism. You and my editor, Miss X, will get along perfectly."

The invitation sucks the air right out of me. Work for this amazing man? Escape my mother? Foil Comstock's lackeys? But how will I resist my unwelcome attraction to him? I will have to use every thread of self-control Soph and Iases have taught me. But I can do it. I will do anything to stay out of an asylum.

"I would be most honored."

He pivots back an arm's length. His mouth pinches tight. "One thing. I am a happily married man. You understand, we must maintain propriety at all times?"

For a moment, I am thunderstruck. Obviously, I am not the only one feeling the ripples of desire drawing us together like pins to a magnet.

I tamp down my racing pulse and turn all business. "Of course. You will find me a most competent professional. I was amanuensis for the noted Alexander Badlam, author of *The Wonders of Alaska* and accompanied him on one of the first steamship tours of the Alaskan coast. I can produce a recommendation from him, if you wish?"

"I have no doubts to your secretarial abilities. Mr. Case praised you highly. However, for propriety's sake, I must ask you to travel and work under a married woman's alias. Let's see. How about Mrs. Irene Sophia Roberts?"

It is a plain enough appellation. Just not my own, and that makes me feel like I am abandoning who I am. Disavowing my marital reform work. To those like Dr. Ned, it will seem like I have disappeared into thin air. Still, Stead is right about the danger.

I gather up my courage. "That name will suffice."

He turns distant. "Fine. I will see that there is a ticket for you waiting dockside. So, pack up your belongings and come make England your new home."

I turn and smile at Henrietta. I can't wait to tell her.

I am going to England.

Rechristened.

Perhaps, reborn—

Chapter 20

"Once the mind becomes familiar with foul stories and
criminal deeds, self-respect at length is lost."
Anthony Comstock, *Traps for the Young,* p.8

London, 1895

I tuck in my shirtwaist, buckle my belt, and slip on my new
gray tweed suit jacket. There, the all-new Ida. I kick out a
foot and frown at the ground-skimming hem of the skirt. I
have hauled down my flag of dress reform and put away my
short dresses.

London differs greatly from what I expected—much more
liberal in thought, and much more conservative in manners
and dress. Not that my mother understands that.

I glare at the hat sitting on my desk. My mother may have
come and gone in her whirlwind European tour a month ago,
but she is still giving me grief. She missed me, she
proclaimed—even though she toured the capitals of the
continent before deigning to visit me. And she made no

attempt to hide what she wants. She needs me home to help with the business now that Decker is completely invalided.

Ha. I wish I had never given her my address.

I glance down. The suit she bought me to lure me back onto her leash is acceptable. The hat is not. The black straw, with its massive bunch of cherry-red silk flowers, is boldly fashionable, but absolutely the wrong color for someone like me with my graying blonde hair and pale skin. And definitely unsuitable for maintaining the quiet inconspicuousness Stead expects of me. Nevertheless, I plop it atop my head and poke in an army of hat pins to keep it in place.

Last night, as I lay in his arms, Soph insisted I wear it today for some reason, and no matter what Stead desires, I will do anything to please my dear husband.

With a quick check to make sure I haven't forgotten anything, I pick up my bag and rush off to work.

The sidewalk outside the dull brick building that houses the out-of-the-way editorial office of Stead's *Borderland* is in turmoil when I arrive. A group of women has come for a book club meeting at one of the other offices in the building and are drawing stares and jeers from the passersby as they maneuver their all-the-rage bicycles up the steps and into the lobby where they will be safe from thieves.

I wend my way around them, tamping down my envy at their good fortune. I love bicycling as much as I do riding horseback. But, while Stead pays me a salary adequate for my needs, it is far from enough to afford the purchase of one of Starley's shiny new Rovers and the biking costume to accompany it.

I give myself a shake. If only Mother had consented to invest in something I wanted, instead of this horrid hat and a wardrobe of frilly shirtwaists I will never wear.

I stride up the stairs and pop into our small office on the second floor. The editor, known as the notorious Miss X, but who is actually the tiny, angelic-faced Ada Freer, looks up from the page she is proofreading.

"Late again?" She gifts me a grin.

Good. She is in one of her better moods. Although, sometimes those are worse than when she is possessed by spirits.

I pull the pins from my hat and hang it on the hook by the door. "Not by much."

She shakes a finger at me. "I bet you wasted time fussing with that outfit."

I peer down at the nipped-in-the-waist jacket with its neat, sewn-down seams and matching fabric-covered buttons. "It's just a simple, ready-to-wear from Harvey Nicols. Nothing special."

She looks at me sideways. "Something your mother chose?"

"No. I selected this one."

She tucks her pencil behind her ear and walks around me. "It will do for your meeting later. Quite sophisticated for you."

I shrug. "At least it is easier on the eyes and less likely to dirty than the magenta suit my mother wanted to buy me." I smooth my palm down my hip. "I like the gored skirt, though. Plenty of room to move."

Ada laughs. "Handy if you have to run from that dragon you're meeting today."

"Miss Gillen is all right. She's been very kind to me."

She frowns. "I wish I never introduced you to her. She's worse than an evangelical, the way she has gotten her claws into you with that Theosophy nonsense."

"It's not all nonsense. I've learned a lot from attending their meetings, even if I've had to constantly question them about their doctrines."

Ada kisses me on the back of my neck. "That's for certain. If there is anyone who can henpeck an argument to pieces, it's you, my sweet. So, are you going to join the Theosophists or not?"

"Not sure. I cannot abide the idea of reincarnation when the glories of heaven await us. And it is ridiculous how they treat the mahatmas as if they are gods when they are merely human teachers. Still, I am tempted. The Theosophists are so passionate about what they believe."

"I could show you true passion, Ida, if you would just let me." She kisses me again.

I brush away the kiss. "You know I'm a married woman."

"Doesn't your spirit husband believe in sharing?" She presses up against my back and snags her arms around my waist. "I bet he doesn't touch you like this?"

Her body rubs against me, her living warmth so much more real than Soph's ethereal touches. It has been a long time since another human being has touched me with kindness and love. Not once in the two weeks Mother was here, did she so much as hug me. I might be middle-aged, but far as she is concerned, I will always be a doll to be dressed and admired from a distance. Nothing more.

Then I remember that today is the end of my tapu time, and Soph and I will join in heavenly union.

I suck in a breath and wiggle out of Ada's hold. "Work's waiting."

Ada pinches the tender skin of my upper arm then strides back to her desk. "You can't keep running away from me. Together, we could be a spiritual phenomenon."

I rub my arm. I like Ada well enough. Her investigations of ghostly infestations are meticulous, and her mediumship quite impressive. But it is her ability to communicate with Stead through automatic writing that irks.

Miss X has mastered the occult in a way I fear I never will.

I tuck on my dust apron and head to the *Borderland's* library. The bite of envy gnaws at my belly and bodes ill for a successful union with Soph tonight. My spirit guides insist I come to our love making with a clear and wholesome mind, free of fleshly temptations and human failings. I am beloved of the angels, they tell me, and they have high expectations for me.

I glance back at Ada, bent over her desk. Have my borderland guides put her physical magnetism in my path on purpose? Does she get her spiritual power from black magic? I have delved deep into the history of witchcraft at the British Library and have learned that it is hard to tell.

I skirt around the table in the center of the bookroom and return to the work I love—typing up brief reviews of the new books on spiritualism that arrive daily and then shelving them. The *Borderland* library has to be one of the most marvelous repositories of works on the occult in the world. And fortunately for me, it is totally private. No one will disturb me. Stead has made certain that no one knows where the magazine office is located nor who the editor Miss X is. No one can find me here. Not even my mother. It is the one place I feel safe.

I take the top book off the pile and thumb through *Madame Blavatsky and her Theosophy*, a paean to the woman by Arthur Lillie. It is nothing special. I skim the table of contents, type up a brief summary, and move on.

The next book, *The Veil Lifted* by James Robinson, deals with spirit photography. I page through it then set it down with a sigh. As real as I know Soph is, I have never seen my angel husband. Stead says that does not matter. He devours my diary entries about the nights Soph comes to me. Tells me I am one of the luckiest of women to be so privileged. That I will be seen as one of the greatest spiritualists of our day. That soon my books will sit on the shelves of this library.

That's what he says.

But I know what he really thinks. He thinks my work fantasies—sexual fantasies written privately just for him. I imagine Stead reading my notes and picturing me naked, in the grip of an orgasm. We have been well behaved, the two us. Nothing inappropriate has ever passed between us. Not a touch, not a sideways look. Not a breath of desire. He is faithful to his wife. I am faithful to my Soph.

I clench my fists. But in another world . . .

"Irene."

I jump then settle. I always forget who I am pretending to be. I straighten and peer over my shoulder.

Ada, wearing her raised-eyebrow Miss X face, stands in the doorway, waving a letter. "Stead's wife just sent this over."

The air becomes heavy. If there are spirits present, they are evil ones.

I rise slowly, resting my weight on the tabletop. "His wife?" Have I conjured her out of my desire?

Ada hands me the letter. "It seems our William's away, traveling on the continent. The wife and son are running the enterprise."

My stomach twists tighter than a corset lace. I open the flap and extract the note. A second piece of paper falls out. I scan the contents of the first. It is worse than I imagined.

It has come to their attention, it says, that I am a fraud—a shady, disreputable character and a lying, spiritualist crank known as Ida C. Craddock—who is pretending to be a Mrs. Irene Roberts, and my services are no longer needed by the Steads.

My hands tremble as I fumble for the second missive. I unfold the sheet and pound my fist. I knew it. My mother has been at work. She has sent a letter, addressed to me, under the name of Miss Ida Craddock via Stead's *Review of Reviews* office with a note that I am working on the staff of *Borderland* and misrepresenting myself as Irene Roberts, a married woman.

My heart withers in my chest. I flop back down in my chair. How could she destroy me so?

Ada huffs, and I look up.

She comes and puts an arm around me. "I'm so sorry, my dear."

I push her arm away, but she does not move. "You knew this was coming?"

"I had a spirit message from William."

I glance at her. Her pudgy hands clasp her shawl. Her eyes avoid mine. She is hiding something.

I open my mouth to ask, and then I know.

"This has nothing to do with my being unmarried. His wife found my diaries, didn't she?"

Ada runs her fingers through my hair. "Don't worry; Stead has rescued them. They are safe now. But you must leave. He doesn't want a scandal. He loves his children."

"Scandal?"

"Well, the diaries *are* graphic."

"You've read them?"

"Just the bits Stead has sent me via telepathy."

I stand. "*Bah*. All you know is what I have told you."

She takes a step back. "How dare you question my psychic ability? People think you're crazy, you know."

"I am no more crazy than you. You're the one in trouble over the Clandon House haunting. You plagiarized the servants' statements."

"I did not. And you're Stead's little pet sex project that he keeps all tucked up nice and safe."

I grab the letter from William's wife, crumble it up, then toss it across the room. "Safe? Letting his wife see my diary was keeping me safe?"

She throws up her hands. "Enough. I don't know the details of what happened. I am sure it was an accident. Maybe he left a page in his suit pocket or something. And his wife figured out you were the author when she got your mother's letter. Don't be angry with Stead. He cares about you, Irene."

The fake name grates in my ears. I knew it was wrong to change it. A follower of correct living must always be honest and true to themselves.

"Then, why isn't he here to defend me?"

Ada shrugs. "He can't and keep his wife happy."

I stomp out of the library, seize my hat off the hook, and slam the door as I flee.

I have never been happier living here in London. Why did my mother and Stead's jealous wife have to ruin everything?

By evening, I have laid most of my resentment to rest. But not all. I roll my shoulders and swing my arms to rid them of the tension and hurts of the day. I pray my Soph comes. It is nature's appointed love-night out of the twenty-eight days of the menstrual month. But I am so afraid he won't.

So, I take extra care in my preparation. I bathe myself using the finely milled lavender soap Katie has sent as a gift then move through a course of harmonic grace poses until my body assumes that weightless state of full relaxation. I spend precious minutes combing out my hair so that it flows down my shoulders like a filmy veil.

Only then do I blow out the paraffin lamp and make sure the window sash is open a crack. Soph hates the smell of the burning oil as much as I.

Chill evening air floats in from outside and removes the last of the day's sun-accumulated heat from the room. I slip beneath the bedclothes and lie on my back, my eyes closed. Gently, I inhale through my nose and exhale through my mouth as I have done so many times before until I feel at one with the world.

I am ready. Waiting.

The clock ticks its way through the night.

Yet he does not come.

I shift on the mattress, unease prickling at my most tender places. I know what is wrong. *You are trying too hard*, my guide, Iases, would chide. Thoughts of William Stead and the temptation of making love with a flesh-and-blood man distract me. Would he and I rut like animals in our passion the way Euclid maintained, or would my dear William treat me with the same care and kindness as my Soph?

I flick the covers down. It doesn't matter. Stead has abandoned me to ignominy, despite our innocence. And it is wrong for me to be tempted so by worldly lust. I have the best of lovers, my Soph, and I never want to lose him.

Oh, but what a difference it would make if I could but see and touch my spirit husband as though he were a person in the flesh. What a joy it would afford both of us and make a wonderful contribution to psychical research.

I dig my fingers into the sheeting. I must hold on to my patience and clear my mind of such lowly thoughts. I am chosen of the angels and must exist on a higher plane. My spirit husband will never forsake me or treat me cruelly. He insists he cannot enjoy our sexual union if I do not.

I must be patient. In five or six years, he has foretold, I will fall asleep and be taken from this earth to heaven where we will be joined together as husband and wife for all eternity in the glorious gardens of paradise. The thought calms.

Mind at rest, I roll over on my stomach the way Soph likes and hum under my breath the affirmations the Theosophists have taught me.

I am calm.

I am serene.

I am one with the Divine.

Something touches the small of my back. A hand, cool, and ghostly, and familiar. I let out one smooth exhale of delight. He is here—my angel.

He is no earthly man who will use me as chattel like Euclid. No hypocrite like Richard who would betray the woman who loves him. No traitor like Stead who abandons me to the petty outrage of his wife. My angelic husband is mine alone to love and be loved by.

"I am ready," I say in my richest voice, "to give you pleasure."

A cool breath brushes my ear. "*I know. And I am here to give you the same.*"

I slide my hands up and down my sides. I am no longer the lithe, coltish girl Charles admired. My breasts are heavier, my thighs plumper, my stomach rounded from too many chocolate bonbons—my one great weakness.

But for my angel, I can be as voluptuous as any siren of myth. I can be Venus to his Adonis. Chloe to his Daphnis. Parvati to his Shiva.

"Everything I am," I promise, "every pleasure I receive, is yours."

His voice peals in my head like the chiming of bells. "*I know, my love. You have learned much. Now hush and let us fly.*"

He hovers. His nearness sets my body thrumming. My breathing comes faster. My heart pulses. Longing fills me.

Still, he waits.

I spread my legs in welcome and focus all my magnetism on the deliciousness of physical union.

"*My sweet Ida,*" he soothes. "*So willing. So ready.*"

"Yes—my love."

We come together, and I still. I barely feel him, but I know he is there. I move my hips and belly in the seductive Danse du Ventre. Soph moves with me. My orgasm starts with tiny ripples that flow through me like ocean currents lapping at the shore. I grow heated. My breath quickens. Tension tightens my muscles. I am on the verge of orgasmic climax.

"*Not yet,*" Soph whispers.

I deepen my breathing and still my movements, hovering on the edge of release, enjoying the growing tremors sparking inside me and the pleasure flowing from me to Soph. Male continence at its best. What delight!

At the same time, I try something new that I have been thinking about based on my research. I use all my willpower to focus on my inner joy and open myself to the Divine presence. For has not God given all creatures the capacity for great joy, and surely, He yearns to receive it back?

So, as the powerful waves of sexual ecstasy magnify and crescendo, I share my inner pleasure with Soph and with God. My breath deepens. My mind lets go. Time, space, and all the human concerns that tether me to Earth disappear, the air shudders, and I am transported to some higher plane of existence—one of light, and air, and freedom. We merge. The triad becomes one.

I think I have never been so close to feeling what it is to be bathed in God's love.

When my mind refocuses and my throbbing body quiets, I feel only love for my husband. I lay on my back, my head nuzzled against Soph's intangible shoulder. I reach up to where his face must be. "I am so in love, my husband. If only I could see you? Just once? Though if I have to wait until I join you in your heavenly paradise, I do understand."

"*Come, my dear. You deserve a reward for the pleasure you have given today.*"

My skin chills as he moves above me. And like clouds clearing to reveal the fullness of the moon, I see an ethereal vision of Charles's face looking at me with wide-open eyes, just as he had when he was alive and was trying to cover up those feelings he held for me by assuming a serenity he didn't feel. And like that day so long ago, his eyes search mine, vainly seeking, poor fellow, for some token or signal that I will take his proposal seriously.

"I'm sorry I hurt you," I say.

"*You were not ready.*"

I reach up to cup his face, but it is already disappearing.

My hands flop down at my sides, and I mourn the loss.

But not for long. Soph will return. Of that, I am sure.

For now, I must focus on how to survive until I can join him in heaven at last. I must leave London. But where will I go?

To India, the continent, or home?

Chapter 21

"But worse than any cyclone or tornado is this silent
influencer."
Anthony Comstock, *Traps for the Young*, p. 48

Race Street. Philadelphia, 1895

The carter unloads my trunk and hefts it through the
familiar doorway. After weighing and reweighing my
options and my pocketbook, I have come home to take
up residence in my mother's house. The question is: will I
stay?

Mother waves to me, and I follow the man up the steps
and into the place I swore over and over never to return to. I
stop in the vestibule and sniff the sun-heated air, redolent with
memories of my childhood. I run my sweaty palms down my
bodice. All at once, all my fears come tumbling back. It is a
mistake to be here.

"So glad to see you home safely. And looking so darling
and respectable in the hat I bought you," Mother gushes. "Did
you have a fair crossing?"

I unpin my distasteful, red-flowered London bonnet and abandon it on the hall table. I will never wear it again. "Fine weather, all the way."

"Good, good."

"I had the most pleasant companions to converse with. Thank you for paying for the first-class fare."

"Haven't I always treated you well? Now, come into the parlor and rest."

I trail after her, surprised to see her limping. "Are you injured?"

She plops down in her newly upholstered wing chair and raises her foot onto a footstool. "It's my toe. The doctor says it's gout." She adjusts her position. "A minor case, though exceedingly painful. I can barely sleep. The burning and aching are so bad I had to stop attending my temperance meetings."

"I'm sorry to hear that." And I truly am. If she is confined to the house, I will never escape her oversight. I sit down on the sofa. "What treatments have the doctor prescribed?"

"Oh, I am just dosing on our own bitters."

"And is our famous concoction working?"

She places her hands on her considerable paunch. "I hope so. But now that you are here, you can be of much assistance with my foot baths and taking care of my dear Thomas, who is quite bedridden with the cancer, I am sorry to say." She lifts her foot slightly. "As you can see, I am incapable of climbing the stairs every time he calls."

Foot baths? Tend the Interloper? Does she think she has acquired a live-in nurse? I have to escape now, before she ties me to her apron strings again.

I clasp my hands tightly together. "I will not be staying here long. I will rent rooms, as I did before."

Mother raises an eyebrow. "But you have no funds."

"I thought to borrow something to tide me over until I find a secretarial position. A friend of mine who works at City Hall knows of an opening there."

Mother taps the arm of the chair. "But why go into debt again when you can stay here? You can fix your old bedroom into a pleasant study for yourself, where you can read and write to your heart's content. Take in typing if you become too bored caring for your elderly parents."

My pulse throbs at my temples. Has she forgotten her attempts to incarcerate me? I certainly haven't.

"My living here did not work out too well before. I think we will do better under different roofs."

"But I need you, Ida. Please, Thomas is dying. I cannot bear it alone."

I wish my heart was harder. I wish I had never stepped over the threshold. I wish I had chosen Italy or France, or any place in the world rather than come home. But just like the leashed dog she thinks I am, I cannot say no. She is getting older, and I feel some filial duty. Not much, but not enough to storm out the door.

"I will stay a short while," I say. "And see that you find a proper nurse to care for you both."

Mother smiles. "That's my good girl. I will even buy you a new desk to replace the one you had to leave in England. Though, why you had it shipped over I could never figure out."

"I hadn't planned on coming back."

Her mother 's mouth twists into a smile of sorts. "Well, I am so glad you did. You've made your loving mother happy."

Her words please me at some deep-seated level I do not even want to understand.

I rise to my feet. "I best get to unpacking then."

Mother nods. "I had the room prepared for you with fresh bed linens and a soft mattress. I want you to be comfortable." She hesitates. "I want you to stay and be the daughter I have dreamed of. The one I saw in London. You were such a . . . a fine lady—quiet, staid, conservatively dressed. I couldn't believe the transformation."

Transformation? That woman wasn't me. That was a woman in hiding from her threatening mother.

I rise from the sofa. "I will see to my things then."

"You do that. And let me know if you need me to purchase anything else."

I tip my head and hurry up the stairs. The stink of the sick bed assaults me as I turn on the landing. I peek into Decker's bedroom. His balding head lolls on the bolster, his skin as white as the sheeting draped over him. He is dying.

I slip down the hall. Why hasn't Mother hired a nurse? She can well afford to. Surely, she hasn't been waiting for my return, planning to trap me here out of the kindness of my heart? Though I wouldn't put it past her.

I throw open the windows in Mother's parlor to rid it of the foul stink and take refuge in my old sanctuary. Although the linens are new and fresh, and there is a bare spot where my desk used to sit, nothing else has changed. The faded beige and burgundy wallpaper still sports what is likely a floral pattern, but I still see the demonic heads that petrified me as a child. My small bookcase holding the classic stories from my childhood tempts, but I focus instead on unpacking my trunk. I hang up my old friends—the dress-reform outfits I'd been too shy to wear in England.

I finger my favorite cotton tea dress with its smocked neckline. Then, throwing caution to the heavens, I remove my oh-so-conventional tan linen suit and annoying stays and slip into the gown. The filmy cream material floats around me, and my body feels free for the first time in months. I tie a pink ribbon at my waist, set my old broad-brimmed straw atop my rather messy hair, and head for the front door.

"You're not going out, are you?" Mother calls from the parlor as I pass. "You just got here." She pushes up from her chair.

I know it is a mistake to pause, but seeing her grimace with pain tugs on my heart. She did pay my ship fare.

I stop in the doorway. "Yes, I can't wait to see my friends."

She grabs her cane and takes a step toward me. "Dressed like that?"

"Why not? It is hot day."

"It's a lovely dress to wear at home, but not on the city streets. It's . . . it's too short, too revealing."

I lift my chin. I will not let her turn me into an overly mothered child again. "I saw plenty of women wearing similar dresses on my way here."

"Ida, I thought you'd changed—"

I do not hear the rest of what she says. I'm already out the door and striding down the street.

"Ida, I need you," Mother's piercing voice cuts through the night.

Not again? Living with Mother would try the kindest of souls, and after six months, I am not feeling kindly, nor patient, nor dutiful. If this is my spirit guides' idea of a way to test my ability to carry out correct living, I am surely failing. I can get nothing done. Between the two invalids, I'm kept running day and night. I need a place of my own. A life of my own.

"Ida, quick."

I pull the application for the job at City Hall from my typewriter then push up from my desk and drag my way to the sickroom.

One look is all it takes. Decker wears the blue cast of death. His breath rattles in his throat. The stink of his decaying flesh smothers even Mother's reeking perfume. It will only be a matter of hours.

I resettle the covers and wipe his brow with a damp cloth. Then I glance across at Mother, sitting with her hands folded in her lap, her head bent down as if praying. Always so pious. Always doing the socially accepted thing. Silhouetted in the darkened room, half-lit by the turned-down gas sconce, she could model for a painting of the grieving widow—not that she's lifted one hand to care for the man she took as husband.

I purse my lips. And what in the world is she praying for?

Not Decker. She might call him her "dear Thomas," but she's had no use for him for years. He was a consummate failure at controlling me and ran the apothecary in a totally lackluster way. The only reason Mother is still a wealthy woman is because patent medicine, heavily laced with laudanum and cannabis, sells well despite poor business decisions and clerks skimming from the till.

Mother blots her eyes with one of her Point de Paris lace handkerchiefs, a memento of her visit to France. "I will miss him."

I let out a sigh. I should at least show some comfort.

I drop the cloth in the basin, wipe my hands, and circle the bedstead to put my hand on her shoulder. "Mother, ought we call the doctor?"

"Too late for that, I fear. He will soon be in heaven."

"Will he?" I remove my hand and step back. That such a man will be welcomed into the glories of heaven, where my angel and I will someday live in blessed wedlock, makes my stomach turn.

"He was a resolute churchgoer. Something you should consider, my dear. Some religious morality would serve you well." Mother sniffs through her soggy linen nose wipe.

"Have you understood nothing I have told you about my beliefs?"

She clenches her fancy hankie in her hand. "That garbage you spout? Your radical, half-cocked, ungodly ideas."

"You dare question my relationship with God? Me, who has earned so much favor through right living and progress in mediumship that I have an angel husband who loves me?"

"Mere fantasies."

"Soph is not a fantasy.

Mother grasps my arm and hauls herself to her feet. "You promised we would not discuss this delusional marriage of yours anymore." There's something in the tone of her voice that I do not like. "I need you, Ida. I can't bear the thought of being left alone. You will stay with me . . . after he passes?"

I glance at the deathbed and bite my tongue. Decker still breathes. As angry as Mother makes me, I cannot argue in front of a dying man, no matter how insensate he appears.

The words nearly choke me, but I force them out. "Yes, Mother, I will stay."

For a while.

Mother is far more devastated by Decker's death than I could have imagined. Silence and loneliness hang over the black-draped rooms. She truly misses having a man to guide her life and cater to her whims. It remains for me to see that the fresh flowers Decker had sent her daily still arrive, and for me to order the special candied treats he used to keep her sweet.

She can't walk, she says. She is in constant pain, she insists. Day and night, I am called to wait on her. No serving girl will do. Only dear Ida can help her dress and undress. Only darling Ida can assist her from parlor to bedroom and back again. Only the world's best daughter Ida can fetch her a glass of water in the middle of the night. I am so tired of hearing her call my name I want to scream.

Time passes, and I get little writing done—just two little folktales and a long essay on the nature of heaven. Worse, Soph does not come. How can he when I am either exhausted or furious? My mother's house has never been a place of right living. Then the acceptance letter from the city highway department arrives. It is like a ticket to freedom.

No, it *is* a ticket to freedom. I will no longer need Mother's doled out largess. I will be able to move out. I will have my freedom back again.

I take a moment to smooth down my hair then carry the letter into the parlor and sit down beside Mother.

She puts down her teacup, eyes wide. "News?"

"I have been offered the secretarial position at the Bureau of Highways at City Hall. It is the type of job you have always dreamed I would have. The salary is topnotch. I could do no better as a woman."

Mother frowns. "But I need you here."

"Not as much as you did right after your dear Thomas passed. City Hall is within walking distance. I can come home for lunch, if you wish. And the new Irish girl is excellent. She comes the second you call."

Her mouth firms. "It's a secretarial job?"

"Yes. I will be working for the head of the highway department. Most respectable."

"You are not doing it for the money?" She touches the back of my hand. "You must admit I have treated you well, haven't I? Bought you fashionable clothing and such. And you have been able to live here instead of those horrid, rented rooms where who knows what foul persons have resided." She glances around the room then waves toward the piano. "All these lovely things will be yours someday."

"I appreciate that, Mother." But I don't and never will. She has given me everything that I never wanted and blocked me from everything my being calls out for. I want no bric-a-brac from her.

I have a different need—to speak my gospel of happy marriage to the world. Now. While I'm still young and full of imagination and vivacity. Not when I'm old and my creativity and energy are gone. If Mother were poor and unable to afford servants, then I might feel differently. But she is not.

Still, I nod in agreement with her. I do try to be grateful for the many little kindnesses she has shown me. Besides, it better furthers my cause.

"In your new position, you will wear the lovely London suits I bought you?"

I stifle a sigh. Freedom is worth more than personal comfort. "Of course."

She smiles. "Excellent. With your fine figure dressed fashionably, I am sure you will attract the eye of one of those well-heeled government officials in no time. It would be so nice to have a man in the house again. And grandchildren. You are not too old to bear a child or two. Promise me you will not turn away any interested gentleman."

I open my mouth to protest.

"And don't you bring up that imaginary husband of yours, or I will declare you insane for sure."

I snap my mouth back closed. No matter how hard Mother yanks my leash, there will be no civil servant sleeping in my bed. No babes lying beneath moldering tombstones. I have another mission in life.

I refill my mother's teacup. Only a few more weeks of being her personal lapdog. Once I have saved enough of my salary, I am moving out.

I set the teapot back on the tray and study her face. Poor Mother. She has aged so much in the last months. It must be awfully hard for her at times. She would so like to have me be conventional, and I can't be what she wishes.

I can't.
And I won't.

It takes far longer than expected, but I finally have a private place to escape to when caring for Mother becomes too trying. I look up from the book I am reading and survey my dear little box of a room. I can't believe my luck. A space where no one can bother me while I write or scream in orgasm.

There is no Mother calling for help every minute and constantly peeking at my drafts. No nosy fellow tenant looking for a chat. No well-meaning friends to stop by and steal away my precious hours. I clap my hands and give a shout, stamp my feet and do a few pirouettes remembered from my childhood dancing lessons. I can be as noisy and wild as I wish. There is no one in this building to hear or complain.

No one knows I am here, and I plan to keep it that way until I start my marriage counseling business.

I have it all planned out.

I slowly close Alice Stockham's new book, *Karezza*. It is beautifully written, but it doesn't go far enough. And it is way too long and wordy. Most married men have no desire to read a one-hundred-page poetic on divine loving. Like Euclid, they just want to get on with it, regardless of the emotional and spiritual heights they and their wives could aspire to with some gentle training.

And if Annie's George Whitby, Euclid Frick, and Katie's Mr. Wood are typical, instructing men is key. What is needed is a short, low-cost pamphlet written with male self-importance in mind. And I am the one to write it.

Unlike Stockham or her medical cohorts, I have spent many hours teaching some of the most recalcitrant of male students. I already have a title: *Helps to Happy Wedlock*. And unlike Alice's book or Edward Carpenter's *Love's Coming of*

Age, my little pamphlet will be brief, with the directions written in plain English.

I lie down on my improvised mat on the floor and peer up through the skylight above me. Pigeons loop and swirl across the sky. Clouds float by. I run a lazy hand down the pale blue wall. My new studio isn't beautiful. It isn't warm. Merely an unused bathroom with the fixtures removed. But the wood floor has been refinished, and although only a block from City Hall, it is as private as can be. What a delicious find at seven dollars a week and the owner glad to get it. Who else but solitary me would want to pay any amount of money for such a tiny space three stories above a failed mercantile?

I push up to my feet and survey my domain. All my years of living frugally have paid off. I spent mere pennies fixing up the place. My typewriter rests on a folding table that must date back to the Civil War but was only a few cents at the used furniture store. My collection of colorful paisley shawls drape my second-hand chair and curtain the windows as a reminder of my time in London. My notes, and books, and treasures are all here. I pick up my silk ribbon bookmark commemorating the World's Fair and let out a long breath. It took me weeks to sneak my belongings out of the house—a few items every day.

Best of all, Soph has resumed his conjugal visits now I am free of Mother's toxic influence. Not that I can sleep here at night.

I glance at my watch. Time to get moving. I straighten my pallet, heft my bag, and trot down the four flights. Then, gritting my teeth, I wend my way to Race Street, my mood sinking the closer I get to home.

I stop on the top step and unlock the front door. I only have to stay a little longer. Just until I find a live-in maid for Mother and until my bank account is flush enough to afford the kind of rooms I've always wanted. A place where I can entertain friends. Hold a salon. Organize a book club. How lovely that will be.

In the vestibule, I smooth down my hair and skirt. Time to be on my best behavior and resign myself to catering to Mother's every whim.

Perhaps, if I please her enough, she will dole out some pocket money to buy a treat or new hat. Not that I would waste the money on such foolishness. After scraping by for so long, I do not need luxury. But each penny I can squirrel away speeds up my escape from the stupefying desk job at city hall and Mother's choking apron strings.

I step into the parlor. The holder of those strings has fallen asleep on her chair in the dark, the perfect image of the caring mother. At the sound of my footsteps, however, she raises her head.

"Ida, is that you?"

"Yes, Mother." I strike a match, lower the chandelier, and light the gas.

She shuts her eyes against the glow. "It is late. Past dinner. Could you have not sent a note around? I waited for hours. Ate my meal cold."

The lie trips off my tongue, sweet-toned and cruel. "Oh, a fine gentleman from work got me into conversation. We stopped and bought meat pies from a street vendor."

Mother huffs. "Most improper. If a gentleman is interested, he should call on you properly."

"It was completely unplanned. And you do so like me to pay attention to the gentlemen."

"Whosoever he was, that man was no gentleman, Ida. Do not see him again."

I open my mouth to argue that I am well old enough to make my own choices then shut it again. I will always be a feckless child to her, and there is no need to stir her up. I have played being normal too well to spoil it now.

"I'm sorry. It's just, I thought . . . But no, I will not see him again." I sit down, pat her hand, and change the subject. I pick up the manuscript from the end table. "So, did you have a chance to read my new piece, *The Heaven of the Bible*?"

Mother nods. "It is a bit overwrought, and you say too much about nakedness and sexual behavior—I am sure that spirits in heaven are much more demure—but yes, I think it is the best thing you have ever written. I am pleased to see that all the hours you spent reading the Bible have had such a beneficial effect on you."

I run my hand over the typed pages. "Lippincott's have agreed to publish it."

"Wonderful news, my darling. See? You need not spout off all that sexual rubbish to gain recognition."

After thirty-nine years, I have, at last, pleased my mother.

I set the manuscript down. If only she knew the turn my life's work has taken now.

Chapter 22

"When Satan's claws are plainly as seen. . .let not men, or those who call them themselves men, sit indifferent."
Anthony Comstock, *Traps for the Young*, p. 92

Craddock residence, Race Street, 1898

Two years of being proper. Two years of tolerating my mother. All for nought. Comstock has found me again.

A second letter from the Philadelphia postal inspector arrived today. Today, when I am feeling so low and poorly, and when dealing patiently with the furious woman at the foot of my bed is beyond my ability.

I have been sick-a-bed for days. Despite the blankets heaped over me, every part of me is icy-cold except where I'm burning hot. My head pounds, and every other minute, I sneeze. I dab my running nose. This is the worst of times to have succumbed to the grippe. I am so rarely ill and to be so now sets my pulse racing.

Mother presses her hand to her bosom. "You will be the death of me yet, Ida. You're incapable of behaving in a respectable way. First, you get fired for writing obscenity at work, then ridiculed in the newspaper." She rolls her eyes heavenward. "My goodness. I can barely look my dear friends in the eye when we pass on the street. But that wasn't enough. You drive the nail in deeper by doing it again—sending those obscene writings of yours through the mail."

I put up a hand to stop her tirade. But that has never worked, and it doesn't now.

She spews on, "I have spoken with the district attorney, Thomas Barlow. Such an upstanding man. I don't know why you couldn't have landed a gentleman like that. You were a pretty girl, accomplished in all the graces. But no hope of that now. No sensible man will marry a notorious woman who's in Comstock's record book."

I clear my throat. "Well, at least that's something we can agree on. But let me make something plain. I haven't"—I stop to sneeze—"sent any more pamphlets out. I returned all the remittances my ads brought in. Even gave up my precious office. Which is why I am lying here, being harangued by you."

"Mr. Barlow wants to make sure you have stopped. He is threatening to arrest you. But I agreed that in return for suspending the indictment, you would turn over your entire stock of pamphlets and—"

My breath locks in my lungs. She is doing it again—smothering me. How could she come to an agreement with one of Comstock's closest allies against her own daughter? I struggle for air.

"You have no right to hand over my marriage guides. I paid for them out of my hard-earned salary."

Mother's face hardens. "That rubbish. I glanced at the ones you left lying around the house. The awful language you use. Deserves to be burned."

I wipe my nose and strive for calm. "Every word can be found in medical books, sold at any bookstore. Sex shouldn't be a mystery."

"Well, it certainly doesn't belong in polite company. You promised to give up this craziness of yours. To be a loving, respectable daughter."

"Marriage reform is my life's work, Mother. Too many women are treated contemptibly by their husbands. Like you were by my father."

Her lips pull back from her teeth. "You know nothing of marriage, *Miss* Craddock."

I rub my throbbing forehead. "I know plenty. I have read and researched and, as much as you deny it, lain with my angel husband. Women come to me for advice. I receive ten or more letters a day from desperate brides willing to pay fifty-cents for one of my pamphlets. The same price as one of your bottles of Craddock Bitters."

"Their husbands will teach them all they need to know. If you had one, you would have given up this idiocy a long time ago."

"Men know nothing about how to please a woman."

"*Bah.* Is teaching men what *you* think they should to do in the bedroom worth going to jail? If you believe that, you will fit right in at the asylum."

"Asylum?" The pounding in my head grows stronger. "What else did you and that snake Barlow agree on?"

"That you will voluntarily admit yourself to the asylum for treatment."

I push up on my elbow. My head spins. "I am not insane."

"The postal inspector thinks so." Mother puts her hands on her hips. "I think so."

I pinch the bridge of my nose, but the headache only worsens. I sit up and lower my feet to the floor. "I am leaving. I planned to leave for Chicago in two days. One of my friends will put me up till then."

"If you don't go along with the arrangements Barlow and I have made, you will need a lawyer to get you out of jail, not a bunch of liberal fools who want to use you as an example."

"My friends have the right of it. There are no freedoms in this so-called democracy." I stifle a sneeze. "Not even the right to suffer a cold in peace." I draw in a raspy breath. "I have a First Amendment right to post anything I want through the mail. Comstock and his cronies have no business opening my sealed letters and accusing me of obscenity merely because I use perfectly acceptable medical terms for body parts. Words women need to know." I hiss them at her, "Penis. Hymen. Vagina. Clitoris. Orgasm."

Mother presses her hands to her ears. "That is more than enough. Get up and get dressed, you foul-mouthed hussy. I have arranged for you to be admitted to Friends Asylum in Frankfort. You will be out in the country with plenty of fresh air and light. You will surely be happier there than in jail."

"Perhaps *you* will be happier. 'Out of sight, out of mind,' as they say. You just don't want to see my name in the papers again. That's all you have ever cared about—appearances." I throw off my blanket. Cold air slaps at me. Goosebumps travel up and down my body.

She comes around the bed. "I'm done mollycoddling you. Letting you live here and trying to instill manners and sense. Paying off your debts. Listening to you spouting off your bizarre ideas and offending every friend I have. No more. You are going to the asylum."

I sit up and glare at her. "I spent precious months of my life nursing you and that man you married to spite me. I've kept your books. Dressed to please. Brought you foot baths in the middle of the night. Typed your correspondence and worked at a job I hated, and now I have some trouble with the law, and you would abandon me?"

"I'm not abandoning you. I have arranged to keep my sex maniac daughter out of prison. Get up." She hands me my shirtwaist. "Put it on."

"I am not a sex maniac, and I am not going to an asylum." Huffing and puffing, I grab the wrinkled shirtwaist and sway slightly as I fumble the buttons closed. Mother slips a skirt over my head, then holds up the jacket. I slide my arms into the sleeves, every movement an effort.

"Stop being difficult. For the price they charge, you will be well-cared for. And if you are not receptive to the treatment of the fine doctors there, I'll put you in the Philadelphia Institute. You can consider the fees I am paying toward your keep as your inheritance. You will never get the rest. I have made up my mind. The Craddock fortune will be donated to the Temperance League."

Despite my fevered brain, my insides turn to ice. I recognize truth when I hear it. Her protestations of love have always been lies. Only her hate is real. Any lingering tenderness I have for the woman who birthed me dissipates like fog on a hot summer day.

"Thank you for paying for *my keep*. At an asylum. Like a horse put out to pasture."

Thunk. Thunk. Pounding on the front door echoes up the stairs.

Mother seizes my arm. "Excellent. They are here."

My thoughts scatter. "Who?"

"The gentlemen from the asylum."

Down below, the maid opens the door. Heavy footsteps clomp into the vestibule.

I pull free. "You cannot make me go. I am a free woman. A sane woman. You cannot force me into a madhouse because of what I say or write. I'm leaving and never coming back." I rush down the stairs. At the bottom, a burly man reaches out and grabs my shoulder. Another seizes me by the arm.

"Ida Craddock, come quietly now," he says.

I have no intention of submitting.

"Let me go," I yell. "You have no right to commit me against my will."

I jerk against my captors' hold. Kick them in the shins. But a pebble has no hope of toppling a boulder. The goons shuffle me outside and toward a carriage with blackened windows.

In the light of day, the fog in my brain dissipates, and it hits me. This is really happening.

I let out a scream, and then another, hoping the neighbors will hear. But all I earn for my efforts is a sorer throat and a gag in my mouth.

That foul-tasting piece of cloth is all it takes to bring me down. My mother has finally achieved her goal. I am silenced.

No.

That's the only word you need to describe an asylum for the insane. I request books to read. The answer is no. I demand paper and pen to write. The answer is no. I ask to use the telephone to call Henrietta. The answer is no. I ask to send a telegram to Stead. The answer is no. I ask to speak to my lawyer. The answer is no. I ask to be released because I am perfectly sane.

The answer is . . . no.

I stroll down the path and inhale the overpowering fragrance of the roses. Mother was right about the light and the air. What she neglected to mention was the spiked-topped iron fence, the grates on the windows, and the sly attendants who follow me around day and night.

A carriage pulls up in front of the main building. I peer over my shoulder. Some lucky person is leaving, or maybe an unlucky one is being delivered. The only way in and out is through the barred gate. And since nobody knows I am here, I am sure the visitor is not for me.

I face forward and continue down the pathway. Maybe if I walk long enough, I will sleep tonight without black-hearted demons pricking, poking, and prodding every time I close my eyes.

My fingers twitch, and I clasp them into fists. I am not crazy. I am not bewitched.

I glance over my shoulder at the white-shirted orderly pacing discreetly among my fellow patients out enjoying the sun. The man's sneaky eyes meet mine, and I turn away.

Everyone keeps waiting for me to do something bizarre in order to justify my being here. *Let it all out. You'll feel relieved,* the doctors admonish. *Tell us your fantasies. Your dreams. Your deepest fears and desires.*

I know better. They want me wild-eyed and raving, hysterical like so many here so they can dose me and douse me, and charge higher fees. But I'm too wise in the ways of psychologists and medical doctors. I am one myself, if not by degree, then by self-study. And once I convince them of my sanity—

"Ida. Ida, stop."

I spin around.

Henrietta runs down the path toward me, one hand holding her amply feathered hat to her head, her skirt flying out behind her.

I open my arms and draw her to me, squeezing her tight. Tears fill my eyes. "You've found me."

"I knew you wouldn't have left for Chicago without saying goodbye. And then, when Alice telegrammed me that you never showed up on the fourteenth, I knew something rotten had happened and your mother was at the root of it. I finally weaseled the name of this place out of her. So proud of herself she was."

"She would be." I side-eye the orderly then loop my arm in Henrietta's and stride toward the semi-privacy of the greenhouse. I must not show anger. I lean over and whisper, "She made a deal with the district attorney—that blowhard Barlow—to commit me."

Henrietta gazes out over the gardens then back at the elegant mansion. "At least she chose a lovely place. Very expensive, you know. There are worse institutions."

I keep my voice calm. "A few thorny roses don't change the fact that I am trapped here with a bunch of true lunatics. Mother has done what she always wanted—silenced me."

I open the door to the greenhouse and step inside. Henrietta follows me in.

The straw-covered walkways are spongy beneath my feet. The rich scent of loam and growing things hangs over us, a warm, damp blanket that pastes perspiration on our brows.

The cherub-faced greenhouse attendant looks up then returns to watering trays of young green plants. He's the image of innocence, but the boy is prone to tattle as much as any other employee. I put a finger to my lips.

She reaches out to touch the speckled leaves of some exotic plant. "I do think your marriage advice is much needed. But it was unwise to have sent out those pamphlets after being warned. Comstock has many allies."

"Which obviously includes my mother. But what could I do? My clients were begging for them—many of them doctors. How could I refuse to mail such important information to a physician? Why, somewhere tonight, a young bride may be introduced to pleasure instead of frightened to death because of my work."

"Still, I thought you were going to limit yourself to face-to-face consulting. Sometimes, I think you want to be a martyr." There is censure in her voice.

I walk deeper into the greenhouse. Sunlight streams through the panes. Vines overflow their pots. All around me is light and life. Inside me, however, the dark knot of fury I have kept tucked away uncurls and threatens to overwhelm me. But I do not want to offend my staunchest supporter and friend. Nor draw the watchers' attention.

I keep the tone of my voice in check and apply the salve of reason. "I thought you liberal-minded, an advocate of free love and free thought. It is wrong what they are doing to me. Can't you see that?"

"Of course, it is wrong. But we must be satisfied with small steps, Ida. You can't change the marriage relationship overnight. Look at the battle for suffrage."

"Yes, look at suffrage. Women have been demanding it for fifty years, and we still can't vote."

"But it's changing, Ida. Women do vote in some states and, little by little, we will in all."

"I am forty-one years old. I can't wait fifty years to share my knowledge or dribble it out to a woman here or woman there. The women of the world can't exist fifty more years without the basic information every girl and boy should learn from their mothers. Think of all the pain and suffering my simple pamphlets can alleviate. Alice agrees with me."

Henrietta brushes a lock of hair off her perspiring brow. "Let Alice be your guide. She has managed to stay clear of Comstock with her writings."

"Not really. She's had her problems. In fact, Barlow banned me from sending *Karezza* through the mail, too."

Henrietta halts. "I didn't know that." She bites her lip. "The censorship is getting worse, isn't it?"

We have reached the working end of the greenhouse. I pick up a forgotten trowel from the potting bench. "One man. One single man stands in the way of our First Amendment rights." I drive the tip into a pot of dirt. "There has to be a way to bring Anthony Comstock down."

"He has Congress wrapped around his little finger. What politician can argue against protecting children from obscenity?"

I pull the trowel free. "And there's the crux. One man, under the cover of religious piety, has stifled all discussion of what is a perfectly natural process. The church and the state need to get out of the bedroom. Women are suffering. There has to be a way to take him down."

Henrietta holds up her hand. "Ida, think. Attacking Comstock will only make your life worse."

I raise an eyebrow. "What could be worse than having your own mother commit you to an insane asylum?"

She rolls her lips. "Rotting in prison."

"What's the difference? I will be silenced either way."

Henrietta shakes her head. "Ever been in a prison?"

I remember the high walls of the Eastern Penitentiary, and a wisp of fear sweeps over me. "No. Have you?"

"Yes. I attend female patients delivering their babes at the city jail." She waves her hand around. "This is heaven compared to that dirty, miserable swamp of despair."

"An insane asylum is not heaven." I shake the trowel at her. "You have no idea what heaven is. Nor despair. Heaven is freedom. Freedom to read and write what one desires. Freedom to contact friends and let them know you are safe."

My voice rises. "Despair is hearing the key turn in the lock night after night after night. Despair is circling around a fenced-in garden until you have worn away the soles of your shoes. Despair is being willing to sacrifice your soul to become one of the birds that flit over that gate you drove through so easily."

I run the rusty edge of the trowel across my wrist. The metal is rough against my skin, too dull to cut.

"Ida, don't." There is high-pitched horror in Henrietta's voice.

I throw the tool down. "Henny, you are all I have. Help me get free, please."

Henrietta puts her hand over mine. "What can I do?"

"Get me a new lawyer. I do not trust the one Mother hired. Thing is, I have no money. Mother has cut me off. For good, she says."

Henrietta sighs. "Caroline Kilgore might do it, but not for free. I'll take up another collection among the congregation. But, Ida, this has to be the last time. Spring Garden Unitarians cannot keep rescuing you from yourself. Too many of them believe you have overstepped the bounds of respectability, especially Richard. He bewails what has happened but thinks you should have been more discreet."

I purse my lips. Richard Westbrook has no idea what discretion is. It is a miracle that his wife is here, standing by my side, after how he behaved toward me. I owe Henrietta so much.

I gift her my sweetest smile. "I so appreciate your help and support."

From behind us, the attendant coughs, invading our semblance of privacy.

I wipe my hands on my skirt and move closer to Henrietta, as if she can save me from demons, real and imaginary. We amble to the door.

"One more favor."

Henrietta's head jerks around. "What?" She is plainly overheated, tired, and ready to leave. Dare I ask?

I think of all those stacks of pamphlets I had printed up. At fifty-five cents apiece, they will provide an income of sorts when I get out. And my phallic worship manuscript. It is irreplaceable. I must ask.

"My papers are at my mother's, and"—I suck in a breath—"and she's threatened to burn them. Could you retrieve them and keep them safe until I am free of this place?"

Her answer comes too quickly. Too harshly. Too out of character. "No."

The word jars the good humor from me. I stop dead in the pathway. Did I hear wrong?

"No? Why?"

She avoids my eyes. "I don't believe you are insane, and I will help get you released. But have you thought about dropping your marriage counseling plans and pursuing your interest in folklore and ancient religions instead?"

The hairs on the back of my neck rise. "Be more discreet, you mean? More respectable? Like Richard wants? Like my mother wants?" I can barely draw breath. Has Henrietta's praise for my work been merely lip service?

She nods. "You're smart, Ida. Make the wise choice."

I close my eyes. I need Henrietta. She is the only one willing to help me escape this thorny mental prison masquerading as a rose garden.

I clasp my hands behind my back. "I will consider it. But I must have my books, my research notes. Surely, you can convince Mother to turn them over to you. She did before."

"I can't. That is something for you and your mother to settle."

My legs wobble. "But . . . she will destroy everything."

She shakes her head. "I can't have your banned works in my house. Richard would . . ." She presses a knuckle against her lips. "You ask too much, Ida. No. Just no."

I stand in the sun as the carriage pulls out of the drive and passes through the gates. Then I sink down on a bench and listen to the bees zipping from flower to flower, sampling one then another, as I have the new religions. Quaker reform. Evangelism. Unitarianism. Theosophy. Christian Science. Yoga. All of these are taken seriously. All considered respectable pursuits.

What difference is there between the Holy Spirit descending through a preacher's hands and setting a young girl a-tremble and loving couples asking God to participate in the pleasure of the sex act?

I rise to my feet and gaze up at the heavens.

If I can have no freedom of speech, then I will claim freedom of religion. I am sure my angels would approve.

It takes two months to win a semblance of freedom. I walk down the steps of the federal court house, reeling from what I have done. The grand jury dropped my indictment. In return, I agreed never again to send my four pamphlets through the mail. I have officially declared to the world that my work is an obscenity. My stomach roils at the thought.

"You did the right thing, Miss Craddock," my lawyer, Caroline Kilgore, babbles in my ear, thrilled with her legal success.

That is fine for her. First woman lawyer in Philadelphia, she's accomplished what I could not—graduation from the University of Pennsylvania, and now she is living the good life while I am sinking lower and lower.

I hesitate on the steps. I have to decide where to go. I can't stay anywhere near my mother. I can't go back to where I was staying. One of the few friends I have left, Voltairine de Cleyre, was kind enough to take me in. But when I show up at her door this evening, she will give me one of her icy looks for refusing to sacrifice my freedom for my cause and kick me out of her rented rooms.

And I will go.

I am not as brave as Voltairine. She has given up her child and aborted another to maintain her presence on the lecture platform and rail against governmental tyranny.

I wrap my arms around myself. My fear of being locked up and silenced forever is nothing compared to the guilty hell she lives in.

Welling tears blur my vision. I miss a step and nearly tumble to the pavement below.

"Careful, my dear." Caroline loops her arm in mine. "I know it was a hard decision to make, but at least you can still do face-to-face counseling."

"Mother won't be happy about that."

Caroline slows. "About your mother, I will get a legal order to make her release your belongings. But I advise you to leave the state at once. She is serious about having you recommitted to an asylum."

The skin beneath my eye twitches. "She told you that?"

"It was mentioned."

I search up and down the street for a too-familiar, blackened-windowed carriage. My mother may have disowned me, but she has sat in court throughout the whole nasty process and still holds my belongings hostage. I wouldn't put it past her to have men waiting to take me captive again.

I turn back to Caroline. "Legally, she can do that? Just to stop me, her forty-one-year-old daughter, from pursuing my occupation as a marriage counselor?"

"If she finds two doctors to agree and sign the papers."

"Outrageous. I think my anarchist friends have a point—all government is corrupt."

Her lips fold in. "Depends on which side you are on."

We stop at the bottom of the steps. She holds out her hand. I give her a quick shake then start down the street. The overheated September air reeks of rotting manure and spoiling garbage, but I breathe deeply. At least there are no gates, or locks, or thorny rose bushes to impede my way.

Only Comstock and his bigotry.

PART 4

"Selfishness is a sin.
Self-sacrifice is blind, ignorant.
Altruism is intelligent."

Ida C. Craddock, Diary entry, August 8th, 1894

Chapter 23

"To educate the public mind by lust is to deaden the public conscience."
Anthony Comstock, *Traps for the Young*, p. 171

Church of Yoga, Chicago, 1899

What a difference a year makes. What a difference embracing religion makes. Chicago is far more liberal than Philadelphia. The World's Fair has left people craving new ways of understanding the world. The more exotic, the better.

I dust off the table in my presentable office waiting room with its reupholstered forest-green loveseat and second-hand oriental rug and arrange my pamphlets in a row. There are the four banned-from-the-mail ones and two new ones—*The Wedding Night* and my best yet, *Right Marital Living*.

I run my finger over the reprint. I dare anyone to criticize this one. With Alice's help, it's been published in the *Chicago Clinic Medical Journal*. Quite a feat for a degreeless marriage counselor.

Next, I make a last check of the small inner room I use for private consultations. With its fine, ripple-glass window in the door to let in light, the substantial oak desk left behind by the former tenant and the anatomical charts lent by Alice on the wall, it is as impressive as any doctor's surgery.

I give the desktop and my typewriter a quick wipe down then return to the waiting room and unlock the main door. The Church of Yoga is open for another day of business. If the success of my lectures and classes over the last four months continues, my schedule book will soon be full of paying patrons.

For the first time in my life, I am confident of being able to support myself in the manner I have always dreamed. Physicians, newlyweds, unhappily married mothers, and the curious are as eager for my counsel as much as they were for my father's patent medicine concoctions. And, like him, the more I advertise and the more fifty-cent pamphlets I write and sell, the more the money will pour in. But not yet. First, I need to establish my reputation and solidify my finances.

Heavy footsteps clomp up the stairs. My first client of the day has arrived.

I make sure my collar is buttoned, my tweedy London skirt straight, and my breath freshened with a peppermint Chiclet. As High Priestess of the Church of Yoga, I am all that is respectable. I slip my longest hatpin into my tightly wound-up braids, and always prepared.

"Mrs. Craddock, could I see that illustration again?" Client Forty-Nine runs his pudgy hand up and down his thigh as he takes the seat opposite me.

I bite the inside of my lip and draw out the medical book from my desk drawer. I turn it so he can see it right side up

Joan Koster

and pray he doesn't drool on it. Young men wanting instruction in divine sexual intercourse are the worst.

Sensualists, I call them, always looking for a thrill. But they pay the best. And someday, there will be a young bride who will thank me, I hope.

My client places his index finger on the vulva. "So, that is how a woman is made? So strange."

"But remember, you must never touch with your hand, only your male organ. A quick salute to the clitoris, and then gentle rubbing with your finger of love until she is wet with the dew of Venus. If you are patient and lover-like, and gentlemanly and considerate, and do not seek to precipitate matters, you will find that Nature will herself arrange the affair for you most delicately and beautifully."

I note the bulge in his trousers. "And this may take a while," I emphasize. "In some women, up to half an hour or more. But if you have prepared her well with kisses and gentle touches to her bosom, and maintain your self-control while praying to the Divine, the reward for both of you will be great."

I slip the book from under his finger and blatantly check my watch. A few minutes short, but his face is too flushed and his breath coming too fast for my liking.

"That ends our session for today. Shall I put you down for another five-dollar lesson next week? I believe our next topic should be sexual self-control during coition." I pick up my date book and come around the desk. Pen in hand, I turn to face him. "Next Monday at one? Just before my lecture on 'Man and Woman as They Were; As They Ought to Be,' which I heartily encourage you to attend."

He has risen, too, but makes no move to the door. "I would like to see, madame."

My stomach clenches. Forty-Nine bodes to be difficult.

243

I suck in a breath and try misconstruction. "You wish to see the illustration again?" I slide around him and sidle nearer to the door.

He closes the distance between us. "No. Just a peek under your skirts. I want to know if that picture you have there is accurate."

I wrinkle my nose at the foul stink of his sweat-infused suit and rub the back of my neck. "Very accurate, sir. *Grays' Anatomy* is used in the best of medical schools."

His jowls quiver. "You're no shy virgin. Not the way you talk. Now be a good woman and open your legs. I'm not going to hurt you. Just look for a bit."

My hand creeps toward my hat pin. "I provide counseling services only. You might consider visiting a prostitute and paying for a . . . an exhibition."

"Why would I want a diseased whore when I can see a nice clean lady such as you? I pay you good money, don't I?"

Blood pounds at my temples. "I thought you a gentleman, sir."

"I am, ma'am, I am. You'd be lying on the floor under me, if I weren't. I'm paying you five dollars a session for instruction in sexual relations. Figure that entitles me to a good, long look so I can see what's what. You don't want me embarrassing that sweet bride you are preparing me for now, do you?"

My fingers find the hairpin. I ready myself to let loose a walloping stab.

The outside office door opens. A shadow flashes across the milky glass.

"Mrs. Craddock," a low, melodious voice calls.

Thank heavens. Otoman Za-Adusht Hanish is early.

"Be right there," I call back.

I slide closer to the door. One more step, and I will be close enough to turn the handle. "You must leave, sir. My next appointment has arrived."

Mr. Have-A-Look lets out a snort and blocks the door. "He can wait. I want my money's worth now, or I will tell the world you are not just a foul-mouthed whore, but a thief, as well."

I do not need bad publicity nor Comstock's Chicago acolytes banging on my door. I rein in the anger thrumming through me and mentally calculate the amount of money in my pocket, minus the rent owed.

Surely, I can recoup the loss. "I'm sorry my services have disappointed you. I'm prepared to issue a full-refund."

"Double."

"What?"

"I want double back—for the humiliation and trickery. You sitting there, talking filth while rustling those skirts of yours. Revealing a tantalizing ankle. Bouncing your corset-less bosom. Showing me those obscene pictures."

"Fine." I slip all the money I put aside for the rent from my pocket, praying it is enough to keep his mouth closed.

I fight back tears as he wraps his hand around the bills and stomps out with a sneer. If my new lecture series doesn't fill every seat, I will be living on water and crusts again.

But I have a recourse—Otoman Zar-Adusht Hanish and his sunbathing lectures—if I can stomach associating myself with the infamous huckster who waits in the outer office. But Moses Harman sent him, so he can't be all bad, right? Besides, I have no choice. I need the money.

I take a moment to wipe my eyes, reseat the hairpin, and then make as grand an entrance as possible.

Hanish leaps up from the loveseat and seizes my hands, kissing each in turn. "That whelp give you trouble, my dear Mrs. Craddock? Just tell me, and I will have that smirk removed permanently from his fat face."

I retrieve my hands, surprised to find them trembling. "No. All is well. I dealt with him."

"Bravo. I so admire brave women. But what a shame that a light of heaven be treated so vilely."

I roll my shoulder in what I hope appears to be airy nonchalance. "He is not the first bounder I have had to deal with." I glance at the man before me. *And probably not the last.*

Dressed in a flowing, gold-embroidered, high-collared silk robe, such as worn by Hindu priests, the fair-haired, whiskey-eyed Hanish has to be the most attractive man I have ever seen, and the showiest.

He holds out a neatly manicured, beringed hand. "Still, you are upset. Come sit next to me. Let us talk of your fine work." With a sweep of his robe, he seats himself on the loveseat.

I perch beside him, as far away as I can. "Moses Harman was insistent that we meet."

He tips his head. "And I am glad of it. I have been reading your articles and pamphlets, and as a practitioner of Tantric sex, I find your description of the love act perfectly delineated for the understanding of the ordinary man and woman. Though I am sure you are far more knowledgeable of the higher joys of sexual union yourself." He winks. "The secrets of secrets?"

I bite my lip. How can this stranger be so attuned to my way of thinking?

"But I see you are still ill at ease. May I . . .?" He reaches for my hand and cradles it palm up in his. "Let us share the pleasure of our meeting with the Divine Spirit you so love."

He smooths his palm over mine then runs his finger along each line. He peers up. "Have you ever had your palm read?"

"Only by a gypsy at a fair once." My voice comes out too breathy. I clamp my lips closed.

"Ah. Then I will tell you what I see." He starts at my wrist and traces around the outside of each finger and thumb. "You are air and light, my dear Mrs. Craddock. Beloved of the spirits. Deep of heart, marred by fate, and destined for great things."

I shift, uncomfortable with his intensity. "You need not stoke my pride."

"Oh, but I do. My golden tongue is my gift, you see." He trails the tips of his long, elegant fingers across my palm and wrist. Each sweep threads deep into my inner core and, for the first time in months, I relax. My breathing slows. My worries fade. My whole being concentrates on the sensations flowing through me. I never want him to stop.

But he does.

"Come, my child. I see we are kindred spirits." He clasps my hand and guides me to my feet. "Kneel with me and let us find enlightenment together."

I sink down on the carpet, facing him, unable to look away from his mesmerizing eyes. Is he hypnotizing me? I do not care. There is promise in his touch. Promise in his voice. Promise in his partially open lips.

"Take my hands."

I slip mine into his. They are warm, and enfolding, and grounding.

"Now, move closer."

I slide forward until our knees touch.

He lets go and turns his hands palms up. "Press your palms against mine to complete the circle of energy."

I hesitantly press my hands to his. It feels odd, binding and yet freeing, in some intangible way.

"Now breathe in concert with me. In through the nose. Out through the lips. Long breaths. Deep breaths. Smooth breaths. Always with reverence."

I inhale, exhale, then inhale again. His breath, lightly scented with sen-sen, mixes with mine. Our chests expand and contract in harmony. Warmth flows through my palms to his and back again. I have never been so in rhythm with another human being.

Time slows. Slatted sunlight moves across the wall. Our matched palms rise and fall with each inhalation and exhalation. Our bodies rock forward and back. I close my eyes. I am so light I no longer feel my knees pressing against the carpet.

"Now," he hums, "let the energy flow free."

Pins and needles crawl along my scalp and stream downward, raising every hair on my body. Waves of cold and heat roll over me. Intense joy fills me and settles deep in my belly. Fire flickers in my womb, hotter than I ever felt before.

I have been here with my Soph. I know what to do. I open myself to the Divine and offer my soul's joy to Him. And it happens, just as I have imagined it. Every part of me pulsates in a slow, even rhythm. My skin tingles. My blood courses through me like a thundering river.

The Divine Spirit blossoms, and I am filled with light, and power, and joy. I am one with Creation, and it is the most heavenly feeling in the world.

But every wonderful thing must end.

The pleasure tapers off and dissipates into the universe. I let out a long breath and open my eyes. Hanish's confounding eyes peer back.

I dip my head, even as the heat still flames through me. "Thank you."

Hanish lifts his hands and genteelly folds them in his lap. "The pleasure was all mine." He rises gracefully to his feet, his golden robes swirling before me.

I am irrationally tempted to kiss his hem. Instead, I concentrate on the small aftershocks still rippling through me, the utter relaxation of my body, the slow thrumming of the blood in my veins.

"Shall we discuss our lecture plans?" He extends a hand and helps me to my feet.

I am still breathless, but I firm my spine, set my shoulders, and raise my chin, glad to see he is having trouble controlling his breathing, too. "Of course."

We sit again on the loveseat. This time, I rest mere inches from him, fully aware of the heat of his body and the faint hint of jasmine and other exotics that scent his robes and skin. I curse my garments and stifle the longing to be free to rub and nestle against him.

"You may wish to loosen your collar—"

My fingers fly to the neck of my shirtwaist. Has he read my mind?

"To aid your breathing, of course." He leans back, putting more space between us.

I undo the top pearl button, hesitate, and then unbutton the next three. It does help. My breathing settles into an easy rhythm.

I fiddle with the fourth button. If I were a braver woman, I would undo them all, let down my hair, and enslave myself to this man. But I am not one of those foolish female disciples who trail after him. Though, having felt the man's magnetism, I understand why they do.

"Now"—he rests his hands in his lap, palms up like a Buddha in repose—"I believe you will find us eminently matched to share our respective gospels on the same platform."

I turn my head away, trying to make sense of how two people could have shared such a momentous experience and now be conversing about business.

I look back at him.

Hanish raises an eyebrow. "So, shall we be partners?"

"I wasn't sure before . . ."

"And now you are?"

I can't help smiling. "Yes. You have shown me the true power of sexual self-control between man and woman. So many men have denied its possibility to me. Tell me about your sunbathing method."

He smiles back. "With great delight. One begins with a cold bath—as I am sure you are a practitioner of—followed by a vigorous rubbing of every part of the body to invigorate the blood. Next, lie down in the sun on a sheet of silk, preferably as blue as the sky, but any comfortable surface suffices. Expose every part of your body to the sun's healing rays, including the generative organs—though you may protect the face and eyes with a parasol or soft piece of cloth, again preferably silk for its magnetic properties. Lie there, absorbing the light of God's creation while, using the ball of your hand, you trail a circle around your navel for at least ten minutes and—"

"But," I interrupt, "this is not what I heard at all. The newspapers say you advocate complete nudity for everyone— men and women together—"

"And Comstock's followers call you the Lecturer of Filth. Are you?" He tips his head and waits.

I pinch my lip between my teeth. "I apologize. Of course, I ought to know better than to believe what is written in the papers."

"All it takes is one disgruntled client, one denied woman, one reporter wanting to make a name for himself, to set the rumor mill a spinning. When one is a Prophet of the True Light, attacks are unavoidable."

My mind flashes back to Client Forty-Nine. "It is. In order to do good, though, one must take risks."

"Assuredly. But one must do more. One must face one's attackers boldly. One must proclaim the truth, no matter how much one is laughed at or tormented. That is the fate God has given people like us." He holds out his arms and extends a curled-toed Turkish slipper. "Look at how I walk the streets of

Chicago. One must assume the outer garments that reflect not who you are but what you wish others to believe about you." He rises to his feet. "Consider what a high priestess of the Church of Yoga might wear. Perhaps a flowing white gown, hair loose, a circlet on your head like a Bouguereau angel."

This man's golden tongue will seduce me if I am not careful.

I avoid his eyes and study the florets on the carpet. Could I dare be so bold and free?

I look up. "Perhaps, Mr. Hanish."

He bows slightly. "Surprise me, then. And please, as kindred souls, let us drop any formality between us. Call me Otoman."

"Of course."

"And may I call you Celanire?"

"How do you—"

"I know much about you, especially your passionate nature."

I dip my head to hide the flush on my cheeks.

"Now, are you willing to plant your feet on the stage beside me—a charlatan, a fanatic, and a sexual guru?"

I stand. "I would be honored."

"Sunday at one at the Unitarian fellowship assembly hall?" He sweeps to the door then stops. "Will you be trying my sunbathing practice?"

"I'm intrigued. But where can a person living in filthy-aired Chicago find a sunny place where it is safe to bare oneself so?"

"While a mountain meadow or private beach is ideal, I, too, live in the city, and we must map out our own square of sunlight." He points. "That window faces south. Draw your blinds and lie beneath it."

I glance around. "This office is not the most private space, though the door does lock. Perhaps on Sunday after the service."

"Sunday. Perfect. As I lie on my silken pallet of blue, I will imagine you unclothed, your golden hair spread like a halo around your face, your skin warm and vibrant, and your heavenly angel hovering close."

"My angel?"

"Of course, your angel, Celanire. Who do you think sent me?"

All the light and warmth leaves with Hanish. I sink down on the loveseat, my inner self a world of confusion. Is Hanish a man of truth and power? Or did the power and will to believe come from inside myself? It is no secret that I have an angel husband.

I lay my head back and focus my mind on the waves of energy still swirling through my body. No matter what Hanish's purpose, my tantric orgasm was real.

I let out a calming breath of air.

If only every woman could experience the same pleasure.

Chapter 24

"Evil reading bears fruit in all seasons."
Anthony Comstock, *Traps for the Young,* p. 46

Church of Yoga, Chicago, 1900

I twirl around the waiting room. This Sunday's Church of Yoga service was a grand success, every seat occupied, the collection plate filled. My dear friend, Otoman, was in top form. One more Sunday like this one, and I will be debt-free.

I remove my gold amulet and throw my precious India silk shawl, a gift from Otoman, over the loveseat. Then I untie the sash of my flowing white tea dress. Yesterday was dull and gray, totally unsuited for sunbathing. But today, the sun is shining in my window. The air wafting in is spring fresh, washed clean by yesterday's rain, and I feel younger than I have in a long time. I can't wait for the warm rays to soak into my skin.

"Mrs. Craddock." A blonde-headed young woman peeks in the door.

I spin around. I wasn't expecting any clients. Still, I should have locked the door, even if the building is empty on Sundays and no one has ever shown up before.

I straighten.

I can do nothing about my hair hanging loose or my unbelted dress, but maybe Otoman is right. Time I embrace the epithet the rabid press has dubbed me with—Chicago's High Priestess of Sex. Cowering under a pseudo-mantle of respectability while counseling hasn't saved me from threats of jail nor lust-crazed men's advances.

I smooth down the filmy cloth of my skirt as I approach my next potential customer. One thing is for certain, a light cotton tea dress is certainly cooler than English wool in this summer heat.

I paste on my most welcoming smile. As much as men need my instruction, I prefer female clients.

"Yes. Come in, please. Are you here for a lesson?"

"I saw your ad in the paper and . . . and I'm engaged, and I'm not sure . . .."

I hold out my hand. "You have come to the right place. I offer advice on how to have the wedding night of your dreams and how to establish a loving and Divine relationship with your husband. My fee is ten dollars for three lessons. Five dollars for the full course in Right Marital Living."

Her hands flutter. "It's just . . . just that I don't have much money. My parents would never approve of my coming here. All I have is the pocket change left over from the marketing."

The heels of her shoes are scuffed and worn. Her clothing, though neat, is not of the highest fashion. I may be desperate for money, but I cannot deny poor souls in need of my teachings. Sexual pleasure and wise lovemaking are not only for the well-off but for everyone.

"I can give you a brief overview for a dollar."

The girl relaxes slightly. "I would be most grateful."

"I am officially not open on Sunday. Can you come back tomorrow?"

The girl flinches and shakes her head. "I dare not. I must work in Papa's store."

My heart goes out to her. I recognize a girl sneaking behind a parent's back. I was once that girl, too. It has taken every ounce of courage for her to climb those stairs.

I extend my hand. "Come into my consulting room where we will have privacy." I stand aside and let her enter.

Once she is seated, I move around my desk and try not to picture how I look with my hair falling loose over my shoulders. With all the dignity I can, I repose myself with my hands folded on the desktop. "So, you are engaged to be married?"

Her lips tremble. In her lap, her fingers twist and turn. "Yes. In a month."

"And you love your future husband?"

Her countenance brightens. "Oh yes. He is kind and respectful, and oh so handsome. Son of the baker down the street from where I live."

"But you are hesitant?"

"Well, there was a man—a married man—who used to come to my parents' tobacco shop, so elegant and sweet-spoken. Wealthy, too. I was just a girl at the time, and his attention excited me. But after a while, he wanted, uh . . . more. I thought he loved me, and my heart caused me to make the mistake of sneaking out and going walking with him, and he got me alone and tried"—she hesitates, then forces the words out—"to make advances of the most horrid kind, but I fought him off and somehow got away, thanks to his landlady. He filled me with such disgust—disgust at what he wanted to do, and disgust at myself for being fooled into loving such a man and allowing him those liberties he took."

"But now you have found a good man, worthy of marriage?"

She avoids my eyes. "Yes. He is completely different. But sometimes, I see the same lustful look in his eyes, and he is always wanting to kiss me and touch me. How do I know he truly loves me, or if he just wants my body like . . . like the other one?" She wipes away a tear.

I use my softest voice. "It is natural for a man to be attracted in that way. It is how nature made them. He wouldn't be normal if he did not hold your sexual attractiveness a great deal in his mind. Just be careful not to let him caress your bosom, as it will arouse a tingling desire in your genitals, which would make full joining with him seem so right and so beautiful. Which it will be once you are married and in the marriage bed. That is part of the gift of sexual pleasure nature has given woman. Now, if he is a good man, as you say, he will respect your wishes when you ask him not to touch you in those ways until after the wedding. Do you think he will listen to you?"

"Oh yes. He will, I am sure. Thank you. You have relieved my worries so."

For the pitiful dollar, I should stop here, but I cannot. I pull out my medical book and show her the illustrations, explain the sex act to her and, for good measure, throw in two free copies of *The Wedding Night*.

"Now, give one to your fiancé," I say, "and if he has questions, have him come to me."

The girl gives me a tentative smile. "You have filled with me with such hope and awe. Everything explained so clearly and openly. Why don't they teach these things to us? I would never have gotten in trouble with that rogue if I understood the love function."

The look in her eyes, and perhaps the passionate experiences I have had with Otoman, weakens me, and I extract from beneath my shirtwaist my most precious belonging. "The first man I loved gave me this." I click open the catch of the bee pendant. "If I had known what I do now, we could have married and lived in wedded bliss. But out of fear of the marriage bed, I turned him down." I snap it closed. "That's why I have dedicated my life to teaching others the joys that my beloved Charles and I missed. Though he comes to me now as an angel, soon he promises that we will dwell together in heaven and walk with God."

The girl presses a hand over her heart. "You can see angels? And one loves you? How romantic. Just like in a storybook."

I think of my cold bed. The nights I sleep alone. What I would give to have my dear Charles with me again—alive, warm, and breathing, our bodies curled in embrace.

A ball of anger forms in my stomach. If only Otoman had not given me a glimpse of earthly passion that can never be mine fully.

I push away from the desk and rise. "It is better to have a loving spouse here on earth. Someone to share your joys and hurts with. Someone to hold you in his arms at night. I wish you a happy marriage."

The girl stands. "You are a good woman, Mrs. Craddock. I can't wait to share your teachings with my fiancé."

Then she is gone, and I am left to contemplate the empty night ahead. Soph and my angel companions, it seems, have not deigned to follow me to Chicago. They have sent Otoman Hanish, instead—a sweet-tongued conman they know I will never trust with my love, to show me the earthly manifestation of my teachings. I paste hope over the small tear in my heart and send a prayer of thanks to my spirit husband.

I sprawl across the loveseat and drift off into half-dreams of reunion with Soph. But not for long.

Loud voices echo up the stairwell. Footsteps thunder up the steps. Seconds later, two men burst into the room.

I jerk upright, half-dazed. "What?"

The older man shakes my *Wedding Night* pamphlet at me. "Did you give this obscenity to my innocent daughter?"

"Look." The younger man sweeps up my neat stacks of printed materials. "There's more. She's a purveyor of this filth. Selling it on a Sunday, too. She dared ask Gertie to have me come here so she could ply her trade with me. My poor innocent, lured in by this witch."

"We will have the authorities down on you, whore. Zachariah, take that garbage and fetch the police. I'll make sure she doesn't flee." He seizes my arm.

I yank myself loose. "How dare you attack me? I am an upstanding woman. A professional marriage counselor. My work is praised by physicians. I am published in medical journals."

He looks me up and down. "I see a harlot before me. No respectable woman would write such unspeakable things."

I gaze at the open door. Every part of me is screaming, *Run*, but I could never outmaneuver the girl's father. The man is the size of an ox and furious. So, I sit on the loveseat and let my anger out as tears. Not that they have any effect on the brute. I pity Gertie with such a man for a father. And from what I saw of him, her fiancé will not be much better.

Still, she is better prepared for marriage than if I hadn't talked to her. Despite the pitfalls of untrusty clients, teaching right living through proper marriage relations is the most rewarding work I do.

By the time the authorities arrive, I am done with crying. The ball of anger in my belly has turned to a twisted knot of fear. The last time they arrested me, Mother bailed me out.

This time, there is no one coming to rescue me. No one knows where I am, and being Sunday, the bulbous-nosed cop gripping my arm and dragging me deep into the bowels of the station house informs me that my arraignment will not occur until the following day.

I am thrown into a dank holding cell, full of other women in various states of dress. They circle me.

"Look at this one," a harlot wearing only a corset and petticoat says. She tugs on my sleeve. "Some hag got up as a virgin. But don't worry; it won't be white for long. Not in this pit."

Another picks up my hair. "Quite the hussy, aren't you?"

I wrap my arms around myself to hide my trembling. "Excuse me. I don't belong here. I am a marriage counselor—Mrs. Craddock. Perhaps you have heard of me?"

My question is met with guffaws and snickers.

My tormentor wraps a length of my hair around her hand and yanks.

I slap my hands at hers, squealing with pain. Tears fill my eyes. "Let go, please." I look around for help but meet only hard, twisted faces. I pray for one woman here to have kindness in her heart.

As if in answer, a rotund woman, dressed in shabby red satin, pushes through the crowd.

"Oh, stop teasing the lady." She looks down. "How about you donate those lovely shoes to Mellie over here? Look to be her size. And then we can all get back to our game of Hearts."

I glance down "My shoes?"

"Mel had to leave hers behind when the police raided our place."

I bite my lip.

"Oh, come on. I'm sure you have another pair. I've heard of you. You're the high priestess of yoga. Always in the papers. Must rake in the money with your fancy way of enticing men."

She laughs. "Imagine, girls, she teaches frigid wives how to enjoy sex so their husbands won't come visit us."

The women around her laugh.

She waves her hand. "Help the lady make her donation to a good cause."

In minutes, my shoes are gone, and I am abandoned in a foul-smelling corner near the overflowing pee bucket. I want to curl into a ball and hide, but the floor is too dirty. If Mother could see me now, she'd be wearing her I-told-you-so expression, and she would be right.

Come morning, I am a disheveled mess. My hair is a rat's nest of tangles and knots, my dress is stained and stinking from my attempt to relieve myself in the bucket, and my bare feet are numb from standing on the cold concrete for hours.

But there is nothing I can do.

The officers herd me into the courtroom with the rest of the denizens of what I have learned is Mrs. Mabley's House of Comfort, augmented by several pickpockets and a house burglar.

I am first on the docket.

"Mrs. Craddock."

I rise and face the judge.

"Not only have you corrupted a minor, and resisted arrest, you are on the postal inspector's list of purveyors of the obscene." He adjusts his glasses. "And I see here that Mr. Comstock himself has put a special watch on you for sending your pamphlets, *Wedding Night* and *Right Marital Living*, through the mails. Bail—five-hundred dollars. Trial set for August ninth."

I suck in a breath. Five-hundred dollars? I have no hopes of raising such a sum of money.

My whole body turns numb. I will rot away if I am condemned to Cook County jail for months. Henrietta was right; jail is far worse than an asylum. Mabley's girls had filled me in on its horrors.

I'm given no chance to defend myself but am hustled out of the courtroom and back to the same jail cell where I am ordered to empty the bucket and swab the floor. Before I am halfway done, a matron appears at the grate.

"Nice friends, you have."

I wring out the mop and glance up.

"Some crazy man in a gold dress has put up your bail."

I suck in a breath—Otoman.

Thank God.

I am saved.

But I am not.

I fold my hands in my lap and scan the law office. Row after row of case books line the shelves. I wonder if my case will ever end up in one of those volumes. But based on my welcome, I think not.

I glance over at Alice. "Why have you saddled me with this dour lawyer? I think he hates me."

She pats my hand. "He doesn't hate you. He's frustrated with your case. Moses recommended him highly. He fights for the underdog, and he is a strong believer in spiritualism."

Clarence Darrow strides back into his office. With the high forehead of an early-balding man and the sleeked-down black hair of a would-be politician, Darrow radiates annoyance at having to deal with me. But I am stuck with him and he with me. He has taken my case pro-bono, and a beggar high priestess facing prison can't be choosy.

But I am not a murderer nor a corrupt tycoon, and dressed in my most staid suit, I am nothing like the outrageous spiritualist in diaphanous dress and flowing hair he expected.

He sits down and shuffles the papers in front of him.

"So," I begin, "do you think I will win?"

He sorts through the papers again then presses his lips together. "Honestly, no. Comstock is too powerful, and you are at the top of his villains' list. I don't know what you did to anger him so much, but he wants to grind you into dust."

"But what about my right to freedom of religion?"

"If we claim your First Amendment right to freedom of religion, the district attorney will just add blasphemy to your obscenity charges. Church of Yoga? Won't fly higher than a pig's snout. You gave explicit materials to an unmarried girl. You will be lucky to avoid a twenty-year sentence at hard labor."

"So, what do you suggest? I don't want to go to prison."

He gives a guttural laugh. "None of my clients do. And in your case, I doubt you would survive such a sentence. Look, I support your work, and I would love to give Comstock his comeuppance. I subpoenaed both him and Henry Blackwell. What an event that would be to have both of them testify. But the district attorney will put that young girl on the stand, and no matter what argument I make, the jury will convict."

I twist my hands, the darkness of prison looming over me. "I did nothing but tell her what every mother should tell her daughter."

He shrugs. "Your intentions don't matter. The law declares what you wrote is obscene. It's an unwinnable battle. I can pull some political strings and probably get a plea deal. But everything must be kept hush-hush. No one wants to run afoul of Comstock and his followers. They will stop at nothing— outright lies, mobs in the street, prayers in the churches. Reporters love him. Gives them a reason to write all the salacious garbage they want and provides their readers an excuse to read it."

Alice captures one of my twisting hands. "I am so sorry, Ida, but you must think of your future. Don't let Comstock win by locking you away. You have a book to write."

I nod, the fight sapped from me.

"All right." Darrow pushes a paper toward me. "Sign here, and I will have your plea switched to guilty."

The word slices through me. I am going to do it again—deny what I believe, deny my life's work. But Alice is right. I have a book to write. When it is done, Comstock will discover Ida Craddock is not a wimp.

I shake away that thought, pick up the pen, and scrawl my signature at the bottom. "Now what happens?"

"I will consult with the district attorney's office. Meanwhile, I suggest you not draw attention to yourself in any way."

"Can I leave Chicago?"

He nods. "As long as I can find you."

I choose Denver as the place to wait out my sentencing.

For the moment, only three people in the world know where I am—my Katie Wood, dear William Stead, and soon, Clarence Darrow. And that's the way I plan to keep it. At least, until the money Stead sent me from his oh-so-generous heart runs out and I have a manuscript on sexual worship to hand him in repayment.

I step out onto the porch of my rooming house and take a deep breath of clear mountain air. I have spent too long in the lowlands of Philadelphia and Chicago. It is the West that I love. Maybe tomorrow, I will rent a horse and ride toward the Rockies. There is so much I want to see before I die. For now, I have work to do. My typewriter waits, worn and battered, like me.

I am writing my masterwork on Sex Worship at last.

And when I am done, book-burner Comstock will hear from me again.

Chapter 25

"To assault their enemies in an underhanded and base manner, and take every advantage over those they oppose, is their peculiar delight."
Anthony Comstock, *Traps for the Young*, p. 197

New York City, 1901

My Chicago case lies behind me. The first part of my tome on sexual worship, all four-hundred odd pages, is in the mail, heading for London and Stead—the most frank and explicit book on the marriage relation ever written—soon to be in safe hands.

And I've come East.

It is time to be brave and do what has been inevitable since Comstock grabbed me by the arm—time to bring the King of Smut and his Draconian law down—and there is only one place to do that.

New York City.

I will face the lion in his own den. But not alone. I have friends there. Edward Foote and the New York Liberal League will help me.

I hope.

But hope is a flighty thing. Despair a shroud.

I gaze around the mean little office I have rented on the fourth floor of a building on 23rd Street. The only object in it— my sadly battered trunk, full of the books and tiny treasures I have lugged from coast to coast, across the Atlantic and back.

Have I been foolish? Will I earn enough money to live on until the inevitable occurs? Where will I sleep? How will I eat?

I roll my shoulders. I have dealt with the same problems before. I will survive.

I sit down on my ancient trunk and fan my face with my most recent letter. I sent my new post office box number to Mother out of some misguided sense of familial duty. I crumple the paper in my fist. Now she is coming, arriving this afternoon on the ferry from New Jersey. Well, there is no way I can stop her. I will make do as I always have.

I get up and throw open the trunk, pull out the London suit, draw the blinds, and retire as far from the street-side window as possible to change into it.

I slip into the jacket with a grimace. The wool itches through my silk blouse. I know I will soon be roasting on this sweltering day in June, but that is nothing compared to dealing with Mother.

Stuffing that thought away, I hurry down the stairs and out onto 23rd Street. Luckily, the ferry depot is only a few blocks to the west.

Two hours later, I am caught up in a whirlwind. Mother settles herself in the Park Hotel on Fourth Avenue then whisks me off to the Ladies' Mile to shop. By the time we have traversed Lord and Taylor, Henri Bendel's, and Seigel's Big Store, I have a pair of medium-heeled Manhattan side-button shoes in tan and brown, a nubby gray linen street suit with an Eton jacket, and another ridiculous hat. This one is a satin-ribboned, wide-brimmed boater, more suited to a schoolgirl than a middle-aged radical.

So attired, Mother treats me to dinner on the rooftop garden of the hotel. I order a wide variety of vegetable dishes with spaghetti on the side, just to spite her. But she is in too good a mood after the shopping spree and my makeover into something respectable-looking to nag at my dining choice.

She peeks over her crystal water goblet. "So, what are your plans, my dear?"

I spread a pat of shell-shaped butter on the delectable soft white roll. I have already slipped the rest of the rolls in my pocket for a lean day. "I will continue my counseling and teaching of Sexology."

Mother blinks at the last word but soldiers on. "And your pamphlets?"

I know what she wants to hear, so that is what I tell her. Once she is gone, there is no way she can put a lie to my words.

"I am withdrawing them all from the public."

She smiles. "How sensible. I am sure you do not wish to risk arrest again. That was such a close call in Chicago, and then again down in Washington. You did the right thing letting them burn all those horrid leaflets." She toys with her fork. "But will you make enough money consulting? The economy has barely recovered from the stock market panic of last month."

"Men and women get married every day, and my fees are low."

"If you came home and gave up the abominable Mrs. Craddock, stopped the oral teaching, and signed a paper promising not to distribute those filthy papers, I would reconsider . . ."

"What? My inheritance?" I grip my knife so tightly my fingers cramp.

"Well, wouldn't having a roof over your head, some good food to eat, your comfy bed at night—"

"Mother," I interrupt, "I will not give up my life's work for a mattress."

Her mouth snakes into a smile. "How about coming for the summer? Relaxing? Looking for a respectable job for the fall?"

"No, Mother. I am set on this course." I glance around at the fine appointments of the rooftop restaurant. Fresh flowers. Glittering crystal. "You know, the Park Hotel was originally for working women. Five hundred rooms and the best culinary department of any hotel in the city. Such a lovely idea. Two women could share a room for six dollars. If only I had a place like that to stay." I shake my head and pop the rest of the roll in my mouth before I blurt out that the rented room I claim I have is a fantasy. "But things will work out. My new office is right here, in the center of things. It just needs a few furnishings."

Mother blots her lips. "How about we trot over to some used furniture places in the morning and pick up a desk and chair? I'm scheduled to leave at two."

Thank the heavens.

"That would be most kind. I thank you for your support and the new clothes."

"As long as you keep yourself out of the papers, I am sure you will thrive. If you wish, I will help you with the wording for your advert, so it is all that is fine and respectable. Just like my Craddock Bitters ads."

I twist my lips into a smile. Mother wants to be helpful with my career. But only to the point where I am collared and leashed, ready to be reeled into my cage.

I study her as she cuts her rare roast beef into dainty pieces. Blood puddles around the meat the way her pseudo-love oozes around me. If she knew what I was planning to do, she would not be sitting here, offering to help me furnish my office.

I force myself to swallow a forkful of string beans, but they wad in my throat. I press my hand to my mouth and try not to gag.

What would our lives have been like if Mother had loved me more and my dead sister less? But it is too late for regrets. I have already set in motion my future, and no one can stop an inquisitor on the hunt.

Hours later, I am finally at peace, locked in my tiny office. Mother gone—I pray never to return. Tomorrow, the scratched but sturdy oak desk and two reupholstered side chairs she purchased for me will arrive. Tomorrow, I will put my ad in the newspapers, take my circular to every doctor's office in the city, mail out pamphlets to whoever asks, and, with pride, affix my *"Marriage Counseling"* sign to the door. And then—I peer around the shadowed office—I will wait for Constock to come. For now, I have the whole space to myself.

I string a curtain at the far end of the room to make a place to hide my dresses discreetly from the eyes of delivery men and clients then spread out my blankets on the floor.

Thank heavens, it is summer.

I remove my hairpins and undo my French braid. Then I lie down on my back and stare out the window. Above the rooftops of the buildings across the street, only a few stars twinkle through the city haze. I miss the clear, starry Denver nights, but not the loneliness.

I shift on the blanket. A faint sheen of perspiration covers my skin. I unbutton the front of my nightgown and wing out my arms. The cool of the tile floor sends goosebumps crawling up and down my neck.

I control my breath. Inhale through my nose. Exhale through my mouth. And search for the calm and rest that has been so hard to find. Soph has not come to me in months. I have been too weak. Too worried. But not anymore. I have food in my belly and a vision to carry me forward.

I clear my mind and prepare to welcome in the Divine Celestial. I know so much more now. Only through union with the Central Force of the Universe can a mere human fully control one's mentality, or as Sigmund Freud calls it, the subconscious. And from that mental plane will come the orgasm magnified and made powerful through the willing giving and receiving of sexual pleasure.

"*Soon,*" Soph says.

Ah. He has come at last.

My angel lover rests his head on my breast—light, ethereal, mine. I know better than to touch my dear heavenly husband. Touching is not needed—Otoman has taught me that. All that is required is the mind in its readiness, the body open to pleasure, and the heart given to our Heavenly Father.

I push my spine against the hardness of the floor and lift my hips. Anticipation gathers. Slowly, I rotate my pelvis in the *Danse du Ventre.* I am more than ready.

We merge. My limbs tremble. My pulse speeds up. My blood pounds through my veins. Sparks shoot from the soles of my feet to top of my head.

At that supreme moment, my body thrumming, I breathe out a prayer of gratitude for the pleasure I have finally achieved with the one I love.

I don't remember when Soph's presence fades. I do not have to. He will come back now whenever I wish.

We no longer need to talk.

I no longer need instruction.

I am a master.

Chapter 26

"The message of these evil things is death—socially, morally,
physically, and spiritually."
Anthony Comstock, *Traps for the Young*, p. 131

New York City, 1902

Summer has changed to winter. Still, the villain has not
come. Snowflakes float down outside my office window,
turning the city white. I huddle under my London paisley
and pick at a hangnail. That self-righteous bastard better come
soon.

I'd thought Comstock would whisk me off the street back
in the fall when the decoy letters started arriving. Then at
Christmas when I mailed out handfuls of booklets to clients
from one end of the country to the other so I could afford to
buy a few holiday treats for my friends. Then after the warning
letter that arrived in January.

But no. The Censor-in-Chief intends to make me suffer
through the coldest days of February.

A shiver snakes up my back and wraps around my neck. The little gas heater, bought with money Stead sent, cannot penetrate the winter cold. Not that a jail cell will be warmer. I burrow deeper beneath my shawl. But at least the waiting and worrying would be over.

I glance at my stack of leaflets. A quarter of the five hundred each of *The Wedding Night* and *Right Marital Living* I ordered after the first warning are gone, spread across the city and its environs. Pearls pushed under the snout of the biggest pig of all. Surely, one of them has landed in his mailbox or in the slimy hands of one of his spies.

Footsteps rattle up the staircase. I lay my shawl over the chair back, smooth down my hair, and rise. Whether it is Comstock or a client, I will maintain my dignity.

A woman bustles in, a snow-covered hood drooped over her head. The hood drops, and I rush to her.

"Henrietta? What are you doing here?"

"I've come to take you home."

I fall back. "Home?"

Her mouth twists into a sour-lemon frown. "This is no way to live, Ida. Sleeping on the floor. Barely eating." She gives me a look that is almost pity. "You've lost so much weight."

"I'm fine. I had plenty of pudge to lose. And I'm not going back to Philadelphia."

"Why, Ida? Why are you doing this? Mailing out those booklets after you said you would never—"

"I am going to bring Comstock down."

It is Henrietta's turn to step back. "You're mad."

"Perhaps. My mother has always thought so. But I believed you different."

"He will put you in jail."

I turn and look out at the falling snow. "I am not afraid. I've been in jail. I've plea-bargained away my freedom to speak, to write, to teach. What I haven't done is faced him down in court and won." I spin around. "He must be stopped."

Henrietta gives a quick shake of her head. "You won't win. He has the law on his side."

"My voice will be heard. My First Amendment rights will be defended. And with the right lawyer, maybe we can take the case all the way to the Supreme Court. Healthy information about improving sexual relations within marriage is not an obscenity."

"Lawyer? Be reasonable. You can't afford to eat. How will you pay a lawyer?"

"I have my supporters—Foote, Stead, the New York Liberal League. I have you, don't I?"

Her eyes meet mine. "You can't expect people to always be saving you from yourself."

I straighten. "You don't believe, do you?"

"Believe?"

I suddenly see her for what she is—a hypocrite.

"In my battle for marital reform, you never have . . ." I am no longer cold. My voice strengthens. "You have a man who knows how to please you. No children to wear you down. No little tombstones to lay wreaths on. A life of comfort that allows you to play the liberal, like so many wealthy women. You have it all. Why should you care for the poor, abused women who come crying to me for help finding pleasure in the marriage bed, and the men who love their wives but don't know how to please them—the help I give to them?"

Henrietta forces her lips into a snarky sort of smile, the kind pretending to be trustworthy. "But, Ida, is it worth going to prison? Think of the embarrassment. The shame. The press will drag you through the mud. Wouldn't an asylum be so much better?"

My fingers curl into my palms. Those are my mother's words. She is not merely a hypocrite; she is my mother's stooge.

"Mother sent you, didn't she?"

The smile flees, leaving behind bloodless lips. "I talk to her on occasion. But I am here as your friend. I am worried about your health living like this—hand to mouth."

I give her a chance to prove her friendship true. "So, make a donation to the Church of Yoga. Buy some pamphlets to gift to your rich friends. You and Richard can afford it."

"Ida, that won't—"

"Won't what? Assuage your conscience for all the ill you've shown me because Richard fancied me once?"

"I never—"

As all the pieces fall into place, I point my finger at her. "You did. You played me false with kind words and cozy chats. Tricked me into thinking you cared about me. You told my mother I was having an affair with Richard and lost me the position at Wagner. You encouraged me to go to San Francisco. Hurried me off to Chicago. Just about hoisted me onto Stead's ship. Always so helpful. Sending my things to me. Conniving with my mother. Doing anything you could to get me far away from your Richard."

Henrietta huffs. "Ingrate. I have come to your rescue more times than I can count. Maybe a long time ago, when you and Richard worked together every day at the Institute, I was jealous. But now?" She presses a hand to her bosom like a Broadway actress. "Why would I be? You are a haggard forty-year-old sleeping on the floor. He disdains you. Says you wasted all your talent."

"I am sure you convinced him of that. After all, you aren't legally bound together. He could have left you for me anytime." I know it isn't true, but I shout it anyway. I want to hurt her so badly for allying with my mother. "I have always been prettier than you. More attractive. More intelligent."

"Little fool. I have stood by you when no one else would. I sent you to Alice Stockham's. Introduced you to William Stead. Got you released from the insane asylum."

"Did you really? Or were they ready to release me, anyway? And that lawyer, Kilgore, you hired, her task was to silence me, wasn't it?"

Henrietta lets out a raspy breath. "You are beyond reason. I should never have come."

"No, you shouldn't have. Soph and I are doing just fine."

"Soph? You're still living in that fantasy world?"

"He's a better husband than the one you have. Soph and I are bound forever. Your husband, old as he is, can't be trusted."

Her face turns red. "I don't even know why I am standing here, still talking to you."

"Neither do I. The door is behind you."

She clasps her hands in front of her. "Look, Ida, I can't just leave you like this. Let me take you out for dinner for old friendship's sake."

My stomach grumbles at the hope of a hot meal. Hunger pains uncurl. But remaining in her traitorous company is the last thing I want to do.

"No," I say. "I've already eaten."

She fusses with the bow of her bonnet. "Then I guess I am done here."

"So it seems." I whip a copy of *Right Marital Living* off the display table and offer it to her. "Some reading for you and Richard. Might make believers of you yet."

She hesitates then plucks it from my fingers as if it is covered in slime and stuffs it in her fine Russian leather handbag.

"Goodbye, Ida." She hurries down the stairs, and I hold my breath to keep from calling her back.

I rush to the window, press my forehead to the icy glass, and watch her trot out of the building and disappear into the falling snow, fading away like a lost spirit.

I pull back and swallow hard. I'll never see her again, I'm sure. For all the love I still have for her, her tampering with my life is over.

For days after she leaves, I am full of regret. In her own way, Henrietta has helped me hone my resolve.

"I shouldn't have been so mean to her," I say to Soph. He and I have had the sweetest lovemaking. No words. Only heat and joy, and communion with the Divine.

He does not answer, but I know I have not lived up to his angelic standards in my dealings with Henrietta. The angel-bound must do no disliking. But the heat of passion running through my veins tells me I have been forgiven.

I sit up on my new, second-hand folding cot, bought with an unexpected windfall from a client who'd heard me speak in Chicago and has prepaid for the ten-dollar, three lesson series. Mother would be happy to know I am no longer on the floor, but I refuse to write and tell her.

The downstairs door slams.

I roll on to my side. The sky is still dawn-shadowed—too early for someone in need of counseling.

My heart does a funny little skip. Is it Comstock at last? The only other tenant in the building is a photographer, and he is away. So, whoever is clumping around down there is coming for me.

Multiple steps trot up the staircase. More than one person, for sure.

I sit up and quickly twist my hair into a bun then pin it up. I wiggle into my wool day dress—plain gray with a tiny, white lace collar that would have looked appropriate on my grandmother, if I'd had one. I sweep my beloved paisley shawl from the chair.

I am ready to face the world.

The door smashes open, and the man monster who has haunted me for years peers straight at me. The world is Anthony Comstock, come at last, accompanied by three hard-eyed, broad-shouldered constables, one of whom clamps his hand around my upper arm so tightly I fight back a gasp of pain.

"Let me go," I protest, chagrined at the tremble in my voice. I twist right and left in a vain attempt to free myself. My shawl slips to the floor. My hair tumbles out of the hastily assembled bun and falls over my shoulders. I tug again against the steel grip on my arm and strive to put my mother's haughtiness in my words. "You have no right to manhandle me. I am a lady and deserve to be treated as such."

My captor laughs. "Says she's a lady."

"Does she now?" Comstock approaches, wearing a gargoyle of a smile. He fingers a lock of my hair. "Doesn't look like a lady."

He takes out a pair of handcuffs and dangles them in my face. "Ida C. Craddock, you are under arrest for violation of section 1142 of the New York State Penal Code and under section 211 of the Federal Criminal Code for the distribution, advertisement of, and the sale of obscene materials."

I jerk against the officer's hold. "My writings are of the utmost spiritual and religious nature, and you are abridging my First Amendment rights to freedom of speech and religion." I stamp my foot. "Let me go this instant."

Comstock's smile widens. He swings the handcuffs back and forth. "I think not. I have been waiting for this day for a long time, Miss Belly Dancer." He signals his minion to spin me around.

My pulse races. My teeth clench. I have never been handcuffed before.

Sweaty hands wrench one wrist then the other behind my back. I can feel Comstock's sour breath on my neck, the fat of his belly jiggling against me. While he fumbles with the locks, he hums the "Hootchy Kootchy," that annoying dance hall song that has nothing to do with the sensual elegance of the *Danse du Ventre*.

It takes him more than a minute to arrange the cuffs to his liking. Finally, with a clank, the rusty iron bands snap closed. The edges cut deep into the tender skin of my wrists, and I can't help but wince. He threads a chain through them, tugs and pulls, then loops it through the cuffs and around my waist. His hands brush beneath my breasts, his thigh presses against my buttocks. I can't miss the sexual excitement he is getting from manhandling me.

Vomit rises in my throat. I choke it back down. Better the burning aftertaste than the added humiliation.

Comstock steps back to admire his work. "That's the way I like them—trussed up like a fowl." With a laugh, he deposits me back into the untender graces of my first captor.

Humming the grating tune louder, he stalks around my tiny office, nosing here and there. He flicks out his hand toward the table with my pamphlets. "Seize them all, gentlemen." He looks over my shelves of books. "These, too."

I can't lose my hard-won books, my ever-present companions.

The words sputter out. "There's nothing in those. They are harmless—medical works, histories, dictionaries in French, German, and Latin."

Comstock turns his cutting blue eyes on me. "Silence, woman." He waves again. "It's evidence. Take it all. Then search the place. These old spinsters love to hide things away."

I cringe as my notes and manuscripts are swept to the floor and trampled by the bulldogs nosing through my belongings. Hungry as Jersey mosquitoes for my blood, his goons overturn my cot, dump out my trunk, and toss my dresses and underthings to-and-fro. Splatter ink over all.

I close my eyes to the destruction, but I cannot shut out the sounds. Every crash, every rip, every stomach-turning laugh cuts as deeply as a horsewhip. By the time Comstock has had his fill, my cheeks are wet with tears I could not dam back.

But I have no time to recover.

Comstock seizes me by the shoulder and hustles me down the stairs. My feet stumble and slide. My ankle twists. His fingers dig in, half-supporting me, half-threatening to send me flying head-first down the stairwell.

On the landing, I risk a glance back. Behind us, his men ferry burlap sacks full of my treasured books and pamphlets. The last man hefts my faithful typewriter, now dented and missing keys.

We emerge out onto the street. The sun has risen, but the feeble winter rays cannot penetrate the cold that has taken up residence inside me. I expected some man-handling, but not this purposeful cruelty. They have not even allowed me to don a coat or throw on my shawl, and the wind whipping down the tunnel between the buildings is bitter.

I pause, shivering, looking for The Inquisitor's carriage, but Comstock grasps my shoulder harder and jostles me to the left. My foot catches on an uneven paving stone, and I trip.

"Walk, Priestess," he snarls in my ear. He pulls me upright and herds me down the pavement like a lamb on its way to the butchers, followed by his officers loaded down with their evidence bags.

Early morning pedestrians on their way to work stare after my parade of shame. Some give Comstock the victory sign or call out a "God bless." A few frown. One calls me a slut and spits on my hem. Most give us a wide berth and hurry on their way.

I try to catch their eyes. *You don't know who I am*, I want to scream. *I am doing this for you.*

I roll my shoulder under Comstock's powerful grip and straighten my spine. I will not let the King of Filth win the fight before it has begun.

By the time we board the Ninth Street elevated line, I have regained my confidence. Comstock uses his bulk to push me down the aisle, but I smile at the people sitting in the rows we pass. One well-dressed woman smiles back.

My jailer stops beside her, tips his hat. "Keeping your children safe, madam."

"Really, sir?" The woman glances from him to me and back again. "A gentleman would not treat a lady so, Mr. Comstock."

He sucks in a breath. "No lady, this one. A purveyor of obscenity." He shoves me forward.

Other occupants of the car turn our way. A few catcall. One snickers.

But my obstinate defender is not deterred. She peers over her shoulder and raises her voice. "But that is Mrs. Craddock, sir, the renowned marriage counselor. I have heard her speak. Not a common criminal to be cuffed and manhandled."

The Censor growls and hustles me into a seat in the back end of the car. At that moment, the train takes a curve, and I lose my footing. Without my hands to catch myself, I slam into the back of the bench. The world spins, my ears go deaf, and my vision flashes black.

I rouse to The Inquisitor's grotesque face, with its bulbous, red-veined nose and bristling muttonchops just inches from mine.

"Good. You're not dead. I'll get my day in court yet." He pulls me up to my feet. "Move."

Everything whirls wildly. My stomach cramps, and I curl over, only to jerk back as the steel cuffs send pain shooting through my shoulders. But I am allowed no time to find my balance.

He wraps his hand around the chain at my waist and jerks me from the bench and out into the aisle. I wobble forward, barely aware of my surroundings, tripping down the steps, scraping my ankle on the metal treads.

By the time I arrive at the booking desk, I no longer care what happens to me next. Somewhere in the depths of my intellect, I know I must not show weakness. All I want is him gone so I can find peace in the arraignment cells with the other unfortunates.

But it is not the waiting cell they take me to. I am hustled into an interrogation room. My hellish morning is not over.

Comstock saunters in and plops down on the opposite side of the table, his hand in his trouser pocket like some swell at a party. Another officer undoes my cuffs then stands by the door.

I draw my hands forward, arms stiff and numb.

The Censor waves a pad and pencil at me. "Your clients—everyone you ever mailed one of those obscenities to—I want their names."

Despite the hazy mess of my mind, outrage boils over like an unwatched stew pot. "How dare you? That is confidential information."

"Make it easy on yourself, Craddock. We know everything about you."

For a brief moment, I believe him. Then I give myself a shake. He doesn't know anything. My manuscripts and important papers, along with all but my most recent case studies, are across the Atlantic in William Stead's protection. The names, I keep in my head.

I sit back, and despite the shooting pains in my temples and arms, I fold my hands neatly on the tabletop. "I demand my lawyer."

"You have one, Craddock? Only a fool would take your case. You can't win."

"All the powers of heaven are on my side," I hiss. "Not yours. You might style yourself a Christian, sir, but what you do to people is nothing the Divine Spirit would ever condone."

He leans forward and laughs in my face. "Pray all you want to your Divine Spirit, or whatever you want to call it. People want their children protected from purveyors of filth like you, Priestess."

"Sexual pleasure within marriage is not filth. I pity your poor wife."

His nostrils flare, his face turns the color of a raw beet, and he rises up to tower over me like the angry beast he is. "You will *never* mention my wife with that whoresome mouth again." He swings his arm out as if to slap me. Then stops mid-stroke. "Craddock, you are not worth an ounce more of my attention." He spins on his heel and heads to the door. "Throw her in the lower drunk tank and lose the key."

Then he is gone.

My pleas to contact a lawyer fall on unhearing ears as I am hurried along dank, lightless corridors and down slimy steps, deeper and deeper into the bowels of the police station. The cell they lock me in is foul with vomit, excrement, and surrender. The occupants curl or flop on the cement floor, more bundles of rags than anything else. Their glassy eyes and the occasional groan, the only sign of their humanity.

There are no benches. Nothing but the overflowing necessary bucket. I hold my breath and gingerly make my way to one of the few empty spaces. I sink down on the fetid concrete, sorry I donned my best dress this morning. Mother would be most upset.

The thought of Mother haranguing me over a spoiled ensemble while my rights are taken away sends me into gales of laughter. I laugh and laugh until the tears come, and all I can do is cushion my aching head on my bent knees and dream of walking hand-in-hand with Soph in heaven.

"Soon," I whisper. "Soon, we will be together."

Chapter 27

"Enforce the laws in every instance; make no exception."
Anthony Comstock, *Traps for the Young*, p. 127

Law Office, New York City, 1902

Lawyer Hugh Pentecost doesn't approve of me. I can tell by the way he taps his pencil and rolls his eyes every time I mention sexual union with the Divine. I am not sure if it is the sexual union part or the Divine part he objects to. I fold and refold my hands in my lap. Probably both.

Dr. Ned says I should be glad such a liberal-minded man has taken my case. But Voltairine has written me a damning indictment of Pentecost's about-face on his anarchist and socialist views just to get offered an appointment as Assistant District Attorney. A wishy-washy politician is all he is. He might hate Comstock, but he couldn't care less about my First Amendment right to teach right marital behavior between husband and wife.

I wiggle in the uncomfortable chair in his overheated office. At least, for the moment, I am clean, properly dressed, and no longer in that horrid jail cell, thanks to Dr. Ned paying my bail. The dear man retrieved my typewriter from Comstock's evil hands and even tried to rescue my books from the police, to no success. I fear they are gone forever. The books probably burned up with my marital guides.

Not that my lawyer cares. All he does is drone on and on about the marvelous plea deal his friend the district attorney has offered and why I should take it.

I hold up my hand. "No. Stop. I will not plead guilty to promulgating obscenity. It is the Comstock Law that is illegal. Does not the Constitution say, *'Congress shall make no law respecting an establishment of religion, or prohibiting the free exercise thereof; or abridging the freedom of speech?'* But the postal law against the use of the mails for obscene literature has been twisted so as to exclude my religious teachings. I have a God-given right to practice my religion and preach Divine sexual enlightenment to the common people."

Pentecost fiddles with his spectacles. "You will lose."

"Then I will appeal. I will to take this to the Supreme Court."

"That would cost a fortune, if you can even find a judge to rule in your favor on an appeal."

"I don't care. What Anthony Comstock is doing is viciously wrong. One man should not be able to force his personal religious beliefs on me and everyone who believes as I do. Marriage and the sexual relationships within it are a matter of privacy between the couple and their God."

"If you bring up religion, you will be accused of blasphemy, and there is nothing that riles up The Inquisitor more."

"What is blasphemous about believing in a loving God who wants His children to enjoy the pleasure He has gifted us with?"

"What is *blasphemous*? How about a Church of *Yoga*?" he sputters. "Nude sunbathing? Belly dancing? Spirit husbands? This is a Christian country. The Supreme Court said so in 1892. The virtuous Comstock, arrayed as a warrior for Christ, will crucify you in the press and convict you."

I rise to my feet. "Maybe I need a different lawyer."

Pentecost snaps upright in his chair. "Sit down. Too late to change lawyers. The trial is just days away. Besides, I am the best you are going to get in this city. If you want to plead not guilty, it is your right to do so. Comstock is a clever fellow—you will most certainly lose. But if you don't mind a stay in jail, then go ahead and use the witness stand to preach your message to the deaf ears of the prosecution and the judges. The reporters will eat it up."

I shift in my seat. I have had enough of jail cells to last a lifetime, and I hate the press. But this is my chance to bring Comstock down, and I cannot afford to search out another lawyer.

"I don't understand. If I am found guilty in the state court, won't I be out of jail on appeal until the federal trial?"

He taps the top of his desk with the end of his pencil. "That is up to the judges."

I close my eyes and remember lying in my angel's arms. Soph wants me to do this. I must be brave, he says. It is the only way we can be together at last.

I gather up my courage. "I understand the risk. I insist on a not guilty plea."

Pentecost frowns then shuffles through his papers. "Impossible woman. All right, let us plan your defense."

The criminal case in the New York Court of Special Sessions is lost before it starts. I can see my doom written in the narrowed eyes, pursed lips, and clenched eyes of the three judges arrayed before me. The wood-paneled dais surrounding the judges pretends to be grand, but like my accuser, it is all show. The walls are ersatz marble, the ceiling stained, and the nervous rubbing of hundreds of defendants' clammy palms has worn away the finish on the arms of the chair on which I perch.

I glance behind me. Plenty of supporters have come. The Manhattan Liberal Club members have shown up in force. Strangers, outraged at the harsh treatment I have received from the police, fill the back rows. Dr. Ned sits in the front and gives me a nod, which only serves to rile Comstock, sitting to my left, to greater heights of Christian indignation.

Ned's circular *Comstock versus Craddock* has made my name a household word in the city and raised a surfeit of funds for my defense.

Comstock has his backers, too. The Society for the Suppression of Vice has turned out all their zealots. They are just the kind of men who need my teaching—rude, crude, self-important blowhards. The banes of womanhood, proclaiming their morality with badges and Bibles while they trample over God's commandment to love thy neighbor as thyself.

I turn my back on them and ignore the gutter names they call me. Everyone can see I am a lady, dressed tip-to-toe in the height of fashion, thanks to a gift from one of my sympathetic clients. I lift my shoulders and smooth down the placket of the pleated maroon velvet jacket. I have even donned a corset and the horrid red cherry-trimmed London hat for the occasion.

The only people in attendance who really matter are the reporters from the dailies. I cannot win in the halls of justice. I can see that now. Pentecost was right about that. Men of prejudice hold sway over my future.

If I am to destroy Anthony Comstock, it must be through public shame.

The lead judge pounds the gavel, and it begins.

Pentecost does his best to defend me. The witnesses he calls on my behalf do a fine job. Three kind doctors take the stand and attest to the medical importance of my work. William Stead, writing as my former employer, has sent an incomparable letter attesting to my morality and condemning my cruel treatment for giving needed medical advice in the land of the supposed free.

"The persecution of Ida Craddock's writings is an outrage," Pentecost reads aloud from William's letter and, for once, the lawyer's voice carries some conviction, "to the principles of religious liberty and freedom of the press."

Then it is my turn to take the witness stand.

No mention of sex or sexual relations must slip from my lips, Pentecost reminds *sotto voce* as I pass by him. I must present myself as the woman my mother always wished me to be—upright, moral, well-spoken, and rational. A delicate and fawning foil to the monstrous King of Smut who, on the stand, called me a purveyor of vile reading matter intended to corrupt the young.

And I try. I really do. I sit straight with my head held high. Even though my gospel of sexual enlightenment wants to fly from my lips, I talk about my work as if it is a small matter. Basic medical advice. Spiritual counseling. Coming closer to God. "I have only put forth facts," I say at the end, "which every person ought to know. I am not ashamed to speak plain truths plainly."

The prosecutor holds up *The Wedding Night*. "This booklet was confiscated from your office on 23rd Street. Did you write this?"

How can I deny the work of my heart?

I purse my lips and nod.

He scans the courtroom, his face forcefully grim. "Any ladies present must clear the court."

I sit and wait as my fellow females file out without a word of protest. Then he opens my pamphlet and begins to read.

> *"You will, by reflex action from the bosom to the genitals, successfully arouse within her a vague desire for the entwining of the lower limbs, with ever closer and closer contact, until you melt into one another's embrace at the genitals in a perfectly natural and wholesome fashion; and you will then find her genitals so well lubricated with an emission from her glands of Bartholin, and, possibly, also from her vagina, that your gradual entrance can be affected.*

"And it goes on." He flips the pages as murmurs of outrage rise in the courtroom.

> *"It is your wifely duty to perform pelvic movements during the embrace, riding your husband's organ gently, and, at times, passionately, with various movements, up and down, sideways, and with a semi-rotary movement, resembling the movement of the thread of a screw upon a screw—"*

"Enough." The head judge's gavel smashes down. "I have never heard such indescribable filth. No woman in her right mind, gentle-born and well-educated, as the literary style of this book shows, could conceive such filthy phrases. And to cause such trouble—in Chicago, and Washington, and Philadelphia before she came to our great city—to spread her blasphemous obscenities." He confers with the other two judges then strikes the gavel again. "I and my fellow judges hereby sentence the defendant, Ida C. Craddock, to three months in Blackwell Island Prison."

I stare straight ahead, any words of anger smothered in the horror of the sentence. Three months in the notorious Blackwell Prison where so many other women have suffered. I will be stifled. Silenced. Forgotten.

I rise to my feet as if underwater. I turn, and all my anger comes flooding back. The Inquisitor stands inches away. He raises up his arms and shakes his fists, as if calling on God to exult his success at bagging his prey.

He presses close. His smile triumphant. "You are going to the hell you deserve," he spits in my face.

But despite the pounding of my heart, I refuse to wilt. I refuse to cry. I will survive the sentence, and we will meet in court again, three months from hence.

I firm my chin and imagine I am a marble angel—cold, unyielding, emotionless—sitting on his grave.

His face closes down, and his errant hand wriggles faster in his pocket. He has a wooden snake in there, Dr. Ned has told me. I think it something else entirely.

I hold his gaze as the court officers seize me under my arms and march me out the side door to the paddy wagon. I am not a bug to be crushed beneath some bully's shoe. I have Divine Purpose and angels watching over me, and Mr. Smut-Sniffer knows it.

I will win in the end.

But first, I must survive Blackwell.

There are no angels in Blackwell Prison, only poor souls whom society has intentionally forgotten. A community of which I am soon a member.

On arrival, I am stripped, shorn of my hair, doused in icy water reeking of stomach-turning carbolic acid, and garbed in the coarse, gray-striped uniform of the incarcerated. Then the real hell starts.

Every day, I march in file from the dank cell I share with three others to the sewing room. Well, they call it a sewing room. But the sewing we do is nothing like the fine hemstitching my mother instilled in me.

A row of battered Singer sewing machines, dating back to the Civil War, runs the length of the stone-cold room.

I slide in on the narrow, rough-sawn plank that serves as a bench and face my assigned torture machine. Three weeks' experience has taught me to thread the needle swiftly before one of the battering-ram female guards snaps my fingers with her cane. It is not an easy task in the pale light streaming through the iron-barred windows.

I squint, find the tiny slot and, for once, get the thick thread in on the first try. I bite my lower lip and pick up a rough canvas strip from the workbasket. My role is to sew strapping for the straitjackets that will be used on the poor souls inhabiting the asylum at the other end of the island— though I am told by my cellmates they are used here in the prison, too. My skin crawls at the idea of having one's limbs and body so confined.

I lower the presser foot and use my feet to rock the treadle down and up, settling into the mind-numbing rhythm that will soon turn into a battle of will against pain. After one strip, my fingertips are raw from shoving the coarse canvas under the needle. After ten, my backside is one miserable ache from lurching to-and-fro. After fifty, I can no longer feel my feet or hands, nor think of anything but the distant reprieve of the dinner bell.

I rotate my neck to relieve the stiffness in my shoulders and spine then pick up another strip. Assignment to the sewing room is considered a tolerably easy labor—the task reserved for the least violent and depraved inmates—young prostitutes swept up in raids on the city's brothels, pickpockets, non-English-speaking beggars arrested for preying on the wealthy strolling along Park Avenue, and me, Comstock's prize purveyor of obscenity.

The Priestess of Filth, the guards call me with a sneer and a snicker. My fellow inmates call me Comstock's Bitch. Neither epithet bothers me. I could be called far worse. The bad-complexioned, rather dumpy woman sitting next to me has been dubbed by the guards as Pissypot. The rest of us call her by her real name—Else.

I glare at my stack of finished straps and then the pile remaining in the workbasket. It looks to be enough for an army of straitjackets. Are there truly that many insane people in the asylums of this country? The thought depresses me.

Another prisoner comes by and sweeps my contribution to the abuse of the insane into her basket. "Watch out, everyone," she whispers as she passes. "They're coming."

I look up from my sewing. "Who's coming?"

"The vaccinators," Else says under her breath. "Here to give us the pox."

I stop treadling, shocked at the thought. "The pox? I don't understand. Why would they want to infect us with syphilis—"

Whop. The cane slashes across the back of my hands.

"Back to work," the matron hisses.

I wince away the pain and start treadling again. The needle rises and falls. The strip edges through. The guard moves on.

Else tips her head and murmurs into her chest. "Not the pox, idiot—smallpox. There's been an outbreak at the madhouse. Every time that happens, the needle doctors show up to give us a poke. I've been stuck ten times in the last six months. Got scars up and down my arm."

"Why, that's outrageous. You only need to get vaccinated once."

She juts out her chin. "Not what those bastards think. Doubt it's a real vaccination, anyway. Probably injecting us with some poison or such."

"They can't do that. Our bodies belong to us."

Else laughs bitterly. "Honey, a woman's body is fair game. You'll see. They can do what they want to us. Prisoners have no rights."

Two men in white jackets push in through the door.

My co-worker hunches over. "Here they come."

The guards start at the far end. They grab an old woman who speaks no English and drag her out of the room. Her screams trail after her.

The poor immigrant has no idea what is going to happen to her. Probably thinks she is being dragged off to be tortured.

My stomach churns at the unfairness of it all. I shouldn't be here, subjected to the cruelty and unhealthiness of this jail. My First Amendment rights have been violated. And I don't care what these women did—they are human beings and American citizens, they shouldn't be treated this way either.

I stop treadling. "We can't let them do this to us," I proclaim in my loudest voice. I find myself standing. I raise my arm in the air. I shout even louder, "Fellow prisoners, stand with me and refuse to work until this awful vaccination process ceases."

I pick up my workbasket and dump the contents onto the floor. I tip over my hated sewing machine. It lands with a most satisfying crash. Bobbins, and spools, and metal bits go flying. "Strike with me, ladies. They have no right to vaccinate us against our will."

The guards hurry toward me, canes held high. I glance around at the rows of guarded eyes staring up at me.

Have I made a mistake? Are these women too beaten down by life?

"Join me. If we stand together, we have strength."

"She is right," Else yells, rising to stand beside me. "Rise up, ladies.

The clack of the machines stops. First one woman, then another stands. Voices, at first wary and then stronger, cry out, "Strike, strike, strike."

One machine topples over. Then another, and another, and another crash to the floor in a thunder of sound. The benches follow. A wall of wood and iron rises between us and the two prison matrons.

We stand behind the fallen machines, a raggle-taggle group of women, breathing hard, breathing scared.

The guards glare, confer, then one goes running, surely to fetch the whips and batons.

"What are we going to do?" the woman closest to me murmurs.

"Be brave. I know some people in the Anti-Vaccine Movement. They will raise a ruckus in the press. Get us support."

"When?" another girl asks. "They'll be bashing in our heads in minutes."

Running feet resound through the prison.

Blood pounds through me. I think back to what I have read about strikes and workers' empowerment, what I learned from Voltairine about being heard, and I know the battle is already lost. But hope is better than despair, and even trapped rats fight back when cornered.

"Join arms," I yell, looping mine into that of the woman nearest me, "and shout so that the whole prison hears us." I start the cry, "No vaccinations. No vaccinations. No work until we have justice." I have never shouted so loudly in my life. "Justice!" I scream. "Justice!"

And I pray that Comstock in his cozy parlor, being fawned on by his pitiful wife, hears me. I will have my justice. I will destroy him for what he has done to me and all the others.

Slam. Bam. The male guards from the men's side of the prison burst through the doors, batons at the ready.

The women press closer together.

"Be brave!" I shout encouragement, more for myself than for them. "Refuse to work. Refuse to eat. Do not give in. Do not let them abuse your rights."

"Her." The matron points at me. "That's the leader, the Filth Priestess. Get her first."

I yell at the top of my lungs. I shake my fists. "You cannot vaccinate us without our permission."

The guards tug the tangle of machines and benches apart and break through our barricade. The other women pull back behind me. Billy clubs swinging, the men stream through.

I'm seized by my arms, but I do not give in. I kick, and bite, and scream. The clubs rain down. Around me, my fellow prisoners cry out and moan.

A guard raises his arm and whips his weapon at me.

Whack.

My head swims, my limbs fail me, but I continue to scream as I am dragged away until I can scream no more.

I come to flat on my back. A medical man—I would not deem him the title doctor—stands over me, a guard on each side. He is jabbing at my arm with a smallpox needle.

I flail and yank against his hold. Kick at him with my feet.

"Stop. You can't do this. Get me my lawyer."

He tips his chin like some entitled king. "Guards, restrain her."

One moves to the foot of the wood plank table I lie on and seizes my legs. The other leans over and presses my arms to my sides.

The doctor tries again.

I snap my teeth at him, knock his hand away with my head. He draws back then comes at me full force. This time, he succeeds.

The needle pricks hard.

My eyes tear, and my stomach rebels. My head reels. Vomit rises up and spills over his hand. A bucket of near freezing water is upended over me.

Coughing and sputtering, I am yanked up and half-carried, half-dragged back to the cells by two matrons. But it is not to my former cell we go.

The matron yanks me past the row of shared cells to a narrow door at the end. "I'll see that you don't rile up my girls again, you witch." She shoves me into a windowless cell no bigger than a closet, one of the prison's infamous Black Cells. "There you go, Priestess. I hope you enjoy presiding over your own filth." The door slams.

The cell is pitch dark and reeks of its previous inhabitant. I lean against the wall and let my eyes adjust, but there is nothing to see. The tiny ray of light streaming through the eye hole in the door reveals nothing. I circle the narrow space and find the empty but heavily encrusted piss bucket. Nothing else. There is no cot or chair, only the cold concrete, wet with condensation and spilled excrement.

I stand near the door as long as I can but, eventually, my toes go numb and my knees weaken. I slide down slowly onto the fetid floor.

The revolting odor swirls around me and fills my lungs. I am in hell on earth, and I am glad that Mother and Henrietta cannot see me here and feel vindicated in their narrow-mindedness.

Time passes. The dinner bell rings, but no one brings food or drink. Cell doors slam open and closed, but no one opens mine. Worries twist their way inside me like venous snakes. Have they injected me with poison? What happens if I die here in prison? Will I be forgotten? Will my work be lost? Will Comstock win?

I smash my fists into the cement wall. If someone were inventing a torture designed to drive me insane, this is it.

I fight back my demons by cataloging my physical hurts. The lump on my head from the guard's baton aches. The noxious air in the cell burns my scream-sore throat with every breath. The swelling wound on my arm pricks.

Closing my eyes, I compose letters to Dr. Ned, Pentecost, and Voltairine. I pen notices to the dailies about the assaults on my person and my conscientious objection to government compulsion. For William Stead, I place my fingers on my thighs and type, sentence by sentence, a plan for completing the final part of my thesis on phallic worship.

In the end, sleep comes at last, and with it, Soph.

I rest my head on the chest of my angel and meditate on the wonder of his love.

My ascent to heaven can't come soon enough.

Chapter 28

"You cannot handle fire and not be burned. Neither can the black fiend Lust touch moral nature without leaving traces of defilement."
Anthony Comstock, *Traps for the Young*, p. 169

New York City, 1902

Three months later, I step off the ferry from Blackwell Island and have to fight the urge to kneel and kiss the grass. The warm June sun feels like magic on my prison-pale skin.

During the three months I have been imprisoned, the world has blossomed into spring. Green leaves flutter on the trees. Dandelions poke their way between the cracks in the pavement. And the female members of my welcoming committee are gaily festooned in the latest gingham and chambray Gibson Girl summer fashions.

For a moment, I hesitate in my progress toward the smiling faces awaiting me. Blackwell Island has reformed me into a different person. My teeth are loose. I have lost weight.

The maroon velvet suit I wore on the day I entered Blackwell hangs like a sack. Beneath my hat, my hair is unfashionably short, thin, and noticeably white. I have a persistent cough and a multitude of scars running up and down my arm from my losing battle with prison authorities over their right to vaccinate me over, and over, and over. Nevertheless, I have survived, and I will get to face The Censor again in court.

I straighten my shoulders and tip up my chin. This time, I will win.

I hold out my arms and rush into Edward Foote's embrace. I owe everything to this one man who may not always agree with me on proper sex relations but will defend my right to my beliefs with every dollar and friend he has.

Dr. Ned pats my back. "My dear woman, Comstock should be torn apart by vultures for the evil that has befallen you." He turns to face my supporters and holds up my arm. "Here she is, our brave martyr for the cause of freedom of speech."

A young girl steps up and shyly hands me a bouquet of daisies. The reticent gesture is so reminiscent of the bouquets Charlie brought me all those years ago that tears gather in the corners of my eyes.

I blink them back—now is not the time for sentiment—and address the people pressed around me.

"Thank you for your support over the past three months. Without your voices raising awareness of my abuse and hardships, I would have surely died, locked away in the horror of that hellhole." I glance back at the island, a world of evil so near and yet so far from these people's lives. "And we must not forget the women," I say, surprised at how scratchy and broken my voice sounds, "who remain imprisoned and suffer every day."

The crowd claps. A few come forward, shake my hand, and express their indignation on my behalf. I barely hear them.

Maybe it is the unfamiliar sun on my head or the rattle in my brain leftover from the baton whack that has never gone away, but the ground sways beneath me, the faces blur together, and my knees turn rubbery.

"Come." Dr. Ned props me up as I lean against his suited shoulder. The dapper man with his elaborate mustache and still chestnut hair smells like wintergreen and cleanliness, and a life of wealth and ease. But I do not begrudge him. He has spent freely of his fortune and risked much in defending me.

"Let me take you to my house where you can rest for a few days," he says, using a tone soft and soothing, like one would use with an injured child, "where your mother cannot bother you."

Despite my lightheadedness, I swivel my head around. "Mother? She's here?"

"No. But she has written she is coming, and I fear her motives in regard to you."

I fear her motives, too. Since the day I entered prison, she has refused to communicate with me because of the shame I have brought to the Craddock name. Shame? I glance down at my diminished self. It is well she cannot see me now.

Ned bundles me through the crowd with the efficiency and lack of fanfare he is noted for and assists me into a waiting hansom cab. The horse lurches forward as the driver pulls out into traffic then settles into a steady trot.

The kind doctor pats my hand. "You have been very brave, Ida. I did my best to spread word about your distress. We raised quite a bit of money for your defense and stoked the press to fever pitch. Your upcoming federal trial will be a sensation."

A sensation. That is just what I want.

I peer up into his kindly face. We have been friends for over twenty years, always at odds over the practicality of male continence, and yet never in all that time has he wavered in supporting my right to teach what I believe.

"I owe you so much . . . "

"You have been foully treated, my dear woman. It is time Comstock gets what he deserves. And I am excited to say that I and Walker, and members of the Manhattan Liberal Club, have created an organization dedicated to doing just that—the Free Speech League. On Friday, we will hold our inaugural banquet, and you are to be our honored guest. But first, you must rest and restore yourself."

The cab slows to a stop in front of a brownstone as plain as the quiet, unassuming man who owns it. A pleasant-faced housekeeper greets me at the door and hustles me off to the simply decorated but comfortable guestroom, looking all the world like heaven to my prison-tuned eyes.

I sink down on the cushiony bed and smile at the garments hanging on the back of the door. Someone, mostly surely Dr. Ned or one of his servants, has retrieved my summer suit and a shirtwaist from 23rd Street and had it cleaned and pressed. Soon, I will feel myself again.

I luxuriate in the huge porcelain bath, feeling clean for the first time in months. I catch a glimpse of myself in the mirror over the sink and bemoan my destroyed hair but quickly shake the feeling away. I have never been a vain woman, and the ragged mess is nothing one of the monstrous hats currently in fashion cannot hide.

I return to the bed and curl up beneath the covers. When I feel stronger, I will walk the few blocks to my office and see what Comstock managed not to destroy.

It takes two days to gather up my strength and courage. I climb the stairs Comstock had so callously dragged me down three months before and unlock the door. The carefully hand-lettered sign I'd taped to the glass almost a year ago still hangs. I trace the black and gold letters. *"Ida C. Craddock, Instructor in Divine Science."*

Comstock tried to shut my teaching down. The guards tried to take away my identity in prison. But they have both failed. I am here. And I am back.

I step inside and swallow hard. Despite the efforts of the servant Ned sent to tidy the place, all I can see is what is missing—the near-empty bookshelves, the missing stacks of my now-burned pamphlets. I press my hands to my stomach and make a vow. Comstock will pay for what he has done.

I open the blinds and, using a piece torn from my ruined paisley shawl, dust off the desk and sit down. There is no obscenity law against oral teaching in New York City, as much as Comstock tried to get that charge hurled at me. With my newfound infamy, I am sure to have customers lined up outside the door just to get a glimpse of the Priestess of Yoga, late of Blackwell Island Prison.

I compose a large advertisement for the local papers then set that aside. Some of the funds collected to support my defense will pay for publication.

Now—I place my hands on my thighs—I must prepare my speech for tonight.

I begin to write.

The banquet room at the turreted and towered Clarendon Hotel in Brooklyn is overly aristocratic for the crowd here tonight. From the platform, I look out over one hundred of the most open-minded freethinkers in the country. I grip the podium with white-knuckled fingers to keep from sinking to the floor. It should be my moment of triumph. But it is not.

If my life had gone the way I had planned, they would have come to hear me present a scholarly discussion on the mythic origins of sexual worship, presented by the first female graduate of the University of Pennsylvania, and they would have bowed in my honor.

Instead, I have been told to avoid all mention of sex.

Apparently, Walker whispered in my ear on my arrival, some attendees at my contentious lecture all those years ago to the Manhattan Liberal Club are still offended by plain talk about a basic human function.

I glance down at my prepared plea for the freedom to speak openly about sexual union then carefully fold it up. I need these people and their money, and their vocal support, to destroy The Censor. So, instead of speaking from my heart, I speak of the First Amendment and Comstock's illegal pursuit of freethinkers and how I will carry on my fight for free expression.

I rap the stand. "I have all confidence in the success of liberalism and free thought," I proclaim. "I have an inward feeling that I am really divinely led here to New York to face this wicked and depraved man, Comstock, in open court and to strike the blow that will start the overthrow of Comstockism. No pious scoundrel will bring me down."

Behind the shield of the podium, I curl my fingers and struggle to draw a breath. Because he will. He already has. Even here, I am censored.

I return to my seat at the head table.

The applause that follows me is warm. The speakers who rise testify to my courage, affirm their support, and show proper indignation.

Then League President Walker rises.

He towers over the podium, a handsome man accustomed to fawning to a crowd. He tips his head toward me. "Some say Ida Craddock's utterances are spiritualistic and unscientific. This may be true, but she is being persecuted because she speaks out on a tabooed subject." He gazes out over the audience. "Her opinions need not concern us. We simply stand for liberty."

I fold my hands in my lap. I keep my chin up and ignore the twitching in my shoulders. In two sentences, he has relegated all my work to oblivion. All that matters is The Cause—freedom. But freedom for whom?

Certainly not me.

On my way out, Hugh Pentecost pulls me aside. "All this enthusiasm for your legal defense is most heartening. But I remain quite pessimistic about your prospects. Comstock has all the judges in his pocket."

I never cared for the man and his wishy-washy support. I shift my weight and give him the same look I gave the guards who held me down against my will. "But not the jury, I should think."

He takes my hands. "I admire your courage, but perhaps you should take a plea deal if they offer one."

Dr. Ned comes up and, in his off-handed way, settles beside me. "Hugh, do not put fear into our dear Ida's heart. She has already suffered greatly." He loops his arm into mine. "Come, Ida; let the Free Speech League worry about your defense. Your job is to rest and regain your strength. I will see you back to your room."

Ned means well, but I have had enough of politic kindness.

I shake my head. "You are too considerate, my friend. You stay and work on winning my court case. I will take a cab back to Manhattan." Then, before he can protest, I push out the doorway of the hotel and flee.

By the time I get back to my room, my whole body is shaking. I throw myself down on my cot and stare at the stains on the ceiling. What am I going to do? Pentecost is right. My imprisonment is assured.

There is no way I can win against Comstock in court.

Censored Angel

How else can I bring the man down?

Chapter 29

"The turgid waters speak louder with the death stillness which they promise than does hope, with its promise of a better life."
Anthony Comstock, *Traps for the Young,* p. 133

New York Federal Court, 1902

October tenth, nineteen hundred and two, the day of my federal trial, burns bright. Sunlight streams down through leaves turned gold. Blue sky reflects off last night's rain puddles. I, on the other hand, have never felt so bleak. My feet drag. My head hangs. My empty stomach cramps.

"Stand up straight, Ida." Mother transfers her burgundy leather handbag to her other wrist and loops her arm in mine. "You brought this on yourself, you know. I always said you were soft in the head. Having those fits. Writing all those filthy pamphlets."

I don't even consider tugging my arm free. Why bother? Mother's been berating me since she arrived two days ago, and she surely isn't going to let up now. Dr. Ned urged me to send her away, and I should have. But I can't. She is old. Her gout is bad, and she did come all this way to offer what she considers love and support.

Right now, I am the one offering support as she leans her weight on me, shuffling up the courthouse steps, one step at a time.

"I hope you appreciate my being here today," she huffs. "My toe is far from better. Though you did prepare that nice foot bath for me last night. You can be such a good daughter sometimes."

"I care about you, Mother." And the sad thing is I do. Despite everything she has done.

"Slow down, Ida." She presses a hand to her chest and stops to catch her breath. "Of course, you care for me. That is why I do not understand why you won't consider committing yourself to one of those pleasant private institutions I told you about. Why, you could go back to Friends Asylum. The rose gardens are so lovely there."

I bite deeply into my lip to avoid screaming at her and use the soft, controlled tone I usually reserve for young women fearful of their wedding night. "I am not insane, Mother. I am a rational, intelligent woman."

I pull free, continue up the steps, and push open the door. The marble lobby echoes with hundreds of footsteps hurrying here and there.

I hesitate. Maybe she is right. Maybe I am crazy to take Comstock on.

Mother catches up to me, and we fall into step. If her toe is sore, she has suddenly forgotten about it.

She shakes her head. "You poor, deluded thing. I worry so. The horrid things they say about you in the papers . . . terrible. Just terrible."

Her words ring in my ears, drill into my brain. "If my pamphlets hadn't been banned and burned, I could be making a fortune with all the publicity I am getting."

"That's all you ever cared about—money."

"No. If I had cared about money, I wouldn't be here." I open the door to the courtroom.

She grabs my arm and yanks me around to face her. "Promise me you will be demure during the trial. Anthony Comstock is too well-admired to be roasted by a little sniper like you. He's a Christian Temperance man who protects children from the evils of this world."

Her words slice through me. Deny it all I want. Hope all I might. My mother truly believes I am one of those evils. And I should hate her for it.

But my angels demand that I not dislike anyone if I am to be a Godly woman. And I try. I do.

In the end, I say nothing, turn my back, and stride down the aisle to where Anthony Comstock waits to bring me down.

My new lawyer, Edward Chamberlain, looks up at me as I slide in next to him. The League-supported lawyer is fiery enough—a regular showman, the onetime defender of Moses Harman and Ezra Heywood. But even with all his legal acumen, they both went to jail. I look up as the jury files into the courtroom. And looking at those smug male faces, so will I.

"Ready, Ida?" he asks, his eyes bright with anticipation for the fine theater he imagines will happen here. "Are you ready to bring the loathsome rogue to his knees?"

I nod. I am all set. But not how he imagines. Everyone admits my chance of prevailing is less likely than Sisyphus conquering his rock. To win, I must elicit the sympathy of the jurors through my testimony.

I draw out my wrinkled notes and pray that the Divine Spirit takes pity on me.

I have never been much of a public speaker. But today, I need all the fiery righteousness I can muster.

The next hour or two is a repeat of my previous trial. Despite Chamberlain's vigorous defense, my vibrant call for freedom of speech, and of the press and of religion and whatever other freedoms my supporters advocate, the judge throws out all the charges except mailing an obscenity.

I'm a dangerous woman, he declares, and my writings are lewd, lascivious—he's referring to the pelvic movements Comstock so hates, I'm sure—and of course, *dirty*.

Unlike the state court, he dismisses even having the prosecutor read aloud any selected passages to avoid offending the sensibilities of the jury. So, in the end, my testimony about freedom is moot. Chamberlain's glowing defense of me, useless. All that is left for the jury of my peers to decide is whether or not Ida C. Craddock, Priestess of Obscenity and Filth, sent sex manuals through the United States mail.

And, since that is the truth that no one, least of all me, denies, I am convicted.

The jury doesn't even leave the room. The sentencing date is set for seven days hence.

Comstock does his cock-a-doodle strut out of the courtroom. I sit and stare, my stomach twisting into a Gordian knot not even Alexander the Great's clever sword could vanquish.

The jaws of injustice are clamping down, and I have no idea how to escape being trapped.

I have seven days of freedom left.

Mother is waiting for me in the hallway outside the courtroom. She pushes through my disgruntled supporters, my commiserating friends, and the burdensome press and wrings her hands. "What are we going to do?"

You would think she was the one condemned to prison. But if she expects me to gather her in my arms and console her, she is mistaken.

"You will appeal the sentence, will you not?" one of the jostling reporters asks.

I firm my stance. "Of course. Mr. Chamberlain will be filing the papers. I intend to continue my educational mission to the men and women of this country in spite of a dozen Comstocks."

But my words are false bravado. I mailed the pamphlets. Broke the law. Any further trial will merely be more theater for the liberal cause. The result will be the same. I will be imprisoned, silenced, my voice gagged by justice's blindfold.

I push my way through the crowd, looking for Dr. Ned. I could use his calm, steady presence right now. But he is gone, I am told. The news zings through me. Has he given up on me at last?

"Ida." My mother's shout echoes in the marbled hall of injustice. Her footsteps resound on the stone beneath our feet.

Ah, yes. The one person who will never give up.

I wait and let her take my arm. She is wearing her I-know-what-to-do expression that always bodes me ill.

"Shall we go eat something at my hotel? The restaurant is quite decent."

My stomach lurches at the thought. I was unable to swallow any breakfast, but I'd be a fool to turn down a delectable meal with prison slop lying in wait.

"That would be lovely," I answer.

"Then come along," Mother says. She strides away, and I follow her like I always have—her puppy on its leash.

I peer back at my dispersing supporters. There are other people I could ask to help me. Others I trust more.

Have I made a mistake letting my mother lead me away?

I poke at a diced apple in my Waldorf salad and glance around the elegant little restaurant. Being here is definitely a mistake. Mother is the most dangerous person I know, especially when she has truth on her side. I can see the glee in her eyes. She knows she has won.

"Now, I have talked with that lawyer of yours." She takes a bite of her steak. "He agrees that you could avoid jail if you commit yourself to an asylum."

I shrug as carelessly as I can. "Doesn't matter. As soon as I am sentenced, I will appeal. During the legal process, I will be free to speak out. Chamberlain has promised to fight for me with all his might, all the way to the Supreme Court. I will continue counseling and spreading word of my work across the country. With all the publicity, I will be able to stir up interest and more support. Look at all the letters I have received from former clients and other clear-minded people, outraged at my treatment by Comstock."

Mother lays down her fork. "For once in your life, face reality, Ida. You will never win an appeal. You mailed your filth, broke the law, and you will go to jail unless you do what I advise—plead insanity."

She is right about the appeal. Judge Thomas has scuttled my defense by throwing out every charge except the postal offense. It is not a reality I want to face.

I force myself to stay calm. "But I am not insane, Mother."

She shifts on her chair and turns her lips up into the smile she uses on potential clients. "I have found a lovely asylum in the Hudson Valley that will provide for all your needs at a fairly reasonable cost. I will pay the fee for you to remain there as long as needed. You'll be able to write letters to me and your friends, walk the grounds, enjoy decent meals, talk to the kind doctors. Think, daughter, wouldn't that be so much better than a prison cell?"

I stare at Mother's animated face. She makes an insane asylum sound like a vacation resort.

I shake my head. "It is not better. I have been locked in an asylum. An inmate is no freer than a prisoner. I would be lucky to be allowed to write a censored letter or two. I would have a guard hovering over me day and night. I would be forbidden to do my Divine Science work or preach sexual enlightenment. In an asylum, my goal of sexual reform will be as effectively silenced as if I were in prison. And Comstock wins."

She shakes her head so violently the feathers atop her hat sway. "*Win*? Do you know how crazy you sound? The man is an honored crusader for morality. And you . . . you are out of your mind if you think to bring him down. You have been convicted three times. I have it on good authority that Judge Thomas will give you the harshest sentence—five years at hard labor. The judge thinks you a dangerous woman. He said so in court."

"I *am* a dangerous woman. Do you know why I have been pursued and reviled by the postal inspector and his goons? Comstock wants me locked away forever because he fears me. I know his secret—he is as impure as any man."

I have told no one this. I don't know why I am telling my mother. I lean across the table and whisper loudly, "The man is a sex pervert and sadist. He gets aroused when he sees or reads obscenities and when he manhandles women like me."

"Ida." Mother slaps her hands over her ears. "I refuse to listen. How dare you spew such vulgarity. You should be on your knees, thanking me for caring about you enough to try to save you. Five years in prison, is that what you want to have happen to you?"

"No, but . . ." But what? I will never survive one year, let alone five. It is a death sentence.

The strangling knot in my stomach tightens, and I push my uneaten salad away.

Mother looks at my plate with distaste. She is probably calculating how much money she has wasted on my discarded meal.

She folds her hands and takes her I-am-superior pose. "I will be returning to Philadelphia in the morning. A shipment of bottles is coming in, and I don't trust the clerk I left in charge of the apothecary to count them accurately. But I will be back for your sentencing on Thursday, and we can have a light repast before the hearing." She pinches her lips together. "In fact, why don't you stay here at the hotel tonight instead of in that awful room of yours? You can give me a foot bath and see me off on the ferry."

Does she merely want a nurse, or does she have some doctor at the ready, waiting to whisk me off to an asylum once I fall asleep?

I have no idea, but my trust in her is nonexistent.

"Not possible. I have things to do—articles to write, clients to say goodbye to."

"Unnatural child. You care more for strangers than you care for your poor mother."

I stand up, kicking my chair back. "No more. I refuse to listen to you revile me any longer."

She slams her hands down on the table so hard the silverware rattles. "Ida Craddock, sit back down this minute."

I turn my back and weave my way between the tables, ignoring the sudden gasps of recognition.

In minutes, I find myself out on the street. I swerve to my left and take off at an unladylike run. I have no idea where I am going. Pedestrians bump around me. Carters throw curses.

Men leer or tip their hats. I ignore them all. I need space. I need sky. I need air.

I end up at the Hudson River, the Chelsea Piers looming in front of me. A steamship bound for the Far East prepares for departure. If only I could join the passengers filing up the gangplank and travel to India where no one would question my beliefs.

But I have no money for a ticket, and I must consider Dr. Ned and my supporters who have put up my bail. They would think I'd turned my back on them and lose all respect for me and my work. I would be vilified, not Comstock.

I peer out at the river. Sunlight glitters off the water. Ships and ferries churn back and forth. Everyone is free to go where they will, except me. Asylum straitjacket or prison cell, I am going down no matter what happens.

But I refuse to suffer alone. The Inquisitor of Smut must topple down with me.

But how? I have four days until I am locked away, one way or another.

I look up and let my thoughts drift. The sky is brilliant blue. Fluffy clouds waft overhead. It looks like an artist's rendition of heaven. All that is missing are angels and cherubim.

I take a slow, cleansing breath, tamp down the hatred twisting my gut into knots, and open my heart and mind to the Divine. A breeze tiptoes over me. My head clears. My stomach settles. There is one thing I can do. One idea I have refused to consider seriously until this moment.

I could join my angel husband.

My whole being lightens. It is the perfect plan. I could free myself from this life and, in turning martyr, cast shame on Comstock at the same time.

I spin around and retrace my steps. This time, I know where I am going and what I must do. I place my hand on my bee pendant and relish the cool feel of the metal against my skin. I will bring The Censor down. Just not in the way everyone imagines.

I can't imagine it myself yet.

But Soph and Iases have been preparing me to join them for a long time.

I gaze up at the heavens and whisper, "Soon."

Then I hurry back into the heart of the city, plans forming, and solidifying in my head. Shopping is at the top of my list. But I need money.

I finger the pendant. It has carried me through so many hard times, but I do not want my mother to have it, and I will need no earthly link to Soph once we are angels together.

I stop at a jeweler's and finagle a better deal than I expected.

The next morning, I pocket my windfall and set off toward the Ladies' Mile to make my purchases—a new dress and hat, wrapping paper, string, glue, parchment, envelopes, and a long rubber tube. At the confectionery, I choose a large assortment of chocolates in my favorite flavors. Everything I purchase is of the finest quality; I have no need to penny-pinch any more.

I arrive at my building, climb the staircase to the fourth floor, and spread my purchases out on my desk. Then, while savoring my chocolates, I create some order out of what remains of my belongings.

I unpack my trunk; only a few books and trinkets of worth have survived. I make a package of some spiritualist papers and a fairly new history of religion to send to Ada Freer as a remembrance of our time together. She has been kinder to me than many in this world. Perhaps she even loved me a bit.

My social reform works, I pack up for Voltairine. They are in miserable condition but will be much appreciated. The poor dear rarely has money to spare for books.

An expensively bound book of Gabriel Rossetti's love poems I purchased in London and which miraculously survived the Comstockian melee, I designate for Henrietta as a way of showing forgiveness for our mutual betrayals.

My heart aches as I pull out Katie's letters from the side pocket of my trunk and read them over and over. I bind the precious missives together and, on top, cushioned in my shawl, I place the seashell collected back when we were young. Then I fold the brown paper around them and set them aside for my dearest Katie, who is somewhere on the other side of the ocean again.

I stare at the bundle. Such a small package for a lifetime of friendship. Our souls were so aligned. If only we could have set our life courses so that she had never married. With a boon companion at my side, how different everything might have been.

I scoop from the floor the few medical texts, charts, and papers that survived The Inquisitor's tramping boots and address them to Dr. Alice Stockham. My dear Alice will know what to do with them and is less likely to be questioned about the content.

I leave directions for the parcels to be sent via the Adams Express Company over on Fifth Avenue then tuck the money for the shipping on top of the folded clothes in my trunk. I will not be beholden to my mother, even after death.

Lastly, I pry up the floorboard under the desk and retrieve my 1902 diary and my case studies from the last three months. These and all my letters must go to William Stead, but not directly. Mother will surely destroy them if they fall into her hands.

I carry them downstairs to the photography studio on the first floor. I knock loudly. Lawrence Vogt is an excellent portrait photographer but not always clear-headed.

The door opens, and Vogt sticks out his shaggy gray head. "My goodness, an angel come to visit. Come in, come in." He sweeps me inside. "Here to have your photo taken?"

The sun still streams in the windows. I have time. I have a little money left.

"Why not?" I answer. I have had so few photos of me. It will be a bittersweet remembrance for my mother.

He guides me to the princely velvet chair, selects a softly clouded background, then disappears behind his camera. I clasp my hands in my lap and wait as he prepares the plate, all the while dreaming of the coming night.

The scent of cedar rises around me. My pulse quickens. Soph is with me. Our time draws closer.

The shutter flicks open and shut. Vogt peeks over the camera. "I have no pressing orders at the moment. I will develop this and bring the photo up to you when it is ready."

"That would be lovely." I pay him generously then arrange for him to mail my package to Stead.

I tread up the stairs. After a quick check that all my bundles are clearly labeled, I sweep the books and papers I have no more use for to the floor. Tomorrow, I will start on the letters. I have many to write. There have been so hundreds of wonderful clients over the years and, of course, there are my supporters.

The day before my sentencing, I awake early, unfulfilled. Soph has only deigned to bestow a few feathery touches and an almost kiss in the night.

"Soon you will know true joy," he murmurs then leaves me to my preparations.

I open the blinds and peer out the window. It bodes to be another beautiful fall day.

I don my newly purchased cream tea dress, tie a bright blue ribbon round the waist, and tuck my scraggly hair under the jaunty, summer boater I couldn't resist buying. A passing glimpse into the one fragment of mirror, which survived Comstock and his wreckers, tells me I am dressed to perfection. Not even my mother could complain about my appearance.

I arrange the paisley shawl I bought to replace the one Comstock destroyed over my shoulders and slip my market basket on my arm. Then, head high, I descend the four flights and step out onto the pavement.

The early morning air is not yet contaminated by the stink of the city—that distinctive blend of horse manure, and garbage, and hundreds of unwashed people all hurrying somewhere.

I take a deep breath and set off.

In the fresh breeze off the Hudson, my body comes alive. My blood pumps evenly. My heart beats calmly. The silky crepe de chine dress flows elegantly around my ankles as I stroll up Fifth Avenue, find a seat at a small, elegant restaurant, and order my favorite foods. I am sure heaven will have even greater delights, but I can't resist the sweet rolls spread with butter and drizzled in honey, nor the baked caramel custard. All downed with a lovely cup of coffee. I purchase a half-dozen cinnamon buns to sustain me through the day, tip the waiter generously, and then start back.

By the time I return to my office, I am more content than I have been for years. Money in your pocket makes all the difference. If only Mother had let me live with her and carry on my work in peace under her roof, I wouldn't have had to traipse the country like an itinerant peddler cobbling together an existence and selling my pamphlets to pay my way.

My writings ought to have been offered for free. Right marital living through sexual passion is vital medical knowledge, not a fad or a dose of patent medicine.

I type my way through the day, cursing the sticking Comstock-bent keys. Slowly, the letters pile up. The second to last is for Mother. I place my fingers on the chipped keys and consider how disappointed she will be in me. But then she has always been disappointed in me—I run my hand over my bare neck—and wrong.

Nevertheless, I regret we did not have a pleasant leave-taking. A chance for me to tell her that, despite the pain she has caused, I do love her. But it is not to be. She will always think me insane and, vicious men like Comstock, the sane arbiters of morality. Still, there is no place for hate in a heart bound for the angels.

I smooth out the paper, insert the sheet in my typewriter carriage, and recount all the things I have told her so many times before. Maybe my death will open her eyes, and we will find reconciliation in heaven.

"We shall be very happy together someday, you and I, dear Mother," I write. *"There will be a blessed reality for us both at last. I love you. Never forget that. And love cannot die. Someday, Mother, you will not be ashamed of me or my work. Someday. you will be proud of me."*

I fold the letter and place it in the envelope. The long rays of sunlight streaming through the window warn that time is passing faster than I expected.

I start my final missive. I write out my tale in all its truth and horror for the public.

"Awake America, to the danger which threatens from Comstockism. I have faced social ostracism, poverty, and the dangers of persecution by Anthony Comstock for your

sakes. I have a beautiful gospel of right living in the marriage relation that I wanted to share with you. And though I am going to a brighter and happier land, I shall still look down upon you, and long and long and long that you may know something of the radiantly happy and holy life possible for every married couple. Even in Paradise with my angel, I cannot be as happy as I might, unless you share in this beautiful knowledge."

There is a knock on the door, and my heart jumps. Is it my mother come with the men to cart me away?

I peer through the glass and recognize the old photographer from below. I unlock the door.

Vogt holds out an envelope. "The angels love you, Mrs. Craddock. Putting you in prison is a sin. He's a vile man, that Comstock."

I give him a quick hug. "Why, thank you for your support, Mr. Vogt. Let us hope The Censor is soon gone for the good of us all."

He nods then disappears down the staircase. I remove the photograph from the envelope and sink to the floor in amazement. It is a spirit photo. Soph is there, standing behind me. I can see his face, his wonderful, glorious face. I clutch the picture to my bosom, knowing I am doing the right thing, and call out to him, "I'm coming."

Epilogue

"I maintain my right to die as I have lived, a free woman, not
cowed into silence by any other human being."
Ida C. Craddock, suicide note to her mother, New York,
October 16, 1902

Woodland Cemetery, Philadelphia, 1912

Katie Wood clutched the pot of pansies she'd brought
and stared up at the tombstone. There should at least
have been an angel. Ida would have liked that.

Instead, a plain obelisk marked Ida's shared resting place
with her mother and her first stepfather, James M. Brown.
Where Decker had been interred, she had no idea. For
someone who caused Ida such distress, for him to be lying
elsewhere seemed a suitable ending.

"You ready to go, Katherine?" Guy scuffed his feet on the
cemetery path and tapped his watch. "We have to pick up the
children from your mother's."

"In a minute." She stooped and set the pot of pansies at
the foot of the stone. The small purple blossoms were barely

visible in the scraggly grass. She removed her gloves and pulled out the tufts around the base.

Guy came up behind her. "What a waste. I told you to get lilies."

"Pansies were special to Ida. They symbolize thought." And if anything best characterized her dear friend, it was the brilliance of thought.

She touched one of the tiny purple blossoms. How like her dear friend—flamboyant in thought, delicate on the outside.

She picked up her gloves and stood. It shouldn't have ended this way. Ida should be standing here next to her, beguiling her with the latest book she'd read, reveling in her latest success educating a soon-to-be-bride, sharing her ideas for a new article or pamphlet.

She ran her fingers over Ida's engraved name. Annie Shoemaker would have been proud of her. Despite it all, Ida had fulfilled her promise. More women knew they deserved pleasure in the marital relations and control over childbearing. More women were speaking out for women's equality in all spheres. The suffragettes in Britain were raising a fuss. There was a new National Women's Party, and a woman named Margaret Sanger, following in Ida's footsteps, had just begun publishing sex education articles in the *New York Call.*

Katie turned to go. But there was one thing lacking— recognition for Ida's beloved scholarly work on sexual worship. She pulled the letter from where she had tucked it in her jacket pocket and studied the sender's address. Theodore Schroeder of the Free Speech League wanted Ida's letters.

Her breath pinched tight in her throat. How could she give Ida's missives away? Every sentence was precious. Every word a memory.

Still, Ida had been gone ten years. Gone with the same determination that had characterized every decision her dear friend had ever made. Her dying a martyr might have let some air out of that pompous Comstock's balloon, but it had not brought her the scholarly acclaim she had so longed for.

Katie refolded the letter—but maybe it was time for her to make a sacrifice, too.

This Schroeder planned to publish her manuscripts.

Ida would have been thrilled.

And she would still have the shells.

Guy always frowned when she unpacked the shells from their tissue nests and placed them prominently in whatever house they leased, in whatever country he was serving as diplomatic lackey. But he knew better than to say anything. He owed his son to crazy Ida Craddock.

Katie whirled around. "Guy, I have changed my mind. We must go the New York City and see this man, Theodore Schroeder."

A feather of air, light as the wings of an angel, skimmed over her, carrying with it the faint scent of fine-milled lavender.

Katie closed her eyes. Could it be?

Ida had been so sure. Sometimes she thought—

She placed her hand on the stone. "Ida? If you are here, know that you are not forgotten. Someday, we will be together in that heaven of yours. Together with your angels."

Author's Note

"I would lay down my life for the cause of sex reform, but I
don't want to be swept away. A useless sacrifice."
Ida C. Craddock, Letter to Edward Bond Foote, June 6, 1898

In researching women who have struggled for social
justice and yet been forgotten, I came across *Heaven's Bride*,
the biography of Ida C. Craddock by Leigh Eric Schmidt. Here
was a woman who took a radical approach to changing the
marriage relationships of the middle class in late nineteenth
century America. Yet, she is barely known today.

Ida Craddock lived in a time of flux. Like the present day,
the country was sharply divided between rich and poor,
Christianity and secularism. At the time, Christianity held
sway. On February 29th, 1892, the Supreme Court went so far
as to declare the United States a Christian nation. At the same
time, a growing secular movement and the call for women's
equality in marriage and politics were challenging the status
quo. The life of Ida Craddock was at the center of this battle.

I soon discovered it was not an easy story to write. What
Ida Craddock was fighting for—the free discussion of sex and
the right to publish and disseminate information about sexual

intimacy remains a controversial subject today. In fact, I suspect readers of my novel may be offended in parts.

Here are some background materials for those who wish to dig deeper into this time period and the power and weakness of censorship.

Comstockery

Anthony Comstock was a crusader who believed himself more Christian, more moral, and more pure than other men. In his campaign to remove any reference to sex from books, from literature, from visual art, and from any and all publications, he went far beyond the bounds of commonsense. He burned medical and anatomy books, along with pornography; attacked doctors, as well as booksellers; railed against nudity in works of fine art; and took it upon himself to define what was an obscenity so that juries, such as Ida's, never even saw the material they were to judge as obscene.

Ida Craddock's claim that he was sexually aroused during her arrest outraged Comstock. Still, the fact that he enjoyed the violence and derived pleasure from manhandling women is clear from the news reports and records kept by his victims, as well as from entries about his sexual shame found in his personal diary.

After Ida's suicide, the men and women who had come to her defense vilified Comstock for hounding a "bright, brainy" woman to death. Excerpts of her suicide letters were published in the newspapers. Fair-minded religious leaders spoke from the pulpit. Comstock was heckled when he spoke in his own defense, especially when he called Craddock a "mad dog" and stated it was "imperative that mad dogs of all sizes should be killed, before children are bitten."

Ida's Legacy

Emma Goldman, in her autobiography, *Living My Life*, called Ida one of the "bravest champions of women's emancipation."

One important result of Ida Craddock's persecution by Comstock was the formation of groups specifically focused on First Amendment rights, such as the Free Speech League, the antecedent of the American Civil Liberties Union. These groups challenged the arbitrariness of the Comstock obscenity laws. Why were some works, such as the poetry of Walt Whitman banned, they asked, but not Shakespeare? Their defense of our First Amendment rights continues to this day.

Another effect of Ida Craddock's battle against censorship was to awaken Americans, especially women, to new ways of talking about marriage, sexuality, and reproduction.

Researching Ida

Because Ida Craddock was an ardent correspondent, diarist, and author, many details of her life are available for anyone wishing to learn more about her. In *Censored Angel*, I have relied heavily on her diaries and letters in creating my imagined version of her character.

The fact that so much of her work has been saved is due to the interest that Theodore Schroeder took in her. Schroeder, although a founding member of the Free Speech League, never met Ida Craddock.

Starting a decade after her death, Schroeder, an amateur psychoanalyst, began collecting her writings and interviewing those who knew her. Ida C, as he called her, became the star example of his theory of the primitive confusion of sexual desire with religious passion. He proceeded to tear apart her writings and accuse her of being obsessed with sex—a nymphomaniac.

William Stead believed Schroeder's views would have been abhorrent to Ida and refused to turn over her papers and materials to Schroeder. Only after Stead drowned in the sinking of the Titanic, did Schroeder obtain her papers from Stead's daughter.

Schroeder went on to publish her work and numerous articles in which he expounded on her obsession with sex, titling one article "One Religio-Sexual Maniac."

Despite Schroeder's particular take on Ida's writings, the work he did collecting everything about her has benefited modern researchers. All her papers are currently in the Ida Craddock collection at Southern Illinois University.

Works by Ida Craddock

Lunar and Sex Worship by Ida Craddock with an Introduction by Vere Chappell (2010).

Sexual Outlaw, Erotic Mystic: The Essential Ida Craddock edited by Vere Chappell (2010).

Ida Craddock's letters and diaries can be obtained from the Southern Illinois University Special Collections Research Center at Southern Illinois University Carbondale

Digital copies of her articles and her suicide letters to her mother and to Comstock are available at Vere Chappell's https://www.idacraddock.com

To learn more about Ida C. Craddock's life:

Heaven's Bride: The Unprintable Life of Ida C. Craddock, American Mystic, Scholar, Sexologist, Martyr, and Madwoman by Leigh Eric Schmidt (2010).

Ida Craddock: A Religious Interpretation of Sexuality (1877-1902) by Elizabeth A. Green, master's thesis, Southern Illinois University (1995).

To learn more about Anthony Comstock's war on Ida Craddock and her compatriots:

Frauds Exposed by Anthony Comstock (1880).

Lust on Trial: Censorship and the Rise of American Obscenity in the Age of Anthony Comstock by Amy Werbel (2018).

The Man Who Hated Women by Amy Sohn (2021).

The Mind of the Censor and The Eye of the Beholder by Robert Corn-Revere (2023).

Traps for the Young by Anthony Comstock 3rd edition (1883).

Weeder in the Garden of the Lord: Anthony Comstock's Life and Career by Anna Louise Bates (1995)

To learn more about nineteenth century women's views on marriage and about tantric sex:

Disorderly Conduct: Visions of Gender in Victorian America by Carroll Smith-Rosenburg (1985).

Tantric Orgasm for Women by Diana Richardson (2004).

Questions for Readers

1. In 1973, the Supreme Court upheld that obscenity is not protected by the First Amendment. However, it modified the definition of obscenity, which previously condemned a work if even merely a paragraph was judged prurient. This led to the banning of works such as *Catcher in the Rye, The Grapes of Wrath, Ulysses,* and many other literary works.

    Under the 1973 ruling, to be judged obscene a work had to meet all three of the following criteria: would an average person, using community standards, judge the work, taken as a whole, prurient? Does the work depict or describe sexual or excretory functions in an offensive way? And, does the work, as a whole, lack serious literary, artistic, political, or scientific value?

    Based on this set of criteria, would Ida's work be judged obscene today?

2. Book banning is becoming a divisive political element in our society. Why do you think people are afraid of having books they disagree with freely available to others? Why were people in the nineteenth century,

like Comstock and his followers, afraid of Ida's plain talk marriage pamphlets?

3. How comfortable were you reading the quotes from Ida's pamphlets and her blunt sexual language? How far have we come from 19th century mores in terms of publicly discussing sexual relations?

4. There is no mention in Ida' s personal diaries of a sexual liaison with a man. Do you think Ida made up her relationship with her angel husband to cover her own hidden sexual misconduct with men, or do you think she truly experienced Divine orgasm through tantric sex?

5. Have attitudes to sex education changed since Ida's time? Where did you learn the facts of life? Was it from your mother or somewhere else?

6. The definition of nymphomania is a morbid and uncontrollable desire for sex in women. During Ida's lifetime, women having an interest in sex were viewed as abnormal, diseased, or insane. Is contemporary society more accepting of women who are openly passionate about sex?

Acknowledgements

My early readers provided important feedback and motivation for me to refine Ida's story. I especially want to express my gratitude to Veronica, Lillian, and my sister, Jeanne, who read some of the earliest versions and offered astute comments.

My critique group at *From the Heart Romance Writers*, including Lisa, Victoria, Diane, Doreen, Renee Ann, Ana, Todd, and Wendi spent many hours fine-tuning the wording.

Final feedback on the almost completed manuscript by my beta readers, Diana Rubino and Joyce Carroll, helped me bring more sensitivity to the characters. The book is better for their feedback.

Much research went into the writing of this story. I deeply appreciate the efforts of the librarians in the Southern Illinois University Special Collections Research Center at Southern Illinois University Carbondale for providing access to the Ida Craddock Papers. The Woodlands Cemetery in Philadelphia provided needed information.

Publishing a book requires the assistance of many skilled people. Kristin Campbell proofread and designed the interior of the book, and cover designer, 100Covers, created a cover that truly reflects Ida's appearance and story.

Writing and publishing a book takes far more time than one imagines. I owe my family everything for the patience and support they showed as I buried myself, and our home, in research and spent hours at my computer. My husband's constant support, his construction of my beautiful writing studio by the sea, and the wonderful give and take about history and writing we have engaged in over the years has only deepened our love and commitment to each other.

Thank You for Reading *Censored Angel*

If you enjoyed learning about a forgotten woman who played a major role in the fight for our First Amendment rights, I would love to hear from you. Honest reviews on Goodreads, Amazon, Barnes & Noble, Kobo, and BookBub are always appreciated. If you would like to know when the next book in the *Forgotten Women* series is available, sign up for my newsletter at joankoster.com.

Thank you!

Joan

About the Author

Joan Bouza Koster is an award-winning author of fiction and nonfiction works in the fields of ethnography, education, anti-racism, and the arts.

She blogs about women who should not be forgotten at JoanKoster.com (about daily life during the Civil War at AmericanCivilWarVoice.org, about romance at ZaraWestRomance.com, and about ways to write better at Zara West's Journal (zarawest.me). She also teaches numerous online writing courses. Find her current teaching schedule on her website, joankoster.com.

Other Books by Joan Koster

Historical Fiction
The Eve of Love Anthology

The Forgotten Women Series
That Dickinson Girl

The Skin Quartet
(Romantic Suspense under the pen name Zara West)
Beneath the Skin
Close to the Skin
Within the Skin
Under the Skin

The Write for Success Series
Fast Draft Your Manuscript and Get It Done Now
Revise Your Draft and Make Your Writing Shine
Research Your Subject and Validate Your Writing
Power Charge Your Language and Make Your Writing Sing

.

Made in the USA
Monee, IL
06 August 2023

40523280R00204